Praise for Bonnie K. Winn
and her novels

"Bonnie K. Winn's *Promise of Grace*
is an uncommon romance novel,
stirring the deepest part of the heart
with tenderness and compassion."
—*Romantic Times BOOKreviews*

"In *Protected Hearts*, Bonnie K. Winn provides
warm romance with a touch of suspense."
—*Romantic Times BOOKreviews*

"*A Family All Her Own* by Bonnie K. Winn
has some wonderful moments."
—*Romantic Times BOOKreviews*

"Bonnie K. Winn has done a fantastic job with
this story, showing readers how
Laura blossoms and realizes that she is able
To Love Again."
—*Romantic Times BOOKreviews*

BONNIE K. WINN
Family Ties

Promise Of Grace

Steeple
Hill®

Published by Steeple Hill Books™

If you purchased this book without a cover you should be aware that this book is stolen property. It was reported as "unsold and destroyed" to the publisher, and neither the author nor the publisher has received any payment for this "stripped book."

STEEPLE HILL BOOKS

Steeple Hill®

ISBN-13: 978-0-373-65123-8
ISBN-10:   0-373-65123-6

FAMILY TIES AND PROMISE OF GRACE

FAMILY TIES
Copyright © 2002 by Bonnie K. Winn

PROMISE OF GRACE
Copyright © 2003 by Bonnie K. Winn

All rights reserved. Except for use in any review, the reproduction or utilization of this work in whole or in part in any form by any electronic, mechanical or other means, now known or hereafter invented, including xerography, photocopying and recording, or in any information storage or retrieval system, is forbidden without the written permission of the editorial office, Steeple Hill Books, 233 Broadway, New York, NY 10279 U.S.A.

This is a work of fiction. Names, characters, places and incidents are either the product of the author's imagination or are used fictitiously, and any resemblance to actual persons, living or dead, business establishments, events or locales is entirely coincidental.

This edition published by arrangement with Steeple Hill Books.

® and TM are trademarks of Steeple Hill Books, used under license. Trademarks indicated with ® are registered in the United States Patent and Trademark Office, the Canadian Trade Marks Office and in other countries.

www.SteepleHill.com

Printed in U.S.A.

CONTENTS

Books by Bonnie K. Winn

Love Inspired

A Family All Her Own
Family Ties
Promise of Grace
Protected Hearts
Child of Mine
To Love Again

BONNIE K. WINN

is a hopeless romantic who's written incessantly since the third grade. So it seemed only natural that she turned to romance writing. A seasoned author of historical and contemporary romance, her bestselling books have won numerous awards. *Affaire de Coeur* chose her as one of the Top Ten Romance Writers in America.

Bonnie loves writing contemporary romance because she can set her stories in the modern cities close to her heart and explore the endlessly fascinating strengths of today's woman.

Living in the foothills of the Rockies gives her plenty of inspiration and a touch of whimsy, as well. She shares her life with her husband, son and a spunky Westie terrier who lends his characteristics to many pets in her stories. Bonnie's keeping mum about anyone else's characteristics she may have borrowed.

FAMILY TIES

To every thing there is a season, and a time for
every event under heaven…a time to weep, and
a time to laugh; a time to mourn, and a time to
dance…a time to embrace…a time to love.
—*Ecclesiastes* 3: 1-8

Dedicated to my husband, Howard, a man of faith *and* romance, an irresistible combination.

Prologue

Houston, Texas

The day was too bright, the sun too cheerful, Cindy Thompson decided. It should be gray, overcast, perhaps drenched with rain or swept by relentless wind. But only a mild breeze stirred the sweet, spring air. It was the best time of year in Houston. Plagued by heat and humidity, the near-coastal city could rarely boast of mild, pleasant days. But it was something Cindy had been accustomed to, growing up there alongside her sister, Julia.

But Julia no longer had to worry about hot and cold, about sunshine and rain. Still the light shone mercilessly on her mahogany coffin, revealing the grain of the highly polished wood and the creamy hue of the pure white floral spray. Two lone ivory ribbons proclaimed "wife" and "mother."

Cindy swallowed another rush of tears, her gaze sliding yet again to her brother-in-law, Flynn Mallory, and his three tiny, identical daughters. Julia would be pleased, Cindy thought irrationally. The girls were dressed beautifully. Matching dresses of deep green velvet, no doubt from Houston's finest children's store, shiny black Mary Janes, spotless ivory tights.

The triplets were just barely twenty-two months old, matching bundles of endless energy. Cindy wondered how Flynn had managed to ready them with such precision. From what she'd known, Julia had been their sole caretaker since Flynn was always working, striving to improve his already-prosperous business.

Cindy had offered to help with the girls, but Flynn had firmly refused. Not much had changed. Flynn was still holding her at arm's length. Shaking away the painful memories, Cindy bent her head for the closing prayer, offering one of her own for her beloved sister.

Silence sliced over the crowd now as they waited for Flynn to rise. He did so slowly, trying to hold three tiny hands with his own larger ones. Taking that cue, Cindy reached for baby Alice's hand, since she was seated beside her. Flynn didn't protest, for once looking out of control and a bit lost.

"Mommy?" little Beth asked, looking as lost as her father.

Flynn's face worked, his lips seemingly trying to form words his heart refused to utter.

Seeing his pain, Cindy knelt down beside the girls, enveloping them in a hug. Then she gave each of them a single pink rosebud, Julia's favorite. Quietly she led them to the casket, allowing each to place a flower on the sun-warmed wood.

Flynn watched helplessly, barely acknowledging soft-spoken condolences of friends as they filed past. Clearly his world had been shattered. Julia had been a rock, the nucleus of their family. Cindy had always imagined her sister growing old, surrounded by Flynn and a passel of adoring grandchildren. But that wasn't to be.

Any more than her own happiness was to be.

Cindy shook away the thought, immediately ashamed of her pettiness. Her only concern could be the children. Cindy intended to delay her return to Rosewood. She wouldn't abandon her sister's children. She owed it to Julia and even Flynn's resistance wouldn't stop her. She knew, however, it was only temporary. She couldn't hope to be included where she wasn't wanted. But in the meantime she would shower the girls with love…and pray they wouldn't forget her.

Chapter One

Rosewood, Texas
One year later

Driving slowly, Flynn Mallory surveyed the main street of the small Hill Country town he'd chosen to call home, a hamlet far different from Houston. And incredibly far from the only roots he'd ever known. He and Julia had never visited Rosewood. Cindy had made the infrequent trips to Houston, saying she could combine business with pleasure. It had suited Flynn. It wasn't easy to travel with the triplets and he'd felt no need to survey Rosewood until now.

But Rosewood offered what his daughters really wanted—their aunt Cindy. For the millionth time, Flynn regretted the loss of his family...his entire family. There was no loving family member to turn to.

No one who could offer help or advice. No Mallory grandparent, aunt or uncle who could help the girls know they were loved. Cindy wouldn't have been his choice if he'd had anyone else to turn to. But his relatives were all dead and Cindy was the only member left of Julia's family. Cindy was irresponsible and fun loving, but he could provide the stability his children needed. They could visit with Cindy once a week and get the emotional bonding they craved while he ensured a secure environment.

For a moment Flynn thought he'd taken a wrong turn. The eclectic, charming neighborhood was old and well-worn, the yards filled with ancient oaks and carefully pruned rose gardens.

Expecting a sleekly modern condo, Flynn looked for a place where he could turn his vehicle around. But then he spotted Cindy's address. There was no mistake. The numbers sat atop a nameplate of swirling letters that spelled out Thompson. But he still wasn't reassured. The softly faded old Victorian house didn't fit his image of Cindy.

Climbing out of his SUV, Flynn strolled up the red brick sidewalk. A magnificent aged magnolia tree perfumed the air, its dark glossy leaves looking as though they'd been polished by hand. Flynn knew the slow-growing tree had to be at least one hundred years old. But the house looked that and then some.

Unable to stop staring, he climbed the steps to the

wraparound porch. Flynn reached for a doorbell and found an old brass knocker instead. He glanced upward at the gently curving eaves, pounding a bit more loudly than he intended. And within seconds the door whipped open. A disheveled, startled-looking Cindy stared at him.

Since she looked flustered, he offered a smile. "I *did* call."

Cindy pushed at a lock of flame-colored hair framing her forehead. Then she pulled back the door, opening it wider, looking surprisingly flushed. "Of course. I'm sorry. I got caught up in some painting and lost track of time." She held up a brush covered in bright yellow paint, then glanced down at her paint-splattered overalls. "Give me just a minute to wash my hands." She gestured past the foyer to an inviting room. "Make yourself comfortable."

Not surprised that the irresponsible Cindy was off schedule, Flynn nodded, walked in, then went down the single wooden step into the parlor.

It was the only word to describe the room. A huge, leaded-glass bay window kept the old-fashioned room bright. The whimsical furniture was as intriguing as it was impractical. Delicate needlepoint chairs that didn't look as though they could support real humans were drawn up to a table set with translucent cups and saucers, a matching bone-china teapot, and bite-size sandwiches.

Raising his eyebrows, he noted that a fainting couch replaced a more conventional sofa. Nothing about Cindy's house met his expectations.

"I'm sorry," she said, gliding into the room, sounding a bit breathless. "I promised my friend Katherine I'd have the bookcases for the Sunday school rooms painted this week. There didn't seem to be so many when I volunteered," she ended with a smile.

He shrugged, knowing little about Sunday school and its expectations. He'd been a boy when he'd last attended church. And that was a lifetime ago.

She moved toward the prepared table with a teapot. "It's hot." She gestured to the thick fabric covering the pot. "The cozy keeps it warm. Tea?"

"It's not necessary."

Cindy kept her smile in place. "Perhaps not, but it's very civil."

He relented, realizing she was being gracious and he was being ungrateful. There had been little time in the last year for niceties. Every available moment had been spent chasing the triplets and trying to decide whether he was making the right decision in moving to Rosewood. It wasn't Cindy's fault that he was feeling so pressed. She was simply trying to help. He forced himself to relax. "My appointment with the Realtor isn't for another hour."

Cindy poured the tea and handed Flynn a cup. "So you're still certain you want to move here?"

Awkwardly he balanced the small, fragile cup, not ready to admit his apprehension. "I'm ready for a change of scenery. Everywhere I look or go, I'm reminded of Julia." He caught her questioning gaze. "Not that I don't want to remember..."

"I understand. But won't you have to face it sometime?"

He frowned. "I've faced her death, the fact that I have to go on alone. But the girls need a change." Unwilling to share how upsetting this was with her, he switched subjects. "And I couldn't take looking for another baby-sitter."

She offered him the sandwich platter. "That bad?"

He took a few of the crustless diamond-shaped snacks, his hands seeming unusually large and clumsy amidst the fragile delicacies. "Worse. I wanted to be sure that whoever was taking care of the girls was responsible."

She drew her brows together, a shadow eclipsing the bright curiosity in her eyes. "That didn't work?"

He paused for a moment, examining the odd little sprouts that edged the filling of the delicate sandwich. "Depends on your point of view. The first baby-sitter, Mrs. Sanders, took charge immediately. I imagine there were POW camps run with more humor. Even I was tiptoeing around the woman. I didn't want the girls growing up believing they had to snap to attention in their own home."

Cindy laughed. "Surely there was a compromise."

"I hired former schoolteachers, and even a registered nurse."

"Weren't they better than the commandant?"

"Somewhat. But the truth is no professional caretaker's going to love the girls and care for them like someone in the family would."

Cindy's fingers tightened around the handle of her teacup and she paused for a moment before she spoke. "You're right, of course. But aren't you worried about uprooting the girls?"

"From preschool?" Flynn shook his head, knowing it wasn't the girls who would be uprooted. "They're young enough to adjust to a move. More so than to the loss of their mother. The only reason I'm considering relocating is because of them." Even if it meant reconnecting with a woman he considered best forgotten. "Everything I do is in their best interest."

"I know it is, Flynn," she responded, her gaze resting on him intently. "I'm just trying to be a good sounding board. This is a big step, and Julia's only been gone for a year."

"True. But I didn't just wake up one morning with a wild hair. I'm able to provide almost every monetary need my children have, but I can't produce a family I don't have."

Cindy nodded, knowing he, too, was the last member of his family. "I may be one of the few people in the world who can understand that." It had been a devastating blow for Cindy to lose Julia since they were the last two left in their family. Still, something about Flynn's uncharacteristic behavior bothered her. He was not the sort of man who moved to an unseen town on a whim.

"And you can't force a connection," Flynn was saying. "Children either feel that for a person, or they don't. And the girls feel it with you."

Tears misted in Cindy's eyes and her lips trembled, emotion overshadowing caution. "They mean so much to me. Thank you for showing your trust in me."

Flynn hesitated, but knew he had to be honest. His daughters were too precious to him for anything less than the truth. "You won't have to take on any responsibility with them."

She blanched, then recovered quickly. "Of course."

Flynn didn't want to hurt her, but she had to know the real purpose of their move, why he was doing this against all reason. "The girls need an emotional connection with you, rather than help with their upbringing."

Cindy's head bobbed up and down a bit too vigorously. "I understand. And I suppose you've worked out something for your company."

He tried not to remember how much that hurt, as well. "After Julia died, my vice presidents banded together, running things so efficiently that it became apparent I wasn't needed for the day-to-day operations."

"Won't you miss it?" she asked softly. "It's been a big part of your life."

More than she could possibly know. "I'm not content to glide along on past accomplishments." He forced enthusiasm into his voice, guessing otherwise the words would ring with empty truth. "I need something new, something challenging."

"And you can find that in Rosewood?" Cindy asked skeptically.

Flynn managed a reasonable chuckle. "Aren't you being a bit snobbish about your adopted home?"

"Not at all. Just realistic. We're a long way from boardrooms and stock quotes."

"Not as far as you think. With the Internet, you can be in Iceland and have as much access to Wall Street as anyone in New York. But I just want the right place to retreat, one where I can recoup, try to start again."

Her expression softened. "I know it's been difficult for you. I miss Julia terribly every day. I remember her laugh, her way of making the worst situation bearable." Cindy met his eyes. "It must be far worse for you—especially trying to be mother and father to the girls. But the important thing is that the girls *do* have you. The rest will come in time."

Uncharacteristic doubt assailed him as it had since Julia had died. "You're so sure?"

Cindy took a deep breath, the green of her eyes deepening to near emerald. He wondered at the emotion that skittered across her face. "As sure as any one person can be. The Lord never gives us burdens that are heavier than we can bear."

He shrugged impatiently, thinking her talk of faith must be her latest fad, one that would no doubt be forgotten soon. He knew from experience that she'd be better off without that treacherous fantasy. "Church seems like ancient history."

She searched his eyes. "That's too bad. You won't find anything more relevant and timely."

He glanced at his watch. "Speaking of time, would you like to go with me to meet the Realtor? After all, you recommended Linda Baker. Besides, you know the town. You can steer me away from any lemons."

The edge of her mouth curled upward. "Kind of takes the adventure out of the process, doesn't it?"

"You've forgotten, Cindy. I don't care for adventure."

Cindy hadn't forgotten. She'd simply pushed that truth to the back of her consciousness. Along with the cache of emotions Flynn Mallory created. While he waited in her parlor, Cindy reached for a change of clothes, remembering the first time she'd met him.

She and Julia were at a party. Spotting Flynn Mallory, Cindy knew immediately that everything about him seemed larger than life. From his shock of unruly chestnut hair to the fire in his dark eyes, to the fierceness of his determination. She had never met anyone like him. Immediately she was attracted to his strength and purpose. Unlike the other young men in the group, he had a maturity and confidence that set him apart. Cindy hadn't doubted from the moment she met him that he would succeed. Everything about him said he wouldn't allow anything less.

She'd been equally determined to make him hers.

And that remained one of the foremost failures in her life.

After she and Flynn had shared one electrifying gaze that she still couldn't forget, Cindy had fallen hard and fast. Unable to still what had momentarily flowed between them, in the ensuing weeks Cindy had employed every trick she knew to interest him. Not because she wanted a mild flirtation, but because she had truly fallen in love with him.

But the more bizarre and outlandish her efforts, the more he withdrew. She and Julia saw him often in their social circle. But Flynn began to concentrate on Julia. He clearly valued Julia's stability and desire to have a family.

And despite his initial attraction to Cindy, he seemed determined to ignore the adventure she craved. And that was something she'd never understood. For it seemed the fire in his eyes matched hers. It was the first and only time she'd ever felt that way about a man.

Even though it broke her heart, she backed off when he and Julia became serious. And she steadfastly accepted the position of maid of honor for Julia, cheerfully organizing showers, parties and wedding breakfasts.

If there were tears beneath the smiles, no one knew. And Cindy told herself that her feelings for Flynn would fade. That in time, she would come to view him as a brother. But that hadn't happened.

Instead, to extricate herself from the situation, a few months after the wedding she had moved to Rosewood where her best friend, Katherine Blake Carlson, was the pastor of the community church.

In the time that followed, Cindy had seen her sister far less frequently than she would have liked. She made sure she visited when Flynn was away on business, keeping the pain at bay. When she did occasionally run into him, it all rushed back, though. He was unfailingly polite when they met, but she could tell that despite the passage of time he still saw her as flighty, unfocused. And she didn't try to change that opinion. It didn't really matter anymore.

Yet his tie to Julia and subsequent place in their family remained an unhealed wound. So Rosewood became Cindy's escape, her place of peace.

And now Flynn Mallory was shattering that to bits.

Cindy shook back her hair, added earrings, then picked up her purse, feeling strangely nervous about being in Flynn's company.

For an instant she remembered his startling phone call a month earlier—the one that promised to change her life and threaten her secure existence. She'd wanted nothing more than to ask him to stay away—not to move to Rosewood. But she couldn't deny her nieces a chance for happiness. If she truly could help them, she wouldn't put her own concerns ahead of theirs.

And it was nothing short of a miracle that Flynn had asked for her help. It was a complete turnaround for him…and a point she couldn't stop questioning. Why, *why* was he doing this?

Taking a breath, Cindy stepped through the expansive arched doorway that led into the parlor. Flynn turned just then. And despite her best intentions, she caught her breath.

He stepped forward and she exhaled, praying silently for strength.

"I'm ready," she announced, forcing cheerfulness into her tone.

When he glanced at her, she wondered if it was disapproval she saw registering in his expression. Self-consciously, she smoothed the soft fabric of her long, flowing, deep purple skirt. Belatedly it occurred to her that the choice might be a bit wild for Flynn. Julia had always dressed and acted much more conservatively.

Their parents' death had stolen Julia's sense of adventure. Cindy had reacted in just the opposite fashion—she needed excitement and new challenges to feel alive. But then everything about her had been too wild for Flynn.

She tried not to dwell on that as they walked outside and settled into his SUV. Once inside it, however, her nervousness increased. The spacious vehicle seemed oddly intimate.

"So, what do you think of Rosewood?" she asked, trying to chase away her nerves.

He shrugged as he handed her the directions Linda had given him. "Haven't seen much of it yet."

"There's a lot of history here, but not anything too high-tech."

"You have electricity and phone lines?"

She blinked. "Of course." Then she realized he was teasing. "Except on candle day, of course."

He took his attention from the road. "Candle day?"

She met his gaze. "Keeps us from becoming too dependent on technology."

He lifted his brows in acknowledgment. "Guess you hope it doesn't fall on stormy days, then."

She pursed her lips. "So the wind doesn't blow out our candles?"

"Right."

The teasing exchange allowed her to relax a fraction. "It's really a good place to raise children.

People watch out for each other, the schools are filled with teachers who care. And our church pulls together through good times and bad."

"You make it sound idyllic."

Cindy turned to gaze at the crepe myrtle trees in full bloom, their delicate blossoms coloring the landscape. As she did, she thought of her own loneliness, the empty nights, the longing for what would never be. "Not exactly idyllic. But genuine."

"That's rare enough in the world today."

Agreeing, Cindy nodded. Seeing that they were nearing the turn to the address he'd given her, she pointed out the way.

"Linda promised to show me the best Rosewood has to offer," Flynn commented as he made another turn.

"She's a great Realtor, as well as a nice person," Cindy acknowledged. "And hopefully she'll have some decent listings."

Glancing at her, he frowned. "That was said with a bit of doubt."

Cindy hesitated. "Rosewood doesn't have much growth, so there's not a lot of new home construction. People tend to settle in and stay in one place. I think only one new subdivision's been built in the last twenty years. So, not much was available when I started looking. Luckily I was able to stay with Katherine because it took me a while to find my place."

"Is that how you wound up in the Victorian?"

"Oh, no! It's exactly what I wanted. That's why it took so long. I've dreamed of owning one of the painted ladies as long as I can remember. I didn't want to settle for anything else." Or *anyone* else, she added silently.

Flynn glanced at her in baffled astonishment and she wondered why he seemed so surprised. Belatedly she also wondered just what he *had* expected.

Then, rounding the corner, they arrived at the first house. A cheerful Linda Baker waited on the front porch.

As they walked through the house, Cindy found her gaze going more toward Flynn than the smallish interior. Sunshine spilled through the uncurtained windows, brightening the rooms. Flynn turned just then and the light framed his uncompromising features. Despite the fact that his lips didn't rest in a smile, she was so drawn to him, it was nearly a physical ache. What was it about this one man that touched her heart in a way no other had?

His gaze shifted, meeting hers, and for a moment she glimpsed uncertainty. As instantly she knew it to be a rarity for him. Again she wondered why he was doing this. How could he consider moving to this sleepy town so far from everything that was intrinsically him?

Flynn again shifted his gaze, obviously unwilling to share that truth with her. But it didn't stop her wondering, nor her awareness when he brushed by.

She pulled back swiftly, yet she could see his eyes widen in startled surprise. Her vivid purple skirt twirling, she spun away from him, practically running toward the front door.

A few moments later Linda joined her, keeping her voice low. "I really thought he'd like this one."

Perhaps if Flynn didn't find a house to his liking, he would abandon his plan to move to Rosewood, Cindy mused silently. Just as instantly she remembered her bond with Julia, her responsibility to her sister's children.

Soon they were on the way to the second house. Then the third. Again, Flynn patiently outlined all of his needs to Linda, who listened carefully, but not too hopefully.

And it was only downhill from there. Everything they'd seen was in need of major repair. Also, none of the houses seemed to suit Flynn. Even with significant renovations, Cindy couldn't see him in any of these homes, including the one they now viewed.

"This one's a bit on the modern side," Linda told him, obviously trying to interject some enthusiasm into her voice for the not-too-inviting house. "That should appeal to a forward-thinking man."

"Hmm," Flynn replied.

"It has quite a bit of potential," Linda added hopefully.

Flynn glanced at the unusual roofline. "What was this originally? A school?"

"Yes. But it had extensive renovations when it was converted. The kitchen—"

Flynn, however, was shaking his head. "Anything left to show me?"

"I'm afraid not. The only other listings in town are a few two-bedroom starter homes that aren't nearly as large as you've told me you need. Honestly, if I thought another Realtor would have something more appropriate, I would tell you. But there's only one other company in town and we're both on a multi-listing system. I'm afraid that with this temporary housing shortage, there just isn't much of a selection." Linda drew her brows together. "Actually, knowing what you want, especially considering your preference for contemporary, I think you ought to consider building."

"Won't that take a while?" Cindy asked, wondering if this could be the relief she'd hoped for.

"Probably," Linda agreed.

"But I've already sold my house in Houston," Flynn told them in a surprisingly defeated tone.

Cindy tried not to let her breath escape in a huge whoosh. "You did?"

"Yep. I thought I'd find something here."

"Perhaps Linda has the right idea—build a house. Can't you hold off the closing date on your house?"

"Nope." His expression tightened. "We closed last Friday."

Cindy winced.

"I wish I hadn't told the girls we were moving right away," Flynn muttered. "I realize now it was a hasty plan, but I never thought I'd encounter a housing shortage."

Linda brightened suddenly. "Cindy, you've got a ton of room at your house. If Flynn decides to build, maybe he and his kids could stay with you until his house is finished."

Nonplussed, Cindy stared first at Linda, than at Flynn.

"We couldn't impose," Flynn began.

"Well, it wouldn't be imposing," Cindy found herself saying. What could she say with Linda staring at her with those puppy-dog eyes and Flynn looking like a stalwart, if bereft, widower? "It can't take that long to build a house," she added weakly.

"And I have the perfect contractor!" Linda exclaimed. "Roy Johnson—my cousin. He just finished a job, and I know he's available. And there's plenty of land for sale locally."

Flynn still looked torn. His gaze was probing as he met Cindy's. "Are you sure about this?"

Her throat thickened as every bit of her common sense screamed *No!* "Of course. What's family for?"

"But this is a lot to ask," he responded in a tone that made Cindy wonder if he wanted to be talked out of the plan.

"Cindy's always helping everybody in town!"

Linda exclaimed. "I'm sure she'd love to help her own family for a change. She told me about those darling triplets of yours."

Cindy stared helplessly at Flynn, realizing she'd been caught in a trap of her own good works and inability to spit out the truth.

But he was looking more than a bit flummoxed and reluctant himself. "I can rent an apartment while the house is being built."

Linda shook her head. "Not in this town. Everything for rent is snapped up by the oil folks—Adair Petroleum's opened a new regional office here to oversee pipeline and trucking operations. The only housing you can find is for sale. And there aren't a lot of those—well, you just saw them. Because of this small boom, there's a real housing shortage. To be honest, it probably won't last long. Everyone at Adair should be settled in a few months down the road and then things will get back to normal. But that won't do you a lot of good right now."

Flynn looked at the unattractive house. "Then I'll buy something temporary."

"That's ridiculous," Cindy burst out. "Everything we've seen today will take a lot of fixing up just to be livable. By that time, your house could be built." She felt herself digging an even deeper hole, but knew her conscience wouldn't allow her to be quiet. The triplets didn't deserve more disappointment. At their age, a few months' delay would seem like an eternity. "Linda's right. I have plenty of room. You and the girls can stay with me."

"I would like to oversee the construction of the house," Flynn pondered, still not sounding convinced, but rather, trapped.

Which put them both in the same position.

"Then it's all settled!" Linda exclaimed, looking like a Girl Scout who'd done a good deed, and certainly the only happy member of their trio. "I'll assemble lists of available land right away."

Cindy forced her smile to widen as she met Flynn's gaze. "Looks like you're all set."

He considered her words for a moment, looking as though he wished he had another option. Any other option. "I can put the furniture in storage. We could probably be here in about two weeks. That'll give you time to change your mind, Cindy."

Two weeks. The words flashed through her like a bad mantra. Two weeks until everything she knew was turned upside down. Two weeks until the man she loved moved into her life. And her house.

Chapter Two

Flynn couldn't hold three hands at once. He tried, but one always slipped away. He'd taught the girls to hold each other's hands so they wouldn't get separated. But on days like today excitement outweighed caution.

They stood on the curving sidewalk that led to Cindy's house. As they did, Flynn took a deep breath, wondering yet again if moving to Rosewood was a mistake. He'd almost turned the SUV back around a dozen times on the drive from Houston. It didn't matter that the house was sold; he could find another place to live in Houston.

"Swing!" Alice exclaimed just then, pointing to the old-fashioned two-seater that was suspended from the tall rafters on the front porch.

"An' flowers," the softer-spoken Mandy added.

"Mommy flowers," Beth chimed in, referring to the roses her mother had loved.

Flynn felt that subtle clutching of his heart—one that always followed mention of Julia. The girls spoke of her less and less often, their young memories fading already. Yet, each comment was a new wound. However, it was a wound of guilt—one that came from the reminder that he wasn't thinking enough of Julia.

Flynn was appalled that he, too, was beginning to forget little things, that days passed with little or no thought of her. He wondered if the progression was normal, or if he was as unfeeling as his own mother had been.

The front door opened just then and Cindy stepped onto the porch.

"Cinny!" In unison, the girls shouted their name for her. Breaking away from him, they hurried up the sidewalk and then the wide steps. Reaching the porch, three compact bodies hurtled toward his sister-in-law.

Laughing, she caught them, exchanging huge hugs and kisses. "Hello, darlings! I thought you'd *never* get here!"

"Us here," Beth replied, grinning.

"And you're so tall," Cindy continued. She cocked her head, studying them in mock amazement. "By next week you'll all be as tall as me!"

The girls giggled madly.

"Uh-uh!" Alice protested.

"I don't know," Cindy teased, shaking her head. Then she reached down, picking up the toddler.

Immediately, the other two clambered to be picked up, as well. Still laughing, Cindy scooted over to the swing, reaching for the other two, lifting them up to sit beside her.

"Now *there's* a picture," Flynn told her as he neared the porch, realizing as he spoke it was true. Cindy looked as unaffected and natural as the triplets. It was a warm and fuzzy image that could have graced a magazine layout.

"Daddy sit, too!" Beth demanded.

But he shook his head as he bent automatically to kiss Cindy's cheek.

The startled response in Cindy's eyes surprised him. But then it seemed to surprise her, as well.

Cindy spoke quickly to fill the gap. "Why don't we go inside and get you all settled in?"

"Swing!" Beth demanded when Cindy stood up.

Flynn plucked his daughter from the swing, preempting her demand. The more malleable Mandy moved toward the door without protest. Alice, somewhere between mild Mandy and belligerent Beth, seemed to realize it was best to comply, as well.

"Why don't I show you where the bedrooms are?" Cindy told him as she led the way. "Let's grab the girls and head upstairs."

Flynn obliged, picking up Beth and Alice. Mandy was content to latch on to Cindy. Upstairs, Cindy pointed out the room she'd chosen for Flynn. Although small, it was the least feminine one in the house. And directly next to it, she led them into a large bedroom, outfitted with three kid-size beds and an overflowing toy chest.

Squealing, the girls wriggled free and hurried over to the new bounty.

Overwhelmed, Flynn stared at her. "Cindy, you shouldn't have gone to so much trouble. This is too much."

She shrugged nonchalantly. "I do a lot of volunteer work and I bring home kids all the time so I had a lot of stuff."

"In threesomes?"

Cindy grinned. "Well, not exactly. But it wasn't that difficult to do a little rearranging."

He stared at the freshly painted pink walls, a captivating also newly painted mural, ruffled lace curtains and a newly upholstered window seat that matched the mural. "A *little* rearranging?"

"Okay. Guilty as charged. But I enjoyed doing it. And, really, cross my heart, I had the other kid paraphernalia."

Despite her protests, gratitude flooded him. Julia had lavished attention on her children, but they'd sorely missed a woman's touch since then.

"Look, Daddy!" Alice shouted, bringing him a bright pink-and-silver unicorn. The soft stuffed toy was toddler safe with no plastic eyes or nose for little ones to swallow.

He knelt down beside her. "That's nice, baby."

Happy with her treasure, Alice scooted away. Just as suddenly, Flynn felt exhausted. The past year had been an endless succession of trials and emotions. And now, without warning, Cindy had opened her life and home to them. It was as overwhelming as it was gratifying.

To his surprise, when he rose, he saw unexpected understanding in Cindy's expression. But she didn't comment on it. Instead, she smiled before turning to the triplets. "Okay, girls, we have tofu tacos for dinner. Who wants to eat?"

But the triplets were practically headfirst into the toy box.

"Probably should have told them about the tacos first," Cindy mused. "No matter." She glanced at Flynn. "Unless you're hungry?"

"I'd kill for some coffee."

She grinned. "You won't have to get that drastic. I could use some myself. Why don't we put up the safety gate at the top of the stairs and find our caffeine fix?"

"Won't get any argument from me," Flynn replied. But he made sure the safety gate was secure before he joined her in the farm-style kitchen.

He glanced around appreciatively. She had incorporated new appliances that resembled ones of yesteryear next to original freestanding cabinetry. She'd kept the integrity of the original structure, yet updated it enough to make it workable. He wondered what all the fronds of hanging dried herbs were for. Mixed among the bluish and sage green were also dried bouquets of roses and heather. It reminded him of a potently fragrant garden that had been preserved from past summers. "This is some kitchen."

"Thanks. It's one of my favorite rooms. I'm reworking them one at a time."

"You've got a pretty big house, Cindy. Planning on filling it up soon?"

For a moment she froze, her hands filled with a pitcher and carton of cream. Then she laughed, a nervous sound in the otherwise relaxed kitchen. "What makes you ask?"

"Just a comment on your home. I didn't mean to pry. Just thought maybe you were dating someone special."

Her fingers clenched the handle of the pitcher before she relaxed enough to pour the cream. "You have a vivid imagination."

"I thought maybe that was why you moved here."

Suddenly breathless, she made a production of looking for the sugar. "Excuse me?"

"I couldn't see any other reason for a young woman to move to the boonies. I thought it must be love."

"Love?" she asked, her voice sounding strangulated.

"I *am* prying. Sorry."

She fussed with the coffee cups, then added a plate of cookies to the tray before finally bringing it to the table. "No need to apologize."

"Still, it's a great house."

Cindy smiled. "Anything newer or smaller cost a fortune. Not many people want to fix up these old painted ladies. This one needed a lot of gutting and repair. Not to mention horrendous utility bills that are eating into my trust fund."

"You wouldn't trade it for a new one," he mused accurately, surprised to realize how much she seemed to fit with the charming old house.

"Nope. It's drafty, always in need of fixing—and I love it."

He accepted the coffee she offered, studying the rose pattern of the fine bone china cup and saucer. "No generic mugs for you."

Her gaze followed his. "It's one of my weaknesses—collecting china. But I only have one complete set. I collect orphaned cups and saucers—I must have twenty of them, each a different pattern."

Flynn glanced at the other collectibles that lined her glass-fronted cabinets. "You like old things—antiques, I mean."

"They have history. I like to imagine the people who once owned them." She stared upward at the tall ceiling of the kitchen, then the original arched wooden-paned windows that brought the sunshine inside. "I couldn't imagine living in a house that's squeaky new, that hasn't had time to develop character."

"Like the one you convinced me to build," he commented wryly.

She flushed suddenly, not a gentle blush, but a violent wave of color, a shortcoming that seemed to be a side effect of being a redhead. "I'm sorry. I really didn't mean—"

But he dismissed her protest. "I know what you meant. And you're right. This house suits you. I'm just not sure yet what suits me." He'd known once, but everything about his life was uncertain now. Especially this move, the one that had him sitting next to her.

Compassion filled Cindy's eyes. "You'll know again, Flynn. It may not seem like it now, but you'll find your way."

"You sound remarkably certain."

"It's my faith," she explained gently. "It makes me sure there's a path for me. I might stumble now and then, but at the end of the day it's always there."

He nodded out of politeness, his own abandoned faith scarcely a bitter recollection.

Still, in comfortable silence they sipped the strong coffee and nibbled on buttery shortbread cookies.

Flynn cocked his ear, listening for the sounds of his daughters.

"I have a baby monitor," Cindy remembered suddenly. "I'll hook it up after dinner. In fact, it has enough units for all the bedrooms upstairs and one here in the kitchen."

Quizzical, Flynn studied her face. "Why do you have a baby monitor?"

"As I said, I bring home kids now and then from my volunteer work. With a big old house like this, the monitor saves a lot of steps. One of the first little ones I brought home with me kept escaping from his crib. That's when I discovered baby monitors. Of course, with that little curtain climber, I could have used an alarm system."

An unexpected smile crossed Flynn's face. "That bad?"

"Unequivocally. And, of course, to make matters worse, he was an absolute charmer, so I could never stay mad more than a few seconds."

"That *would* be rough," Flynn remarked.

"Especially when it was time for him to go home. The house was deadly dull and I didn't get nearly enough exercise."

A thud from upstairs echoed through the floorboards. "I have a feeling you won't be lacking in exercise now." He stood. "I'll go check on them."

Cindy watched him leave, feeling her heartbeat settle to a near-normal rate. At this pace, she'd be a wreck in less than a day. Watching everything she said, trying not to read something into his words…. Briefly she closed her eyes, masking the questions. But not the big one. Had she made a terrible mistake in agreeing to let Flynn stay in her home? Would he somehow discern her hidden feelings? And could her heart stand this constant assault?

Again she heard a few thuds overheard, then the clatter of many small feet on the wooden stairs. Rounding up the troops, she realized.

In moments, the girls scampered into the kitchen and many of her apprehensions faded. How could she not give everything in her power to them? They were Julia's legacy, the only tangible link she had left. Little Mandy clutched Cindy's leg and the last of her reservations melted even more. Whatever it took, she would help these girls. No matter what it cost her own heart.

The following day, Flynn used a few rocks to anchor the blueprints on a portable camp table. Rudimentary but effective. The breeze was light, yet it ruffled the rolled paper just enough to keep it out of alignment.

Cindy glanced at the papers, then at the lot Flynn had purchased. "Are you happy with them? The architect drew up the plans awfully fast."

His gaze remained on the lot, but he didn't look especially pleased. Instead it was a contemplative expression. "Rand Miller's a friend. And he put together the complex for my insurance company."

"Does he design homes, too?"

"Usually bigger ones than I'm planning, but yes. He's doing this one as a favor to me."

"Has he seen the lot?" Cindy asked, her eyes on the triplets who seemed determined to pull up all the wild buttercups scattered across the field grass.

"We took a ride out here before he drew up the plans. Luckily, Linda showed me this lot first—so it didn't take any time to decide."

"The view's good," Cindy mused, appraising the gently knolled lot. "Are you planning to put the house at the top of the little hill?"

Flynn nodded. "That'll make the best use of the plans. I want a lot of windows—so many, it looks as though the walls are made of glass. Which works out well since I'm going to have a solar energy system."

Cindy pointed to the drawing of the roof. "This looks kind of unusual."

"Good eye," Flynn replied. "That's a cooling pool. With all the brush out here in the fields, there's a higher fire risk. The pool will keep the roof from catching a stray spark."

"Hmm."

Enjoying her polite but puzzled expression, Flynn laughed. "You don't sound convinced. It's not only for safety. We can swim in the pool, as well."

"Ah…" Politeness gave way to pleasure, softening her face in an unexpectedly attractive way.

Not that she wasn't already pretty…. Flynn felt his thoughts jerk in surprise. He'd always known what an attractive woman she was, but that had never mattered in the past. Not when Julia was alive. And because he and Cindy were all wrong for each other, it could never matter in the future.

"You'll be glad of that in the summer," Cindy was saying, her smile nearly as bright as her blazing hair.

"What's that?" he replied, distracted by the wash of unpleasant memories.

She drew her brows together as she glanced at him in quizzical surprise. "That you can swim in the pool."

"Oh… Yes."

But Cindy didn't seem to think his mental detour was significant. "The kids should love it."

His expression mellowed. "I want to build swing sets and a playhouse, too, make the house a place they want to be."

Cindy's smile was at once tender yet nostalgic. "You're a good father, Flynn."

But he couldn't easily accept the compliment. "I spent a lot of time away from them when they were babies. Julia was so competent. She and the girls were a perfect unit. It didn't seem as though she really needed me to be there." As soon as the words were out of his mouth, Flynn realized they were true. He'd never verbalized this vague feeling and it both surprised and embarrassed him that he'd made the confession to Cindy.

"Perhaps it just seemed that way," she suggested gently. "The way our parents died changed Julia forever. You know she blamed it on their incurable zest for adventure." Cindy paused, her expression reflective. "And I always felt that was why she became so efficient and capable. So much so that she no doubt thought taking charge of the girls was good for both of you. And she probably didn't realize she was radiating such a self-sufficient image."

"Maybe," Flynn acknowledged, not completely buying the explanation. Cindy was right about their parents. Julia had confided early on that's why she wanted stability and security, but it didn't explain shutting him out. "I should have seen past that, made sure I was involved in raising my own children."

Cindy moved a bit closer. "The important thing is that you're here for the girls now. As difficult as this sounds, they probably don't remember any of that earlier time."

He nodded glumly, suspecting it wouldn't be long before they lost all memory of their mother.

"Oh, Flynn! You don't think they'll forget their mother, do you?" Cindy exclaimed, obviously only that very moment realizing they could forget Julia.

But he couldn't find any glib reassurances to offer. "I've worried about it. Even now, they speak of her less and less often."

Dismayed, Cindy stared at him, tears misting her vivid green eyes, as she brought one hand to her mouth.

Flynn moved closer, his fingers closing around her arm. "Between us they'll remember." It was as much a promise as a resolution. A promise born of one he'd made long ago.

"She loved them so much," Cindy murmured. "They have to know that."

"They'll see it in you," Flynn told her, the response surprising both of them.

Cindy's chin lifted, her eyes meeting his. "They will?"

"They've held an attachment to you that's remarkable, considering how young they are, how seldom you used to see them. I can't help but think it's your connection to their mother."

Slowly, almost painfully, Cindy nodded. "There was a time when Julia and I were so close, we used to imagine we were twins."

Flynn frowned, the words giving him weighty pause. "You never seemed much alike to me."

A smile rose from the pain on her face. "Probably not to anyone else. We don't look anything alike—I'm the only renegade redhead besides my grandmother. And I'm as boisterous as Julia was refined, but it was something deeper. A connection in our souls. And that only strengthened after our parents died."

"But you didn't visit all that often. And you moved away from Houston," he pointed out, wondering yet again about his elusive sister-in-law, remembering how he'd shut out any thoughts of her once Julia was his.

Cindy turned, her gaze fastening on the gently winding road that was nearly obscured by the great tracts of irrepressible wild grass. Her open expression didn't slam shut; rather it sidled away so subtly, he wondered if he imagined the change.

"People grow up and away," she finally answered. "Distance need not be more than a physical impediment. I don't think it was for us."

"She missed you," Flynn admitted. "Especially since you were the last of your family."

Pain vaulted past subtlety, ravishing her face. "I had no idea."

"Don't take the words to heart. But you should know how she felt, how she always valued your relationship." He couldn't admit that Cindy's absence from their lives had been a relief to him. Flynn hadn't needed or wanted reminders of what she represented, of what he had tried to escape every day since childhood.

Despite his reassurance, only a sparse bit of comfort mixed with the trepidation painting her face. "I should have visited more. I shouldn't have let…"

"What?" he asked, when her words trailed away.

She brushed a tear from the corner of her eye, then shook her head. "Nothing."

"Did you have an argument?" Flynn asked, wondering how he could have not known that.

"No." For a moment her face brightened. "Julia wouldn't have allowed it. Besides, she was my other half. Surely you've noticed that we were complete opposites?"

The fact that Cindy was her sister's opposite in every

way was still Cindy's biggest downfall in his opinion, the reason he'd chosen Julia over her, yet he nodded.

"We seemed to complete what the other lacked. And I feel like my other half's gone forever." Suddenly she looked horrified. "I don't know what's wrong with me. I keep putting both feet in my mouth and tromping around like they're clad in combat boots. I'm so sorry. You truly have lost your other half."

"No need to apologize. We both lost her." His gaze moved to include the girls, who were tossing wild-flowers skyward, then giggling madly as the blossoms fell down upon them. "We all did."

"Children are so resilient," Cindy mused. "It's one of the ways the Lord protects them."

Flynn lifted his eyebrows but he didn't respond, thinking it wasn't worth arguing over. His own faith was long gone, and he still believed it wasn't something Cindy would be spouting for long. "Hmm."

But Cindy didn't argue in defense. Instead, the expression in her eyes was so knowing and certain it defused any debate. At once, Flynn felt old defenses lock into place.

As his thoughts rumbled, he spotted the girls as they started running toward the road. Even though only a handful of cars had passed in the last hour, Flynn and Cindy both bolted after them. It didn't take long to corral the children.

"All right, girls, you know better than to run toward the road," Flynn began in a stern tone.

But the girls laughed as they jumped up and down, cutting off his reprimand.

Since where they stood was still plenty of distance from the street, Flynn tried not to overreact.

"Cows!" Alice hollered, pointing across the road.

Glancing up, Flynn saw a mild-mannered herd of dairy cattle munching on the grass. "So that was the attraction," he muttered.

"You have to be wary of small-town dangers," Cindy agreed in a serious tone. But the twinkle in her eyes gave her away.

"They do look pretty ferocious," Flynn replied, seeing the cattle's only movement was the swishing of hairy tails and the methodical chewing of cud.

A tiny giggle escaped even though Cindy was clearly trying to keep it under control. "We have some wild ice-cream socials here in town, too. Gotta be on your guard all the time."

Flynn glanced down the empty road. "I can see that. There might even be a horse or two in the next pasture over."

"Horsie!" Beth and Mandy repeated in delight.

"Cow!" Alice insisted.

"Just wait until a new movie comes to town." Cindy couldn't repress her grin. "The excitement's enough to do you in."

"I think for now the horses and cows will keep us entertained."

Cindy's expression was knowing and skeptical. "We'll talk in six months when the biggest action in town is the fall carnival."

"I haven't been to a carnival since I was a kid." The thought was unexpectedly warming. But Flynn knew what Cindy was driving at. Clearly she thought he would grow tired of small-town life, that Rosewood would lose its appeal. But everything else that had once held appeal for him was now gone. Yet instinctively he felt that the tiny town was right for him. Was it possible he'd been given another chance? Another place to call home?

Chapter Three

"**I**'m on to you guys," Cindy told the girls with mock seriousness as she wiped one face, only to see another triplet smear granola cereal across her cheek.

They only giggled more.

Each of the girls was secured in a booster seat, bowls and spoons in the same vicinity, as they sat around the breakfast table with Cindy.

"Here you are," Flynn greeted them. Awakening only moments earlier, he'd been startled to find all three girls gone from their beds. Passing Cindy's room, which was next to the girls', he could see it was empty, as well.

Cindy and his daughters glanced up at him in unison. The girls garbled out greetings mixed with cereal and juice, slurry versions of "Daddy."

"Morning," Cindy greeted him.

Flynn was unable to shake the frown from his face. "You didn't have to do this."

She shrugged easily. "No big deal. I was up, they got up. So we're eating."

"But they're a lot of trouble to feed and—"

"Not really. Besides, it's more fun than eating by myself with only the newspaper for company."

"Oh." Deflated, he wasn't certain what to say. For the past year, despite a housekeeper, nannies and sitters, much of his daughters' care had fallen on him. It was disconcerting to see how easily Cindy took over the chore. "They weren't up this early the last few days."

"Takes a while to get settled into a new place. And it's possible I woke them when I got up."

"I didn't hear anything."

"You're two rooms over. Besides, like I said, it's no big deal. Actually, it's kind of fun." Mandy decorated her golden, honey-blond hair that moment with a glob of cereal. Cindy laughed aloud as she reached for a damp towel. "For the most part, anyway."

"I'm up. I can take over."

"Why don't you grab some coffee?" Cindy smoothed the towel gently over Mandy's hair, removing most of the cereal. "No sense jumping in till you're awake." She stood just then, moving over to the refrigerator, drawing out a container of organic apple juice.

His mouth opened as he intended to tell her to back off, that these were *his* children, that *he* would feed them breakfast. She spun around, however, at that moment her face pulling into a tentative look of speculation. "You know, I may have to take you up on that offer. I got so caught up in the girls I forgot today is Tuesday, my Rainbow class day."

Pottery, he guessed, or some similar sort of thing. She'd always been involved in one crazy project after another. Julia had reported on her sister's escapades often enough. But that had only reinforced his opinion. Cindy was fun, reckless and totally without responsibility. He'd finally stopped listening to Julia's tales, having learned enough about Cindy. He had grown up in a home where fun had been valued over stability and it had ruined all their lives. It was the reason he'd always remained detached from Cindy. Now she was offering him back the responsibility for the girls so she could run off to some mindless class. "Fine."

She smiled. "I have a few minutes, though, if you'd like that coffee."

His voice sounded stiff even to his own ears. "It's not necessary. I *have* managed to feed them and drink my coffee for the past year."

Her brows drew together. "Of course, but—"

The phone rang, cutting off her reply.

Flynn could only hear one end of the conversation, but he didn't need to listen long to learn that it sounded as though she planned to meet half a dozen friends for the day's outing.

"Fine, I'll pick up Lisa and Heather on the way, too," Cindy continued on the phone. She glanced at her watch. "But I'd better run." She turned back to Flynn after clicking off the phone. "You sure you're okay on your own? I could make some arrangements if—"

"No. I told you I didn't want our staying here to interfere with your life."

"It's not. It's just that today—"

"Go," he replied shortly, sliding into the chair nestled between the girls.

Looking as though she wanted to continue what she was saying, instead Cindy nodded. "I'll see you later, then."

That was more like it, he thought to himself after she left the kitchen. He hadn't asked for or wanted Cindy's help. Turning back to the girls, he saw that they weren't happy with her disappearance, though.

"Cinny," they wailed in unison.

"Daddy's here." He comforted them.

"Cinny!" they continued demanding.

"Cereal?" he questioned, pushing a measure of enthusiasm into his voice, staring down at the unfamiliar granola, thinking it didn't look very appetizing.

But when he glanced up, three minor storms had descended over their faces.

"It wasn't my idea for her to leave," he attempted.

Beth, always the loudest of the triplets, banged her spoon on the edge of the table. "Cinny!"

"Okay, time to settle down and eat your breakfast."

Although they weren't happy with the request, they eventually complied. Three sticky faces later, he was near the end of his patience. It was going to take forever to get the girls cleaned up, not to mention the damage they'd done to Cindy's formerly spotless kitchen floor. It wasn't how he'd anticipated the day, but there was no getting around the fact. He was going to be scraping up granola for at least part of the morning.

Cindy was tired. Her usually endless supply of energy was running low. It had started draining that morning when Flynn pulled his stiff, get-out-of-my-face act. She'd tried to repump, knowing the Rainbow children needed all she had to give. But his mood had intruded on hers the entire day—even though today had also been filled with rewards.

None of them was the large variety that impressed most people. Rather the small ones, like when Heather offered to share a toy. Not remarkable for most children. But then Heather wasn't the average child. She'd lost her parents and younger brother in a car accident. Now, living with an aunt and uncle who didn't really want her, she'd become hostile, desocialized. A few months earlier Cindy had convinced the child's guardians to allow Heather to attend the Rainbow class.

The class had begun three years earlier with one

lonesome little girl, Lana, the child of a single father who was desperate to round out his daughter's life with the happiness she'd lost along with her mother. Cindy, full of love she'd yet to give anyone, lavished it on Lana, finally coaxing smiles, then laughter from her sad little face. Then another emotionally scarred child had come along. And another.

Katherine had encouraged Cindy when she'd suggested forming a group. And the Rainbow class was born. Children continued to join, all with a variety of needs, no two the same. Yet they came together in the Rainbow class, a healing, nurturing place.

Normally days spent with her "Rainbow" kids were ones of great satisfaction. But the nagging feelings she'd carried with her from the house had stolen some of that pleasure.

As she pulled into her driveway, Cindy couldn't halt a jolt of apprehension. It wasn't a simple emotion, but one tied in to her feelings for Flynn, his obvious dissatisfaction and the grand mess she'd made by inviting him to stay in her house.

For the first time since purchasing the winsome Victorian, she was reluctant to enter. Her throat caught—this, her place of refuge, was no longer a sanctuary. Forcing the dregs of her energy to respond, she pushed open the front door.

And entered chaos.

The triplets, who appeared to have dragged every

toy in the house to the front hall and parlor, were running through both rooms as though flung like buckshot.

Paralyzed for a moment, she watched in stupefied fascination as Flynn entered the hall and tried to harness the girls.

He glanced up just then, all his earlier stiff resentment gone, replaced by a sheepish embarrassment. "It's really not as bad as it looks."

She placed her purse on the hall table. "That's a relief."

"Nothing's broken—I put all the fragile stuff up high." Cindy glanced at her assortment of antique scarves and shawls that normally hung from a brass rack near the door. Apparently the triplets had tugged them free. Now they were strung haphazardly over and across the rich marquetry floors. Sunlight from the second-story rotunda usually shone on the intricate pattern of oak, bird's-eye maple and rare East Texas long leaf pine. Now, however, it was hardly visible under the mess.

"Things got a little out of control," Flynn admitted.

"So I see."

Flynn followed her gaze, releasing a low groan. "I didn't realize they'd gotten into your scarves, as well. To be honest, I thought once I'd put the breakables out of reach, they'd be safe while I mopped the kitchen floor."

Amazed, she stared at him. "Why did you feel you had to mop the floor? I just did it—"

"Breakfast," he explained, the one word conveying paragraphs.

"Oh."

He met her gaze. "I know I said I didn't need any help, rather emphatically if I remember correctly. Truth is, back home we had a housekeeper. While she wasn't their nanny, she kept all the messes and spills cleaned up. I never realized how difficult it would be to watch the girls *and* clean up their fallout."

She felt a chuckle unexpectedly germinating and tried to suppress it. "Sometimes things aren't as easy as they appear."

He glanced around the nearly destroyed area. "I'd say that was an understatement. Unless you have a strong objection, I'd like to find a housekeeper as soon as possible."

Cindy allowed a fraction of her smile to escape. "I don't think that's really necessary."

"You want to live like this?"

"That's not necessary, either." She kept her tone mild, guessing the end of his rope was nearly frayed. "I often have four or five children here at one time. But it does take a little organization, some planning."

He stared at her in disbelief.

"I *do* have a grasp on those concepts," she told him wryly.

"Still—"

She held up one hand. "I'm really not accustomed to depending on others, especially in my own home. To be honest, it would seem like an intrusion. How about if we try it my way for, say, a week? If it doesn't work, we'll look into finding a housekeeper."

"A *week?*"

She chuckled. "You sound about the girls' age. It's a week, not a year."

"Maybe so. But the week I'm anticipating will seem like a year."

Cindy bent down, retrieving a hand-beaded silk shawl that was the prize of her collection. "Look at it this way. Your stuff's in storage so I've got the most to lose."

"Point taken. I just hope you don't regret your offer."

Regret. It was her constant companion, a reminder she couldn't shake with hurricane force winds. But having become an expert at disguising her feelings, she only smiled, edging toward the kitchen. "I'd better check things out, start on dinner."

"The floor's clean," he responded.

She glanced at the wreckage in the parlor and hall and nodded. "Well, that's one positive."

"Don't worry, Cindy. I'll put things back to rights."

She disappeared into the kitchen. It wasn't possible, she knew. Even if the house was fashioned into *Architectural Digest* perfection, things could never be made right. Not while he held her heart in his hands, and didn't even realize he controlled its very rhythm.

Dinner was spectacularly uneventful. Only a few spoonfuls of mashed peas landed on the floor, soon wiped clean. Flynn wasn't certain just how Cindy had accomplished it, but control prevailed throughout the meal. But it wasn't a disciplinary nightmare. To the contrary, the girls were happy, easy to handle.

Perhaps it was a woman thing, he mused. Julia had always had just the right touch with the girls, as well. But that wasn't something he expected Cindy to share with her sister.

Bathtime was also competently and quickly accomplished. Soon, the girls were snuggled in their sleepers, tucked into their matching beds.

More than a bit amazed, Flynn studied Cindy as they reached the bottom of the stairwell. He wondered if she was part magician, making the care of the triplets seem effortless.

Having reassembled much of the parlor, he began gathering some of the scarves still strewn across the floor.

Cindy stooped down, as well, carefully picking up each ancient slip of fabric.

"These are really…different," Flynn finally decided aloud.

"That doesn't exactly sound like a compliment."

He held up one sheer red scarf, threaded with gold, edged with long strands of dark fringe. "They suit you."

Her smile was wry. "Again, I'm not sure that's a compliment."

Flynn paused, the scarf awkwardly filling his hands. "Look, I know we don't see many things the same way." He held up the exotic red silk. "But I don't have any frame of reference for stuff like this."

"Granted," she replied, a touch of a sigh flavoring the solitary word. "Julia was always practical, unlike me. Cotton versus silk, that was us."

He studied the weariness she couldn't quite disguise. "We haven't gotten off to the best start, have we?"

She shrugged. "It's a big adjustment. You're used to running things your way."

"And you're used to being on your own."

Cindy lifted her face, new shadows deepening her obvious fatigue. "Yes. That I am."

Flynn sighed. "I knew this was a bad idea. We're messing up your life, your home."

"I'm not a neat freak," she replied after the barest pause. Then her eyes shifted away. "We knew going in this wasn't an ideal situation, but if it helps the girls, I can manage. How about you?"

He fingered the soft, exotic scarf. "I'll do whatever it takes to make the girls happy."

"Then there's no more to say," she responded.

Flynn wanted to search her eyes, to see how Cindy really felt, but she stood, turning to the brass rack. He owed her an apology, but it was difficult to spit out. He'd spent the better part of his adult life making certain he had nothing else to be sorry for. And he doubted even his unsettling sister-in-law could change that.

Cindy chose to be especially quiet the following morning as she worked in the downstairs conservatory. Not wanting a repeat of Flynn's displeasure, she'd tiptoed around her bedroom as she'd dressed, then slipped silently down the stairs, knowing how to avoid the creaks in the ancient steps.

Her night had been restless, filled with dreams caused by thoughts she couldn't chase away. So she'd risen early to escape them, needing to lose herself in activity.

Picking up a box filled with old photos, she started to put it aside. Then she glanced at the picture on top. Settling the box on top of the table, she withdrew the photo. It had been taken years ago. Her parents, Julia and herself. They were on vacation at Disneyland. Julia and their mother both looked pretty, smiling gracefully. But Cindy and her father were wearing goofy hats and glasses, wide, silly grins covering their faces. She eased a thumb over the slick surface, remembering the good times, the pain of loss that had faded, but never disappeared.

Flynn coughed from the doorway.

Startled, Cindy dropped the photograph.

He entered, reaching down to pick it up before she could. "Nice picture."

She nodded, not willing to delve into her unreconciled loss. "Kind of early in the morning for reminiscing, isn't it?"

"I wasn't actually. Just saw that picture and it brought back a lot of memories."

He looked at it again. "You and Julia were on different wavelengths."

Cindy swallowed the pain of that comment. "She was always more like Mother, refined, graceful, elegant."

"And you were like your father?"

"I guess so. He was the adventurer—the one who wildcatted after the days of oil wildcatting were past. He liked to pursue the impossible."

Flynn's gaze shifted between Cindy and the picture. "I'm not like my mother, either."

Never having heard much about his family, she wondered about them. "What was she like?"

His face closed. Tossing down the picture, he shrugged. "Just a mother." Then he glanced at the newly cleared desk. "What are you doing in here?"

"Making a temporary office for you."

His eyes swept over the newly arranged room. "You didn't have to do this—"

"You're beginning to sound like a broken record," she interrupted. "You need a place to work in until you get the office space you want."

"I'm hoping to get that set up soon."

"Fine. I'll need the room back after a while anyway. It's one I use sometimes for one of my volunteer functions. And in the future it may be the permanent spot for the class."

He frowned. "Then why go to so much trouble?"

This time she didn't shift her gaze, instead meeting his. "It's who I am."

He studied her, clearly baffled.

But then that was the point. She'd always baffled and alienated him. And moving to Rosewood wasn't going to change his impression. Only reinforce it.

Chapter Four

Two days later, Flynn pushed aside the sage-green sheers that covered the tall conservatory windows. Tapestry drapes that puddled beyond the woodwork onto the floor were tied back with thick, silky tassels. It seemed Cindy left no detail unattended. Two pairs of aged leather wing chairs were grouped beside a small fireplace. And a Georgian library table served as a desk, covered by neat stacks of his work papers.

Like the rest of the house, this room was cozy. He was no decorator, but the furnishings she chose reminded him of older homes he'd visited in England and France. Even the landscapes and botanical prints looked as though they could be European in origin.

It was restful, snug and casual, yet he itched with discomfort. He glanced down at the candy bowl filled with sunflower and pumpkin seeds. The house and the temporary office suited him no better than the birdseed she called food.

From the window he could see the swish of a weeping willow in the gentle breeze. And across the street, an elderly gentleman handled his roses with the care usually reserved for rare orchids.

A knock, so quiet it barely penetrated the thick mahogany door, reached him. He turned. "Come in."

Cindy, looking somewhat like a wary redheaded comet, poked her head in. "Do you need anything?"

Flynn shook his head. "I don't know what it would be."

"Enough paper? A snack? Maybe some coffee?"

Although he appreciated her concern, he'd never been comfortable accepting help. "Cindy, I'm not accustomed to having someone make all my decisions for me."

She blanched for a moment. "I didn't realize an offer of coffee constituted interfering."

Flynn drew one hand back across his hair. "That's not what I'm talking about."

Her green eyes still looked stormy. "Then what?"

He gestured around the room, overwhelmed and embarrassed by her generosity. "This. Everything. I didn't ask for an office, but you produced one anyway. Even after I told you I didn't want it."

Cindy's fingers curled around the edge of the door. "You don't have to use it," she replied evenly. "After all, you've rented another office. If you don't mind moving in there while they're renovating, I certainly don't."

The pull and tug vibrated between them.

Suddenly half a dozen small footsteps thudded across the floor. "Cinny! Daddy!"

As the triplets approached, Cindy turned, ending the immediate need for resolution. She knelt as the girls reached her. "Why don't we go swing in the backyard? Let Daddy work."

"You've been taking care of the girls all day. Why don't I take them outside?"

"I want Cinny!" Beth retorted.

Cindy glanced between Flynn and his daughters. "If your daddy helps you swing, I could set the table in the backyard and we could have supper there."

"Supper?" Mandy asked.

"Veggie burgers," Cindy replied. "They're yummy."

Flynn didn't agree, but also didn't want to snap her olive branch in half.

"Yummy," Alice repeated.

He glanced at his daughters, more content in the last week than the last year. For that he could eat veggie burgers and granola. He could also somehow find a compromise with Cindy.

"And I'm about done with work for today," he added, finding a second note of accord.

"Wanna make yummies," Alice was requesting.

Cindy ran gentle fingers through her blond curls. "I can always use a good helper."

"Good helper me," Alice agreed.

"So you are."

"Wanna swing with Daddy," Beth stated more assertively.

"Me, too," Mandy spoke up.

Flynn walked toward them, stretching his hands out toward the girls.

Beth and Mandy readily placed their small hands within his. Seeing the unsettled look that remained on Cindy's face, Flynn relented. "Veggie burgers, huh? I don't suppose we could have French fries with those?"

Unexpectedly her lips twitched. "To cancel out the healthy effect of the meal's veggie portion?"

"Something like that," he agreed. "I'm more a meat-and-potatoes kind of guy."

Her smile widened. "Is that why you pick all the sprouts out of the salad?"

He winced. "I thought I was a touch more subtle."

"Not especially."

Surprise melted away the last of his reserve. "No kind demur?"

"No. That would have been someone else. Not me."

Julia, he knew. Cindy wouldn't say it in front of the girls, but it was true. Julia had always smoothed over any potential bump that could have put a ripple in any conversation. It had been the tone of their entire relationship.

Flynn walked outside with his daughters, losing himself for the moment beneath the cover of towering oaks and ivy-covered lattice work. The yard smelled of honeysuckle vines that poked fragrant blooms through the cracks of the weathered fence.

The swing set that sat on the longish grass was old, not new and shiny. But it was so sturdy, it could hold eight children; now it only needed to support his two small daughters.

Glancing back toward the house, Flynn wondered what it was about his sister-in-law that commanded such affection from his children. Alice had always clung the closest to him, never wanting to be separated. Beth might toddle off on her own, Mandy sometimes only a few feet behind. But not Alice. She was Daddy's girl.

Only, now she seemed to be Cindy's girl.

Inside, Cindy allowed Alice to pat and roll the burgers into shape. They were beginning to resemble small boulders.

"A Flintstones supper, Alice? Good job." After washing the child's hands, Cindy led her to the ancient French doors that opened to the backyard. "Why don't you go swing for a while with Beth and Mandy?"

Happy to be with both Cindy and her father, Alice

scampered contentedly away. Watching her, Cindy couldn't help but wonder if all memories of Julia were fading from their young minds. For a moment she felt a stab of longing for her deceased sister, one more poignant than she'd felt since her untimely death. Even now, Cindy railed against the unfairness.

Colon cancer had struck silently, without warning. And Julia, in typical fashion, had persisted in acting as though nothing could go wrong with her perfect life, her perfect family. Ignoring the final, irreversible symptoms, she had died within six weeks of the diagnosis.

Julia's little family was adrift. In Cindy's backyard. Peering out the large windows, she saw how gentle Flynn was with his daughters. It was a side he showed only with them. Cindy couldn't even remember seeing him treat Julia with the same tenderness. His manner toward Julia had always been filled with deep respect and devotion, but not tenderness. It was as though he'd placed Julia on a pedestal—one her sister had relished. Suddenly she wondered why.

The girls' giggles floated through the open French doors. The low murmur of Flynn's voice accompanied the happy sound. Even though she couldn't understand the walls he constructed or the reasons for them, Cindy could see the joy he brought out in the girls. Although reluctant to cease her uncensored view, she gathered the charcoal lighter and matches.

Once outside, Flynn spotted her as she approached the grill. "I'll start the fire," he offered.

"Great. My least favorite part of eating outside." She handed him the supplies, checking quickly to see that the girls were still safe.

Within a few minutes Flynn had a good fire going. Cindy rounded up condiments and place settings. However, when she brought out the plate containing the misshapen burgers, he raised his brows.

"Pretend we're in Bedrock," she told him breezily.

"I'm still getting fries, right?"

She nodded.

"Fine. We can be in Oz then for all I care."

It was so out of character for Flynn that she paused. Musing, she returned to the kitchen to prepare his French fries.

By the time she brought them to the table, Flynn had finished grilling the burgers. The girls ran from the swings, their short legs pumping with the effort.

Once they were seated, and their burgers assembled, Flynn and Cindy concentrated on their own plates.

He stared at his burger with a noticeable lack of enthusiasm. "Do you have something against regular food?"

"*Regular* food?" she repeated. "As in cholesterol-clogging, energy-draining junk food?"

He took a hefty portion of French fries. "Absolutely." Tasting one, his expression changed. "Are these made some…uh…special way?"

"They're made from potatoes and they're fried," she replied enigmatically.

"In what?"

"Olive and canola oil," she admitted.

He sighed. "Does everything you cook have to be so…healthy?"

She took a moment's pity on him. "We do have a fast-food joint in town. You can always get a fix there."

He picked up another fry, his words hesitant. "You've been doing all the cooking and I don't sound very grateful."

Cindy felt the saddening, one that came from a place she could never quite conquer. "It's not what you're used to." Smiling to hide the pain, she glanced down at the simple dinner. "None of it. Me, this house, the food you think suits birds and squirrels better than people. You probably feel as though you've landed on another planet."

He glanced at the girls, but they were more interested in spearing pickles than the adult conversation. "It is different," he finally admitted. "But I needed a change. And the girls wanted Aunt Cinny."

Caution slid past logic. "They'd have forgotten me in time."

He glanced up, catching her eyes.

"Yes," she replied to the unspoken question there. "Like they're forgetting much of the past year."

In the quiet, the chirp of early-evening crickets mingled with the girls' random giggles and murmurs.

"Are you already tired of us?" he questioned in a low tone that didn't carry down the table.

She could say so much, so very much. Her gaze flew to the girls, cheerfully smearing Cindy's homemade mayonnaise on the table. Correction, she couldn't say anything at all. "No. It's great having the girls here." She paused. "And you, of course. The house is full of noise and smiles and laughter. I wouldn't trade that for anything." She wouldn't, Cindy realized, despite the heartache. It wasn't simply an empty assurance for Flynn.

"Veggie burgers are probably good for us," he offered finally.

Cindy's laugh spilled between them. "Then you'll love the carob-chip cookies."

"I don't suppose you have any genuine chocolate in the house."

She tried to resist the pull of his eyes. "Well, I'm not a fanatic!"

"So you can be tempted?"

Oh, so tempted. She scrambled for a reasonable reply. "I eat the way I do because I like it, not to prove a point."

"Do you ever eat out?"

"Of course. I'm willing to try most anything."

His expression was reflective.

When he didn't reply, she prodded him. "What?"

He shook his head. "Nothing really. Just that Julia never wanted to try anything new."

Of course not. Steady, dependable Julia never made Flynn grimace in displeased surprise. "That must have been a comfort."

"Yes," he agreed.

His reply took away her words, her desire to keep the conversation flowing. She was so everything Julia wasn't. So everything Flynn despised.

The following day Flynn examined the progress on the office space he had rented. The renovations weren't coming along as quickly as he'd hoped. Although they were only weeks from completion, he wished it were mere days. He needed to get his office out of Cindy's house.

Never having had to wrestle with a woman over the issue of control, he found himself uncertain how to deal with Cindy.

Julia had never questioned his opinions, in fact preferring to let him assume all the responsibility and worry of their decisions. It had become their custom for him to decide and for her to comply. It irritated him that Cindy had him wondering if that had always been for the best.

A knock sounded on the outer door. "Hello, anyone here?" a man called out.

"In here," Flynn responded, rounding the corner.

A tall, dark-haired man approached, extending his hand. "I'm Michael Carlson."

"Flynn Mallory," he responded automatically.

"Katherine's Carlson's husband," the man continued.

Flynn searched his memory.

But Michael began to grin. "I see that my wife and her friend didn't tell you about this visit."

Flynn shook his head.

"Katherine and Cindy are friends."

"Oh, the pastor," Flynn remembered.

Michael's grin spread. "Yeah, that's what I thought at first, too."

"Sorry, I—"

"It's okay. Most people aren't used to women ministers. Actually, Cindy asked me if I could stop by, take a look at your renovations. She said your contractor's behind on the job."

"Oh." Flynn issued the solitary word.

"I see she didn't tell you. Listen, if you'd rather call someone else, fine by me."

"I need to get this place operational as soon as possible. But you've probably got a lot of important jobs to be overseeing rather than looking at this dinky office."

Michael shook his head. "I work on all kinds of jobs. I do a lot of remodeling as well as building stores, offices, the new headquarters for Adair Petroleum. And like I said, Cindy asked."

"And that's all it took?"

"Yeah, pretty much."

Flynn couldn't hide his surprise. "Guess things work differently in a small town than a place like Houston."

"I imagine so. All I've known are small towns. I didn't grow up in Rosewood, but a place pretty close in size." Michael looked around at the partially demolished space. "So, what's this going to be?"

Flynn smiled. "Software Development."

Michael nodded. "And you can run that kind of business from anywhere. Rosewood's as perfect as Silicon Valley."

Flynn studied the other man with new respect. "My thoughts exactly."

"You've picked a good town, lots of good people here."

"That's what Cindy's been telling me."

Michael studied him. "But you're not sure yet. That's okay. I don't judge an orange by its peel, either. Get to know us first."

Flynn wasn't accustomed to this much directness, but it struck a chord. "Good advice."

Michael's gaze roamed around the building. "Now, let's see if you like the rest of it."

Hours later, Flynn headed back to Cindy's house. Michael Carlson had carefully examined the office structure. Then he'd offered to have a word with the contractor Flynn had hired. But Flynn wasn't comfortable accepting help from strangers. Or friends for that matter.

Even though he hadn't appreciated Cindy's interference, Flynn liked Michael. Instinctively Flynn believed he was honest, capable.

Still, that brought him round to why Cindy had asked Michael to stop by. Why she felt a need for control, one he hated to admit equalled his own.

Entering the house, he didn't hear anyone; in fact it seemed deadly still. The panic that had struck him once as a child and never fully disappeared now crawled into his throat.

His walk a near run, he traveled through the front rooms, finally jogging into the kitchen. He was ready to turn back and tear up the stairs, when he heard the hum of voices from the backyard. The French doors were closed. Only one kitchen window was slightly ajar, dimming the sounds.

Pulling open the doors, he searched for and saw his daughters. Relieved, he watched for a moment as they played with three children he hadn't seen before.

And in the background Cindy's distinctive, upbeat voice blended with that of another woman's. Flynn took a few steps forward.

It was bright in the yard, the warming spring sunshine pushing past overhanging branches, muted only by the slats of the faded white lattice arbors. And Cindy sat in the sunshine and shadow.

There was something different about her, he realized, walking farther into the yard. Fully animated, unreserved, she was as brilliant as the deep fuchsia azaleas blooming around her.

Glancing up, she spotted him, and some of her vivacity faded. Still, she smiled in welcome.

"Hello, ladies," he greeted them.

Her friend tossed back long dark hair and extended her hand. "I'm Katherine Carlson. I've heard so much about you and your daughters. It's a real pleasure to meet you."

He hesitated for a moment, amazed that this attractive woman was the "female preacher."

She noticed and her grin widened. "Yep. It's true. I'm the woman minister."

He collected his manners, shaking her proffered hand. "No wonder your husband looks like such a happy man."

Confident, unflappable Katherine blushed.

Cindy, to his surprise, winked at him with an equally wide grin. "Then I guess that means Michael found you this morning."

Katherine recovered a trace of her composure. "I hope he was able to help. Michael subcontracts out a lot of the smaller jobs. If your contractor's one of those, he would probably listen to Michael."

Flynn met Cindy's eyes. "I do want to get things going quickly. I'm not comfortable working from Cindy's house."

Katherine shrugged. "Beats me why anyone would rather work in an office building than this charming place, but I'm sure Michael could help if you ask him."

"That's great," Cindy concurred, not relinquishing Flynn's gaze. "I'll be needing the conservatory for one of my groups soon anyway."

Katherine glanced between them, but didn't comment on the visible tension. "Looks like the kids are getting along well."

Belatedly Flynn and Cindy pulled their gazes from each other.

"So it does," Flynn agreed, wishing Cindy wouldn't look at him that way. There was no reason to feel guilty about telling the truth. Then he really looked at the kids. "How old are your children?"

Katherine's face softened. "David's the oldest. He's eight. Annie's six. And baby Danny's fourteen months."

Flynn watched them for a few more minutes. "The older ones are good with your youngest and my girls, as well."

"They've always treated Danny as though they found him under the tree on Christmas morning," Katherine replied with a winsome laugh. "But then, since he was a gift from God, that's not so bad."

Flynn swallowed the comment that sprang to mind.

He didn't have to agree with people to remain polite. "Still, you should be proud of them. Older children aren't always so gentle with toddlers."

Surprisingly Katherine's eyes brightened with an unexpected sheen of tears. "I'm so proud of them I could burst. Annie, David, Danny and their father are the best things that ever happened to me."

Cindy's gaze suddenly held red-hot warning. So he chose his words carefully. "My girls mean the world to me, too."

Katherine recovered her composure. "I know. Cindy's told me about your late wife, and all the sacrifices you made to move to Rosewood."

Startled, Flynn stared at Cindy.

However, her expression didn't lighten. In fact, if he could identify the emotion lurking there, it would be suspicion. And for the life of him, he didn't know what caused that.

"Mommy!" Annie hollered, running up to them, all dark hair and huge blue eyes. Seeing Flynn, she turned suddenly shy.

"Hi," he said first. "I'm Flynn. You must be Annie."

She bobbed her head up and down. "Uh-huh. Can the girls swing with me?"

Katherine stood. "How about if I supervise?" she asked Flynn.

He agreed and in moments he was alone with Cindy. "Is something wrong?"

She studied him. How could she tell him she still had doubts about his uncharacteristic move to Rosewood? She felt a desperate need to safeguard the life she'd built, afraid that her heart would outweigh her caution. Knowing none of it could be said, instead she shook her head. "No. I just didn't expect you home so soon. I thought you wanted to work in your new office space."

"About that… Why did you ask Michael Carlson to come by, without telling me?"

Exasperated, she all but snorted. "Are we back to that again? Are you a total control freak?"

"Not any more than you apparently."

She counted inwardly to ten. "I *know* I'm not like Julia. I'm sure she deferred to your every comment and dictate. But I don't operate that way. I *do* have opinions. And while I don't always insist they're right, I intend to express them." Cindy paused. "Well, unless they hurt someone's feelings, of course. But I'm not retiring and complacent. I have ideas. I make my own decisions." She met his gaze, feeling her chest tighten. "And I'm not going to try to be someone I'm not."

"I don't recall asking you to," he replied mildly. "But I would appreciate a heads-up when you send someone like Michael over."

She frowned. "Didn't you like him?"

"That's not the point."

"*Everybody* likes Michael," she responded in instant

defense, never forgetting how happy he had made her once-lonely best friend.

"Are you being deliberately obtuse?" Flynn asked. "I'm only asking that you not blindside me."

"Then you did like Michael?" she asked hopefully. She knew Flynn needed to broaden his circle of acquaintances. And Michael was one of the nicest people she knew.

"He was all right," Flynn replied.

Cindy took a deep breath, remembering that men didn't verbalize their feelings, that Flynn had probably revealed all that was masculinely possible. "He and Katherine have been my anchors since I came to Rosewood. They're good friends to have."

"Hmmm."

She sighed inwardly. "I mean they could be good friends for you, too, Flynn."

"I'm not especially looking for a wild social whirl."

For a moment the past hung between them, the gregarious, fun-loving social circle they'd once traveled in, the one that had brought the Thompson sisters together with Flynn. Cindy fiddled with a bluebonnet she'd plucked from the grass. "No, but everyone needs friends."

"I don't need to borrow yours."

She wondered if it was Julia's death alone that had created such intense barriers. "They're not trinkets to be lent. One of the best things about a small town is getting to truly know people."

"But it seems most of the ones you know are connected with the church."

She frowned. "And that's so bad?"

"It's not for me."

"Have you considered getting to know them before judging their value as friends?"

The negative motion of his head was reluctant. "Cindy, I appreciate all you've done for the girls…for me. But like the office, or sending Michael Carlson, it's not necessary. You're doing too much already. I'm used to calling my own shots."

Unwanted compassion shadowed her thoughts and her voice. "But isn't that a lonely way to live?"

He raised his brows. "Seems I could ask you the same thing. After all, you moved to a town where you knew only one person, and you live alone in a house big enough for a huge family. Doesn't that seem a bit lonely to you?"

Pain, both past and present, assaulted her. He would never know just how lonely she'd been. How difficult her life had been since he'd pilfered her heart. And meeting his eyes, she wondered how she could continue hiding that from him.

Chapter Five

By Sunday morning, however, Cindy was ready to put that aside. She'd invited Flynn to attend services with her, but he had curtly refused. She had nearly expected the same response when she told him she wanted to take the girls. He'd hesitated, but finally agreed, telling her the social part of Sunday school probably wouldn't hurt as long as she didn't fill the girls' heads with unrealistic ideas. In her opinion, nothing taught at her church was unrealistic, so she took him at his word.

And she chose to ignore the look on Flynn's face when they left. One that said this, too, was simply a fad Cindy would outgrow.

The girls loved Cindy's classic bright red convertible Mustang. Since she had left their curls loose and free, she didn't care that the breeze mussed their soft hair.

"What's at church?" Beth asked.

"That's where we go to learn about God and Jesus."

"Daddy says there's no God," Beth replied innocently.

Still the pain shot straight to Cindy's heart. There was no easy answer, none she could offer that wouldn't confuse Beth. "Not everyone believes the same way, sweetie. As you get older, you'll learn about lots of new things."

"Is God new?" Beth asked.

Cindy smiled despite the pain still squeezing her heart. "No. He's older than the sky and the grass and the flowers and the trees."

"Is He older than Daddy?"

Another trickle of amusement sprouted at the child's guileless words. "Sure is."

"Real old, huh?"

"Yes, sweetie. Real old."

When they arrived at church, Cindy felt the welcoming fellowship like a balm to the wound that was Flynn.

Once the girls were happily ensconced in their class, Cindy was awfully glad she'd insisted on bringing them, despite Flynn's reservations. Again she remembered the look on his face any time she mentioned church. The man knew so little about her, it was pitiable.

It came as no surprise to Cindy that the triplets charmed everyone with their identical heart-shaped faces. It was difficult to withstand twins, impossible to resist triplets. Luckily, they were too young to let all the fawning go their heads.

Katherine popped into the classroom, her eyes lighting up when she saw Cindy and the girls. Crossing to Cindy's side, she lowered her voice. "So you were able to make off with them?"

Cindy nodded, her brows raised in a matching mock conspiratorial motion. "It wasn't exactly the great heist, but I'm happy they're here."

"Any chance Daddy will be joining them?"

Cindy shook her head.

"Has he just fallen out of the habit?"

"I'm afraid it's much more than a broken habit."

"It isn't an unbreachable problem," Katherine reminded her, alluding to her husband's once-lost faith.

"I'm glad it worked out for you and Michael, but I don't know about Flynn...."

"I wasn't certain at first about Michael, either."

Cindy's smile was bleak. "It's not as though this is a break in our relationship. We don't have a relationship to crater."

"I'm afraid you're focusing only on the big picture."

"In what way?"

"I think you need to take it one day at a time. See what unfolds. Learn if Flynn realizes you're no longer a frivolous twenty-one-year-old. You told me that you've scarcely seen Flynn since he married your sister. To be fair, he hasn't had a chance to learn about the real you. Instead, you're an inaccurate memory. Don't you think it's time he got to know the real Cindy? While you're at it, subtly find out if he's in a crisis of faith, which calls for prayer, rather than worry."

Cindy looked at her friend whom she knew to be both caring and wise. "I haven't really thought about it that way. Maybe he's not as sure as he thinks he is."

"Sometimes we're so overwhelmed, we can't see the pieces as they separate and change."

"You know what, Katie-cakes?"

Katherine's grin erupted. "What?"

"I think you're in the right job."

Eyes rolling, Katherine hugged her lightly. "And you, my friend, are on the right track."

Maybe not yet, Cindy realized. But tomorrow was another chance, one she could use to apply Katherine's advice. And she was nothing if not tenacious.

The drive to Houston the following day seemed longer than Flynn remembered. But perhaps that was because Cindy was at his side. He took another glance at her bright red dress, saucy hat and delicate high-heeled sandals. Hardly the outfit he'd expected her to choose for a board meeting. But then, when had Cindy ever done the expected? "You sure that Katherine will be all right taking care of the girls today?"

Cindy didn't disguise her sigh. "She knows it's for a good reason. Her calendar is clear, and to quote her,

'How can I possibly repay you for baby-sitting my children dozens and dozens of times?' It's not as though we have a meeting every day, or even every week. It's only once a month."

Flynn thought about the shares he'd inherited from Julia—half the stock in their family oil business. Ironically, it made he and Cindy unlikely partners, even though he'd ignored his inheritance until now. There had been no time—and it had been too painful a reminder. But Cindy had been insistent about attending the meeting. "Do we have to do much today?"

She shook her head. "Nope. The management staff has been in place for years, they know exactly what they're doing and we're just there to listen and vote if necessary."

He looked at her curiously. "I would think you'd care more about your family's business."

"Did you ever feel that way about Julia's participation?"

Nonplussed, he hesitated. "Well, no. But she—I mean you—"

"What you mean is that Julia had a purpose in her life that you don't see in mine, therefore she was excused. It happens that I chose to focus my life in a different direction."

One of fun and frolic. Just as she had when he'd met her. All motion and energy, but no substance. A flibbertigibbet, his late grandmother would have called her. "It's not up to me to judge your decisions."

Her eyes clouded. "No. But that doesn't stop you, does it?"

He held up one hand. "How about a truce for today? We can enjoy the big city—have lunch at a five-star restaurant without worrying that we'll be wearing half of it courtesy of the triplets."

She relented. "I suppose you're right. I usually do a little shopping while I'm in the city, too."

Flynn grimaced.

Cindy's laughter filled the closed space of the car. "Typical male reaction. I thought we could at least pick up something for the girls."

It was his turn to relent. "I suppose so."

Reaching downtown Houston, Flynn concentrated on the traffic-filled streets. "Gets worse every day."

"I don't know. I find all the people invigorating."

Despite the distraction of tall buildings and hordes of pedestrians, he turned to stare at her. "Yet you moved to Rosewood?"

"Mmm," she murmured.

And she didn't reveal much more as they parked, then attended the meeting. It was only afterward that she brightened again, suggesting they go to the Galleria for their shopping excursion.

FAO Schwarz was a child's fantasy. And Cindy seemed much like a child herself as she oohed and ahhed over the treasures the store contained. She agonized over the selection of three unique stuffed toys.

"Don't you want them to match?" Flynn asked.

She shook her head. "I've never taken to the notion that twins and triplets should be treated as a unit. It's fun to dress them identically at times, but they have to know they're individuals, with different tastes, dreams." Cindy reached for a stuffed bunny, still unable to decide.

"Aren't you going to get one for yourself?" he couldn't resist asking, seeing how absorbed she was in the task.

An unexpected tinge of color warmed her cheeks. "I do have a weakness for them, but I'll resist this once."

Funny, he thought she would indulge her least whim. Maybe she was having an off day.

But the thought had barely faded when she started looking at more toys.

"Actually, I don't want to spoil the girls," he told her. "It's great that you want to be generous, but I think we've gotten enough things for them."

She picked up the stuffed bunny she'd discarded a few moments earlier. "These aren't for the girls."

Once a playgirl, always a playgirl. Flynn was amazed that a woman of Cindy's age would want the bunny. But then her indulgences weren't his concern. Still, he felt a flash of remembered disappointment. One that was reminiscent of their first meeting. He'd seen the promise in her eyes, and had felt the disappointment of learning she was as scattered as Julia was collected.

With their purchases tucked safely in the trunk, Cindy talked him into an exotic restaurant that boasted only the unusual. She had promised to forgo granola and vegetarian fare, but he wasn't sure this was much better.

"So, what do you think?" she asked, excitement deepening the green of her eyes.

"Let me put it this way. I don't recall ever finding myself torn between ostrich and buffalo as my only possible entrée choices."

Her face, bright and mischievous, only sparkled more. "Great, isn't it? I mean any place can offer steak or fish."

Flynn had a sudden longing for just that banality. "So they could." He turned the menu over, glancing at the back. "I don't suppose they have pasta."

She rolled her eyes. "We had pasta for dinner last night."

"True. And what are the chances of finding spinach-and-wheat pasta twice in a row?"

Some of the pleasure in her expression dimmed. "Oh."

He swallowed a sigh. "Most pasta doesn't have that much flavor."

But her former sparkle had disappeared. "That's diplomatic."

"It really was good," he insisted. "I'm not used to a pine nut sauce, but the noodle part was good."

Unexpectedly she laughed. "We really should have gone to a steak place, shouldn't we? It's not too late. We haven't ordered yet."

"No. This is fine. How many chances will I have to try exotic meats?"

"If you stay at my house long enough, you might be surprised."

His actual surprise was the grin he found pushing his lips upward. "So, what do you recommend? Which delicacy won't we be trying?"

She took pity on him. "Both the buffalo and ostrich taste like beef, just a touch milder. And they're lower in fat, cholesterol and calories."

"It must work," he admitted.

Puzzled, she tilted her head. "What do you mean?"

"You're still turning heads, and none of the calories are sticking."

When she didn't immediately reply, he glanced up from the menu. But instead of a warm blush or sly demur, she had paled. "Something wrong?"

Cindy shook her head a bit too quickly and forcefully. "No. Just hungry. I didn't have any breakfast."

Flynn wasn't sure why, but he was certain that wasn't the truth. Still, he didn't argue the point; instead he listened as Cindy asked the waiter for a bowl of soup. He played along deliberately, sensing whatever was bothering her would only be exacerbated by anything else he could say.

It was unusual for Cindy. She normally steamed ahead with unrestricted fervor, energy and an undue need for control. But she never seemed weak.

And it affected him with unexpected emotion. Cindy had never struck him as needing protection.

As he watched, she pushed at the roll on her plate, but never picked it up. So it wasn't hunger. He wondered what it could be, what had so thoroughly shaken her. But throughout the meal she didn't meet his eyes.

And that made him want to know all the more.

A few days later Cindy tucked the new toys into place in the Rainbow classroom. She had chosen each one with a particular child in mind, and she could just picture their faces when they came to the next session.

"Hey, you," Katherine greeted her, strolling into the room. "I thought I saw the light on in here."

"Just getting things ready for tomorrow."

Katherine glanced around the empty room. "And where are your three new appendages?"

Cindy smiled, but her heart wasn't in the effort. "Flynn has them. I think he believes I'd like to take them over."

Katherine's smile was wise, knowing. "Wouldn't you?"

"Absolutely. But not away from him. And Flynn has this all-or-nothing mentality."

"I don't suppose you've considered the possibility that he thinks you might need a break from their constant care?"

Cindy furrowed her brow as she sank into one of the kid-size chairs. "No."

"It's not a competition," Katherine reminded her gently.

"I don't look at it that way!"

"Not even a little bit?"

Deflated, Cindy stared at her friend, the only one who knew her secrets and still didn't judge her. "I suppose I do feel I have a lot to prove."

"Do you remember when I was agonizing about Michael? Trying to change myself into the woman I thought he wanted?"

Cindy nodded.

"And do you remember what you told me? That if he didn't love me for myself, he wasn't the right one for me?"

"All too well," Cindy admitted. "I guess that's the crux of it. I don't really want to change for him, yet I suppose I hoped he'd see me in a new light, realize my value."

"If he doesn't, then he's blind."

Cindy's smile struggled to form, but failed. "Don't you see? He always has been as far as I've been concerned. After he took one look at Julia, I was as appealing as an Easter egg you find in the middle of the summer."

Katherine couldn't stifle a smile. "Oh, Cindy. How can he not see how special you are? How much joy and adventure you bring to everything?"

Cindy shrugged. "He doesn't care for adventure— that's why he chose Julia."

Wincing for her friend, Katherine met Cindy's gaze, her voice gentle. "You also told me that I couldn't be a substitute."

"Believe it or not, that's been the foremost thing on my mind these days. Even if I never find another man to love the way I do Flynn, I won't settle for being Julia's substitute."

"I suspected as much." Katherine hesitated. "Do you suppose now that Flynn is here, some of the illusion of denied love will lose its appeal?"

Cindy couldn't control the tears that spurted, or the trembling of her lips. "That's just it. Now that he's here, it's just worse. I don't know why. I can't explain it. There is something about Flynn and only Flynn that's in my heart and won't go away. I've tried, Kath, I really have." The tears gave way to gulping sobs. "I've tried not to love him, but it's still there, every moment of every day."

Katherine reached out, enveloping her in a hug, one that vibrated with great shaking wails of pain. And one that Cindy was helpless to stop.

* * *

That same evening Flynn tried to keep the lid on the rice cooker, while making sure the girls didn't tug on any of the pot handles on the stove. But that was harder than he'd expected. Fearing they'd pull a pot off and burn themselves, he put them in the next room with a children's video.

He'd chopped and diced for what seemed like hours. He'd found a fairly palatable-sounding recipe in one of Cindy's cookbooks. It was a tofu stir-fry seasoned with oyster sauce. The instructions promised that the tofu would then taste like oysters. He had his doubts, but the dinner he was preparing wasn't for him. It was for Cindy.

Belatedly it had occurred to him that perhaps she was worn-out. She still kept up her hectic social schedule with her Rainbow thing as well as other functions, and she'd also assumed the majority of the triplets' care. Cooking dinner wouldn't make a big dent in that pressure, but maybe it would create a small vent. The girls had loved going shopping for the ingredients. But some of their suggestions had the stir-fry looking a little questionable.

"What's going on?" Cindy asked from the doorway.

Flynn spun around, seeing her gaze take in the messy kitchen. "You're early. I'd planned to have everything cleaned up before you got here."

"Oh," she answered in a small voice.

"But I did get the table set in the dining room."

"The dining room?" she echoed.

"Yeah. The stir-fry should be done soon."

"You're making stir-fry?"

He held up the cookbook. "I found the recipe in here. Between the grocery and health food stores we found everything we needed."

"That's what you were doing today?"

He smiled. "As you pointed out, there's not a lot of action in Rosewood. And the girls enjoyed it."

"Well…"

"I'd planned to have it all arranged in the dining room, but…surprise!"

"Surprise?" she echoed, looking stunned.

"Yeah. To say thanks for all you do for me, for the girls." He walked toward the small sitting room just off the kitchen. "Girls, Cindy's home." As they scampered toward him, he stopped Alice, whispering to her, "Get your surprise."

In a few moments Alice returned and came toward Cindy with a bouquet of daisies.

Cindy's eyes misted as she accepted the flowers, then gave Alice a fierce hug.

"They seemed to suit you," Flynn explained. "The daisies, I mean."

Cindy's throat worked. But Beth and Mandy were rushing at her, as well. Scooping them up in a hug, she hid her face behind their compact bodies. And Flynn couldn't help wondering what was going on in that fiery head of hers.

Finally her face emerged as she settled the girls back on to the floor. "This is really nice. The dinner—" she held up the bouquet "—the flowers. Thanks."

"I don't say it often enough, but you've changed our lives and we appreciate it."

Remarkably he thought her eyes brightened with the suspicion of tears. But that couldn't be. Not freewheeling Cindy. She was all laughter, not tears.

She lowered her face, presumably to sniff the daisies. Her voice was soft, nearly muffled. "And you have changed mine."

The girls pulled at her hands, tugging her toward the dining room to show off the table setting. But Flynn didn't follow, instead remembering the remarkable look on her face, the remembered feelings it evoked. Feelings he thought he'd put to rest the day he proposed to Julia.

Chapter Six

A few days later, Flynn entered his daughters' room. Once again he admired all of Cindy's handiwork, but still he felt she had gone overboard. She claimed she wasn't spoiling the girls, but he was worried about all her overly generous gestures. From experience he knew it wasn't wise to grow up believing life was always this kind.

He reached down to pick up a discarded pair of pajamas the girls had left behind. As he stood, he noticed a new addition to the room. A picture of Jesus.

All the betrayal of his past choked him. It was one thing to spoil the girls, it was another to tamper with their beliefs.

Hearing Cindy's steps in the hall outside the room, he called out for her. "Would you come in here?"

The echo of footfalls on the wooden floor paused, then turned into the room. "Yes?"

"What's this?"

She glanced around the room. "What?"

"Don't play games. This picture."

Cindy looked back at him wryly. "Well, I think that's pretty obvious."

"What's it doing in here?"

She pointed to another picture on the wall—one filled with cartoon characters. "I'm decorating their room."

"The picture of Jesus isn't a decoration. It's a statement."

"I think that's an exaggeration. The girls aren't even three years old yet."

"The younger the mind, the easier it is to brainwash."

"Brainwash?"

"Influence, then."

"Flynn, they're babies!"

"Then why the picture of Jesus?"

She hedged for only a moment. "I like the idea of Him looking over them, protecting them."

"That's a fairy tale," he told her flatly, deep anger and remembered pain darkening his thoughts.

Shocked, she stared at him. "You can't mean that!"

"Don't delude yourself, Cindy. Especially for a craze you'll forget by next month."

Hurt flashed in her eyes. "Is that what you think of me? That I'm chasing fads like a teenager?"

Exasperated, unwilling to face the pain in her expression, he threw up his hands. "All I asked is a simple question."

"Then I'll give you a *simple* answer. Your lack of faith is going to hurt your daughters. If you're having a crisis of faith—"

"You don't know what you're talking about," he responded, with only the slightest grip on his anger.

She studied him, opened her mouth, then closed it again. Nodding, she turned away.

"Cindy?"

She glanced at the picture on the wall. "I'll take it down later. But I can't guarantee that you won't see it somewhere else in the house."

Unable to watch her leave, he turned toward the window. Then he heard the sound of tiny steps, then a tug on his jeans.

Flynn glanced down. "Hey there, Alice."

"Up?" she asked.

He obliged, picking her up until they were at eye level.

"Daddy?"

"Yes, sweetie."

"Why you hate Jesus?"

He hadn't known a fist to the gut could be delivered by a guileless toddler. "What makes you say that?"

Alice screwed up her precious face. "Me heard fight with Cinny. I wanna have Jesus here."

"But it's only a picture."

"How come, then?"

Why not indeed? It was only a picture, it had no power over them. Over him.

Yet the torturous question accompanied him as he went through the motions of the day. It was late afternoon when he finally sought Cindy out again.

She was in the kitchen, preparing a huge casserole.

"That's quite a lot of food," he commented, not certain how to begin this discussion.

"For tonight," Cindy replied. Then she glanced up, catching his puzzled glance. "Remember the people coming over tonight? I told you about them."

"Oh, right. I'll clear out pretty soon."

Exasperation flooded her expression. "Flynn. I invited them over to meet you."

He'd completely forgotten, caught up in hours of rare contemplation, a prisoner of a past he'd never outrun. "Of course."

A buzzer went off and she walked to the oven, pulling out a fragrant tray of rolls. Searching for a place to put them on the crowded tile counter, she glanced up at him. "Did you need something?"

He moved aside the casserole dish at the end of the counter, making a place for the rolls. "I've been thinking…"

Uncharacteristically, she didn't jump in with words to ease his way.

Which made him feel even stiffer, more uncomfortable. "It's about this morning…the picture. You can leave it in their room."

She studied him silently, again surprising him. Flynn wondered where all her fiery words had gone. Especially when she only nodded.

He considered an apology, but the place inside him that held those words had been dammed up long ago. "Do you need any help?"

She seemed to consider this, too. Then she gestured toward the fridge. "You could put the salad together."

"Sprouts included?"

But her usual ready laughter didn't surface. "Whatever you'd like to put in it. The vegetable drawer is pretty full."

They worked in silence for a while. Flynn wasn't certain how to break the strain, how to bring the sparkle and laughter back to Cindy's face.

She glanced up at the clock. "Yipes, I still have to shower and change my clothes before everyone gets here."

"I can finish in here," he offered, surprising himself as much as Cindy.

"Well, I did want to tidy up—"

"I can take care of it," he insisted.

She took a final glance at the food, then nodded. "The table's set and—"

"Go."

"And I—"

"Go."

And she did.

It didn't take long to clean up the kitchen, then check on the girls who were making Play-Doh teddy bears on the faded, terrazzo terrace. Because of the tall, wide windows he'd been able to watch them as Cindy had been doing before he arrived.

He remembered the first time he'd tried to feed the girls and clean up while watching them. It had never occurred to him to put them in the safety of the fenced backyard. An old wooden toy box beneath the awning held a large and varied collection of toys to keep them occupied.

His daughters looked content, having assimilated into Cindy's life and home as though they'd always been here. He thought of the gathering Cindy had planned for the evening, suspecting she hoped to accomplish the same for him. Knowing that hadn't been possible since he was a child, equally certain it would never be possible again.

There was something about a group of people who'd known each other long and well. Their chatter filled the air, snatches of conversation that melded from person to person. It seemed everyone was talking at once, but in a good way. No one was excluded, no one hanging outside the fringes of the group.

And due to Cindy, Flynn was included, as well. She'd introduced him to the collection of people who ranged greatly in age and background. Ruth Stanton, a perky seventy-two-year-old woman, welcomed Flynn as warmly as did people of his own age, and some much younger.

Having met Michael and Katherine Carlson before, Flynn felt a little more comfortable with them. Michael in turn introduced him to Tom Sanders, clearly a good friend, also a casual, warm person. Then he met Gregg Rosentreter, Roger Dalton, Don Westien and Gary Simpson. All the men, obviously good friends, were welcoming.

The fact that it seemed everyone at the party attended Rosewood Community Church wasn't lost on Flynn.

Seeing Cindy heading toward the kitchen, Flynn followed her, relieved to see no one else was in the room. "How'd you go about assembling the guest list for tonight?"

She thought for a moment. "Well, you'd met Michael and seemed to like him. I thought you might have something in common with the other guys he's friends with—also, they're people I especially like."

"No other motive?"

Frowning, she narrowed her eyes. "Such as?"

"They all go to your church."

She relaxed a fraction. "That's where I met my friends."

"*All* of your friends go to your church?"

A touch of exasperation entered her expression. "It's not a requirement. I'm friends with some of my neighbors, other people I've met in town. But, yes, my closest friends are those from the church. You'll notice I did invite most of the people who live on this street, as well."

"To throw me off the scent?"

Something flickered in her green eyes, a flash she quickly disguised. "The sole purpose of tonight's party is to introduce you to people in the town you've chosen to call home. I'm sorry it bothers you that so many of them attend my church. But I could hardly walk the streets and invite total strangers."

Looking at her, the evidence of her temperament, as fiery as her hair, challenged him. Again, he couldn't help comparing her to Julia, remembering how his late wife would never have confronted him. "No, I don't suppose you could. Cindy, I do appreciate your effort but—"

"You didn't ask for a party. I know. Just me being me again."

"Cindy—"

The tall swinging door pushed open. "Here you are," Katherine exclaimed. "Can I help do anything?"

Flynn watched as Cindy reluctantly pulled her gaze away. "Yes," Cindy replied shortly. "Keep Flynn entertained. I'll take some more punch into the dining room." The door swung smartly behind Cindy as she exited.

Uncomfortably Flynn studied Katherine, wondering if he was about to get a sermon.

Katherine strolled over to the oven, opening it to peek inside. "Cindy makes killer crab puffs."

"Pardon me?"

"Her crab puffs—they're great. I know she's into granola and nuts, but she can cook up a storm of gooey, good stuff when she wants to."

"Oh. Well, we've gotten used to her cooking."

Katherine laughed. "Better you than me. When she and I go out, I pick the restaurant and you should see her put away a hamburger and shake."

Flynn suspected Katherine wanted to talk about more than food, yet he stuck to the safety of the subject. "The main course tonight is vegetable lasagna."

"Now that's one of her healthy creations I love." Katherine closed the oven door. "But that's our Cindy, a mass of contradictions."

He should have escaped right after the crab puff remark. Now he was stuck. "Yeah, I suppose so."

"How many trust fund kids do you know who devote their lives to volunteer work instead of shopping and gliding around the world?"

Flynn stiffened. Apparently Katherine didn't know her friend as well as she thought. "For the time being, anyway."

But Katherine didn't immediately rebut the reply. "So, that's how it is."

"Excuse me?"

"Nothing. I'm glad you and your daughters are getting settled in."

"Well, we will when my house is finished."

"Of course. It's always difficult to blend two lives."

Flynn remained cautious. "Cindy's been patient, but we're intruding on her routine."

Katherine shrugged. "I haven't heard that from her. It's a difficult time for you and your daughters and I know she's thrilled to be able to help out. But you know Cindy, she just wishes she could do more."

Flynn studied her, wondering at any hidden meaning. "I'm not sure what that would be."

Katherine's smile, however, was enigmatic. "She probably doesn't, either."

The kitchen door was pushed open again. Without looking at Flynn, Cindy walked over to the oven.

"They looked almost done when I checked them," Katherine offered.

"Thanks."

Katherine nodded, then left the room.

The remaining silence was a palpable thing.

Flynn felt forced to end it. "Katherine says you make killer crab puffs."

"Yeah, well, Katherine tends to be a bit prejudiced." Cindy withdrew the baking sheet, transferring the appetizers to a porcelain tray. "We'd better get back in there."

"Cindy?"

She didn't meet his eyes. "Yes?"

"I seem to have a way of irritating you on a daily basis. I guess I'm just not used to someone taking control of things, offering so much. It was really great of you to arrange this party tonight."

This time, she did raise her eyes, her green eyes darkened to the color of sheltered, unlit forests. "So what else is new? I'll never be like Julia and everything I do is a daily reminder of that."

"That's not what I meant."

Cindy walked toward the door, one hand on the old wood, prepared to push it open. "Yes, it is. Even if you don't want to admit it."

Flynn followed her slowly. Why did Cindy think he would want her to behave as Julia had? Julia was his wife and Cindy was…Cindy.

Walking into the crowded parlor, he was immediately swept into the group of people. Michael made a point of including him in his conversation with Tom Sanders.

It was a friendly gathering. Everyone seemed genuine, most made hospitable offers ranging from baby-sitting services to help on the house he was building. It was rather amazing.

"We start softball practice this Saturday," Michael was telling him.

"I'm not sure I have time to—"

"We don't take no for an answer. Just ask Michael," Tom Sanders added.

Michael's grin was wry. "I can vouch for that. It's a lot of fun. And we can always use another player."

Flynn looked from one determined face to the other. "Why don't we see how Saturday shapes up? I don't want to dump the kids on Cindy for the day."

"Are you kidding?" Tom asked. "She's nuts about your girls."

Puzzled Flynn stared at him. "And you know that…how?"

"She talks about them constantly," Tom replied. "She's as proud of them as any parent."

Unconsciously Flynn stiffened. "She's their *aunt*."

Tom shrugged. "I wish I'd had an aunt like Cindy, someone who makes everything seem like a treat. I think Cindy could make fun out of a pile of sticks in the rain."

Flynn studied Tom, wondering if the man had more than friendly feelings for Cindy. "So, you and your wife have been friends with her for a while now?"

"I'm not married," Tom replied. "Not anymore."

Which meant he and Cindy could well be more than friends. Funny, he didn't seem like her type. Flynn shook away the thought. It wasn't any of his business whom Cindy chose to date. Yet he found himself observing Tom, evaluating the other man.

As the evening drew to a close, all the departing male guests reminded Flynn of the upcoming weekend softball game. And, oddly, he was tempted to go.

When the door closed behind their last guest, Flynn watched as Cindy began to quietly collect bowls and trays. He joined her, filling his hands with the delicate china Cindy treasured. "So what do you think about their insistence that I play softball?"

"I think you should do what you want to."

Flynn angled his head. "That doesn't sound like you."

She turned briefly. "How would you know?"

"What?"

"You don't know me at all. How could you possibly think you would recognize when I'm being myself?" Not waiting for an answer, she disappeared into the kitchen.

Flynn was left holding the delicate china, as deceptively fragile, it seemed, as Cindy herself.

The softball field was much like Rosewood itself, old-fashioned and appealing. A small shack sold ice-cream cones, canned soda and homemade hot dogs.

Cindy made sure the triplets held hands, an uneven line of rambunctious little bodies. She'd been surprised that Flynn had agreed to come to this first practice. Reluctant to the point of reticence, she had expected him to find a thousand excuses not to go.

She wondered if Michael's unscheduled, unexpected visit the previous night had made a difference. Busy with the triplets, she hadn't heard their discussion. And then this morning, Flynn had announced his intention to attend the game.

Seeing her friend, Cindy waved at Katherine, who waved back while angling her head in Flynn's direction.

No need to be subtle, Cindy wanted to shout. But Flynn hadn't seemed to notice. Relieved, she walked the girls around the small field.

Tom approached with a grin. "So, how are the four most beautiful women in town?"

Cindy winked, recognizing Tom's harmless teasing.

He responded by tugging her pert ponytail, making the girls giggle.

Since Tom was much like a brother, she only shook her head in bemusement.

He knelt down, bringing his gaze eye level with the triplets. "So. You going to clap and cheer for Daddy or for me?"

"Daddy!" they chorused loyally.

He whistled. "Tough crowd." Standing back up, Tom reached for Cindy's cooler. "I'll carry this over to the bleachers."

"Thanks. That gives me at least one free hand."

"Cute kids, Cindy."

"Yeah, they really are."

Tom glanced down, seeing that the girls weren't

paying attention. "Lucky break Flynn decided to move to Rosewood."

Cindy withheld the sigh that had been building inside since Flynn's first mention of relocation. "Yeah, lucky."

Tom slowed his steps. "Everything okay, Cin?"

She met his concerned gaze. "I finally have some family here. It's spring. What could be wrong?"

He hooked his arm with her free one. "Remember, you can tell me if something's wrong. I have a sturdy shoulder."

She glanced up at him with a heartfelt smile. "So you do."

"Cindy?" Flynn snagged her attention.

Startled, she glanced at him, not aware he'd walked over to their little group. "Yes?"

He glanced at her arm, still loosely linked with Tom's. "Are you sure you can handle all the girls by yourself?"

Tom discreetly dropped her arm and self-consciously she pushed at the hair that fell across her forehead. "Of course. Why?"

Flynn glanced once again at Tom. "They can be a handful."

She shrugged. "I brought treats." She motioned with her head to the swing set, slide and seesaw in the park beside the softball field. "And there's plenty to keep them busy. Besides, they can't wait to see you play."

"Daddy play!" Beth demanded.

Flynn scooped her up. "In a few minutes."

Mandy tugged at his pants leg, as well, but Alice hung on to Cindy's hand. Flynn obliged by picking up Mandy, giving both girls a hug, then putting them back down.

"We have to let Daddy go practice," Cindy explained.

"Me play, too," Beth demanded.

"No," Cindy told her firmly. "This is Daddy's day."

"She could walk to the field with me for a few minutes," Flynn replied.

Cindy wanted to thump him. And he thought *she* was spoiling them? "I spent quite a bit of time explaining to the girls that this is a grown-up game, that little girls don't get to play."

"I didn't intend to let her play."

"No, but I'll spend the entire time keeping her off the field if you take her out there."

"That's an exaggeration," Flynn replied.

Tom cleared his throat. "I'd better get back to the practice." He held up the cooler. "I'll put this on the bleachers."

"Thanks," Cindy replied, wondering why Flynn was scowling as though he had ants in his shoes.

"Sure," Tom replied, walking away quickly.

"What's with you?" Cindy asked.

Flynn's scowl didn't lighten. "Problem?"

"You just chased away one of the nicest people here. Some special reason why?"

"You tell me."

Puzzled, Cindy grasped Alice's hand a little tighter. "So, are we going to grapple over taking the girls on the field?"

He looked at her for a long moment. "No, I don't guess we will."

Then his gaze shifted toward Tom. "Nothing to argue about at all."

Confused, Cindy stared after him as he stalked on to the field. And for the life of her, she couldn't imagine why he hadn't taken to Tom.

"Men," she muttered.

"Men?" Beth asked.

"Yes, sweetie. We'll talk more about them when you're older. For now we'll stick to Cinderella and Prince Charming."

Mandy drew her brows together. "Like Daddy?"

Yep. However, Cindy was the only girl in the world whose glass slipper wouldn't fit. At least not for Prince Flynn.

Chapter Seven

Two mornings later, Cindy carefully banded the remaining stacks of paper, making certain each was straight and in order. She glanced down at the three nearly filled cardboard boxes, then back at the almost bare desktop.

It didn't take a crystal ball to know that Flynn wouldn't appreciate the fact that she'd packed everything without consulting him. But a late-night phone call had taken precedence over Flynn's makeshift office.

Her Rainbow class, already strained by growing pains, had suddenly acquired six new members. And even Cindy, who possessed an inordinate amount of energy, knew she didn't have enough stamina to spread that thinly. The only solution was to cut the class in half so they would be manageable groups. That meant two different meeting times.

And they had run out of space at the church. Rosewood Community had begun a small private academy in the Sunday school building the last year, and they already needed the space allotted to Cindy's Rainbow class. Obtaining it for an additional day each week wasn't possible.

As her class had grown, she and Katherine had discussed the necessity of relocating the Rainbow group. That's when Cindy had handpicked her own conservatory for the purpose. Then Flynn had needed an office and she'd been able to put off the move. But now there was no other choice. Her parlor, with all its breakable collectibles wasn't suitable. And she couldn't keep the kids in the yard the entire time.

"Hey, what's going on?" Flynn demanded from the doorway, his sleep-tousled hair still a bit wild.

Cindy glanced up, immediately assessing his displeasure. "I need to use this room for my Rainbow class."

He frowned. "So you're just clearing out my stuff?"

"You *did* tell me you wanted to handle your own office arrangements, in fact all your arrangements."

He gestured to the boxes. "Is this what you call allowing me to handle my own decisions? Packing my things without consulting me?"

She rolled her eyes. "Do you want me to remind you how often you've mentioned that you'd prefer the office space you rented to this one?"

"One small point—it's not ready yet."

Cindy shrugged. "Michael offered to help. But you wouldn't even let him make a phone call. If you had, maybe the space would be finished by now."

"I don't impose on strangers."

"Michael's not a stranger!"

"Not to you. I barely know him."

Exasperated, she tossed down a manila folder. "By your choice. My friends have extended themselves, but you purposely remain distant."

"Another thing I don't believe I asked for," he reminded her in a tight voice.

She leaned back against the desk. "Look, Flynn. I don't know how things were done with your friends. But in a small town like Rosewood, we depend on each other and our faith."

"One more strike and you're out."

Dismayed, she stared at him. "I still can't believe you mean that."

Impatiently he smoothed one hand back over his chestnut hair. "And you accused *me* of ignoring what I didn't want to hear?"

She fiddled for a moment with the deep blue antique glass inkwell. "I hate to think of you having such a gaping hole in your life, one nothing else can fill."

"And I hate to think I'm going to have to endure a sermon. If I'm going to move today, I'd better get to it."

But she didn't stir, instead raising her eyes. "I wouldn't have put you out of your office if it wasn't for a good cause. My Rainbow class has nearly doubled and there's no other space available."

Flynn muttered under his breath.

Cindy couldn't distinguish the words, but suspected she wouldn't want to hear them if she could. Turning around, she scribbled on a notepad, then ripped the page free. "We can still call Michael about your office."

"How about if you let me make that *one* decision?"

"Of course." She handed him the paper. "Here's his number." She took one more step toward the door, then hesitated. "I know you think I want to wrestle away your control. But it's never been about that. I feel how much pain you've been in since you lost Julia, then all the responsibility of raising the girls on your own. I was just trying to make things easier for you, to let you not have to worry for once."

Flynn stared at her, not replying.

And so she left him there, not certain what he would have said if he'd spoken. Nearly as certain she wouldn't have wanted to hear the words.

Later that morning Flynn studied the bare, dusty space he'd rented. Not much had been accomplished since he'd examined it a week before. He bent to test one of the outlets. No current. He couldn't even plug in his laptop. The spot where the phone jack was to be installed was still a bare empty hole.

He sighed. He could run his computer off the batteries and depend on his cell phone, but it was hardly an ideal situation. And he was eager to set up the business that had been fermenting in his mind. Details were coming together daily, and he was having new development ideas on an almost hourly basis. He also needed to hire a few employees. Glancing around, he realized he couldn't expect anyone else to work alongside him in this disaster area.

Reluctantly he pulled the wadded-up piece of paper from his pocket. He stared from his cell phone to the number Cindy had scrawled. With equal hesitation he punched in the number.

Michael didn't seem to think it was odd that he'd waited so long to call, agreeing to stop by within the hour.

It was an unusually long hour for Flynn. He couldn't repress the memory of Cindy's face, the seeming sincerity of her words. What was it about her that seemed to be crawling under his skin? Admittedly in a way that had never before happened. Not even with Julia. Safe, unthreatening Julia.

And the realization made him want to run, fast and far. Then he pictured his daughters' precious faces. They adored "Cinny" and no amount of logic or reasoning could change that.

Still the minutes dawdled. It wasn't Michael, Flynn knew. It was his own past pushing at him. A familiar suffocating feeling gripped him and Flynn headed outside.

It was there that Michael found him, as he pulled into the parking lot. He had brought coffee for them both. Sipping from thick paper cups, they canvassed the area.

It didn't take long for Michael to make an assessment. "This should have been finished not too long after we talked the first time," he told Flynn bluntly.

"Can you recommend another contractor?" Flynn asked. "I know you work mainly on big projects, so—"

"I told you I do all sorts of construction. I'd be happy to put a crew on it," Michael interrupted.

"But this is a piddling job compared to what you're probably accustomed to."

He shrugged. "You need an office. I have a crew."

Flynn narrowed his eyes. "Did Cindy call you?"

"No. Should she have?"

Flynn hesitated. "I'm not accustomed to accepting favors."

Michael grinned. "Don't worry. I'll send you a bill." He glanced at his watch. "How 'bout some lunch?"

"I don't want to tie up your entire afternoon."

"Gotta eat."

"Yeah," Flynn agreed. "So we do."

Rarely allowing himself to get close enough to form fast friendships, it surprised Flynn to find himself comfortable in Michael's company. But for once he didn't question it. Cindy had provided more than enough questions to chew on.

Many of the kids in the Rainbow class had been to Cindy's house before. And they were happy to return. She had set up projects in the conservatory, kitchen and on the terrace.

It rarely mattered to the children what tasks she chose. They simply enjoyed the nurturing and acceptance Cindy offered. Originally she had assumed that the boys wouldn't enjoy making cookies, but they had lined up alongside the girls at the big, oak table in the kitchen, eager to roll the dough and cut out shapes.

"I gotta horse!" young Ricky Dunn announced, holding up the sturdy dough.

Cindy couldn't contain a smile as she glimpsed his precocious grin and widened deep blue eyes. Although his shock of thick, dark hair needed to be trimmed, he looked perfect to her. This particular child had endured so much sadness in his young life, it was a thrill to see him excited over something as simple as a cookie. His father had died when Ricky was barely a year old. And his mother had been suffering from cancer for the last few years. Even someone as young as Ricky could see that his mother continued to look worse, rather than better. And just a year before, he had lost his only remaining grandparents in a freak accident when a pilot light was extinguished and they died in their sleep from the lethal, escaping gas. Now Ricky was alone in the world with only his fragile, ailing mother.

So Cindy was understanding when he sometimes acted out, getting in one minor scrape after another. She sensed the fear behind the acts and offered him nurturing acceptance.

Now Ricky's comment had the others offering her views of their own cookies. She kept a huge old basket filled with cookie cutters, some from her own childhood and newer ones she'd purchased to fit even the smallest hands.

Allowing the kids to each pick one favorite cutter, she then encouraged them to trade and share with the others. So many of them desperately needed that social skill, one that wasn't easily acquired in their dysfunctional families.

"What in the world?" Flynn muttered from the hallway.

"Making cookies!" Beth chirped, still slathering sprinkles on her tiny, misshapen mound of dough.

Cindy glanced at Flynn's face, set in lines of surprised disapproval. "So, how'd the move to your office go?"

"Fine."

She thought it would be easier to pull the moisture

from a year-old apple than words from Flynn at times. Holding in a sigh, she smiled instead. "We should have a batch done soon."

"Mmm," he replied.

"Oh, you don't know the kids." Cindy laid down the spatula she held, moving from child to child, resting her hands lightly on each one's shoulders as she introduced them to Flynn.

He greeted them kindly, yet Cindy could still sense his reserve. Seeing the questions in his eyes, she picked up a tray, motioning for Flynn to follow her into the dining room. When they were alone, she turned to him. "Shoot."

Lifting a brow at her directness, he spoke as bluntly as she had. "What's with all the kids? Some sort of charity play date?"

Cindy stiffened in automatic defense. "What's that supposed to mean?"

"A few of them look as though you picked them up at a shelter."

Mild fury blended with her protective instincts. "I didn't realize you were a clothing critic, as well."

He waved a hand in dismissal. "I'm guessing you just didn't know what you were getting yourself into."

"No, that's where you're wrong. I know *precisely* what I've taken on. Why do you suppose the Rainbow class is so important to me?"

His eyes widened in surprise. "*This* is your Rainbow thing?"

She nodded.

Shock battled with disapproval in his expression. "Why didn't you tell me it was a kid class?"

She shrugged. "I assumed you knew. What did you think I was doing?"

"I don't know, pottery or some social thing."

Exasperation literally oozed from her pores. "You thought I'd run off the first day you were here, leaving you to deal with the girls on your own, for a *pottery* class?"

He shrugged. "It really wasn't any of my business."

Frustration fumed, but she couldn't spit out enough words to express it.

Flynn gestured toward the front of the house. "You told me you needed the conservatory. Yet you've filled the kitchen with kids."

"I need both," she explained with what little was left of her patience. "We do story and music time in the conservatory. And the floor's perfect for nap time."

"Music?" he questioned. "Are you hoping to produce another Mozart?"

She counted silently to ten. "Not necessarily. But I wouldn't dismiss the idea, either."

He frowned. "The piano's in your parlor and I haven't heard you play it since we've been here."

"I've been busy," she replied with a renewed touch of exasperation. "Besides, I also play the violin, guitar and mandolin. That's what we use in the conservatory."

Flynn studied her in surprise. "I didn't know you were musical."

She gritted her teeth against the rush of words begging to be spoken. "There's a lot you don't know about me, Flynn."

He glanced back toward the kitchen. "Why did you have to include the triplets in your charity project?"

She might thump him yet, Cindy realized. "I would appreciate you not referring to my Rainbow kids as a charity project. And why wouldn't I include the girls?"

"Well, by the look of some of those kids…"

A big mallet, she decided, one that would pound some sense into that thick head of his. "Are you saying my ragamuffins aren't good enough to play with your children?"

An unexpected look of shame flashed in his eyes, then was gone. "What do you know about them, Cindy? They could be the products of pretty unsavory backgrounds."

"Exactly, Flynn. That's why they need me. Not every child has the luxury of loving parents and a father who can snap his fingers and produce every material need they could ever want."

Another sort of flush infused his face. "I worked hard for every penny I earned. I wasn't a trust fund baby who could play at will and still have a fortune at my disposal."

She felt the stab at his insult and instantly wondered if he'd ever said such a thing to Julia. "Yet you married a trust fund baby."

"You and Julia couldn't be more different if you'd been conceived on separate planets!"

That truth nearly took the breath from her. But she refused to let him know it. "Then, lucky you for picking the right sister. Now, if you don't mind, I have children to supervise." She stalked toward the doorway, pausing to glance back around. "And if you'd like to start teaching your daughters the value of snobbery and condescension, feel free to yank them out of the kitchen."

Three days later Flynn and Cindy were still tiptoeing around each other. Which made him glad that Cindy had taken back his temporary office.

Though he'd expected Michael to complete his space sooner than the previous contractor, he had been amazed by the skill and speed of his experienced crew.

Even now, Michael was checking over the last of the finishing work. "I think you should be set by the end of next week."

"That's great." Gratified, Flynn studied the other man. "How do you manage to oversee all the projects you've got going?"

"I don't," Michael admitted. "I used to try. Then I met Katherine. She convinced me that my children needed to be seen by me more often than a baby-sitter, so I hired a second-in-command. Now I choose the jobs I want to manage, and still have enough time for my family."

Puzzled, Flynn drew his brows together. "I must be missing something. That chronology doesn't work."

Michael nodded. "I guess no one told you. Katherine and I were married about two and a half years ago."

Flynn couldn't hide his surprise. "The way she treats them, I thought David and Annie were her children."

"Yeah. That's part of what makes her so special. Sounds hard to believe, but I honestly think she has the deepest feelings for our two oldest kids. Not that she isn't equally loving with the baby. But I guess she fell in love with David and Annie first."

Flynn considered a polite comment, then pushed it aside. "It's none of my business, but did you divorce or—"

"Like you, I lost my first wife. Never dreamed I'd ever marry again. And Katherine couldn't be any more different from Ruth." He shrugged. "Maybe that's why it works so well. I don't think I could have lived a life of comparisons, accumulating similarities instead of building a new life." Michael pushed his cap back. "I'm beginning to sound like a segment on *Oprah*."

Unexpectedly Flynn laughed. "I've barely talked to anyone besides Cindy since I moved here, so it didn't even faze me."

"Whew," Michael replied. "Katherine and Cindy have a unique way of getting people to think along their wavelengths. But for some reason, I have a sudden need to watch a ball game or drive about a hundred nails in the wall."

Flynn thumbed his hand toward the nearly completed interior. "I doubt your crew would appreciate the gesture. I have a better idea. Why don't we get a card game together?" Then he stopped. "I forgot there for a moment that I don't have a house to offer."

"Cindy wouldn't care. But there's no need. Mine's available. Katherine has a Mommy & Me thing planned for tonight. I can call the guys." He paused. "Guess you'd better make sure you have a sitter for the girls."

"Yeah," Flynn replied slowly, knowing he didn't want to ask the favor of Cindy.

"Why don't we say seven o'clock? Just call if there's a problem."

"Sure." Flynn pulled himself out of his thoughts. "And thanks for getting this place together so quickly."

"It's what I do."

The words had a familiar ring, but Flynn couldn't pinpoint them until hours later when he faced Cindy. They were almost identical to ones she had uttered earlier.

"Can you give me the names of a few baby-sitters you trust?" he asked, watching as she prepared shish kebabs made with chunky vegetables.

"Any special reason?" she asked.

"Michael Carlson's getting a card game together for tonight. I don't want to just dump the girls on you."

She paused, a metal skewer in one hand, a cherry tomato in the other. "Wasn't that the point of moving the Rosewood? So the girls wouldn't be left in the care of baby-sitters?"

"You're right. I can cancel the game."

She made an odd, strangulated sound. "I will be happy to watch the girls."

"You sure you don't have plans?"

She picked up a pearl onion, adding it to the skewer. "Tell you what. I'll watch the girls tonight if you'll be available Friday evening."

Instantly Flynn thought of Tom Sanders, wondering if she and Tom had a date. "Something special on?"

"Not really, but I'm going out. So, do we have a deal?"

Flynn wasn't sure he was ready to see what was behind door number two, but he nodded. "Sure."

Cindy picked up a chunk of green pepper. "Have fun at the card game."

"Yeah, right." Flynn wasn't able to understand why he suddenly couldn't think of the game, only what Cindy had planned for her night out.

Chapter Eight

Cindy rechecked her dangling green rhinestone earrings. They were flashy, but definitely went with the dress. Her makeup, too, was stronger than usual. But on stage, her normal light cosmetics washed out. It was only one of the tricks she'd learned since joining Noah Brady's band.

Despite her lifelong love of music, she'd never considered joining a group. But Noah, once convinced that Cindy had no interest in serious dating, had been relentless, nagging and hounding her until she agreed to participate in a one-time-only gig.

That had been nearly two years ago. Smiling softly, Cindy remembered Noah's disappointment when she'd told him only casual dating was on her agenda. She'd never confided to him about Flynn. No, only Katherine knew of those hopeless feelings. And although she accepted dates, Cindy never encouraged the men to believe she was interested in a serious relationship. If they pressed for anything more, she stopped going out with them.

Noah had been more persistent than any of the others. But also more understanding when he sensed her hidden pain. She hadn't expected to expose that to anyone, and he'd never pressed for details. But she guessed he had figured out it was a hopeless love. So he'd changed tracks, becoming a good and trusted friend. It seemed she'd acquired more big brothers since moving to Rosewood than she could have ever imagined. Michael Carlson, Tom Sanders, Noah Brady. Even though she'd never had a brother, she couldn't imagine a blood relative being any more dependable and concerned for her welfare.

Leaning forward, she inspected her outfit in the cheval mirror that stood in the corner of her room. Tonight's dance was a high school reunion, and the green glitz of her dress would be perfect since it was one of the school's team colors.

Hearing the doorbell ring, she also heard the scrabble of little feet as they trod across the entry hall floor. Although she'd cautioned the girls not to answer the door, they considered it a game, always trying to outrun "Cinny" to welcome whoever stood on the porch.

Luckily it was Noah, who immediately made the girls giggle with delight as he produced three puppets, demonstrating how they worked, then handing them to the girls.

Soon they were settled in the parlor. Noah didn't take one of the chairs or a place on the fainting couch. Instead he chose the piano bench, running his fingers lightly over the keys.

"No late cases?" Cindy asked him, referring to his medical practice.

"Nope. Cleared the calendar." Strong, sculptured fingers that performed with such perfection in the operating room danced over the keys.

Despite their fascination with the puppets he had brought them, the girls were drawn to the music, especially since Noah chose to play a children's song. And within a short time, they were crowded on the bench beside him.

After a few rousing songs, Beth tried to plunk her stubby fingers on the keys. Unruffled, Noah started teaching them the basic notes of "Chopsticks." Delighted, they all reached toward the piano at once. Good with kids, Noah completed the uneven quartet.

Soon, more laughter than music filled the room.

And that was how Flynn found them. He could hear the strains of piano music from the front steps. But it was the laughter that intrigued him. Recognizing his daughters' giggles, his own smile grew.

Until he stepped into the parlor.

Cindy stood directly behind a man Flynn didn't recognize. And his girls were bunched beside him on the bench. It was a cozy picture.

A far-too-cozy picture.

Flynn's jaw tightened. Who was this man now charming both Cindy and his daughters?

Laughter and music continued to fill the old house, drowning out the sounds of his entrance. Although the girls kept their attention on the pianist, Cindy turned suddenly.

It surprised him. Why was she the only one to notice him?

Her hand came down lightly on the man's shoulder and he stopped playing. The girls, finally sensing Flynn's presence, jumped down from the bench, hurtling toward him.

He knelt down, accepting their hugs, gratified by their response.

Then Beth held up a small puppet. "Look what Noah gave me!"

"We played piano, too," Mandy added also holding up her puppet.

Even little Alice displayed hers, a soft bunny-shaped toy.

"Well, isn't that nice," Flynn managed as he stood back up.

The man had risen from the piano bench. He approached, extending his hand. "Noah Brady."

Flynn accepted the handshake, offering his own name. "Looks like you've won over my daughters."

Noah shrugged. "I love kids. Don't have any of my

own so it's a pleasure to spend time with someone
else's."

"Right," Flynn agreed, wondering who he was.
What he meant to Cindy.

Belatedly he realized Noah was dressed in a tux and
Cindy was wearing a sparkling deep green gown, one
that made her hair look like fire. It was equally clear
they were dressed for a very special evening. Ignoring
a squiggle of unwanted, insensible resentment, he
reached for the anchor of his daughters' hands.

But Beth wriggled away. "Dr. Noah's gonna show
us more piano."

Dr. Noah? Flynn glanced pointedly at Cindy.

"Noah's a surgeon," she explained. "Which is
probably why he has the right touch for music."

The right touch. Perhaps that wasn't confined only
to music. It seemed the man was capable of making
Cindy smile and laugh with abandon.

Cindy corralled Beth. "Dr. Noah will have to show
you how to play another time. Otherwise we'll be late."

"Me go, too!" Beth demanded.

"Not this time, sweetie," Cindy replied. "This is a
grown-ups-only evening."

Flynn wondered why the words felt like ground
glass beneath tender, bare feet.

"You come back?" Mandy asked Noah.

"Sure. I love having a captive audience. But Cindy's
right. We'd better be going." Again he extended his

hand to Flynn. "Good to meet you. Hate to steal Cindy away, but the evening wouldn't be complete without her."

No, Flynn supposed, it wouldn't.

Cindy pulled an exquisitely beaded shawl from the hall rack, then picked up a tiny jeweled bag from the hall table. "We shouldn't be too late."

Flynn stared at her, wondering who this dazzlingly beautiful woman was. Normally dressed in jeans or overalls, she now looked like an exotic stranger. One who was going out with the handsome doctor. Struggling to maintain his composure, Flynn nodded. "Fine. The girls and I will probably order a pizza."

"Whatever you think," she replied easily.

Where was her normal lecture on the benefits of healthy eating? Had the good doctor turned Cindy's head so much she didn't give the girls' welfare a passing thought?

But before the notion could process, Noah swept Cindy outside, the duo looking perfectly suited. Flynn bit down on the thought, but it escaped nonetheless.

He should be glad, happy Cindy had found such a person. Instead, all he could feel was a growing wall of resentment.

Cicadas and bullfrogs filled the night air with their own sort of music, accentuating the solitary hoot of a secluded owl.

The lonely sound fitted Flynn's mood. Any other time he would appreciate the scent of the native honeysuckle that roamed through the trees and over the weathered fence. But he'd been restless most of the evening. That had only increased since he'd put the girls to bed. Because then his mind could wander without distraction.

Flynn took a deep breath, inhaling clean air that wasn't tinged with big-city smog.

Flynn wondered if Cindy and Noah were dancing beneath the stars that stood out so clearly in the uncluttered sky. No reflection from thousands of lights dimmed the deep midnight color. Everything about this place was so different than what he was used to.

And he didn't want to dwell on the fact that Cindy was the most different of all.

He stood that way for a long time, hearing the quiet neighborhood sounds, ones that were now familiar to him. Mr. Elliott next door put out his cat. Mrs. Anderson whose backyard aligned with Cindy's, called for her little poodle, then closed and locked her door once he was inside. And somewhere not too far away, he could the distant strains of a teenager's music.

The theme for the evening—music.

The thought barely surfaced when he caught the drifting scent of a new fragrance. Recognizing it, he spun around, not willing to be part of a possible goodnight kiss between Cindy and her date.

But she stood alone, framed by the ancient French doors, before cautiously stepping out on the terrace. "Flynn? Is that you?"

"Yes. Didn't mean to get in your way."

She stepped closer. "I'm not sure what you mean."

"Isn't Noah with you?"

She shook her head. "Well…no. Are the girls asleep?"

"Hours ago. Although I still can't get them settled in as quickly as you do."

She shrugged a slim shoulder, partially exposed by the narrow straps of her dress. "It's not a contest."

"So it isn't."

Silence slithered between them, broken only by another call of the distant owl.

Cindy stepped out of her strappy high-heeled sandals, her voice as soft as her face. "My feet are killing me."

A night of dancing would do that. "I imagine so."

"It's pretty out here at night, isn't it?" she mused, her face dreamy beneath the partial moonlight.

Flynn wondered if Noah had put that expression on her face.

"I'm usually so caught up in one thing or another that I don't appreciate what's literally in my own backyard," she continued.

Mr. Elliott opened a side door and coaxed in his cat. One final meow was cut off by the closing door.

"So, does this Noah guy go to your church, too?" Flynn asked, hoping he sounded appropriately casual.

She paused for a moment, crickets filling in the silence. "Yes, that's where we met. He's the musical director."

Flynn frowned into the darkness. "I thought he was a doctor."

"He is. A plastic surgeon. But he volunteers as the musical director for our church. We don't have a large budget—certainly not one that would stretch to include a paid musical director. We had a fire a few years ago that we're still paying for. Besides, Noah's incredibly talented. He once considered music instead of medicine."

"And which profession suffered the most from his choice?"

She laughed, a quiet, skeptical sound. "Neither. He gives his all to his patients when he's at the hospital. And he absolutely inspires the kids and teenagers at church. He's helped to turn around more than one wayward child by including them in the choir."

"Practically a saint," Flynn muttered.

"What?"

"The girls were very impressed by him. They want you to invite him over again."

She shrugged. "No problem. I see Noah often. And if he's coming to pick me up, and his schedule permits, he can arrive a little early, see the girls."

Flynn stiffened, glad that the blackness of the night hid the motion. "I'm sure they'd like that."

Another silence vibrated between them. But the crickets weren't enough to fill the gap this time.

"Is something wrong, Flynn?"

He shook his head. "Nah. There's something about the quiet that makes a person think, evaluate."

"Funny, we fill up nearly every moment with television, music, computers or conversation. One of the downfalls of modern technology, I suppose."

But Flynn wasn't in the mood for small talk. "Why didn't you invite Noah to the party you gave to introduce me to your friends?"

"I did. He had an emergency call and didn't leave the hospital all night. It's hard for him to know if he'll ever be able to keep plans he's made."

"That must be annoying," Flynn remarked.

She shrugged. "He doesn't really seem to mind. He's so dedicated. And he just shuffles other commitments. He has a lot of friends who step in when there's a real crunch."

"He sounds almost too good to be true."

She laughed again. "I thought the same thing when I met him. But now I know him well enough to realize he's the genuine article."

So Cindy was infatuated with the town hero. That should be a comfort. He wondered why it wasn't.

He glanced over at her, realizing she was only a

handspan away. Again the subtle scent of her perfume snagged his attention. He had only to reach out and he could touch her, catch her hand within his.

She turned, meeting his gaze. "I'm glad we've been able to work things out, that we can trade off watching the girls as we need to. I want you to feel that Rosewood is really becoming your home, that you can find wonderful friends here, as well."

"Friends like Noah?" he questioned, watching her face.

But her pretty features didn't give anything away. "Exactly. You couldn't ask for better people than Noah or Michael or Tom."

It was an innocent statement, absolutely guileless, equally unrevealing.

She hitched up the shawl, covering her arms. "I'd better head inside. As much as I enjoy the night sky, the girls will be up early." She smiled. "And I need my beauty sleep."

He watched as she walked away and into the house. That's where she was wrong. With or without sleep, Cindy was a beauty. And it seemed the men in this small town weren't blind to the fact. Staring again into the ever-deepening darkness, he wondered why that, too, was a thought he couldn't shake.

Chapter Nine

Cindy finished snapping the last overall strap in place. She grinned, just looking at the triplets, thinking surely they were the most lovable children on earth.

Alice, the child who clung the closest and had bonded inseparably with her, reached for her hand.

"You all look great," Cindy complimented them, glad she'd picked different color T-shirts for each one. Purple, kelly green and bright yellow.

All of the clothes Flynn had brought with him were things Cindy considered more appropriate for dress-up occasions.

"Daddy!" Beth hollered, seeing Flynn in the hall.

He turned into the room with a smile that faded faster than ice cream on a hot summer sidewalk.

"Me pretty?" Mandy asked again, this time directing the question to Flynn.

Seeing the displeasure on his face, Cindy motioned

with a shake of her head for him not to say what was obviously on his mind. "I'm sure Daddy always thinks you're pretty."

"Sure, punkin," Flynn replied. "Why don't you and your sisters head downstairs? You can get the granola out. But no running."

They took off with typical toddler speed, but the sound of their sneakers slowed down as they reached the stairs, having been properly impressed by the danger of falling down the wide, wooden steps.

"What's with the overalls?" Flynn asked as soon as they heard the girls successfully navigate the stairs.

Taken aback, Cindy stared at him. "I'm not sure what you mean."

"I don't consider overalls proper attire for my daughters."

Cindy hesitated, remembering all too well the frilly dresses Julia always put them in. "How do you expect them to run and play if they're dressed like porcelain dolls?"

He waved away the concern. "It's never been a problem."

Cindy wouldn't criticize her late sister if it meant biting her tongue until it sliced clear through. Yet, she couldn't relent on this point. "They're not fragile dolls meant to be put on a shelf. They're real children who need to run and get dirty, and maybe scrape a knee." A new thought prodded her. "Is that what you're worried about? That they'll get hurt if they play like other children?"

His mouth tightened and Cindy wondered what past demon still possessed him.

"I'm not blasé about my children's safety. And I don't understand your attitude. Why are you so willing to assume they'll be all right?"

Cindy blinked, nearly taking a step backward from the wrath she saw in his eyes. "Flynn, I care terribly about their welfare. I, too, have lost everyone in my family. I don't want to lose anyone else. Especially the girls. But you can't lock them away, either." Taking a chance, she continued. "I know that's what Julia tried to do. She never got over the fact that if Dad hadn't insisted on so much adventure, he and Mom would be alive. But they had to live as they did, including that last boat ride. There was something in Dad that pushed him to carve every bit out of every minute. And Mom loved him enough to understand that. It was an accident, a dreadful, sad, unfortunate accident, but it wasn't some sort of morbid legacy. I'm sorry if Julia brought that worry to your marriage and transferred it to the girls. But keeping them from life won't keep them alive."

His jaw tightened even further. "Don't meddle in things you know nothing about."

"Nothing? They were my parents, too, and—"

"But the triplets are *my* children, not yours. I'll decide what's best for them."

Cindy pushed past the pain of his reminder, one that said no matter how she'd grown to love the girls, they would never be hers. "Of course they're *your* daughters. But I do care desperately about them, as well. And I certainly don't think wearing overalls and T-shirts will scar them for life."

He snorted impatiently. "What's next? Jeans and cigars?"

She smiled, despite the unresolved tension. "Jeans maybe. But I'll hold off on the cigars."

Flynn's glance lifted to encompass the picture of Jesus that still hung on the wall. The unspoken reminder of his displeasure lingered between them.

He pivoted toward the door.

But Cindy reached out, catching his arm.

The contact seared between them.

As quickly she dropped her own hand. "I—I was wondering if you'd like to go with us to the park. I promised the girls. We could make a morning of it, take some lunch along."

Flynn's eyes remained dark, unrevealing. "I have to go into the office. I'm interviewing some applicants today."

She nodded. "I see."

His gaze searched hers again. However, just when Cindy thought he was about to say something, he turned, leaving the room.

And again she wondered.

* * *

The park was perfect. Spring in the Texas Hill Country meant mild temperatures, often sunny skies. And wildflowers colored all the fields beyond the manicured lawns of the park.

The girls spotted the seesaw and squealed as they headed straight for it. Cindy didn't mind. She knew they would all try to get on one side and they'd be safe until she put the cooler on a redwood table beneath the shaded canopy of tall oak trees.

Beth, Mandy and Alice all sat on one side as she'd predicted. Plucking Mandy from the trio, she put her on the other end, using her own weight to help Mandy move up and down. When they finally tired of the seesaw, they were off to the swings, then the slide, the sandbox and the monkey bars. By then they were ready for the seesaw again.

She put Mandy and Beth on one end this time and took her place with Alice, reaching out to pull the child down so Mandy and Beth could rise.

"Any room on there for me?" Flynn asked from beside her.

Startled, she let the board go, snapping Alice back into place. "Sorry, sweetie."

"Tell you what," Flynn offered. "I'll sit with Alice and you sit with Mandy and Beth."

He looked as though he expected her to refuse. But she'd seldom met a challenge she'd capitulated to. So she walked to the other end, pulling the girls down and sitting behind them.

Flynn easily pulled down all their weight with one arm and climbed on the seesaw behind Alice.

Cindy tried to be cautious, but Flynn's strong legs pumped them quickly up and down. Within a few minutes, she was laughing along with the girls, their giggles and hoots filling the quiet playground.

Nearly winded, Cindy was ready to call for a time-out. But a new, unexpected twinkle flashed in Flynn's eyes. And she couldn't resist the dare lurking in them.

It felt as though they were almost flying as the seesaw moved up and down, again and again. Even so, they were careful to keep a secure grip on the girls. It was Flynn who finally slowed the pace when the girls began to tire.

"No, Daddy!" they chorused.

But Flynn plucked them off one by one.

"Okay, girls. Let's head to the table. Time for some lunch."

"And a nap," Cindy said quietly, reaching down to pick a wildflower, knowing the girls would be so exhausted they'd probably fall asleep in the car on the way home.

Although they protested, each one came to the table. "I thought you had to be at the office," Cindy commented, pulling at the stem of the buttercup.

"The interviews didn't take long."

Cindy wondered if he'd rushed the interviews so he could join them. As quickly she dismissed the notion.

"Did you find anyone you liked?"

"Actually, all three that showed up."

"Is it going to be hard to choose?" she asked.

"No. I hired all of them."

Surprised, Cindy glanced up at him. "Do you have that much work for them to do?"

"If my concept's valid."

Concern mixed with her other feelings. "Do they know it's a risk?"

"Sure. I wouldn't let someone assume a sense of security that's not certain. But they seemed to think it was a risk worth taking."

Cindy nodded. "I only asked because new jobs aren't that plentiful in Rosewood. Even Adair Petroleum brought in their own people for the new regional office. I'd hate to see someone give up a secure job and then wind up unemployed."

"I may not be a member of your religious circle, but I don't cheat or lie, either."

She bit back at the exasperation bubbling to be heard. "Of course you don't. And belonging to a church isn't about judging others. In fact, it's just the opposite."

"Not in my experience."

"What is that experience, Flynn?" she asked quietly.

"Doesn't do any good to dwell on the past. It's gone, unchangeable."

She searched his eyes, seeing a wealth of pain he

usually concealed well. "If it would help you to deal with today—"

"I have to depend on myself, Cindy. Myself alone. I learned that a long time ago. And talk of church won't change that."

"It's not just talk, not to me, despite what you believe."

"Has your faith brought back your mother, your father…Julia?" Bleakness so cold, it stole away the warmth of the day, surfaced in his eyes. "I didn't think so."

"But—"

"And you'll move past this phase too, Cindy. You think I'm saying this to be cruel, but that's not it. You shouldn't be sucked in by a myth any more than I should. Myths don't protect and nurture."

Feeling the pain of his tortured soul in her own, she reached for his hand. "Despite what you think of me, my scattered ways, the way I poorly compare to Julia, don't let that stand between you and the truth."

He glanced down at their clasped hands.

Feeling the heat of his gaze, she slowly withdrew her own.

"The truth is I haven't believed God existed since I was nine years old. Meeting all your church friends, even liking them or considering them my new friends, allowing the girls to attend Sunday school, playing on the church softball team, none of that will change how

I believe." He glanced at the table where the girls were happily digging into the chips and cookies. "You live a fairy tale, Cindy, and I don't want to take that away from you. But don't think you'll change me. Ever. Because it won't happen."

Cindy forced her stiff legs forward, her body numb from his words. Was that truly how he felt? Would he never, never change his views about his faith? And if not, where did that leave her love for him?

Closing her eyes, she remembered the past painful years, ones spent silently loving him. Reality struck like a slap across the face. Even if he could eventually come to love her, she couldn't spend her life with a man of no faith.

And she'd thought convincing him that she'd changed was her largest obstacle. Now, it seemed a minor bump in the road in comparison. Yet, it, too, was a mammoth barrier. For the first time since she'd met Flynn Mallory, Cindy faced the truth. They weren't meant to be together, not then, not now. Never.

Even though Flynn had no use for religious holidays, he tolerated those with secular meaning, as well. So he had expected Cindy to color Easter eggs and fill baskets for the girls.

But returning home from the office, he was stunned to see Cindy's charity kids all grouped around the kitchen table, as well. A dozen bowls held all shades of dye and it looked as though Cindy had boiled at least six dozen eggs for decoration.

Cindy, like the kids, seemed to be wearing an undue amount of dye, as well.

"Any dye left for the eggs?" he asked, coming closer to the table.

Cindy glanced up at him, then down at her messy hands and arms. "Possibly a drop or two." Quickly she introduced the children. Flynn smiled at them in turn.

The triplets, imitating Cindy, held out their arms, as well. Alongside the light-tinted dye stains were deep streaks of color.

Flynn's tolerant smile faded. "Are you sure that washes off?"

Cindy followed his gaze. Her patient smile dimmed. "That doesn't look like the egg dye."

Ricky held up a black marker. "We found these in the crayon drawer."

Cindy's eyes widened. Reaching out, she took the marker from him, then collected the others. "These are permanent markers, Ricky. We don't use these to color on anything. They're mine for making signs. Are you sure they were in the crayon drawer?"

Six-year-old Ricky shrugged. "I dunno. Paul and me found 'em."

Cindy glanced up at Flynn. "Sorry. I didn't realize they'd gotten into these."

"So they're not going to wash off?"

She shook her head. "Not for a while anyway."

"Great. They'll look as though they've been tattooed."

Cindy looked first at the triplets, then back at Flynn, inserting a placating note in her voice. "They can wear long sleeves till it fades."

Flynn rolled his eyes. "And you plan to take them to church tomorrow looking like that?"

Cindy's smile wavered. "I'll find something for them to wear."

He glanced around the messy, cluttered kitchen, but didn't say anything. What was the point? As though she could pull together this fiasco, clean up the children *and* find them something to wear for the next day. It was of no concern to him. Flynn didn't want the girls to attend anyway. At first he'd considered Sunday school simply a social thing, but he didn't want the girls to make connections that would be difficult to break.

And he was certain Cindy wasn't committed enough to the church to spend the night assembling outfits for the triplets.

Easter morning dawned, bright and beautiful. So much so, that it seemed perfect, Cindy realized, as she hemmed the last small dress.

Flynn had been right. She had scrubbed the girls' arms as vigorously as possible during bath time, yet the stains wouldn't budge. And nothing the girls owned would completely cover the permanent ink marks on their arms. A quick trip to the children's store had been fruitless, as well. Being spring, all the dresses had short sleeves.

But Cindy wasn't ready to admit defeat. Returning home, she'd searched her project closet, unearthing a bolt of white material that had been intended for church tablecloths. Since she'd purchased pink hats and socks to go with their short-sleeved Easter dresses, Cindy was certain she could come up with something appropriate.

Using an older dress for a pattern, Cindy cut out three little dresses. Once sewn, the dresses still lacked something. Rooting through her project materials, Cindy almost squealed when she unearthed two full rolls of wide pink ribbon. She had once used a third roll to make congratulatory ribbons for the kids. Now she was certain it would make the perfect accent for the pristine white dresses. It didn't take long to braid the pink ribbon with a bit of lace, forming sashes.

Although Cindy was tired by morning, she was also pleased. Making dresses for the girls was far more satisfying than purchasing them. And now she decided the pure white dresses with their simple sash belts were far prettier than the short-sleeved floral ones she'd purchased.

Skipping downstairs to grab a cup of coffee, she was surprised to see Flynn in the kitchen. "It's early for you, isn't it?"

"I know you're disappointed that the girls won't be able to go to church, so I'm making breakfast."

"'O, ye of little faith.'"

He frowned. "We're not going into that again, are we? I've allowed the girls to go to Sunday school because it seems mostly playing and coloring and singing at their age. But—"

She held up one hand. "I'm a little tired for a theological debate this morning. Besides, it's Easter. Let's not spoil that."

He handed her a mug of coffee. "Why are you so tired?"

She smiled. "I've been up sewing."

"*You* know how to sew?"

"You really do think Julia and I were conceived on different planets." She waved away his attempt to explain or apologize. It really didn't matter which. "Yes, I know how to sew. I made the girls new dresses for today—long-sleeved dresses." She took a healthy sip of coffee, then glanced at him. "You can close your mouth now."

"Sorry. But what possessed you to do that?"

Meeting his questioning gaze, all she could feel was sadness so immense, it wearied her far more than the sleepless night. "I don't think you can possibly understand." She gripped her mug closer. "And that makes me the one who's sorry."

Turning away before she could see his stunned face,

Cindy jogged up the stairs, escaping the questions, but embracing the day. She took comfort in the beautiful Easter morning, knowing the agony it cost Flynn to stand alone. Also knowing she was powerless to change his unyielding views. But it was Easter, the day of new promises and life. And time to put this dilemma in His hands.

Chapter Ten

The next few weeks were tense. Flynn hadn't wanted to unleash more of his past. But all of Cindy's questions did just that.

Funny though, escaping from Cindy had pushed him into a closer friendship with Michael Carlson and Tom Sanders. He still felt the instant kinship he'd shared with Michael since the first time they'd met. He'd been far more reluctant to accept Tom as a friend, remembering too well how chummy the other man seemed to be with Cindy. He refused to put a name to why that bothered him, but it hadn't made him want Tom as a friend.

Then, during one of their card games, Flynn had learned inadvertently that Tom Sanders wasn't a romantic interest. Tom referred to her as the little sister he'd never had, but one he was glad to have in his life. The words were genuine and true, Flynn realized with a touch of shame.

But that didn't relieve Flynn's thoughts fully. There was still Noah Brady to consider. And the good doctor didn't come to their friendly card games; his crowded schedule too full.

It didn't matter, Flynn told himself. Cindy could date whomever she wanted. That nagging feeling in his gut was no doubt a brotherly concern of his own. An inner voice told him that reasoning didn't ring true, but he ignored it. And each day, like today, it had been on his mind as he worked.

The house was quiet as he entered. It had been a long day at the office—too long. Quietly walking upstairs, he was disappointed to find that the girls were already asleep. It was his own fault, Flynn realized. The same mistake he'd made when Julia had been alive. Resolving not to let it happen again, Flynn passed Cindy's room, seeing that it was empty. He searched the rest of the house, looking for her.

She was out on the terrace. Sitting in one of her aged, fan-shaped wicker chairs, Cindy had a tall glass of what looked to be lemonade on the round wrought-iron table. A pitcher and a second empty glass sat on one of her painted, wooden trays. The arbor shaded the last of the sun's evening rays, creating a dappled illusion of shape and shadow.

Cindy could have stepped out from the confines of a Renoir canvas, Flynn realized suddenly. Her vibrant hair and eyes, the old-fashioned sundress, her clear porcelain skin.

He could tell she didn't hear him approaching, his soft-leather-soled shoes making little noise on the faded red cobbled stones.

Cindy was intently studying a tall, wide book. Without the unceasing tension that normally separated them, she looked gentler…soft even. Nothing about Cindy ever said soft.

Wild, impulsive, adventurous. But never soft.

Still he gentled his own tone, trying to quiet the intrusion. "Hey."

She didn't jump, instead finally looking up at him as though reluctantly pulled from another world. Cindy belonged to another world, he realized suddenly. She could have fit in as easily in Victorian days as she did in the present. Her vivaciousness and quick wit would have made her a darling of society.

As he watched, her lips turned upward gently, not her usual wide grin, rather a soft sloping that revealed tenderness rather than mirth. "Hey, yourself."

He gestured to one of the other chairs loosely gathered around the table. "Do you mind if I join you?"

She shook her head. "I thought you might be coming home soon. The other glass is for you. I made limeade."

Of course. No traditional lemonade for nontraditional Cindy.

As he sat, she tipped the pitcher, filling his glass.

Now wanting to disturb the unusual, peaceful moment, he sipped the brew, finding it surprisingly good.

"It's the maraschino cherries," she told him before he could ask. "Sweetens without being too sweet."

Again he nodded, enjoying the tranquil moment. Relaxing in the oversize chair, he wondered at this woman of many moods. "What are you reading?"

"A party planner. It has all kinds of great ideas for kids parties."

Surprised, he hadn't expected her to need a guide. Her life used to be one endless party. Of course, that was before he'd burst on to the scene, bringing his three children and a weight of responsibility. "You thinking about a party?"

She smiled at him ruefully. "Oh, Flynn."

Calmed by the surroundings, even her tone could scarcely stir him. "Yes?"

"The girls' birthday. Next week. I want it to be extraspecial. The last one…well…you know."

The last one had been too soon after Julia's passing for him to celebrate it properly. Uncomfortably Flynn remembered that he hadn't invited Cindy to the last-minute, toned-down birthday dinner. Only Flynn and the girls had been there. He had been ill at ease in the kiddy pizza place, the girls unhappy without their mother or Aunt Cindy.

And now it was time to plan another celebration.

"Funny. I thought about it for months afterward, how I would make it up to them, taking the time to arrange something really special for the next birthday."

"Perhaps you put it out of your mind because it reminded you of more difficult times."

"Regret." The word was surprisingly bitter in the calm of the night. "I've had my fill of it."

Cindy's gaze softened further. "Flynn, you can't blame yourself for things no one can control."

"Who do I blame?" he asked with less rancor, trying to match his tone to the mood of the night. "Your God?"

Agony darkened her bright green eyes and impulsively she laid one hand over his. "Is that what you want your daughters to believe?"

"I want them to understand you have to be strong on your own, that you can't depend on anyone or anything in this life other than yourself."

Cindy swallowed, her expression so earnest, it was nearly painful. "What about friends, the people who care about you? Ones who like you for who you are, not who you want to be? Who accept you, flaws and all, maybe liking you even more for having them. Do you want to shut them out of your life, too?"

Flynn considered her words, the depth of her sincerity. Depth? From Cindy? The girl he'd met that long-ago night hadn't possessed depth. What she had possessed was like the lure of molten gold. Beautiful, but capable of burning when touched.

"What about you, Cindy? I've listened, observed. But you've never told me. Why did you come to Rosewood? What made you hide yourself so far away from your own friends and only family? You told me that you knew just Katherine when you moved here. Even Julia didn't know about your plans until a few days before you left. What's the big secret, Cindy? Why did *you* run away?"

Her mouth opened, but no words emerged. Instead she handed him the book she'd been reading. Then thrusting back her chair, she fled. Spry and slim, she disappeared into the house.

Left with only the night sounds for company, Flynn dropped his forehead against one splayed hand. What had come over him? Because she had pushed him, he knew, looking for answers. And he couldn't bear to repeat the painful memories. So he'd pushed back, taking the offense instead of the defense.

Lifting his head, he glanced at the book she'd shoved into his hands. A piece of paper marked her place. On it she'd drawn a spectacular rendering of a child's birthday party. One that seemed nearly as magical as the dreams all little girls should have.

And then he wondered what had happened to Cindy's dreams. A passionate person, she must have once held lustrous hopes. And no matter what she said, he doubted those had begun or ended in Rosewood.

Paper lanterns fluttered gently in the breeze, lending an old-fashioned aura to the festive backyard. But they fit well with the antique wicker chairs and long, curving wrought-iron benches. The lattice arbor continued to shade the terrace where Cindy had set up several round tables. Each was covered by a rose-or daisy-patterned tablecloth that trailed to the ground. And she'd scattered just enough iridescent glitter over them that they sparkled in the sun. The largest table was already stacked with presents.

Knowing the kids wouldn't want to remain seated at a long table, she had instead put punch and cups on one table, small plates with nuts and candy on another.

Although three sparkly tables were set aside for each of the girls' birthday cakes, the actual desserts remained inside under wraps. She had chosen three separate shapes, flavors and colors to give each girl a special, individual birthday experience.

"It's coming together," Flynn commented, tacking up a Pin-the-Tail-on-the-Donkey game.

Cindy nodded. "We've planned enough games to keep them occupied, and then of course, there's the pony you rented."

He winced. "Okay, maybe *I* am the one spoiling them. But the pony will only be here for a few hours. It's not like I got them a stable."

She placed a stack of games on a side table. "Only because there's not enough room in my backyard, and your new yard's still being torn up by bulldozers."

"I wasn't planning on a stable for nearly another year or two," he retorted, a smile twitching on his lips.

She grinned, as well.

He glanced at the swing set that she had covered in streamers and balloons, then to the edge of the decorated arbor. She had wound streamers decorated with unicorns and delicate ballerinas among them all.

His gaze traveled to the dozen child-proportioned chairs and tables, which had been set with plates, cups and plastic forks, scattered throughout the yard. The multiple colors of the tablecloths resembled those of a box of spilled crayons. "And you didn't go a little overboard yourself?"

She shrugged. "You know me. I go overboard with everything."

For a moment he didn't reply, the tension that never left them, surging again.

"Besides, I borrowed the kiddie furniture from the church."

He lifted his brow.

"Katherine said it was okay. And you can help me haul it back."

"After scraping up sticky plates and cups, that should be a treat," Flynn replied easily. Then he spotted Noah Brady entering the yard through the side gate, as though he'd done it every day of his life. The man seemed uncommonly comfortable in Cindy's home.

She turned to follow his gaze. "Oh, good! Noah's

here with his electronic keyboard. I thought the kids would like the music."

"You haven't heard of a CD player?" Flynn retorted.

She drew her brows together. "Live music's a little more fun. Besides, I've drafted a few other players. The kids will love it."

Flynn forced his thoughts to settle. This was his daughters' birthday party, not the time to question Cindy's personal life. Still, he watched as she rushed over to Noah, her smile wide and open. It occurred to him that the only time he saw that same smile on her face was when she was with someone other than him. As Flynn had suspected, Noah knew how to make her smile…. Evidently he was a man who came with no irksome baggage that precluded easy smiles.

Katherine and Michael Carlson, along with their children, arrived next. David, Annie and Danny immediately joined the triplets.

Flynn watched the Carlson family, still amazed that the couple had been together for such a short time. Not only did they seem ideally suited, but Katherine was openly loving and tender with all three children. Flynn was certain that no one would take them for a blended family. But then he guessed their relationship was an exception.

Michael raised a hand in greeting. Although Flynn was accustomed to keeping people at a distance, Michael was one of the few people Flynn had met who were simply and exactly what they seemed. No pretense, no agendas. Through softball and card games, he'd come to consider Michael a friend.

Michael crossed the yard. "Katherine and Cindy have their heads together, and I'm guessing we're about to be drafted soon."

Flynn found himself grinning. "That sounds like it was said from experience."

"You wouldn't believe what those two can dream up. You should have seen Annie's first birthday party after we married. You'd have thought our house and yard had been taken over by a Barbie army. I saw pink for days."

Flynn chuckled. "Barbie army, huh?"

"Don't laugh. Wait'll your girls are a little older. We've had tea parties that would send a sane man running for his life. You haven't lived till you've come home to a dozen little girls dressed in hats and high heels and your wife acting as though it's the most natural thing on earth."

Flynn winced in male sympathy. "But you do have sons, as well."

"Don't even get me started on that. For David's party, she had everyone dress like cowboys and cowgirls and she rented not one, not two, but three ponies. My yard looked like I'd been housing a herd of wild mustangs."

Flynn tried not to laugh. "So, you're telling me Katherine has a lot of…um…creativity."

"More than enough. But it's not just her. She and Cindy came up with both plans. Alone they're fascinating. Together they're positively explosive. You sure the circus isn't planning to appear in the backyard today?"

"Nah. I wanted a pony. Cindy wanted a clown, but we agreed the pony alone would be best."

Michael glanced around the yard. "You seen Cindy since we got here?"

Flynn shook his head.

Michael's brows rose. "I was wondering why Katherine brought along an overnight bag. Ten to one, either she or Cindy makes an appearance dressed as a clown."

"But she wouldn't—"

Michael's chuckle cut off his words. "Oh, Flynn, my man. You don't know these women very well yet."

"I don't think Cindy would really do that."

Michael's hearty laugh echoed in the quiet yard. "Are you kidding? The two of them might burst through a flaming hoop!" He clapped a hand on Flynn's shoulder. "Buck up. You just have to realize that Cindy's got an endless imagination."

"A corked barrel of dynamite," Flynn replied.

"I'm wrong. You do know her."

"I did once," Flynn admitted. "I'm not quite so sure now."

Some of the male camaraderie faded from Michael's expression. "I consider Cindy's passionate spirit her best quality. It makes her who she is."

And that was the problem. Yet Flynn only nodded.

Michael, in tune with Flynn's change in mood, glanced toward the yard. "So what can I do to help?"

"Cindy's got most of it set up. She's been up since dawn."

Michael chuckled. "When she was working on the church after the fire, we had to pry her down from the scaffolding. You'd have thought she had experience working on skyscrapers the way she climbed up and around that stuff."

"She mentioned the fire briefly. What happened?"

"Old wiring. It leveled the sanctuary. But with a legion of volunteers like Cindy, we were able to salvage most of the original stone and brick. That's why the building doesn't look squeaky new."

Flynn lifted a brow skeptically. "You mean Cindy was doing the work herself instead of writing a check?"

Michael's face reflected his own surprise. "Why would you think she'd do that?"

Flynn shrugged. "The Cindy I've known never lasted very long with these fads of hers. Julia told me Cindy tried a half-dozen different occupations since we married, never staying with one long enough to see if it suited her. I honestly don't believe this is any more than another craze."

"Then maybe you don't know Cindy as well as you think," Michael replied quietly. "And that's a shame."

Flynn glanced over at Noah, who was running an

extension cord for the keyboard and speakers. "I think there are plenty of other people in Cindy's life who know her well."

Michael kept his own counsel. "Maybe so."

Flynn wasn't sure why, but he sensed disappointment from Michael. Since they were still only new friends, Flynn wasn't certain why this bothered him.

So he directed his gaze back to Noah. However, as he watched, a stream of children entered from the side gate. Cindy's Rainbow kids. And it looked like both sets, from her two classes. Perfect.

"Cindy's worked miracles with these kids," Michael said, following his gaze.

Flynn continued watching them. "Yeah. Cookies and Play-Doh will do that."

Michael shook his head. "You don't have a clue, do you?"

"I don't mean to be rude, but this isn't going to be a religious lecture, is it?"

"That, too?" Michael asked in a knowing tone. "I should have guessed. But maybe it's true, sharing a problem doesn't make you recognize it in someone else. Like ex-alcoholics, smokers…and disbelievers. You'd think there'd be some sign of unity, but I guess we hide it because we don't want to think about it, examine it too closely."

"I don't know what you're talking about."

"Until I met Katherine I was in the same place you

are. Happy as I am now, it's hard to think about that time. But if you need someone who understands, someone who was there, when you're ready I'll be around."

The kids started hollering, clapping madly.

Flynn and Michael glanced in their direction, seeing Katherine stepping through the French doors with a clown.

"It was an even call," Michael told him with a rueful note of glee. "But yours is the clown this time."

Yours. Did Michael really see Cindy that way? As the woman in his life?

Watching her, Flynn couldn't imagine two such ill-suited people.

Cindy had swept her luxurious, flaming hair into a multitude of ponytails. And her face was covered in white grease paint, her eyes, nose and lips blatantly outlined. Two bright spots of red circled her cheeks and she was dressed in orange and purple polka dots and a lime-green checkered plaid. It looked as though she'd wound at least a dozen scarves around her neck and waist. Her hands were covered by oversize cotton garden gloves in a wild floral print. She looked outrageous, unlikely and entirely unique. Much like her personality.

The older kids tugged her toward the backyard while the triplets stared at her with a sort of confused fascination and then started running toward her, as well.

When they reached her, Cindy made each of the triplets stand alone for a moment as she individually introduced them to the other children's cheers.

"Are you going to do magic tricks?" young Ricky asked.

She frowned, walking over to him and bending down slightly. Her hands rested first on his shoulders, then one moved over his ear, producing a quarter. "I'm not sure you can afford my magic tricks," she teased him, plopping the quarter into his hands.

As Flynn watched, Cindy performed a few simple tricks. But the children, unsophisticated and eager, clapped for each one.

Then she and Katherine brought out trays of paints and brushes. Face painting, Flynn realized. The children lined up in front of both Cindy and Katherine, eager to have designs painted on their small faces.

Flynn started to turn away when he saw Cindy beckon to him. Thinking she needed more supplies, he knelt beside her, just close enough to speak lowly into her ear, "I thought we'd decided not to have a clown."

Her black outlined brows rose. "Oh, no. That was you." Then she batted her huge false eyelashes. "Besides, I'm a woman of many talents."

Standing up, he smiled at the next child in line, and started to move away.

Cindy snagged his hand, however. "Not so fast. I need another helper."

He stared at her in disbelief. "I don't know how to do this painting thing."

"You can show him," Annie Carlson suggested helpfully.

"Yes, Daddy paint!" Beth cried out.

"Yes!" Mandy and Alice echoed.

Flynn groaned aloud.

But Cindy was already swiveling toward him. "I think you'll need to sit down so I can reach your face."

"You're going to show me on my own face?"

"What better way?" she asked. She motioned with her eyes to the triplets. "You wouldn't want to disappoint them, would you?" It was only because of his daughters that he complied.

"I should have made my escape when I could," Flynn muttered.

Cindy was already dipping her brush into vivid green paint. "Perhaps a butterfly," she mused. "Or a sweet little pink heart."

He looked at the green paint. "The only reason I'm still sitting here is because that paint isn't pink."

She smiled, her perfect white teeth emphasized by the outlandish clown face makeup. "I think you can brave it through pink or green." She lifted the green-coated brush. "But I won't push my luck." Leaning forward, she touched the tip of the feather-light brush against his cheek.

Flynn hadn't known what to expect, a cold slimy

glob of paint heated only by his embarrassment perhaps. Instead, her touch was incredibly gentle, much like a warm whisper against his skin.

Angling closer to paint the intricate design, she was mere inches from his face. He could smell the sweet rush of her breath, feel the warmth of her touch. Mesmerized, he sat as though paralyzed, his mind and body captive to her spell.

She had brought a small tray of paints with her and she tilted her face to study them, her forehead only a lock of hair away from his. Reaching up to add some final spots of brown, she paused.

Despite the camouflage of her clown makeup, he could discern the green of her eyes, the wisp of pink as her lips parted. And there was something in her face, something he'd never seen before—the true Cindy. Despite the ludicrous grease paint, her naked emotions were laid bare.

Cindy, all fun and fire. And something within stirred in response.

"Frog on Daddy!" Mandy exclaimed.

He tore his gaze from Cindy's. "What?"

"Frog on you," Mandy explained.

Flynn glanced up at Cindy.

She shrugged a bit sheepishly. "I thought the idea of face painting might make you feel like croaking."

The laugh burst out before Flynn could stop it.

Alice tugged at his sleeve. "Daddy funny?"

"Yes," he managed. "I imagine Daddy looks very funny."

The moment broken, he accepted a tray of paints and a brush. "Me first?" Alice asked.

Flynn glanced at Cindy. "I can't paint as well as she can."

Cindy winked at this shiest triplet. "But Daddy paints with love, and that's lots better than anything else."

"Better," Alice agreed.

And one of the cold places deep inside Flynn thawed a fraction. He had about decided that Alice preferred Cindy hands-down to her own father. Now she wrapped chubby arms around his neck. "Love you."

Hastened by a furnace of emotion, the thawing continued. "I love you, too, punkin."

"Make me a clown like Cinny?" Alice asked, with her sweet smile.

Two worlds, Flynn realized. One they shared with him, one with Cindy.

Flynn did his best, turning often to study Cindy's face, presumably to copy her makeup. But he found his gaze lingering a little too long, a little too often.

When the face painting concluded, they rushed to other games. Even with a piñata dangling temptingly as the final prize, the kids still lingered over the other games.

Flynn, along with the other adults, spread out across the yard. So he was surprised to find himself playing Twister with Cindy.

"I could move on to another game," he offered.

She shrugged. It was neither invitation nor rebuff. Yet he stayed.

It didn't take long for Flynn, Cindy, Annie and David to become snarled in the game. The kids giggled as first Flynn hunched over, then Cindy stooped next to him, their shoulders touching.

Flynn felt her soft flesh, remembered the one dance they'd shared so many years ago. Then he took another turn and somehow they were tangled together on the slippery game mat.

As they bent, twisted, tangled, mangled, wound and curved, they were never more than inches apart. Inches that had once seemed like miles, he realized with sudden clarity. Because he had put them there.

The next call sent Cindy and Flynn falling, the kids bouncing on top of them. The game was over, but Flynn was slow to move away.

Cindy studied him curiously. "Are you ready for the cake and presents?"

He cleared his throat. "Sure." And he tried to clear his head. "Whatever you think is best."

She tilted her head. "Whatever *I* think is best?"

"Well, you did plan everything." He couldn't tell her she so distracted him that he could think of little else.

"Fine. Do you want to help me bring the cakes out?"

"Sure. I still can't believe you baked three cakes. And why are they such a secret?"

Her smile was mysterious. "You'll see."

Strangely he wanted to.

Cindy signaled to Katherine, who came to help them carry in the multiple trays that had been hidden away in the small butler's pantry behind the kitchen.

"What?" Flynn asked, staring at the unusual cakes.

"The shapes have a special meaning" was all Cindy would say. "You'll see why soon."

Flynn picked up the cake with Beth's name on it. Cindy and Katherine followed suit and soon all the cakes were positioned on their special tables. Cindy had loaded the kids' wagons with ice that held buckets of ice cream that could be pulled to each small table.

Cindy clapped her hands together. "It's time for cake and presents!"

Three cakes for the triplets on their third birthday. It couldn't be more perfect. At least when he figured out what the shapes meant, Flynn decided.

Candles lit, everyone began singing "Happy Birthday" with Noah and his friends playing in the background.

"Make a wish!" Cindy told the triplets as they pursed to blow out the candles.

"But don't tell what it is," Flynn added, suddenly re

membering the few happy birthdays of his own child-hood, memories he hadn't even realized were still stored within.

Beth's small face puckered in concentration. Mandy's eyes widened. And Alice looked dreamy.

Cindy glanced at Flynn, indicating it was up to him to tell them to blow out the candles.

"All together. Get ready, blow them out…now!"

The girls squealed as each of their tiny sets of candles expired and smoke whirled up from their cakes. Everyone clapped and cheered.

"I'll start getting the gifts," Cindy offered. "If you want to help them cut their cakes."

Flynn had a sudden memory of the girls' first birthday. Julia had organized the party, insisting on doing everything herself. When he'd offered to help cut the cake, she'd waved him away. Capable, he'd thought. But he also remembered the feeling of being excluded, as though his presence wasn't really needed.

Now, however, Cindy stood aside, allowing him to guide each girl's hand in slicing the first piece from each of their cakes.

Waiting until that very special moment was over and Katherine and Michael took over the cake-cutting chore, Cindy pulled out one gift apiece.

"Hold cake!" Beth demanded, pushing her plate at Flynn.

He smiled at her excitement as she ripped open

Cindy's gift. It was a small ukelele. She studied it uncertainly.

"It's to play," Cindy explained. "Like when I make music on the piano."

Beth plucked one string, its twang startling all the triplets. As Mandy and Beth stared intently at the instrument, Cindy handed them each their presents.

Mandy unwrapped hers the fastest. "Music?" she asked, holding up a recorder.

Cindy nodded. "You blow into it."

Mandy did and was immediately delighted by the light woodwind sound the starter instrument produced.

Alice had her own present unwrapped by then, and she held up a small, child-size violin. "Alice music?"

Cindy produced a proportionately small bow. "You pull this over the strings."

Alice did and instead of the terrible yowling sound they expected, the child instinctively pulled the bow gently over the strings. Her face bloomed at the sound.

"That's wonderful!" Cindy exclaimed.

Pleased, but still shy, Alice glanced from the violin to her cake. "Matches!"

Flynn tore his gaze from his daughters to their cakes. He had recognized the violin shape, but now he realized the other two were formed as a recorder and ukelele. Unexpectedly he grinned.

He could see that Alice's name was positioned on the frosting strings, as was Beth's. Mandy's lettering wove in between the recorder's apertures. Each was as unique as his daughters.

Glancing up, he caught Cindy's gaze on him. In it he saw a questioning, as though looking for his approval. He hadn't ever suspected she sought approval, instead acting on her own whims and wishes.

Still she'd done all this on her own for the girls, creating, working…and at the same time making him feel a part of things, rather than a bystander. He raised his hand in a thumbs-up gesture.

The bizarre makeup emphasized her wide grin. Irrationally he wondered how she could look so pretty, clown makeup and all.

Chapter Eleven

Flynn told himself that flying Cindy to dinner in San Antonio was a simple thank-you, nothing more. His plane was hangared in the small local airport that was used primarily for crop dusters and rich oil executives who vacationed in the privacy of the Hill Country. He hadn't expected Cindy to enjoy the mode of transportation; it was simply for expediency when he didn't have the time to drive. Usually he preferred to have his own car, especially in Houston. The commute from the airport to downtown took nearly as long as the drive from Rosewood and wasn't nearly as pleasant.

So it surprised him when Cindy's face lit up at the invitation, then further brightened when he mentioned the plane. Julia had hated his Cessna Skyhawk. He had finally talked her into going up once, but she'd hated every moment, scarcely able to bear it until he'd landed. Then she'd scrambled out, swearing never to get into his plane again. What, she had asked, would happen to the girls if they were both killed in a crash?

Now, as Flynn taxied down the narrow runway, he could scarcely believe the excitement in Cindy's expression. Leaning forward so far that she strained the straps of her seat belt, she stared out the windows.

Building up speed, Flynn took a moment to glance at Cindy. Instantly he recognized the pure adrenaline. The own rush he felt each time he jockeyed into the air.

With a gentle bump and swish, they were off the ground, gaining altitude.

"We're up!" Cindy exclaimed, still peering through the windshield. "This is so cool. Look!" she pointed. "It's like being in *Land of the Giants.* We can see the roofs and the *tiny* people!"

"You've been on a plane before," he commented in mild amusement.

"But not this kind. It's like a ride at Disneyland, only a whole lot better. In a commercial jet, you don't see the details. You get too high up too soon." She leaned even closer to the window, pulling her seat belt to its limit. "Look! Look! You can see the playground!" She laughed aloud. "If I had a plane like this, I'd be up here every day."

"I used to, a long time ago," Flynn admitted. "But not in the last few years."

She tore her attention from the fast-disappearing panorama below. "Why did you stop?"

"Julia didn't like it. She hated being in the plane herself, then worried every time I went up. So I only used it for business."

Cindy's eyes deepened in sympathetic understanding. "I know she felt that way. I didn't realize you'd cut back so much. Julia didn't mention that—only the concern. The way Mom and Dad died in that boating accident— it was tragic, but it changed Julia. She'd always been reserved, but after that, she absolutely detested anything that could even remotely be considered unsafe. She gave up horseback riding, boating, even biking." Cindy paused. "I worried because it was as though she wanted to create this impenetrable shell of safety. I felt she was afraid to have any fun, to really enjoy life because of her fear." Hesitating again, the tone of her voice cracked a bit. "And then to die so young from something she couldn't protect herself from. I don't know…it seemed so cruelly ironic."

Flynn nodded. "I agree. But I'm surprised you see it that way. After all, don't you believe your God could have saved her?"

Pain darkened her eyes, a deep abiding pain. "I won't pretend to understand everything He does. But that's why it's called faith."

Flynn took a deep breath. "I don't want to ruin the afternoon. Maybe we should change the subject."

She glanced through the large windshield at the de- cidedly blue sky, the uncluttered white of the drifting clouds. "We can, but it's all around us."

They rode quietly for a while, then Cindy began to pick out landmarks below, her excitement rekindled, growing by the minute. As they approached the city, she pointed out the Tower of the Americas, a tall needlelike structure that had been erected in the sixties for the Hemisfair. San Antonio was a city of landmarks, historic and new. They flew over old missions, a new stadium and the curving river that defined San Antonio's image.

When they landed, then exited the plane, Cindy was still pumped. "If I were you, I'd fly every day." Her eyes widened. "We could fly to the monthly board meetings in Houston instead of driving, couldn't we?"

Amazed, Flynn stared at her. How could two sisters be so different? "You'd really want to do that?"

"Are you kidding? I'd ask you to fly me to the grocery store every day if there was a landing strip on Main Street."

His laughter erupted on its own again. Before he'd moved to Rosewood, that had been such a rare action it was almost nonexistent. "I've rented a car. We can pick it up and head downtown."

As they drove through the crowded streets, Cindy sadly noted the tall skyscrapers that surrounded the most famous of the city's landmarks. Built as a mission, the Alamo was the shrine of Texas independence.

"Do you know that when I was a little kid, I think I

was about five, my parents brought us to see the Alamo. At that time, it stood all alone, no other buildings around it. I remember thinking it must be the biggest, most magnificent building in the world." She pointed to the mall and office structures that now dwarfed the symbol of the Lone Star state. "It seems sad somehow that all this commercialism has ruined that. When I toured the mission for the first time, the man in charge told us it was a shrine and cautioned us to be quiet. It was easy because there couldn't have been more than a dozen people inside. The last time I tried to visit the Alamo, hundreds of people were squeezed inside, so many that you couldn't even move. Again, the man outside gave the same instructions. Why I'm not sure, because once we were inside, with that many people there was more pandemonium than I imagine they had during the actual last days of the Alamo. I could have cried for what was lost, what would never be again."

Flynn could understand exactly how she felt, he'd had similar experiences. But the vision of Cindy crying over a lost historical landmark moved him beyond measure. Again, he wondered, who was this mercurial woman?

When he didn't comment, she angled her face. "Gives a new meaning to 'Remember the Alamo' though, doesn't it?"

"Tell you what. I know the Riverwalk's changed, but at least the river's still there. You game?"

She sighed, a purely feminine response. "I have to warn you, once I get there, you may have to drag me away."

"I'll chance it."

After parking the car, they crossed the street. Reaching a stairwell, they descended the stone steps. The famed Riverwalk, nestled below street level, lent European character to the distinctively Texas town. People were drawn to the "Venice of Texas" because it was the thread of the historical tapestry that was San Antonio. Deep roots of Spanish, Mexican and German heritage made the town unique and ripe with charm.

The Riverwalk wasn't as crowded as it would be in the coming summer days. Still, couples strolled the old riverbank. Once a secluded, little-known area, it was now a tourist mecca with sidewalk cafés, boutiques, gift shops and galleries. "As long as we're reminiscing, I can remember when there was only one restaurant on the Riverwalk."

"The Casa Rio near the stairs at the end of the sidewalk that goes up to Commerce Street," Cindy agreed. "The oldest restaurant on the Riverwalk."

"You've been there?" he asked in surprise.

"My dad brought me here. I was the one who loved traveling, so I went along when Mom and Julia wanted to stay home. He and I visited La Villita. Back then it was more authentic, not just touristy, and we watched the old glassblower. I remember wondering how he could blow that fiery glass all day, especially when it was so hot outside, but then he blew the most beautiful clear glass ship. And my dad bought it for me. I know it's silly, but I believed that with that ship as my good-luck piece, I could sail around the world."

"The one in your curio cabinet," Flynn suddenly remembered. "It's on a shelf by itself, right at eye level."

She nodded. "I'm surprised you remember."

"It's an unusual talisman," he replied.

"I suppose so." Cindy sighed. "After Mom and Dad passed away, Julia couldn't stand to look at it, so I packed the ship away and didn't take it out until I moved to Rosewood."

Flynn suddenly wondered why they'd all tiptoed around Julia. Probably because she was so delicate, so seemingly fragile. Her own trepidation had made them capitulate to her needs, he realized. Not because she wanted to manipulate them, but because she could never escape the fear.

And that he understood. Fear, even one as old as his own, never disappeared. It always lurked around the edges, threatening to erupt, to maim again. Yet Cindy hadn't shared the insecurity with Julia.

"How is it you escaped all the pain Julia felt?"

Cindy's eyes filled with wisdom and acceptance. "I didn't. But I learned to deal with it instead of hiding, and that's being truthful rather than critical. It's not as though Julia wanted to be frightened. But for me, I felt

I'd faced the worst I ever could. I found comfort in my faith, but Julia had a harder time accepting God's will."

Flynn frowned. "Julia didn't even go to church."

"She used to. Even though she still agonized over losing Mom and Dad, she was still attending until she met you."

Shocked, Flynn stared at her. "That can't be true."

Cindy shrugged. "You offered her security, safety, stability. She thought she needed that more at the time."

"Doesn't say much for me, does it?" he asked wryly.

"Oh, I didn't mean that! Julia loved you."

Maybe so. And maybe she really had only needed what he had to offer. But Flynn put the thoughts out of his mind as they climbed the steps, paused at the arches that crossed over the river, looking down into the water, the slow-moving boats. The Arneson River Theater still remained on the now fully developed Riverwalk. Once the amphitheater had been one of only a handful of structures.

Despite the commercialization of the quaint spot, it was still incredibly romantic. As evening approached, lights hung up and down the banks illuminated, strings of fairy lights that twinkled over the brackish water.

"There's nothing like dusk on Paseo del Rio," Cindy murmured, using the Spanish name for the Riverwalk.

He glanced at Cindy, seeing the reflection of the lights on her brilliant hair and sparkling eyes. "No, there's not."

By mutual accord, they strolled to the end of the walk, seeking out the restaurant they'd been to as children. They were escorted to a table beside the water.

"It looks just like it did when I was five," Cindy marveled. "Busier, of course. But unchanged."

It was a new memory, Flynn thought without warning. One they didn't share with Julia. Only each other and a good part of their pasts. And that was remarkable for him.

As they had only a few times since Flynn's move to Rosewood, they enjoyed a few hours unaffected by what usually lay between them. The food was as they'd remembered, but the conversation wasn't.

Flynn admitted that he still wasn't sure about the move to Rosewood, also admitted that it had been made reluctantly.

And Cindy finally confessed that she still wondered why he'd made the choice, that it made her distrustful.

They were huge confessions for two such guarded people. But the admissions allowed some of the tension between them to dissipate.

Cindy's finger rimmed the moisture that formed on her glass of iced tea. "Thanks for bringing me here, Flynn. I've loved everything—the flight, bringing back old memories, even my enchiladas."

He had, too. But it wasn't in Flynn to admit that. "I wanted to say thank you. For the girls' birthday party, taking us in, everything."

She shrugged. "There's no need to thank me. I did it because I wanted to. That's why I work with my Rainbow kids. They give me back so much more than I can do for them."

"You never told me how you got into that."

Explaining, Cindy's face took on that rare softness he'd glimpsed, but when she spoke of what she would do to protect them, she grew equally fierce.

"Isn't it kind of unusual for a church to take on a project like that?" Flynn questioned.

"I'm not really sure," Cindy replied. "I was the one who formed the group, with the kids I just told you about. They're kids who need extra care and attention for more reasons than I can name. The church just lets me use space in the Sunday school building."

"This was *your* idea?"

"Yeah. The kids needed someone. I had lots of time and energy to give."

"Still…"

"Why me?" she asked wryly. "Doesn't fit your picture of me, does it?"

Nothing did anymore. "It just seems like a lot for one woman to tackle."

"No one else was stepping up to bat."

"But why you?"

She smiled. "Because it was the right thing to do."

He stared at her in silence, a thousand questions begging to be voiced. Instead he asked the waiter for the bill. Once he'd settled it, they strolled back down the sidewalk, watching boats gliding by, hearing the gentle slosh of the water as it lapped against the river-bank.

Angling his head, he saw the wistfulness on Cindy's face as she looked at the boats. "Why don't we take a ride on one?"

Her smile surfaced. "Do we have time?"

"You're the one who made the arrangements for the girls with Katherine. Do you think she'd mind if we're about an hour later?"

Grin widening, she shook her head, pulling a cell phone from a side pocket in her purse. "We can call and let her know."

Cindy quickly phoned Katherine as they entered the short line for the next boat, and soon were on board. Since it was still late spring, a cool breeze skipped through the air, disguising the hot, humid days of summer that were just ahead.

The San Antonio River wound through the business district of the town, crisscrossed by quaint curved bridges, the banks beautifully landscaped with native plants.

The ride down the river was near magical, the strings of tiny white lights providing a romantic, winsome background. Overhanging tree branches reached out across the river, teasing but not quite touching the passing boats. Another new memory, Flynn realized. One as unexpected as the first.

Glancing over, he saw Cindy's gaze on his. But seeing him, she looked away, her porcelain skin pale against the deepening night. So different, he thought again. But this time it wasn't a disquieting thought, rather one that intrigued.

Water continued to lap against the sides of the boat, a gentle thrumming that echoed beneath the overhanging walkways, one that whispered to his thoughts.

It seemed the ride ended too quickly. Flynn was reluctant as he stepped from the boat. The allure of the surroundings made him want to take Cindy's hand, to linger, to discover more.

But her expression was rueful as she glanced at her watch. "Katherine will be expecting us soon."

It was ridiculous to be so disappointed. It was only a thank-you dinner, he reminded himself. Yet the thoughts that had begun on the boat echoed as they flew home.

It wasn't a long flight, yet the plane was incredibly intimate in the dark night.

"The lights from the homes and buildings look so snug and cozy, secured for the night," Cindy said softly. "I love that feeling, that all's right with the world."

Flynn's voice was quiet, not wanting to provoke the unique moment. "But you can't know that."

"No, but I can hope it's true."

He glanced over at her. "I suppose so," he replied, settling for the words even though *hope* hadn't been in his own vocabulary for many years. The clear night sky stretched out before them, the evening darkening, the wonder growing.

Chapter Twelve

Nearly three weeks later, Cindy still thought often of their evening in San Antonio, the unspoken repercussions. She and Flynn had shared an uneasy truce since then, but Cindy held no illusions. Nearly every day Flynn went to the construction site of the house he was building. It seemed to her that he wanted to leave her house as soon as possible.

Before he did though, she wanted to be sure the girls had a good religious foundation. Thus every afternoon, like today, she blended songs and stories with a biblical theme into their music lesson time.

Cindy was thrilled that the triplets were still excited about the instruments she had given them. She had taught them some basic notes, which they practiced faithfully. Using her own methods, Cindy picked out simple notes on the piano while the girls followed along. Now they played often in the evenings and also with the Rainbow class.

"The Jesus song," Mandy requested, her shorthand version of "Jesus Loves Me."

When they finished the song, Cindy clapped her hands. "That was wonderful! When your mommy and I were little girls that was our favorite song."

Beth screwed her always inquisitive face into a question mark. "Where's my mommy?"

Although both she and Flynn had tried to explain this before, it was too much for the children to understand. "You know what, there's a book that I'd like to read to you, about a little girl."

She read them the story of a young girl whose mother had died. The girl looked and looked everywhere for her mother and asked everyone she met where her mother was. But no one knew. Until she went to church.

"Was she there?" Beth asked.

"No, but that's when she learned her mommy had gone to Heaven. Just like your mommy."

"Is it nice there?" Mandy asked.

"Yes, because all the people your mommy loved were there, waiting to greet her. She'd missed her mommy and daddy, too, and was very happy to see them." Cindy's eyes misted, her own longing for her lost family never completely at bay.

"Did they hug her?" Alice asked, concern in her tiny face.

"So much, it probably shook up a storm," Cindy replied, smiling at the image.

"I'm happy Mommy's in heaven," Beth finally concluded.

Still smiling, Cindy glanced up. But her happy expression drained away as she encountered Flynn's furious face. He must have come in while she had been absorbed in telling the story. "Flynn," she greeted him quietly.

"Mommy's in heaven," Mandy told him with cheerful confidence.

"You girls go into the kitchen and get an apple," Flynn told them with quiet authority.

"No more story?" Beth asked.

"No," Flynn replied tightly. "No more stories."

Once the girls were out of earshot, Flynn advanced. "What was that about?"

"They wanted to know where their mother is."

"In the ground," Flynn replied, with barely controlled anger.

And something deep, deep inside Cindy fractured. It no longer mattered if Flynn didn't return her love, couldn't see the person she now was. His lack of faith was even more painful than unrequited love. And something she could never, never compromise on. So she kept her silence.

"I thought I'd made myself clear. Don't interfere with my children's beliefs."

"You *want* them to believe their mother is in the ground? That they have no possible hope of being reunited with her?"

"You've crossed the line."

Cindy set her teeth, trying to restrain her own temper.

"I thought your Sunday school thing was strictly social. Since it's not, that's out."

Shocked, she stared at him. "You can't mean that!"

"I've never been more sure of anything. You seem to keep forgetting that *I'm* their parent."

"That's where you're wrong. I've never lost sight of that fact. But I think you have."

The following days were so tense, Cindy considered going away for a while, leaving the house to Flynn. Then one of the girls would climb in her lap, and her resolve fled.

The rest of the week passed and when Sunday morning arrived, Cindy dressed for church. Once downstairs in the kitchen, she picked up her purse.

"Us go?" Beth asked, starting to scramble from her booster seat.

"Not today," Flynn answered for her.

"Sunny school?" Mandy asked, seeing that Cindy was holding her Bible, as well.

Cindy glanced at Flynn, then nodded.

"I wanna go!" Beth wailed.

Alice and Mandy also tried to climb down from their booster seats. "Wait for us, Cinny!"

"You'll have to talk to your daddy," Cindy replied, pain wiping the color from her face.

Feeling as though she were betraying her sister, Cindy turned and fled. But before she could escape through the front door, she heard the girls' voices rising in demand, then the beginning of sniffling cries. Cindy pressed her head against the door as she heard the cries increase to sobs.

Pulling back, it took all of her power to walk through the door, to not turn back around, confront Flynn and console the girls. But this was Flynn's decision. Girding her strength, Cindy made her way to church, knowing she needed His help now more than ever.

Six days later, Flynn rubbed at the throbbing headache that had centered between his brows. He'd thought the previous Sunday had been bad with the girls crying and throwing tantrums because they wanted to go with Cindy to church. But the rest of the week was even worse. Every morning before work and each evening when he returned, the girls were at him, pleading to go back to "Sunny school."

Flynn had been certain they would forget all about it within a day, two at the most. But they hadn't forgotten. They repeated over and over again that they wanted to sing, and hear stories, and color and see their friends.

Now he was facing another Sunday morning of forcing the children to remain behind as they watched Cindy leave for church.

Picking up a bottle of aspirin, he quickly swallowed two, washing them down with one of Cindy's organic juice blends.

He had two choices. He could insist on having things his way and create another round of chaos. Or he could let the girls attend church while they stayed with Cindy, then when they moved into their own house, he could let the habit fade away on its own.

It was his decision.

He pictured the onslaught of three pairs of eyes, ones that had been boring into him all week. And he knew he couldn't withstand them any longer.

Knowing the girls were napping, Flynn sought out Cindy, guessing she had retreated to the quiet of the backyard. She had made a point of being anywhere he wasn't the entire week.

He was right. She was in the far corner of the yard, alternately weeding the flower bed and stretching her hand between two loose boards in the fence to pet the neighbor's dog.

Dispensing with small talk, he resisted the urge to rub at his throbbing forehead. "I've come to a decision."

"Another one?"

He winced. She was still stubborn, still challenging. There was no bending, no complacency. Nothing except her incredible appeal to suggest she was the weaker sex. "While we are staying here, the girls can go with you to church."

She turned around so that she could see him. "And afterward?"

"What difference does that make? They're my children. I'll do what I think is best for them."

"No, actually you're doing what you think is best for you."

Flynn stopped short of throwing his hands in the air. "You can't just win, can you? You have to win *and* have the last word."

But there was no victory in her expression. Only sadness colored her brilliant green eyes. "You just don't get it. Neither one of us wins."

For a moment, Flynn could only stare at her. But he couldn't believe that was true. He had dedicated himself to protecting his daughters, ensuring they would never suffer as he had. "It's up to you, then," he said finally.

"No," she replied, her voice shaking. "This is your decision. I'll take them with me in the morning only if you've told them they can go."

Flynn turned away, unwilling to search her eyes again. That was far too painful. And equally hopeless.

Once inside the house, Flynn kept himself busy, going over some revised plans for the new house. He had an urgent need to finish the house, to move away from all the confusion he'd felt since staying in Cindy's home. Closing his eyes, he could picture the disappointment in Cindy's expression, the certainty that she disapproved.

It wasn't up to her to approve or disapprove, he told himself righteously. Glancing toward the stairs, he thought of his innocent daughters still asleep. He would do anything to protect them, anything. And that's what Cindy didn't understand. He wasn't keeping them from church to deprive them, rather to save them from the hurt he'd known. And now Cindy had put him in an untenable position. Hurt them by denying their attendance, or hurt them by letting them believe a delusion that could only lead to disappointment.

They were only three, Flynn reminded himself. Young enough to forget once they were in their own home. Glancing around, Flynn looked at the comfortable, cozy space Cindy had created. The girls would miss this, he realized. And in their young lives they'd been forced to miss too much already.

With leaden feet he stepped on the first riser. It was time to wake the girls. Time to tell them that he wouldn't force this particular sacrifice right now, that they could go to church with "Cinny" in the morning.

But he made a second resolution, as well. From now

on, he'd spend less time at his new office and more time with his girls. Because it had been easy, he'd allowed Cindy too much influence on them. It was time he took that back. Before it was too late.

In the following weeks, Cindy had taken an inventory of her own, as well. But before she could act on it, crisis struck.

One day she had gone to pick up Ricky for Rainbow class and had found an ambulance parked in front of the house. The young boy was crying as they loaded his mother into the ambulance.

Sweeping the child into her embrace, Cindy put him in her car, following the ambulance to the hospital. Using her cell phone, she alerted Katherine who promised to take the class for the day.

Once at the hospital, Cindy held Ricky's hand as the doctors worked on his mother. The child clung to Cindy, terrified.

And when the doctor emerged from the room, his face was somber.

No, Cindy prayed. *Don't take this child's only parent.*

"I'm sorry," the doctor began, looking first at Cindy, then down at young Ricky. "We knew it was inevitable. But we did try everything."

"My mommy?" Ricky asked in a wavering voice.

Cindy knelt beside him, still clasping his hands. "Mommy's in Heaven now with Jesus."

"But I want her here with me!" Ricky shouted. "Not with Jesus!"

The tears came then, huge gulping sobs. Cindy pulled him close, holding his shaking body next to her, feeling her own tears wetting her cheeks, salting her lips. While they both cried for what Ricky had lost and could never regain, the doctor quietly moved away.

As Cindy smoothed the hair back from his forehead and searched her pocket for a tissue, Ricky finally spoke. "Why did she have to die?"

Cindy searched for the right words, but couldn't find them. "I don't know. She just got very sick."

"Did she want to go to Heaven?"

Cindy felt her own heart breaking. "She didn't want to leave you, but now her pain is all gone."

"She won't take no more pills?"

"No more."

"She couldn't breathe sometimes," Ricky admitted, the tears thickening his young voice. "And she hurted."

"Well, she doesn't hurt anymore."

Ricky nodded, then looked up again. "Where will I go, Miss Cindy?" His face crumpled. "I don't have nobody."

And in that instant, she made another binding and final decision. "Yes, you do. You have me. You'll come and live with me."

Tears still ran down his cheeks, wetting his T-shirt. "For how long?"

Forever, she thought to herself, if it was within her power. "For as long as you can. I think your mother would like that."

He glanced back at the room that held his mother's still body. Again his mouth trembled. "Mommy said you were the nicest lady she ever knew."

Cindy's own tears started again. "And your mother raised the nicest little boy in the world." Clasping his hand, she led them down the hall.

Speaking quietly and briefly with the doctor, Cindy told them she was taking Ricky home with her and to notify the mortuary that she would be paying for the funeral.

Once back at her house, Katherine met her at the front door, having made sure the kids were playing out back, rather than inside.

Cindy knelt beside Ricky one more time. "I have to make some phone calls. Can you stay with Miss Katherine for a few minutes?"

Ricky didn't want to release her hand, but finally nodded.

Katherine picked up his other hand. "Let's have a glass of milk, okay? Miss Donna, one of the Sunday school teachers, and the other kids are in the yard and we can stay inside if you'd like."

Again Ricky nodded, the motion wobbly and uncertain.

Katherine hugged him close, as well.

Cindy met her friend's gaze, signaling her grati- tude, before disappearing into the privacy of the con- servatory. Quickly she called her attorney, who promised to notify child services and file an immedi- ate petition for temporary custody along with her request for permanent adoption.

Then he hesitated. "Are you certain about this, Cindy? Permanent adoption?"

"Very certain," she replied without hesitation. "Can you let me know if there's any problem with the im- mediate permission to keep him?"

"I don't anticipate any since there are no relatives. It was wise of you to investigate the family situation while his mother was alive and could give you the in- formation, dismal as it is." He hesitated. "This is a lot to take on, Cindy."

"Not as much as a six-year-old who's just lost his last living family member."

The attorney rang off and Cindy contacted the mortuary, verifying that she was paying for the funeral, also requesting that everything be elegant but tasteful.

Drained, Cindy sat back in her chair, her heart breaking for this small child.

Hearing a noise at the doorway, she glanced up, meeting Flynn's curious expression. True to the resolve he'd informed her of, Flynn had been returning home from work in the early afternoons, determined to be a bigger part of the triplets' upbringing.

"Why is it so quiet?" he asked, entering the room.

She didn't answer at first.

Flynn's own expression turned downward as he examined her pale face. "Has there been an accident? Are the girls all right? Are—"

"They're fine," she said finally, her voice as low as her spirits.

"Then what is it?"

"Ricky Dunn's mother died today."

Flynn drew his brows together. "The little kid in your class that's always stirring something up?"

"Yes, that would be him."

"Tough break," Flynn sympathized. "Did you cancel the class today out of respect?"

She shook her head. "The kids are in the backyard. Katherine and Donna took over."

"Oh. Well, I can see why it'd be hard for you today."

She met his gaze. "That's not the reason." Briefly she explained how she'd come to be at Ricky's house, then the hospital.

"Where is he now?" Flynn questioned. "With the grandparents?"

Again she shook her head. "He's remarkably like you and me, Flynn. He has no other family."

Shocked, he stared at her. "This little kid doesn't have *anybody?*"

"Not exactly. He has me."

"Well, that's fine on a temporary basis—"

"You don't understand, Flynn. It's not temporary."

"You're taking this child in to raise?"

She nodded. "He needs me."

"You plan on taking in every other orphan in the state?"

"I probably would if it were possible. But I don't know them as I do Ricky. And I won't let him grow up without a single person to watch out for him."

Flynn drew his brows together. "You mean you're going to adopt him?"

"What would you have me do, Flynn? Turn him over to strangers who don't care about him? A child who just lost the mother he cherished, and who has no one else?"

"Well, no, but you've never had kids of your own and—"

She ignored the sharp if unintentional barb of his comment. "Maybe not. But this isn't a game to me, Flynn. I know you still see me as a scatterbrained twenty-one-year-old with thoughts of only parties and fun. Well, yes, I did like parties and I did like having fun. But that wasn't all there was to me then. And it certainly isn't all there is to me now. I intend to give this wonderful little boy a home. I'm raw, knowing the pain he's suffering, but I'm also grateful I can be here for him now, that the Lord gave me this opportunity."

Confusion settled over the surprise in his face. "You really see it that way? As an opportunity?"

"Yes," she replied quietly. "I do. Flynn, we've both known our share of loss, we know how it feels to be the one left behind. Can you imagine how it would be if you were only a child?"

He blanched, something Cindy had never seen, not even at Julia's funeral.

"Flynn?"

Pulling himself back to the moment, he met her gaze. "Yes, maybe I can. Where's Ricky now?"

"In the kitchen with Katherine." She glanced down at the phone. "I wanted to be alone while I talked to my lawyer and then the funeral home."

He nodded. "Do you want me to clear the girls out for a while? I could take them to Houston for a visit, let you have some space."

Knowing the offer was sincere, she felt only gratitude despite its misplaced intent. "No. Actually, I think it would be good for Ricky to have them around. He already feels so alone."

Flynn again looked at her questioningly. "What happened to his father? Were they divorced?"

"No. He died when Ricky was a baby."

Unconsciously, Flynn winced. "And you're sure there aren't any grandparents?"

"All gone. His father had one sister who died in childhood. His mother was an only child. You know the equation, Flynn. It's just like our own."

Flynn glanced in the direction of the kitchen, even

though it couldn't be seen from the confines of the conservatory. "How old did you say he was?"

"Six."

For a moment Flynn's jaw worked. Then he nodded.

And silence stood between them for several long moments.

Flynn lifted his head at last. "What can I do to help?"

Unbelievably touched, Cindy couldn't stop the tears that suddenly erupted, the trembling of her lips. Blinded by the onslaught, she didn't see Flynn walk around the library table until he stood in front of her. Then his arms were around her, holding her close, offering the comfort she hadn't experienced since before the loss of her parents.

The stiffness of her shock cracked as she laid her head on Flynn's sturdy shoulder and let the tears flow. Tears for all their losses. Things that could never be made right again.

Flynn's hand was gentle as he stroked the back of her head, and for just the moment she gave in to the need to remain like that, buffeted from all the pain that was ahead. Pain made worse by the fact that he couldn't shelter her from the biggest loss, that of his love. And again she issued the same silent prayer she had been repeating for weeks, that the Lord would soften Flynn's heart and show him the path back to his faith.

Chapter Thirteen

Determined to keep his promise, in the following weeks Flynn often returned home by late afternoon to see his daughters and Ricky. He had hired six more employees to keep up with the growth of the business. Within little more than a month, their volume had quadrupled.

He had resolved to devote more time to the kids than to his software development business. And now it weighed on him that he had the responsibilities of both work and family. Due to Rosewood's stagnant job market, the positions he had offered meant life-altering changes to his new employees. If he dropped the ball, it wasn't just a financial loss for him; it could harm the people he'd hired, people who had placed their trust in him. He knew two had already purchased small homes, based on their new earnings. And Flynn couldn't live with himself if they lost their homes due to his negligence.

Which put him squarely in the middle again.

But this afternoon, he'd been able to leave early, reaching the house just after four o'clock. He could hear the babble of young voices coming from the backyard. Cindy's Rainbow kids. He couldn't believe she was insisting on keeping both classes intact, but she said these emotionally scarred children needed her. Flynn had argued that she was stretching her energies in too many directions: Ricky, the triplets, the Rainbow kids. But Cindy wouldn't budge.

Stepping through the French doors, he was appalled to see Mandy crying, sprawled out on the terrace, blood gushing from her mouth. With a cloth grasped in one hand, Cindy was holding the child's head.

Fear had Flynn beside his daughter in mere seconds. "What happened?"

"The kids got a little rambunctious," Cindy explained, pressing the cloth gently around Mandy's mouth.

"Rambunctious?" he demanded. "What's that supposed to mean?"

"They were running, Paul pushed her a little and she fell."

Fury nearly blinded him; still Flynn reached for his daughter, intending to pick her up. "I knew something like this would happen."

Cindy laid a restraining hand on his arm. "What are you doing?"

"Taking her to the hospital, of course!"

"Flynn, you're overreacting. One of her teeth poked her lip when she fell. It's not serious."

He motioned to Mandy's swollen mouth and the blood that had dripped on her T-shirt. "It looks pretty serious to me!"

"Flynn, have you ever seen one of the girls bleeding before?"

"No... Why?"

"Because the first time it's terrifying. But trust me, she's okay. We'll put some ice on it to stop the swelling, and see, Mandy's already stopped crying."

Flynn studied his daughter's face, seeing her tears had indeed stopped. "Still, better safe than sorry."

Cindy kept her tone mild. "Taking her to the hospital would be pretty scary. And the bleeding's almost stopped."

But Flynn hadn't spent his store of protective impulses. "I knew that letting them run around in jeans wasn't a good idea."

Cindy didn't rise to the bait, instead widening her eyes in mild disbelief. "She'd still have fallen if she'd been wearing a dress. And then she'd also have scraped knees."

"If you hadn't insisted on bringing these ragamuffins into your house..." Flynn began, but the words trailed away as he watched her face transform to one of wounded incredulity.

"It's good to know how you really feel," she said in a tone that was as quiet as it was livid. "Before Ricky discovered it the hard way."

Flynn wished he could bite back the words. "I didn't mean him."

"No? Then which particular *ragamuffin* were you referring to? They're all either scarred emotionally or in desperate need of nurturing. Take your pick."

Flynn passed a hand over his forehead, then glanced down at Mandy. "I think we'd better discuss this later."

Cindy thrust the moist cloth at him. "Be sure to wrap the ice in this or it will burn her skin."

"Cinny!" Mandy wailed when Cindy rose.

Flynn met Cindy's determined gaze, then watched as her eyes closed briefly.

Then she held out a hand to Mandy. "Let's go in the kitchen. We'll show Daddy how to fix the boo-boo, okay?"

Trailing her, Flynn knew he'd been given one last reprieve. Glancing into the yard, and catching sight of sad-looking little Ricky, Flynn knew he had to make good on this final chance.

Cindy watched as the sun surrendered to the far horizon. It never ceased to her amaze her, this show the Lord provided them on a daily basis, its beauty never matched by even the most talented artists over the centuries.

Night sounds began as darkness tried to slip past twilight's final barriers. It was that indeterminate time of day, not daylight, yet not dark. A calm time of day, Cindy always thought, one that bordered between the worries of day and the loneliness of night.

The sounds of crickets and baritone bullfrogs were equally comforting. She needed this sameness in her life. As much as she craved adventure, she was deeply rooted to this community, to the things in her life that had become so important.

Things Flynn Mallory would never understand.

She was glad the triplets were safely tucked in bed, the crisis over Mandy's minor injury past. Having agreed to let Ricky lose himself with the PlayStation game in the sitting room off the kitchen, she kept track of the time, not wanting him to be left on his own. Flynn was in the house, but that wasn't a particular comfort.

And to think she'd believed his offer to help with young Ricky. Then again, she had always believed her white knight would eventually find her, as well.

Hearing footsteps on the terrace, she turned, wondering if she'd miscalculated the time. To her surprise, Flynn and Ricky were walking outside together.

As she watched, Flynn was clearly not at ease, yet he sat with Ricky at the old wrought-iron table. From her spot deep in the back of the yard, Cindy couldn't hear their conversation, but she could see the look of concern on Flynn's face, one that also seemed beset by some unknown pain. And again she wondered about the mystery who was Flynn Mallory.

She watched them for the next hour, sensing that Flynn was trying to draw out the boy. Ricky had been terribly quiet since he'd come to their home, his grieving a visible thing.

For days after the funeral, he'd hardly spoken. It had surprised Cindy when Flynn had attended Mrs. Dunn's funeral with them. But he'd stood solidly beside Cindy and Ricky. And she was sure that the service had brought a wash of unwelcome memories, yet Flynn had remained stoic. Cindy had been the one to put Ricky on her lap, then comfort him through the painful service. But she had appreciated Flynn's silent show of support.

She'd thought it meant he had a genuine change of heart, that perhaps her prayers were working. But then this afternoon…

Now she wondered again. Did Flynn have two sides that battled for dominance? One that shut out compassion, and one that offered it? Or was she still a lovesick girl who couldn't get a grip on her own heart?

The questions haunted her for days as she watched Flynn with Ricky. First he'd brought home a soccer ball and net to practice kicking. Then he'd asked Cindy if he could sign the boy up for the soccer team. She'd commented that since it was late spring, there was only a month left of the sport. But that didn't faze Flynn, who told her that they could sign up for Little League to fill the summer days.

It confused her in many ways. Because this wasn't an instant bonding. In fact, the more Flynn offered to do for Ricky, the more tortured he appeared. Flynn's appetite had lessened to the point that Cindy urged him to eat hamburgers and French fries, but he insisted he just wasn't hungry. His face grew more gaunt. And each time when he thought no one was looking, he studied Ricky as though watching a ghost.

After this went on for two weeks Cindy decided it was time to confront Flynn. She chose the one time she knew they would be alone—as they traveled to the board meeting in Houston.

Although Cindy continued to love the sensation of flying in the small plane, this time she didn't marvel about it. And she guessed that discussing Flynn's past wouldn't be wise while he was piloting the plane.

After the meeting concluded, Flynn asked where she wanted to have lunch. But a crowded restaurant wasn't what Cindy had in mind.

"Why don't we walk for a while?" she asked.

They strolled along the sidewalks, filled with rushing pedestrians. Cindy glanced up at Antioch Baptist, the city's oldest black Protestant church. It sat between half a dozen mammoth structures, yet it wasn't dwarfed by any of them, instead remaining the most beautiful building in the circular street's crown. Its grace reinforced her resolve.

"Let's head toward Sam Houston Park," she suggested. "It's just a block away."

"Fine," Flynn agreed.

The park was an oasis in the crowded city. Although bordered by towering skyscrapers, the park itself was tranquil, populated only by historic buildings from the state's past that had been relocated to the one central spot.

A small store in the park, run by the Heritage Museum, sold sandwiches, chips, cookies and drinks. Flynn and Cindy purchased enough for a small, but substantial picnic.

Since it was nearly two o'clock, most of the downtown lunch crowd had dispersed. Cindy and Flynn found a bench that offered privacy.

She felt her nerves building as she waited to approach the subject. They were nearly finished with their sandwiches when she took the plunge. "Flynn?"

"Hmm?"

"I need to talk to you about something."

He seemed relaxed by the surroundings, and unaware of her nervousness. "Shoot."

"It's about Ricky."

"What about him?"

She swallowed. "I'm wondering why you offered to help me with him."

He hesitated, and for a moment she wondered if he would answer. When he did, his voice was hoarse. "He reminds me of my brother."

Surprise nearly stilled her as well. "I didn't know you had a brother."

"I never talk about it. Todd died when he was six."

"Ricky's age," Cindy murmured.

Flynn nodded.

"Can you tell me what happened?"

This time his hesitation was much larger, less surmountable. "I don't think you want to hear it and I certainly don't want to dig back that far."

Earnestly she met his gaze. "I *do* want to know. I *need* to know, to understand. And if it's tormenting you this much, *you* need to talk about it."

For a long time Flynn didn't say anything, his eyes taking on a faraway expression. He gripped the remainder of his sandwich, unintentionally crushing it in his clenched hand.

And when he finally, reluctantly spoke, his voice was gruff. "My mother wasn't like any of my friends' mothers. She was always scattered in one direction or another, off on some new quest. I guess some people would call it an incurable zest for life. But it's hard to see it like that when you're a kid, watching out for your younger brother, and you find yourself standing in front of school, the rec center or the movies waiting for her, realizing she had forgotten about us. Oh, she always showed up eventually, apologizing, explaining she'd been caught up in one thing or another." He laughed, a caustic, raw sound. "Something that interested her more than either Todd or me. Then she'd insist on buying ice cream cones or hot dogs to make it up to us. She'd laugh and cajole us into believing the makeup treat was far better than her timeliness. And it usually worked."

Cindy swallowed the sudden dryness in her throat, dreading what was to come. "And then?" she prompted gently.

"I was nine years old. I had a bad case of chicken pox so I was confined to bed with calamine lotion and comic books." Again Flynn hesitated, his jaw working. "Since I couldn't go to school and watch out for Todd, I made sure Mom left on time to pick him up. But on the way she detoured to a flea market. I guess she only planned to stop for only a few minutes. But, as usual, the time escaped her. When she realized she was more than an hour late to pick up Todd, she sped off toward the school." Flynn's voice thickened. "But Todd had gotten tired of waiting and I wasn't there to make sure he didn't wander away."

Bending his head, Flynn rubbed at his forehead. "It wasn't too hard for Mom to find him. Flashing emergency lights lit up the street next to the school. Todd had walked in front of a car." Flynn swallowed as he raised his head, again staring hard at the same faraway place. "He was killed instantly."

Tears misted in Cindy's eyes as she reached for Flynn's empty hand. At first he didn't respond, his own hand rigid. Then he glanced back at Cindy, seeing the tears roll silently down her cheeks. Unfurling his hand, he took Cindy's. And the fragment of sandwich dropped unnoticed from the other.

"I'm so sorry, Flynn. That must have destroyed your family."

"It was the beginning."

Even more horrified, she gripped his hand more firmly. "The beginning?"

"Mom committed suicide the day after Todd's funeral. She took a handful of pills that my dad didn't know she'd gotten from the doctor...and never woke up."

Anguish sliced through her and she couldn't control the tears that continued wetting her cheeks. "Oh, Flynn. That must have been horrible for you."

"My dad did his best, but he was never the same. For all that was wrong about my mother, I guess she was the love of his life. By the time I was nineteen, he died of grief, a broken man."

Cindy couldn't find words of sympathy that didn't fall miles short of how she felt. Instead she wrapped her arms around him, pressing her tear-soaked cheek against his.

When they finally pulled away, Flynn looked at her with a bit of wonder. "I never even told Julia the whole story. She was already filled with so much of her own pain…well, it never seemed the right time."

"I'm glad you told me," she said softly, knowing it was true. "I remember when I first met you. Even though you were five years older than me, I remember thinking you seemed decades older in maturity. No wonder. You had to grow up when you were only nine."

"I never thought about it that way."

Cindy continued to hold his hand, offering her support. "It sounds as though even before Todd's accident, you were older than your years, watching out for him. Then I suspect you watched out for your father after your mother's death. That's an incredible amount of responsibility for such a young child."

He shrugged, clearly uncomfortable with the praise. "If I hadn't been home sick, if I'd been there for Todd—"

"Flynn! You were a small child yourself! And you couldn't help having chicken pox! Surely you can't have carried around that guilt all these years?"

"Some of it. Most of it rests on my mother's shoulders. She should have behaved like a responsible adult. Instead she valued fun more than her family. And look what happened. It destroyed everyone but me."

Cindy chewed on her bottom lip. "It's destroying

you, too, bit by bit. Don't you see that, Flynn? You've carried this burden alone for too many years."

"And who do you suggest I give it to?" he asked bitterly. "I doubt there are many pack mules looking to take it on."

"I know you don't want to hear this, but you need the Lord to lean upon, to help you carry your pain."

"The same God that turned His back on us? Where was He when Todd was hit by that car? And when my mother swallowed a bottle of pills? And my father died of a broken heart? Where was He then, Cindy?"

But she knew that she didn't have the answers that he needed. Only the Lord did. And now she was even more uncertain whether Flynn could ever accept Him again.

Chapter Fourteen

A week later Flynn was hammering a backboard onto the pole he'd had installed beneath the large oak when he heard a car pull up. He glanced over to see who it was.

Noah Brady, dressed in an impeccable tux, stepped out of the sleek Porsche. Cindy had told him she would be out for the evening. She'd failed to mention it would be with Noah.

An untenable kernel of jealousy knotted his stomach, and Flynn turned back to the pole.

"Planning on a little basketball?" Noah asked as he approached.

Flynn shrugged. "The kids should like it."

"Yep. Hey, why don't you join the church team? We could use a decent player."

"I'm not much into church stuff."

Noah nodded. "Fair enough. But the invitation's open. We want to make you feel welcome."

"Because of Cindy?" Flynn asked tightly.

"Sure. We like to keep her happy."

"I bet you do," Flynn muttered beneath his breath.

"I'm sorry. I didn't catch that."

"Nothing." Flynn drove the final nail into the back-board. "Come on inside. I'll see if Cindy's ready."

"Thanks. I don't want to be late."

Flynn looked up and down Noah's formal wear. "Little early for going out on the town, isn't it?"

Noah laughed. "Good one."

Flynn had no idea what the other man meant by that, but led him inside anyway, by way of the back door.

His daughters were grouped around the table, Ricky keeping an eye on them. Flynn wanted the basketball hoop to be a surprise, so he'd invented an excuse for Ricky to watch the girls.

The triplets squealed with delight as they spotted Noah, begging for him to play the piano.

"Now *this* is the ideal audience," Noah replied with a wide grin. Then he glanced at Flynn. "Do you mind?"

Hiding his thoughts, Flynn shook his head. "No, go ahead." Quickly he stabbed the button on the intercom. "Cindy, Noah's here."

"Thanks!" she replied cheerily.

His good mood out the window, Flynn helped Ricky clean up the mess the girls had made with their watercolors.

"Are you mad?" Ricky asked.

Flynn withheld a sigh, immediately regretting causing the child more concern. "No. Just have a lot on my mind. You know, I was thinking a basketball hoop might be kind of fun."

Ricky's always saddened face lit up a little. "Really?"

"Yeah. But I'd need someone to help me put it up."

"I could do that!" Ricky offered eagerly.

"Hmm." Flynn pretended to consider. "I guess you could. Why don't we head out to the driveway and take a look?"

Once outside, Flynn walked companionably with Ricky, waiting to see his reaction.

Ricky stopped suddenly, his eyes growing wide and round. "Wow!"

"You like it?"

"It's swell!" Then he turned to Flynn, his six-year-old eyes far too wise. "You don't need my help."

"Sure do. The pole's set. But I need help hanging the hoop."

Ricky brightened as Flynn took the ladder from the tree he'd leaned it upon.

"I tacked up the backboard," Flynn explained. "But we need to center the hoop."

"Cool!" Ricky exclaimed.

Originally he'd offered to help Ricky because of the guilt he still felt over Todd. He'd never considered that the child would come to tread on his heart, as well. Yet the connection remained painful, as though each step closer picked at the wound that was his past.

But today, standing beside the young boy who looked up at him with something nearing hero worship, another barricade tore loose.

Picking Ricky up, he sat him on his shoulders. "Okay, you center the hoop."

"By myself?" Ricky asked excitedly.

"Sure. When you get it in the center, we'll mark the spot with this thick pencil."

"Okay." Screwing his face into lines of concentration, Ricky carefully centered the hoop.

Flynn handed him the carpenter's pencil and the boy made two marks as Flynn instructed him.

They turned, Ricky still on his shoulders, just as Cindy and Noah stepped out of the house. She was dressed in a gold sequinned evening gown. With her silky red hair streaming down her back, she looked like a gorgeous flame.

And Flynn felt an invisible fist to the gut.

Noah took Cindy's elbow, guiding her down the sidewalk. Again, she looked relaxed, happy. No angst, no uncertainty.

Nothing as she looked when they were together.

Glancing up, she spotted them.

Ricky waved.

Cindy lifted her arm, as well, studying Flynn and Ricky.

"See you later!" Ricky called out.

"Yeah, have a great time," Flynn managed with notably less enthusiasm.

She nodded. "Thanks. I will."

Flynn watched as she got into the car, then as Noah pulled away.

"She looks pretty, huh?" Ricky asked.

Flynn swallowed. "She sure does."

"She's nice like Mommy," Ricky added quietly.

Flynn lifted him down from his shoulders. "She is?"

"Yeah. To the triples, too," he replied, using his own version of triplets, a word he couldn't quite conquer. "I thought they were her babies at first."

"You did?"

"Uh-huh. Excepted I knew they didn't always live here."

The world through a child's clear vision, Flynn realized. A rare and remarkable gift. "She loves them a lot," Flynn admitted aloud.

"Cindy makes us feel special," Ricky said. "Even Heather, and she hates *everybody.*"

Flynn felt an unexpected smile emerge. "Is that so?"

"Yeah. She used to do mean stuff before we had Rainbow class. Our Sunday school teacher said she couldn't come back never."

But Cindy had rescued that unlovable child. He had been a fool, Flynn realized. Purposely not seeing Cindy's depth and caring, her commitment to a group of children who had no one else to be concerned for them.

The fact was that she still drew him as she had the first moment he'd seen her.

But Julia had been safer. She hadn't threatened a true hold on his heart. And Cindy had held just such a promise in her eyes. One he guessed had been like the jolt his own father had felt when meeting his mother. A love that took precedence over everything else. One he'd been fleeing since the day Todd had been killed.

Flynn stared down the now-empty street. But this time he had run straight into that phenomenal and rare love. And she'd just driven off with another man.

Nearly four weeks later, Cindy hummed softly under her breath as she checked on the waffles she was preparing for Flynn's birthday breakfast.

In the past weeks she had pumped the girls, finding out his favorite breakfast foods. She'd listed all the traditional items, knowing he would prefer them to her buckwheat pancakes or granola and berries. Between the girls, they had remembered waffles, sausages and orange juice. Cindy had purchased regular syrup, and creamy butter, as well. It wasn't that she didn't know how to prepare traditional food, she simply preferred healthy eating.

She added a freshly cut early summer rose to the

tray. Covered by her finest linen, silver, crystal and dinnerware, it looked especially appealing, she decided. Seeing the light go out on the waffle iron, she placed the waffles on the plate in a matching diagonal fashion. The sausages and juice were already on the tray.

Cindy turned to the kids. "Okay, guys, do you have everything?"

"Yes," they chorused, barely able to contain their excitement.

They trooped upstairs, but Cindy paused as she reached Flynn's doorway, her nerves clicking into overdrive. She'd never before entered his territory. It didn't matter that it was her house. This was still his room.

Heart pounding, she pushed open the door. From behind and around her, the kids shouted, "Happy birthday."

Flynn's sleep-tousled head popped up. He stared at them in surprise.

Then to Cindy's relief, he grinned.

Still nervous, she approached the bed, offering the tray.

Accepting it, he glanced at the contents, then up at her in amazement. "What did I do to deserve this?"

Her eyes brightened despite her anxiety. "You were born."

He smiled. "Waffles *and* sausages?"

"We told Cinny you liked 'em," Beth offered.

"And orange juice," Mandy added.

"We have another surprise," Cindy added, motioning to the kids.

They scampered out to the hall, returning quickly, carrying musical instruments. Although Ricky didn't really play one, Cindy had found a tambourine for him.

"You going to serenade me, as well?" Flynn asked in pleased surprise.

Cindy picked up her own mandolin that Ricky had fetched from the hall. On her signal, they began to play. Flynn continued smiling, but his eyes widened when the girls' sweet voices added the words "I'm so glad you're my daddy."

Even Ricky sang along, and Cindy saw Flynn's jaw work.

When the song ended, Flynn set the tray on one side of the bed, reaching out to hug his daughters and Ricky. His voice when he spoke was gruff. "Thank you. That was the best birthday present I ever got."

"We boughted more stuff for you!" Beth revealed.

"And wrapped it all up," Mandy added.

Alice smiled sweetly. "It's surprises."

Flynn lifted his eyes, meeting Cindy's. "I don't think I need any more surprises. This was the best."

And her heart weakened, as the hold he held on it strengthened. Pulling her gaze from his, she glanced down at the children. "Okay, you want to go get the presents?"

They clapped and squealed in agreement, scampering away.

Flynn looked at the carefully prepared tray. "How did you possibly know all my favorites?"

Despite the tug-of-war in her heart, she grinned. "Some little fairies told me. You have to be careful. These little fairies are encyclopedias of information."

He returned her grin. "Even better than the Internet."

Their gazes met and lingered, the grins giving way to something else.

"Thank you," Flynn told her quietly.

It seemed to Cindy that the words resonated beyond what they appeared on the surface. She knew her own did. "You're welcome."

"Look, Daddy!" Beth hollered, skidding into the room. "Presents!" She dumped her own awkwardly wrapped gift on his bed.

The other children followed, piling presents on the bed.

Flynn picked up Beth's, using great care to open the clumsily assembled package. He held up a T-shirt emblazoned with a picture of Donald Duck.

"I picked it!" Beth exclaimed.

Amused, Flynn lifted his gaze to meet Cindy's. "Really?"

"She had a hard time choosing between that one and Winnie the Pooh," Cindy explained, unable to hide her own smile.

Flynn hugged his daughter. "Well, this is the one I would have picked, too. It's perfect. Thank you, Beth."

Pleased, Beth grinned as Flynn opened the next one, which was from Alice.

"Oh, this is great," he replied, holding up a huge chocolate bar.

"You like it?" Alice asked.

He hugged her, as well. "It's almost as sweet as you."

"Mine now," Mandy demanded.

Obliging, Flynn unwrapped two coloring books and a huge box of crayons. He glanced between Mandy and Cindy, clearly trying not to sound either puzzled or amused. "Wow."

"We can color together," Mandy told him, beaming at the prospect.

"So we can." A third hug was dispensed. "What a great idea."

Ricky shyly pushed forward his present next.

"I'm getting pretty overwhelmed," Flynn admitted.

He was, Cindy realized.

Flynn unwrapped the present, revealing a baseball cap.

"It's got the Rangers on it," Ricky explained. "Your favorite."

Flynn's throat worked. "You're right. They are my favorites. Thanks." More awkwardly this time, Flynn offered Ricky a hug, as well.

Cindy's own emotions tumbled as she watched them, thinking how perfect they looked together.

"Yours now!" Beth told her.

"Oh, yes." Cindy handed him a small, neatly wrapped box.

His gaze touched hers. Then he opened the gift, unfolding the tissue that was tucked inside, then lifting up the present. He held up a framed portrait of the triplets. They were wearing dresses Flynn had chosen for them, a triple play of perfection.

"How?" he asked in wonder. "When?"

"I have my ways," Cindy replied. "We snuck off when you weren't looking."

"It's wonderful," Flynn said softly. "Really wonderful."

"There's something else in the box," she told him.

He dug beneath another layer of tissue, uncovering a second framed picture. Again his throat worked as he turned it around to show the others the picture of a shyly smiling Ricky.

The girls clapped and Ricky stubbed the toe of his tennis shoe into the thick rug, his pleasure overshadowing his timidity.

"You really are a magician," Flynn said finally.

And his hold on her heart gripped even tighter.

Chapter Fifteen

"What are you guys doing here?" Flynn asked, looking up from his work to the crowd standing in his doorway.

Cindy touched the glass block wall that separated Flynn's office from a large working area, one that had half walls of the same material to give each employee a degree of privacy. "This place looks great! Michael did a wonderful job on the remodeling. Looks kind of retro.

"To answer your question—I've got a scheduling conflict," she explained ruefully. "Katherine's booked solid and I've called everyone else I know. I can't find a sitter, so…"

Flynn glanced down at his daughters' expectant faces. "Oh, sure. I'll find something to keep them busy."

Ricky held up a canvas tote bag. "We brought markers and Play-Doh and blocks."

Cindy raised up a second bag. "And snacks and juice."

Flynn wriggled his brows at the children. "I don't know. We might just get crazy, bust out of here and get some pizza."

But Cindy only grinned. "Great. Give them plenty of sugar, too, because you'll be in charge of naptime, as well."

"You must have a long date planned," Flynn probed in what he hoped was a casual voice.

"Actually, it's a photo session. Can you believe it? Noah says someone caught our act, and he actually thinks we can promote the band."

Flynn caught only one word at first—*Noah*. So that's who she'd ditched the children for. Then he shook his head. "What did you say?"

"I know. It doesn't seem possible. But apparently some people from Dallas were at our last gig and really liked the sound. Personally, I don't want the travel involved in band commitments that far away, but I don't mind posing for the publicity pictures. Noah can always replace me if he decides to get that cosmopolitan."

"Band?" Flynn managed to spit out.

She cocked her head, drawing her brows together in a puzzled manner. "You know, the one Noah and I play in. The one that came to the girls' party."

"You weren't in the band that day," he replied, still not grasping her explanation.

Cindy looked faintly exasperated. "No, I was a little busy with the party and being the clown. Why?"

Flynn cleared his throat. "How often do you play in this band?"

She shrugged. "I never kept track of exactly how often. But you've seen me dressed in costume when Noah picks me up for a performance. It's not like Rosewood has enough proms, parties and anniversaries to keep us busy every day. To be truthful, since you and the girls moved here, I've cut back on my participation a lot. Noah's real understanding about it." She laughed. "He only pleads when he can't find a backup player and singer."

"Doesn't that intrude on your relationship?" Flynn asked, pushing the envy from his voice with great effort.

She blinked. "Our friendship's fine. As I said, Noah's very understanding. I guess it comes from being a doctor. He has to back out on so many social commitments because of emergencies that it's hard for him to even find time to date. I think that's why he doesn't have a girlfriend."

Buzzers and whistles clamored so loudly in Flynn's head, he wondered if he'd imagined her reply. "He doesn't have a girlfriend?"

Expression sad, Cindy shook her head. "No. And I think he's lonely even though he's so busy. You know what I mean?"

Flynn knew exactly what she meant. The longing for that one special person to be in your arms, the need for a true partner. The feeling maybe it would never be possible. At least…not until now.

"Flynn?" Cindy asked, her eyes puzzled again.

"Right. Yeah, I do know what you mean. So, what are you doing after the photo shoot?"

She shrugged. "Nothing. We don't have a gig tonight."

"But you have to dress up for the pictures?"

She rolled her eyes. "Full tilt. That's why my dress is in the car. I'd look a little ridiculous driving around in the middle of the day dressed in an evening gown."

Flynn studied her face, the sparkle in her eyes. "Does seem like a shame to get all dressed up, then have nowhere to go. Do you think we can find a place here in Rosewood to do it justice? *If* I can locate a baby-sitter."

Clearly taken aback, she stuttered at first. "We-well I guess so. There's a little Italian restaurant with a dance floor that's only a little bigger than a half dollar, but it's dressy for Rosewood."

"Then it's a date?"

She flushed, not a gentle warming, but a wave of red. "A date?"

"You know that thing where two people go out—" he lowered his voice to a mock whisper "—*without* the kids."

Cindy looked at the kids' intrigued faces, then back to Flynn. "Uh, okay. Sure."

"Don't get too carried away with your enthusiasm."

She backed out of the doorway. "No, of course not." She bumped into a chair, then muttered, "Sorry."

Flynn's brows rose and even the children studied her curiously.

"I'd better be going," Cindy told him fervently.

"I'll see you tonight."

"Tonight," she agreed, bumping into another chair, muttering a second apology to the inanimate object.

Flynn watched as she left, marveling at how even her haste was animated.

Beth reached up, tugging on his hand. "What do we do now?"

What indeed?

Nervously Cindy checked her hair, which she'd partially swept up. The insistent curl in its texture escaped to frame her face. Hair okay, she decided, turning to look in the cheval mirror, checking her dress again.

It was ridiculous. She hadn't primped this much for the stupid photo shoot. Picking up the petite gold purse that matched her dress, she reluctantly headed downstairs.

It's just dinner. Dinner with the man you've been in love with for years. Put the brakes on, she chastised herself. He's the man you can't even consider sharing a future with.

Halfway down the stairs, she caught sight of Flynn, pacing in the foyer. She had seen him dressed in suits before, but the one he'd chosen for tonight was of a European cut, adding another layer of sophistication.

She guessed all the female heads in the small restaurant would positively crane in his direction. Willing her nerves to settle, she traveled down the last few steps.

Hearing her, Flynn spun around, then stopped as quickly. "I was right. You do look like a flame."

Pleased, embarrassed, nearly thrilled, Cindy ducked her head. "Flatterer."

He took a few steps closer. "Just telling the truth."

The nerves in her stomach were rattling her brains. "Well, should we go?"

He picked up a solitary rose from the hall table and extended the flower.

"It's nearly gold," she marveled, seeing that its deep yellow petals almost matched the dress.

"I was hoping you'd wear the gold. It suits you."

She bit her bottom lip. "A flame that flickers?"

"And warms everyone in its proximity."

Beyond flattered and touched, she could merely stare.

But Flynn took her elbow, escorting her to the door. Once inside the car, she stole a look at him. "Tell me how you convinced Michael to watch the kids tonight."

Flynn's expression grew rueful. "I promised to play on their softball team the rest of the summer."

"Oh, I see. True blackmail."

Flynn chuckled. "I thought it was worth the sacrifice."

Cindy averted her head, staring out the window. "How's the construction coming on your house?"

"It's close to being finished. I checked the site today."

"That's good," she replied, thinking it wouldn't be long now. Flynn would move his daughters to their new home and her relationship with them would never be quite the same.

It didn't take long to reach the restaurant. Despite the fact that it was Rosewood's most elegant restaurant, Flynn and Cindy's attire still drew glances.

"Do you suppose they'll believe we just came from the prom?" Flynn whispered.

She grinned. "I don't think I can pass for eighteen even in my wildest dreams."

He leaned forward, barely touching one of the runaway curls that brushed her cheek. "I don't know. I think I'd buy it."

"Your table's ready," the hostess announced.

Shaken, Cindy was grateful for the reprieve.

Once their order was taken, Flynn glanced at the small quartet that provided the background music. "Would you like to dance?"

That sounded entirely too dangerous. "Oh, I don't think so. With these fancy outfits we'd probably be awfully conspicuous."

Flynn leaned back in his chair. "You know, Cindy, you never told me why you really moved to Rosewood. If you were running to someone…or away from someone."

And this was even more dangerous. "Who cares if they think we look like escapees from our senior, senior prom?" She stood abruptly. "So, you still want to dance?"

He stood, as well, extending his hand.

Accepting it, Cindy felt the connection the moment her hand touched his. But when he took her in his arms, her heart cratered. She'd dreamed of this moment, longed for it, despaired of it ever happening.

But in her dreams, he wasn't meant to be kept at arm's length. Still, she allowed him to lead her around the dance floor, to feel for this solitary moment how it would be to spend all time with him.

She felt the whisper of his breath on her cheek, the texture of his hair, the strength of his hands and arms, the structure of his tall frame. And for that moment, she let her imagination wander, to envision a future with him.

The music slowed to a halt, its progression matching her hopes. She declined a second dance, instead suggesting they order.

"Is something wrong?" Flynn asked when she continued to be unusually quiet.

She shook her head. "Just thinking."

"Do you want to share your thoughts?"

Cindy searched his eyes, seeing the sincerity, the puzzlement. And for another moment she didn't want to ruin this exceptional evening. She lifted her glass. "Why don't we just enjoy our dinner?"

His expression wavered, then he nodded.

The food came, warm and fragrant. They tasted the homemade linguini, the sauce pungent with fresh tomatoes and basil. Yet, there was more food than conversation.

"It's not quite the same as on the Riverwalk," Flynn mused.

Her gaze met his, that remembered moment stretching between them, begging to be felt again.

"No," she agreed at last. "That was unique…a rare time."

After declining dessert, Flynn suggested they walk along Main Street, a leftover from the previous century with its old false-fronted buildings.

The summer breeze teased the branches of the tall, ancient trees that lined the street, their branches stretching out to meet in the middle of the road. During the day they provided shady relief; at night they seemed to shelter.

"It's a beautiful evening," Cindy remarked, pulling her antique silk shawl closer.

Flynn stopped, turning to her. "Not as beautiful as you." He leaned toward her.

For one brief and dazzling moment she considered letting herself fall into the kiss he offered…into all the romantic fantasies she'd ever had of this moment.

But the pleasure of the kiss would also be like a bruise to her soul. Knowing that, she pulled back, brushing him away. "Please…don't."

He stared at her. "Are you telling me I've misread the signals? That there wasn't something between us that evening in San Antonio? That there isn't something between us now?"

She shook her head, starting to turn away.

But he caught her elbow. "Then why are you rejecting me?"

"Let's stop now," she pleaded, knowing his three children would always remain a connection between them, one that might not take the damage of the truth.

"Why?" Flynn demanded. "Why should I stop?"

"Don't do this," she begged again.

"Look at me, Cindy. Tell me you aren't feeling like I do. That you don't want to take our relationship to this next step."

Her lips trembled with the force of holding in the truth. "I can't tell you those things because they aren't true." She lifted her gaze, willing her heart to settle long enough to spit out what she must. "But it's not that easy."

"Why not?" he demanded.

She swallowed. "I cannot love a man who doesn't share my faith."

"Do you want me to lie?" he asked bluntly.

Her heart fractured with pain. "That would only be worse. I can't live a falsehood, and I can't accept anything less than a man of equal beliefs. I'm sorry, Flynn."

"And that's it?" he asked in disbelief.

She hesitated, remembering her recent prayers for guidance. "Perhaps it's not impossible, if you're willing to try."

He scowled. "In what way?"

She ducked her head, afraid to see the anger she knew was coming. "Maybe by revisiting the past."

His snort conveyed anger and more. "That's not a trip I ever want to take again."

Knowing his reaction was born of pain, she caught his hand, leading him to a bench that curved around a large oak tree in the sidewalk. "I know this is hard for you, Flynn." She met his eyes, willing him to understand. "We've both suffered loss. It hurts, even when you've pushed it to the back of your mind. But I've been thinking a lot about what you told me… about your past."

He started to pull his hand away, but Cindy held it that much more firmly.

"Flynn, have you ever considered that perhaps your

mother took her life because she was consumed with guilt over Todd?" Cindy gentled her voice even further. "Maybe she was afraid that she would cause a similar fate for you. Perhaps it was less of an abandonment, rather a sacrifice." Cindy tightened her grasp on his hand. "Oh, Flynn think how anguished she must have been, the fact that she couldn't have been thinking clearly, rather responding to the love she felt for her sons."

He was quiet, absently rubbing his thumb over her fingers. "She just left. She let Todd get killed, then she died."

"From a nine-year-old perspective," Cindy reminded him quietly. "You're a parent, now. Imagine how you would feel if your negligence cost the life of one of your daughters. Do you suppose you'd be thinking straight? Making responsible decisions?"

"She never was responsible," Flynn replied, the old bitterness seeping out, bit by bit. He lifted his head, meeting Cindy's eyes. "That's why I chose Julia, you know. She was nothing like my mother. I was sure she'd be stable, secure, always there."

"And even that collapsed when she died," Cindy replied, clamping down on her own pain. Flynn *had* chosen the right sister. Julia was everything he needed, everything she wasn't. Yet, Cindy knew she couldn't put her own feelings ahead of his crisis of faith. "Flynn, I think the pain you feel from losing your brother…

your entire family will always haunt you. I'm no Pollyanna. I know the past can't just be erased. But you can put what happened into perspective."

"I don't think that's possible," he replied dully.

"There's one way... Forgive your mother."

Anguished, Flynn stared at her. "How can I possibly forgive her?"

Cindy swallowed, knowing how difficult the next words would be for him to hear. "By reconnecting with the Lord."

"That's impossible!" he railed, pulling away from her. "You don't know what you're asking!"

"I've had an equal share of loss, Flynn. Both my parents, my only sister. But my bond with the Lord is even stronger than ever before."

"How can I hope to forgive? To reconstruct a faith lost in childhood?

"Through prayer." Cindy met his eyes, her own bright with unshed tears. "Just a few simple words... ones from your soul."

But Flynn only stared ahead.

Cindy didn't know if he'd even heard her, if the words had simply washed over him like the fingers of moonlight stabbing through the overhanging branches. Or if he'd already cast them aside.

Chapter Sixteen

Flynn accepted the baseball glove, tucking it into his gym bag. He and Michael Carlson were the last ones left on the practice field.

"Something wrong?" Michael asked quietly.

Distracted, Flynn cleared his thoughts, then shook his head. "Not really."

"That was said with a distinct lack of conviction," Michael noted.

Shrugging, Flynn zipped up the bag. "Just a lot on my mind."

"Want to talk about it?"

For several long moments, Flynn contemplated the problem, the issue of sharing it. "I doubt it's something you can help with."

"Try me."

So Flynn explained his recent discussion with Cindy, briefly outlining why he'd lost his faith initially.

But the other man surprised him. Michael looked neither shocked nor displeased. And he didn't directly address the faith issue. "Do you still think Cindy's as flighty as your mother was?"

"No. I think I've finally taken off my blinders. Cindy…" Flynn chuckled. "Well, you know how she is. You pointed it out yourself." Flynn's quiet laugh turned into a contemplative sigh. "But I couldn't see it then—my past was getting in the way. I've never known anyone like her before. She's caring, compassionate. She has so much energy, it's like being around a constant whirlwind, yet at the same time…" Flynn glanced up sheepishly. "Guess it's my turn for the *Oprah* segment."

But Michael only shook his head. "Nah. You've just gotten tangled up with a wildcat. And I mean that only in a good way."

"Yeah," Flynn agreed. "The rare combination of brains, personality, heart and spunk."

Michael studied him. "So, are you ready to try what she's asked?"

"I'm not so sure."

"That's how I felt," Michael confided.

"You?"

Michael grinned. "Being married to a minister doesn't make me a saint."

Flynn raised his eyebrows.

"Before I met Katherine, my wife, Ruth, died. When

she got sick I prayed, my family prayed, the whole congregation prayed. But she still died. And I couldn't get past the fact that the Lord had let that happen. Ruth was a good person, fair, kind, always looking out for everyone else. I just assumed that meant He was looking out for her. And nothing anybody said or did could change how I felt."

"But you go to church now."

Michael smiled. "It's more than attendance for me. I've regained my faith, but it wasn't easy. The journey back was even more painful than losing Ruth. If it weren't for Katherine, I'd still be stumbling in the dark." He shrugged. "Since I'm back on the right path, everything is right with my life. I have a beautiful wife, a new son, my other children are happy." Michael met Flynn's eyes. "And that wouldn't have happened otherwise."

"You're so sure?"

"I don't have a single doubt."

Flynn nodded. "Thanks."

"Now you just have one more talk."

"With who?"

Michael looked at him pointedly.

"Oh, the prayer thing."

"Yeah. I'll clear out." Michael started to turn away, then glanced back. "You won't regret it, Flynn. I'm sure of it."

Flynn watched as Michael walked away, the field

suddenly empty. The hottest part of the day was past, the sun past the day's prime. The air was still; not even the barest breeze stirred the dry grass or the dusty pitcher's mound.

It was rare for him to be this alone, Flynn realized. There was something oddly revealing about the solitude. It was more difficult to make excuses…to hang on to anger from a past era.

Tilting his head backward, Flynn studied the graying sky. And he wondered. Could Cindy and Flynn be right? Was it only a matter of words?

For an interminable time, Flynn considered and rejected a thousand beginnings. He started, stopped, then started again. Finally the prayer stumbled out… fumbling, unpoetic words. But they were from his heart. Briefly he closed his eyes, wondering if he spoke to an empty field, an empty sky.

Then a warmth he hadn't known since childhood filled his heart. Again Flynn closed his eyes, gripped by the power of this new truth.

And suddenly the field was no longer empty, the shadows no longer growing. Flynn lifted his head, staring into the heavens. One thought penetrated the wonder. He had to tell Cindy how he felt about her. How he really felt about her.

Flynn wanted this incredible woman in his life. The woman who had set him free. And who, he hoped, would share his love.

* * *

The evening sky was settling stars in formation before Flynn reached the house. From the study windows, Cindy watched for him, knowing softball practice should have ended some time before. It didn't seem much could happen to him in a small place like Rosewood, yet she couldn't help worrying.

She'd put the girls to bed, but Ricky was still up, waiting for Flynn. As much as she was growing to love the child, it was Flynn that filled the loneliness in Ricky's life, the one he turned to.

Hearing the front door open, Ricky scooted through the kitchen and into the foyer. Cindy followed more slowly, watching as Flynn scooped up the boy, hugging him. Then he set him back on the floor, ruffling his hair, keeping one hand on his shoulder.

Her gaze met Flynn's. Something about him was different. She couldn't place it, yet she was certain. "I saved you some dinner."

"I don't suppose it's that great veggie lasagna?"

She stared at him in surprise. "Do you really like it?"

"Sure. It's great. Not as good as your crab puffs, but still great."

Cindy considered checking his I.D. Was this really Flynn Mallory? "Well, actually I did make lasagna."

Flynn glanced down at Ricky. "Have you eaten?"

"Uh-huh. But I could eat more," he offered hopefully.

Flynn glanced at Cindy. "Do you mind?"

She shook her head, still wondering at his easy manner. "No, it's fine." Then she glanced down at Ricky. "A small piece for you?"

"Okay. Does this mean we can have more brownies, too?"

Cindy smiled tolerantly. "Why not?"

But it didn't take long for Ricky to start tiring. Soon his eyelids were drooping.

Flynn glanced at Cindy. "Maybe the guys ought to head upstairs."

"I'm not tired," Ricky protested, fighting a yawn.

"'Course not." Flynn pretended to yawn, stretching his long arms upward. "But I am. Want to keep me company?"

Ricky yawned again. "Okay."

Cindy watched them leave, the tall man, the very small child. It shouldn't affect her so, she knew. But it was a tender picture.

She rinsed the plates and stacked them in the dishwasher. Remembering that Flynn had liked her limeade, she pulled out some limes, squeezing them into a pale pink, Depression glass pitcher. Once it was ready, she hung maraschino cherries from matching pink glasses.

Flynn entered the kitchen as she was arranging the tray.

"I thought we could take this outside," she offered as

he crossed the room to stand beside her. Close beside her.

She started to lift the tray, but Flynn took it from her, carrying it out the open French doors. Once she was seated, he put the tray on the table then pulled up a chair right next to hers.

Cindy kept sneaking glances at him, wondering what was up with him. "How'd practice go?"

He shrugged. "I doubt we're ready for the major leagues, but it's coming together."

"Mmm." She let a few moments pass. "So, nothing out of the ordinary?"

He met her gaze. "Such as?"

She shrugged away the question. "Limeade? It's the one I make with—"

"Maraschino cherries." His gaze met hers. "I know."

Cindy licked her lips nervously. "Of course you do."

The limeade was just sweet enough, the night just quiet enough…the tension between them, however, rising higher than the new moon.

"Cindy?"

She jumped, sloshing the limeade. "Yes?"

"There's something we didn't talk about the other night."

"Oh?"

"About how we felt when we met."

She swallowed. "That was a long time ago."

"And we were very different people then."

Her head jerked up. "You think so?"

"Don't you?"

She stared at him hopelessly. "But you haven't noticed that I've changed, that—"

He leaned even closer. Reaching out he took her hand. "Have I waited too long?"

Pain sweltered, its heat dissolving her hope. Now she recognized the new emotion in Flynn's demeanor and expression. He was confusing loneliness for something more. A man accustomed to being married, now adrift on his own. She'd known men and women like him before—people who could not emotionally bear to be on their own, even though they were unrelentingly self-sufficient. And soon he would be on his own—his new house lacked only finishing touches.

But companionship wasn't enough for her. It was a great and true love, or nothing. "It's not a matter of time."

Flynn's expression dimmed, his eyes narrowing. "What then?"

She battled tears and temptation. "I can't be a substitute for Julia."

"I didn't say I wanted that!"

"No. But I've become a comfortable habit. Caring for the girls, doing the things Julia always did, trying to fill the place in your lives that she left."

"Comfortable?" he questioned incredulously. "That's how you think I feel about you?"

But Cindy had tussled with this question far longer than he had. "Let's be honest, Flynn. When we met, you chose Julia, not me. And fundamentally I *am* still that person. Wiser, more mature, more compassionate, but I'm still not demure and refined. I'm noisy, bull-headed and opinionated." She clutched the arm of the wicker chair for support. "And I wouldn't change myself to suit you if I could."

"I haven't asked you to change," he protested.

Sadly she met his gaze. "No, but it's what you would want. I can never be like Julia." She swallowed again. "Let's face it. You've been running from a woman like me since the day you lost your brother. That's why you chose Julia, why you need someone like her. We may be sisters, but as you've pointed out, we're so different we could have been conceived on separate planets."

"Cindy, you're not listening to me. I know who you are…who I want."

She gazed at his sincere face, wishing she could believe him, wishing that for once her heart would overrule her head. But it wasn't to be. She couldn't open herself to more hurt, knowing the ultimate outcome, the disappointment he would feel when he realized how very little she was like her sister.

More important, Cindy couldn't give her love to a man of unequal yoke. "That's just it. You don't know me." She bit down on her lip to stop its trembling. "And neither one of us needs the disappointment."

Flynn searched her expression. "You really believe I just want a substitute?"

Cindy thought of all the lonely nights, the longing for a husband and family of her own, the love she'd hidden for years. Despite that, she couldn't be second best. And so she withdrew her hand from his. Despite the ebony night, she could see the confused disbelief in his eyes.

And knew it matched her own.

Chapter Seventeen

Persistence had always paid off for Flynn. When he'd worked three jobs to put himself through college, when he had convinced a bank to loan him the seed money for his first business, when he'd taken that company from a struggling one-man outfit to a premier international insurance form.

But Cindy was a tougher nut to crack than any of those. And so Flynn decided he had to woo her. As romantically and creatively as ever was done.

For nearly three weeks he had tried chocolates, flowers, perfume, romantic picnics, evening strolls. And one thing was certain.

He hadn't changed her mind at all. It was as though she tolerated the gestures, but didn't take them too seriously, still believing he saw her only in Julia's shadow. She even considered his recent church attendance to be nothing more than a show for her benefit.

It would take more, he realized. Not simple, traditional courting methods. It had to be something that blew her socks off.

And he could think of only one possible choice.

He glanced over at Cindy, uncomfortably scrunched close to the car door on her side. As far away from him as possible.

He withheld a sigh, turning into the recently completed driveway. "Here we are."

Her face was unreadable as she looked up at his new house. "So we are."

Before she could step from the car on her own, he was beside her door, opening it.

Her gaze encompassed the large, modern structure. "It really is lovely."

"Nothing like your house, though."

Cindy stared at the entrance again, a wisp of sadness coloring her expression. "No. Not at all."

"Let's go inside."

She nodded, allowing him to guide her up the walk.

They passed through the arched courtyard that was a mix between a classic Italian style with Tuscan columns and Mediterranean tile and a more casual atrium. It had been designed to be inviting, much like the wraparound porch was at Cindy's house. But at the same time, it offered a bit of privacy.

Once inside, surveying the interior, Flynn tried to see the house through her eyes, ones so very different than his own. He pointed to the unusual striped arches over the doorways in the entry hall. "Dark Texas Pecos sandstone," he explained. "The lighter stone is granite."

"I like it," she responded quietly, the sadness in her face making its way into her voice. "It's different, and I always appreciate using native materials."

"I like contemporary, but I'm not crazy about living in a barren box." He pointed toward the tall windows in the next room. "There's a loggia in the back that I want to be cozy, like your terrace."

Flynn led her deeper into the house.

"The design is good," she commented as they stepped into the great room that seemed all windows and white walls. "With warm decorating, it won't be sterile."

"Glad you brought that up."

She lifted her gaze. "Oh?"

Flynn felt himself falling into that gaze, wishing he could simply offer the shelter of his embrace, that she would believe how much he valued her. "Well, actually, I want to ask you a huge favor."

"What is it?"

"I'd like you to decorate the house."

Clearly stunned, she stared at him. "What did you say?"

He smiled, pleased to see the sadness chased away by surprise. "I think you heard me. I'd like you to decorate the house."

She studied his expression. "I don't get it. My style couldn't be more different than yours."

"Please?"

Swallowing, she turned again to look at the clean lines of the room. "So, what do you have in mind?"

"Put your stamp on it, your distinctive sense of style."

Cindy frowned. "Why mine?"

He shrugged. "Could we call it one last gift in a long list of things you've done for me, the girls?"

Cindy clasped her hands together, the nervous gesture as betraying as the dark pain she tried to hide. "Why don't I copy what Julia chose for your home in Houston? I remember it pretty well."

"No. It wouldn't suit you. I'm not looking for a substitute for Julia. Not in my house. Not in my life. Just as I don't want you to change yourself, to imitate her. You're no substitute, Cindy. It's your style I want in my house."

Her face filled with wonder and disbelief. "But... what if you hate it? What if—"

"What if you let me decide the things I like and want?"

A month later Cindy was still mulling over his words. She couldn't help wondering exactly what Flynn had meant by them. They'd already resolved that she would never be a substitute for Julia. And yet, no amount of arguing would convince him that she shouldn't be the one decorating his new house. When they were at the final impasse, he'd told her flatly that he and the girls would stay at her house until she agreed.

Although part of her would like nothing better, Cindy knew she couldn't take the daily torture of having Flynn in her house much longer, knowing they had no future.

So she'd thrown herself into the project, taking time out only for her Rainbow class which the triplets attended and, of course, the triplets themselves. The rest of her hours were spent studying colors, textures, fabrics and furniture. She told herself that she was spending the time as part of her ongoing endeavor to help the girls. But in reality, she needed the distance from Flynn, from the feelings she couldn't control. Luckily Noah found a temporary replacement for her in the band so that wasn't a distraction.

Thinking surely Flynn would want to ship at least some of his belongings to the new house, she'd pressed him again. But Flynn was unyielding. He had already arranged for an estate agency to auction everything in storage, which should bring in an amount at least equal to his new decorating budget.

When Cindy heard that, she'd gulped in apprehension. What if he didn't like what she chose? What would he replace it with?

Flynn showed no concern whatsoever.

Which made Cindy that much more nervous.

His only specific request was that she decorate the guest room in a style suitable for a young boy, for Ricky when he visited, Flynn explained.

Although she urged Flynn to inspect the house as she chose first the paint colors, then rugs for the wood and tile floors, he declined. Nor would he accompany her to furniture stores or galleries in either Rosewood or Houston, insisting he wanted the house to have her exclusive style.

So the first week she picked out the colors and hired painters. Then she shopped. It was a challenge. She wanted the house to be masculine, yet comfortable for the girls. And, some of her own whimsy and playfulness also incorporated itself in the decorating. She was glad to be putting her own stamp on the house, knowing a small part of her would remain with him.

It was a mixed feeling, the joy of doing something special for the man she loved, tempered by the sadness of knowing how much she would miss Flynn and the girls. And as the long summer days eventually shortened, so did her hope.

Three weeks later, Cindy was ready to show Flynn the completed project. They'd spent very little time together since she'd started working on the house. When Flynn came home from the office, she left him with the children, spending each evening at the new house.

Now, despite the time she'd poured into the work, she was anxious about his reaction.

Glancing over at him, she swallowed. It was a place for play, for living, for love. She was a mass of nerves as they stepped out of his car. "You know I'm a collector at heart, but I also have very eclectic tastes."

"Hmm," he agreed noncommittally.

Entering the walled courtyard, they were immediately shaded and surrounded by varying-sized plants she had nestled into the cool space. She'd also added a nineteenth-century fountain that spilled a calming stream of water near the flora. The now-serene alcove appeared almost European, with its now seemingly aged charm.

"I hope you like plants," she continued, still feeling like a tour guide instructing a reluctant tourist.

"Yes."

Cindy wondered at the brief reply as she used the key he'd given her to unlock the front door. She handed him the key, knowing she wouldn't need it again.

They stepped into the entry hall, which she'd had painted in a warm terra-cotta wash that highlighted the beautiful stonework above the doorways. A simple table in the center of the hall held a sleek vase filled with yellow flowers.

"I know guys don't usually have flowers," she explained anxiously. "But they give such life to a house."

"I like it," he remarked, strolling on to the great room.

It took her a moment to absorb that. Then realizing he was walking forward, she scurried to catch up. Uneasily she watched for his reaction to the main living area. She'd had the walls painted a warm, honey yellow that seemed to glow, almost at one with the light flowing in the ceiling-to-floor windows. A thick, comfortable rug anchored the room.

She had interspersed leather club chairs with a warm fabric sofa. The antique armoire that held the television and VCR was a pleasant contrast to the sleek furniture.

"I was going for warm but modern," she explained earnestly. "For you and three growing, constantly changing girls."

Flynn didn't say anything, instead turning slowly in the space.

"And upstairs," she continued nervously. "Even though you gave the girls a three-room suite, I thought each room should have its own character, so although the colors harmonize, each one's different. Is that okay?"

He didn't answer, still looking around the great room.

"Flynn?"

Finally he turned to her. "No, Cindy, it's not okay."

He reached for her hand, turning it palm up, then dropping the key into her grasp.

Disappointment rushed through her. He really did hate it.

"It's far more than okay." His gaze traveled over the soft lamps, the incredible artwork. "It's like you. Singularly unique. One of a kind. Which is why I love you."

Cindy desperately wanted to believe his words, but the fragments of logic she still possessed overruled her heart. "I can't be a stand-in for Julia. I have to be loved for myself, not because I helped you or the girls." Her words stumbled. "It has to be all or nothing."

"Then let's choose all."

Cindy's eyes pleaded with him. "You had your true love. And I deserve that, as well."

Flynn pulled her an inch closer. "Don't you see that I do? How incredibly unique and wonderful you are?"

Afraid to believe, she shook her head.

His eyes darkened to beyond ebony. "I never knew before what real love was. You're right. I've been hiding from it all my life. But I know now. And it's because you're an original."

Cindy swallowed, wishing…wondering.

"I've grown to know the value of a meteor that streaks through life." He reached out, gently touching her vibrant tresses. "I want a woman with red hair and a personality to match."

"But…I'm so different."

His eyes warmed in a way she'd never seen before.

"Exactly. Don't you understand? I don't want to curtail your enthusiasm, I want to embrace it. I want to squeeze the last drop of goodness from every day like you do." He tucked back a lock of her wildly curling hair. "With you."

Her lips trembled. "Oh, Flynn…"

"Will you marry me, Cindy? In your church? The one I've come to believe in again?"

Cindy's eyes filled and she couldn't control the quivering of her lips. "I must be dreaming, or you are…."

"No, for the first time in a long time I know exactly where I am, where I want to be, who I want to be with."

"Are you sure, Flynn? About your faith? About me?"

He nodded. "You were right. I hadn't prayed since I was nine, so I was pretty rusty. But He didn't seem to mind." Flynn's hands rested on her shoulders. "And I'm just as sure about you. My life will never be the same without you. You're the light that I've needed forever, that I never believed existed. The one I ran away from the day I met you."

"And you're sure you still don't want to run away?"

"I want to run toward you, Cindy, toward a future brighter than I ever guessed was possible."

Cindy's eyes closed briefly in a prayer of thanksgiving, in happiness greater than she'd ever known.

And when he pulled her into his arms, she knew it was no dream, but a reality hoped for...and prayed for.

His lips were gentle as they touched hers. Their joy was as bright as the persistent beams of the late-afternoon sun.

"I love you," she said with wonder, never having believed the words could be uttered aloud to him.

He reached for her hand, his fingers strong, his heart gentle. "Then I believe this is mine."

Epilogue

Sixteen months later

Three matching faces lined up in front of the nursery at Rosewood Memorial Hospital.

"Are you sure ours will be that little?" Beth asked.

Ricky nodded. "Sure, they're always little when they're born." Formally adopted by Cindy and Flynn, he had stepped naturally into the role of older brother, and the triplets both revered and loved him to pieces.

"Will it go live in the children's house?" Mandy asked, referring to Cindy's old Victorian home that Cindy had donated for a children's shelter.

"'Course not. That's why they had that other bedroom built on the house." Ricky glanced up, seeing the nurse's reproving expression. The woman had agreed to watch them until an adult arrived, but she was all business. "We better go sit down."

"Yeah," Beth agreed, second in command to Ricky as the most assertive triplet. "Daddy said we had to be quiet or we couldn't stay."

"Miss Katherine's supposed to be here," Mandy fretted, anxious without her father or Cindy in sight.

"She's on her way," Ricky explained for the dozenth time. "The baby wasn't supposed to come till next week. Dad said she's driving here from Houston. And Miss Donna's sick so she couldn't come." Ricky's face screwed into a frown, peering toward the labor and delivery rooms. "I wonder what they're doing in there. We've been here *forever.*"

Actually it was barely a few hours. But down the hall, Flynn was wondering about many things, as well.

How he'd come to have such an incredible wife, how she'd changed his life in such a short time. He remembered their simple but beautiful wedding. The triplets had all been flower girls, Ricky the ring bearer. Michael had been pleased to be his best man and Katherine, as matron of honor, had beamed the entire time. But no one had radiated like his Cindy. *His* Cindy.

Together they were a family in the truest sense, with Ricky and the girls. Flynn had never before felt such a complete sense of belonging as he did in the fellowship of their church. He could depend on the Lord, as well as his many trusted friends.

It was a funny thing, under Cindy's tutelage he'd

learned that love was the one thing that increased as you gave it away. The more love he gave to others, the fuller his life became.

Cindy's hand squeezed Flynn's more tightly, and he smoothed the hair back from her forehead. "He's beautiful, isn't he?" she asked in a soft voice.

"Almost as beautiful as his mother," Flynn replied, believing no woman could ever compare to his wife.

A few tears spilled on to her cheeks.

"Tears now?" he asked in surprise.

She nodded tremulously. "You bet."

He smiled, delighted as always by her spunk, then kissed her forehead. "Thank you."

Her eyes met his in shared understanding. "This wasn't a solo project."

"Maybe not. But you've given me so much—a true family, Ricky, another new son."

She glanced at the baby, who rested against her chest. "Little Todd Mallory?"

His throat tightened. "You really want to name him after my brother?"

Cindy's eyes were soft, her smile bright. "Can you think of anything more fitting? This way we can embrace the good of our pasts." The baby's tiny fingers clutched hers. "And in him we have the promise of a whole new future."

Flynn stared at her, scarcely able to believe that he had captured this truly mercurial comet, that she was his wife, his love. For a moment he closed his eyes and uttered a now-familiar prayer of thanks.

Then she glanced up again, her bright green eyes so filled with life it made him ache.

Flynn smoothed the back of his hand over her cheek. "I didn't know it was possible for my love to grow each and every day."

Tenderness filled her expression. "We've been given a new beginning, the rarest of gifts."

Their hands clasped together, the pain of the past fading, the joy of tomorrow growing. Just as it had since they'd married a month after he proposed.

Knowing that the feelings they shared were a blessing directly from heaven, their eyes met. In that moment they left the past behind for good, looking to a future filled with hope, buoyed by love…and forever awash in the brilliant light of two hearts joined as one.

Dear Reader,

There are few things more heartrending than love denied. Especially when that love is impossibly out of reach. For Cindy Thompson, a woman of incredible spirit and equally strong faith, it is a road she would never have chosen to travel.

Which is why I was compelled to tell her story, to give voice to these characters who found a place in my heart, as well. I hope they will tread on yours, as they undertake their journey of both love and faith. And in the twining, discover that nothing is more important and binding than the ties of family.

God Bless.

Bonnie K. Winn

PROMISE OF GRACE

Behold, I tell you a mystery;
we shall not all sleep, but we shall all be changed.
—1 *Corinthians* 15:51

For my father, George Yedlovsky,
for making me reach and assuring me
nothing was beyond that reach. I love you, Daddy.

Prologue

Houston, Texas

Wonder wasn't always a good thing.

Not when it was all you could do.

Grace Stanton tentatively tried to reach out, but she wasn't able to feel anything because of the thick layer of bandages wrapped around her hands. Even that small movement hurt. Yet she couldn't stop herself.

Just as she couldn't stop the wondering. How had she come to be in the hospital? What was beneath the bandages? And why had this happened now with the wedding only a week away?

Aunt Ruth hovered, her eyes dark with concern. "Grace, can you hear me?"

"Yes." The word formed in her mind, but emerged as little more than a croak.

Ruth looked as though she was about to cry. And again Grace wondered. Only this time it was mixed with dread.

"The other driver and his family are going to be fine," Ruth finally managed, her voice a bit shaky, "because of your sacrifice. If you hadn't driven into that concrete barrier when they drifted into your lane, none of them would be alive."

Grace wanted to ask questions—about the crash, her injuries...but she couldn't summon her voice. Instead she blinked her eyes.

In turn, Ruth swiped hers.

Exhausted and confused, Grace wanted to comfort her aunt, but mind and body refused to cooperate. And the beeping and whooshing of all the machines frightened her.

Ruth, who had taken Grace's parents' place after they died, leaned forward. "I know you're scared, Gracie. But remember, the Lord is with you. He'll take care of you."

Tears collected in Grace's throat. Unable to shed them, she began to wonder yet again. Was He really with her? She'd been uncertain about that since her mother and father had died.

A procession of nurses and technicians rotated through the room. Grace was relieved that they didn't expect a response from her, instead speaking to her aunt, some poking and prodding, others simply making notations.

Her aunt leaned close. "Gracie, the doctor's here."

Although her eyes were swollen, she opened them, studying the man.

"I'm Dr. Jamison, Miss Stanton. And you've had quite a bang-up." He studied the chart. "Which means you're going to be with us for a while. Your internal injuries are manageable, but you're in for a number of restorative surgeries."

She held up one of her heavily wrapped hands in question.

"You've severed a tendon in your right hand. But don't dwell on that. Many people find they can compensate very well by using their left."

She gasped. She knew that her injuries were significant, since Ruth had driven from where she lived in the small town of Rosewood to be with her in Houston. But Grace hadn't guessed how bad the injuries were. To think she wouldn't be able to use her hand—

The doctor's words interrupted the thought and jarred her at the same time. "I understand your hand isn't your major worry. But we'll have to wait for the results of the first plastic surgery to determine how much of your face can be repaired."

Terrified, she turned slitted eyes, searching for her aunt.

Ruth stepped forward, her look censoring the doctor. "Grace hasn't been awake long enough to be told how much recovery time to expect."

The doctor scratched his balding head. "Sorry to be blunt, but this is an extremely busy hospital, Miss Stanton. Our touch may not be very personal but trust me, it's extremely skilled. It may take you some time to adjust to the gravity of your injuries, but that's also normal. Don't be discouraged. You're in for a lengthy process, but you'll have to take it a day at a time. I'll be back to check on you this evening." Dr. Jamison carried the chart with him as he exited.

Ruth laid a very gentle hand on Grace's shoulder. "It'll be all right, dear. There's a lot to take in at once. Don't worry. We'll sort everything out."

A nurse entered before she could reply, injected something into one of the many tubes, and Grace felt herself fade.

When she awoke hours later Grace struggled to speak, and one word emerged, raw but audible. "Patrick?"

Ruth appeared swiftly at her side. "He's not here yet, Grace. He called the nurses' station a short while ago and he should be here any minute. It took a while for his office to reach him, but he headed here as soon as he heard."

Grace had to know. "What will he think?"

Ruth's chin firmed. "He'll be worried about you, I'm sure. But he loves *you,* not your face."

Grace closed her eyes. Unknowingly Ruth had confirmed Grace's worst suspicions. Holding on to consciousness, she heard more footsteps nearing the bed.

As she opened her eyes, her fiancé, Patrick Holden, paused at the end of the bed.

Relief started to warm her. But then it faded. And in that sickening moment she realized she no longer had to wonder. She knew. It was written on Patrick's stricken face.

"Grace..." Patrick stared at her in horror for an instant, then shuttered his eyes so she couldn't read them.

She wanted him to come closer, to stand by her in every sense. And after a moment's hesitation he approached, his expression sorrowful.

Ruth slipped quietly from the room.

Patrick leaned close, his manner changing abruptly, becoming hearty. "You're going to get better. I know it's scary right now, but doctors can do so much now for... Well...doctors can work miracles."

Grace blinked yes, again struggling to speak. "Why now?"

Patrick looked blank.

"Our wedding," Grace whispered, thinking of the picture-perfect day that she had been planning for months. Actually years; she'd dreamed of this day since she was a child.

"Don't worry, Grace. We can postpone it. Everyone will understand why." He smiled too brightly. "Then you can have the fun of picking out new invitations and flowers. You know how much you enjoyed that. You're like a kid in a candy shop with all the wedding preparations."

She could see, despite his show of bravado, that he was overwhelmed. Grace found her voice; however, it was still a mere whisper. "But it's not candy. It's bad, Patrick."

He reached for her hand, then paused when he saw the thick bandages. After an awkward moment he patted her shoulder. "It's okay, Grace. We'll get through this."

Grace met his eyes, trying to see beyond the forced cheerfulness of his words. And there she saw apprehension and fear. "It won't be that easy."

He swallowed visibly. "The doctor says you've got a lot of surgeries ahead of you, that it's going to take a long time to recover. You'll have to be patient…we'll have to be patient."

Patrick was giving his best, saying all the right words. But there was no fire in his eyes or determination in his voice. And somewhere deep inside, she knew he wouldn't stand the test. How strange that it took something like this to show her his true mettle. Awash in pain and despair, she slowly shook her head.

"Grace, you can't give up. I…I know how difficult this is for you." He paused, clearly in far over his head. "I don't know what else to say."

But what he couldn't say was plastered over his perfect face. And she recognized the other emotion in his expression. Pity. He stared at her with unrelenting pity.

And beneath the swaddle of bandages, she flinched. Yet she had to know it all. She couldn't stand to wonder about anything else. "Do you still want to get married?"

His pause was barely perceptible. "Grace, we weren't expecting anything like this. It's going to take adjustments…for both of us."

And something inside Grace that the accident couldn't reach to damage suddenly crumpled.

"I'm sorry," Patrick continued. "I'm probably saying all the wrong things. Truth is, I don't know what to say."

I do. Even though you're fighting it, I see it. Grace wasn't sure she would ever view him in the same light again. And she wondered how the breaking of her heart could be so silent. There should be a great crashing noise, louder than cymbals, more wrenching than a bitter blast ripping apart the tallest structure.

He patted her shoulder again. "Things will look better as time goes by."

She pushed herself to speak past the tears collected in her throat. "I'm tired."

Patrick looked immediately remorseful. "Of course you are. You need to get some rest. I'll stop talking and just sit with you."

Somehow her heart continued to limp on despite its mortal wound. "There's no need. Ruth will be here."

"Are you sure?"

Relentlessly sure. "Yes."

"All right, then. I'll be back in the morning. You'll see. Things will look better after some time." He leaned forward, then slowly pulled back. "I'd kiss you goodbye, but I don't want to hurt any of your wounds." More pity filled his eyes. "I hate that you've been hurt like this."

Knowing how eager he was to be away from her, Grace couldn't bear to respond. Instead she half closed her painfully swollen eyes.

Patrick turned away, quickly looking back one more time before walking away. The door closed behind him as the first hot tear dampened the gauze covering her cheekbones. The tears turned to sobs, ones that pulled at her wounds, both emotional and physical.

As her sobs finally dwindled, the room became unbearably silent. Then Ruth pushed open the door. "Grace?"

"He's gone."

"I know, Gracie. But he'll be back tomorrow. I'll be here, too. And don't forget, the Lord's always with you."

Grace gathered the last of her draining energy. "Is He?"

Ruth didn't wince at the bitter question. "Yes. But I know it's hard for you to see that right now."

Everything rushed at Grace and she couldn't control the sobs. "My life is over."

Ruth cradled her as much as possible without pressing against Grace's injuries. "No, sweetie. It's just beginning. I'm going to take you home with me to Rosewood." Silently Ruth vowed to do everything in her power to help her beloved niece. "We have a wonderful plastic surgeon, Noah Brady. All the big-city hospitals are always trying to lure him away. But Rosewood's his hometown and he's staying put. It might be easier for you there, all things considered. And we'll see things through." She patted her niece's shoulder. "Don't give up hope, Gracie."

Hope. That was gone. Along with Patrick and her faith. Everything was gone. Including the wonder.

Chapter One

Rosewood, Texas

Noah Brady reread the last pages of Grace Stanton's already massive chart. The woman had been through a horrendous experience. While he'd worked on equally damaged people, this case brought his own memories close to the surface. And instinctively he knew Grace had even more pain ahead of her.

He remembered Ruth Stanton's call from Houston, her plea for his help. Despite knowing her for most of his thirty-three years, Noah had never heard her cry before. But she had broken down, her love for her niece cracking through her usual resolute demeanor.

Since the call, Noah had been consulting with Grace's attending physician. She had already been through four surgeries to repair internal injuries. Her surgeon was convinced that she wouldn't require further operations for those injuries. But her restorative plastic surgeries would be extensive.

Now that Grace was stable and her internal injuries on the mend, she was being airlifted to the small Rosewood hospital. A short time ago he'd been apprised that the helicopter would be setting down soon.

Although the hospital staff could capably transport her from the landing pad, Noah wanted to be there. Ruth had phoned him that morning, worried because she didn't want to leave Grace on her own to be loaded into the helicopter. But by staying with her, Ruth wouldn't be able to drive back to Rosewood fast enough to outpace the helicopter. So Noah had promised Ruth that he would personally greet her niece and situate Grace in a room.

Rising from his desk chair, Noah made his way from his office in the building adjacent to the hospital. He bypassed the core of the hospital, heading to the emergency-room exit. The helipad was located just beyond the ambulance driveway.

Although Rosewood wasn't in the hub of a medical center, Noah had worked hard to ensure that the facility had what was needed for the small town. Since he had turned his back on his lucrative job in Houston, it had taken a lot of fund-raising to keep the community hospital current.

As he walked outside, Noah could hear the distinctive whir of the incoming helicopter. As it approached, winds from the blades flattened thickly leaved branches and sent errant spring buds scattering.

Accustomed to the forceful currents, Noah didn't blink as the wind slicked back his hair and tugged at his lab coat and scrubs while the helicopter landed. His concentration was focused on the woman inside the copter.

Grace had been sedated for the journey, and as expected, she was nearly obscured by heavy bandages. Despite her medication, the jolting of the stretcher as it hit the ground must have jarred her.

Grace's eyes flew open. And as Noah looked into their blue-gray depths he saw terror. When she noticed him, the look changed, hitting him with unexpected force. It was a raw plea.

Unable to resist the compelling pull of her gaze, he let her know with his own eyes that she'd made the connection. Then he nodded, guessing she wouldn't be able to hear him clearly with the noise from the copter and the barrier of her bandages.

He walked beside her as the attendants rolled her inside. Noah made sure he was in her line of vision as they took the shortest route to the room that had been readied for her.

Although he could easily prescribe more medication that would sedate her, he wished there was another way to erase the fear and uncertainty in Grace's eyes. Ruth hadn't indicated whether there was anyone else to stand by her niece. But Noah's instincts told him that Grace Stanton was alone except for her aunt.

Once Grace was settled in a bed, her vitals taken and recorded, Noah adjusted the blinds and the overhead lights so they wouldn't glare into her eyes. He saw her lids flicker in relief.

And it occurred to him that he hadn't yet heard her speak. Her records hadn't indicated damage to the vocal cords, but he wondered if emotional trauma was silencing her.

"Grace?"

She didn't answer right away. Instead she lifted her eyelids with what seemed to be great effort. "Yes."

Her voice surprised him—the clarity, the bell-toned sound of the single word.

"I'm Dr. Brady."

"Ruth told me about you."

Despite his usual reserve, he smiled, lifting his eyebrows. "I doubt you could have stopped her."

Surprise lit her eyes.

The past had taught Noah to maintain only a professional relationship with his patients, yet he wanted to put Grace at ease. "I've known your aunt since before she started planting blackberries."

"Blackberries?" Grace echoed.

Seeing her focus on something other than her pain,

he continued. Besides, with the medication he'd just di-
agnosed, he was fairly confident that Grace wouldn't
remember his words. "I told her the pears on her tree
weren't worth snitching. The next spring she planted
blackberries. Over the years she's complained how
they sprawled out in the yard, climbing up her ivy
lattice and taking over." He grinned, remembering that
easy time. "They're so big, one berry fills your mouth.
Better than caviar. And to this day Ruth hasn't ripped
them out. Between you and me I think she likes
knowing she can make the best blackberry pie in town."

A fraction of relief eased into Grace's eyes. He
guessed few people still spoke to her as though she
might enjoy a normal conversation.

"Her pie's the best," Grace finally replied.

"This is making me hungry. Do you feel like
eating?"

"No." The word was small, seeming to match her
damaged spirit.

"Have you had much appetite since the accident?"

She sighed. "The doctor questions begin."

Noah studied her, having acquired a second sense
about victims. He didn't need to see her expression to
guess what it would reveal. "Had enough of those
already?"

She nodded.

"You're going to have a lot more," he told her. His
tone was uncompromising, but she needed to hear the

truth. "We're going to be a team, Grace. But I can only function as the captain if you're an able navigator."

Her eyelids closed again.

He recognized the action as a defense, one he'd seen many times before. Noah turned away. But an inner voice nagged him to turn back. And his words seemed to come from a source he no longer thought he possessed. "I'll make you a deal. You drink your broth and I won't ask you any more questions today."

It took a moment, then she nodded.

Noah made a quick, unprecedented decision. Leaving Grace, he called the cafeteria. It took only a few minutes for a worker to bring up the tray from the kitchen.

Grace was resting quietly when he returned to her room. He adjusted her bed carefully, knowing her body was a mass of pain. Once the broth was in place on her bed table, Noah situated the straw. Then he pulled up a chair, placing the tray across his knees. He'd only spent this much nonwork-related time with his young patients. And still then, he kept his distance. Not because he didn't care, but because he'd learned his lesson well in the past.

Grace glanced over at him, then down at the loaded tray. "I can't eat all of that."

"I'm pleased to hear it. This is *my* dinner."

Surprise lit her eyes again.

"You don't mind my eating with you?" he asked, retrieving a french fry, acting as though he routinely shared dinners with patients.

Cautiously she shook her head.

Noah ripped open a packet of ketchup. "Hospital life can get somewhat intrusive. It's difficult to make a phone call or eat a meal without interruption. People assume if you're a doctor you don't have a life." He took a bite of his hamburger. As he swallowed, he acknowledged how true that was. His complete commitment to the hospital only emphasized the empty holes in his life.

"I never thought of that," Grace replied softly.

He was pleased that she had offered a complete reply. "Most people don't. But you take the good with the bad. When I first decided that I wanted to be a doctor I didn't think it was possible." Pushing away the difficult memories, he stood, placing his tray on the bedside table. "You're not keeping up your part of the bargain." Grasping the straw, he held it up to her mouth. Seeing she wasn't motivated to eat, Noah hoped it wasn't an indication of a complete loss of will. "You don't want me to start the inquisition again, do you?"

Her eyes, darkening pools of sorrow, met his.

An unexpected fist of emotion clobbered him. The danger that feeling held made him pause. But he couldn't ignore the agony in her eyes. "Can you manage a small sip?"

She parted her lips.

Noah held the straw for her. She drank about a tea-spoonful of the broth. Even that movement seemed to fatigue her.

"It's okay, Grace. Your appetite will return as you heal. I'll keep prodding you so the healing process goes more quickly." He gently encircled an uninjured patch of her forearm. "We're in this for the long haul, Grace."

A new uncertainty flashed in her eyes.

Noah wondered why she had no one except Ruth to care for her. Was it possible she had no family? No special man in her life to stand beside her?

As Noah watched, Grace moved the fingers on her left hand, the less injured of the two.

Momentarily ignoring his own defensive instincts, he grasped her outstretched fingers.

While the noise of carts rattling down the hall and the paging of doctors persisted outside the room, Noah continued to watch her.

A solitary tear escaped from her tormented eyes. Noah gently wiped it away, the echo of the busy hospital receding. And her fingers cautiously tightened around his.

The pit of his stomach tightened. It was his duty as her doctor to heal her. It was his duty to himself to remain uninvolved. At all costs.

Chapter Two

The lights were bright. But they always seemed that way since the accident. Grace watched the nurse's expression as the woman carefully unwrapped the bandages covering her face.

Most of the professionals who had performed this task hadn't commented on the condition of her face. Grace supposed it went with the medical training. *Don't let the patient know she looks grotesque.*

Grace knew she should be accustomed to the process, but it wasn't getting any easier. If anything, it had become more and more difficult as the reality sank in.

"You're lucky," the nurse declared.

There was that word again. The same one her new doctor had used before he left. That blackberry doctor with the gentle but supportive touch.

"The left side of your face has a few scratches remaining, but the bruising and swelling has diminished from what's noted last on your chart in Houston."

Part of Grace wanted to reach up and touch the allegedly undamaged portion of her face. A larger part of her couldn't stand the awfulness. She supposed half a face was better than none, but it was difficult to be grateful for that small reprieve. And so she remained quiet as the nurse continued the bandage change.

Grace was surprised to feel coolish air against her exposed cheek when the nurse started to leave. "Aren't you going to finish?"

The nurse smiled. "I did."

Grace still couldn't bear to touch her cheek. Instead she leaned the bandaged side of her face against the pillow. It all seemed so unreal, so unbelievable.

Occasionally she still dreamed that everything was all right. And in the brief moments as she awoke she would feel the relief of knowing the accident wasn't real. But then the darkness set in.

Other times she would dream of Patrick's face, remembering his halfhearted attempts to deal with her injuries. And the bitterness of her waking hours invaded the deep of night, as well.

She had expected Patrick to stand beside her. Not motivated by obligation, but rather strength and love. But he'd folded in the first instant. How had she misjudged him so?

Perhaps no such man of strength existed. Wasn't

love supposed to bear all things? She needed Patrick to say he loved her no matter what, not to set a new world's record for coming up with excuses.

He hadn't spoken of visiting her in Rosewood. He had muttered something about business commitments. Besides, she would be in the hospital, undergoing numerous surgeries, he'd added.

He had suggested she might prefer to have Ruth with her during this difficult time. But Grace had seen through the excuses. Patrick wanted her to disappear, to take the ugliness she had become out of his well-ordered life.

Closing her eyes, Grace listened to the sound of footsteps in the corridor, wondering if any of the technicians or doctors were headed her way. Ones like the blackberry doctor. Silly to think of him like that. But he was the only medical professional Grace had encountered who hadn't treated her as though she was only a mound of bandages.

She didn't place any value in his words or actions, though. It was simply his job. Beyond that, he was a man.

The following day Noah strode toward Grace's room. He'd had her on his mind most of the day. And strangely, when Ruth had come to relieve him the previous evening, he had been disappointed, reluctant to leave this fragile woman. It was an atypical reaction for him. He couldn't survive becoming involved again.

Quietly he pushed open the door to Grace's room, careful in case she was asleep. His breath caught as he saw her unbandaged face for the first time. Aware from her chart that the damage was limited to the right side of her face, he'd left instructions with the charge nurse to leave the other side exposed so that air could reach the skin.

However, Noah wasn't expecting the lovely lines of the undamaged side of her face. He'd met his share of beautiful women. But this was different. Grace Stanton was different.

Even so, she would think he was either crazy or lying if he told her he thought she was beautiful. But that's what he saw.

A beautiful woman.

The impression had begun with his first glimpse of her eyes. She had spoken more with her eyes than her voice. And more than most women did with both.

This one woman struck him far more strongly than any in his memory. So much so that Grace had been in his thoughts since the previous evening and throughout his morning rounds. He'd purposely made her the last patient on his rounds in case she needed extra attention.

Grace moved her head, and he realized she was awake.

"Hello, Miss Stanton."

"Hello." Her reply was soft, hesitant.

Noah was certain Grace had long since tired of being asked how she was feeling. Instead he approached the bed, studying her exposed face carefully.

She averted her eyes.

He picked up her chart. "Did you eat your Wheaties this morning?"

She turned her face back toward him, her eyes blinking in surprise. "Wheaties?"

"Yep. You're going to have to be a champ today. I've scheduled a full day of tests."

She looked at him in silent inquiry.

"The sooner you're ready for surgery, the sooner you'll be dancing on tables."

Her eyes reproved him. "I don't do that."

"Maybe not. But you'll be able to if the whim strikes you. The last tests you had in Houston show a marked progression. So my instincts are optimistic that we can begin surgery in a few days."

"Oh."

He glanced up from the chart. "You don't sound very encouraged."

"I don't mean to seem ungrateful. But it's difficult to be enthused."

He met her gaze, noticing that today her eyes seemed gray. He wondered if it was a trick of light or if she possessed changeling eyes. "I don't expect enthusiasm, Grace. You've been thrust into a life-altering experience with little time to absorb what's happened. Many of your friends probably haven't known what to say or do."

He saw a flash of recognition.

So he continued. "You're going to have to take the lead in your recuperation. I can captain the medical care, but if you steer us into a reef, we'll go aground."

"I'm not feeling much like steering."

"No. I don't imagine you are. But it does get better. It's not easy. In fact, it's frustrating and painful."

"Don't feel you have to use kid gloves, Doctor."

"I don't. I could tell you a lot of soothing lies, but I respect you too much. I suppose I'm making a big assumption, but I'm guessing you're made from the same stuff as your aunt Ruth. And she'd take a switch to me if I fed her cotton candy instead of the truth."

Grace briefly closed her eyes, then met his. "You're right. But…I'm scared."

Noah gave in to his unexpected instinct to take the unbandaged portion of her left hand. "I know you are. But you're not in this alone. Your aunt Ruth has the stamina of a dozen people."

"I suppose you're right," she murmured softly, her voice cracking.

He suspected there were buckets of unshed tears in her. There would be times she needed to cry, but he couldn't let her slide into self-pity and depression. Her recovery depended on a strong spirit. "You'll probably be ready to throw rocks at me before we're through, but like I said, I'm tough."

Tough enough to disregard the appeal she evoked in him, he reminded himself, seeing her fingers curled inside his. Yes, tough enough.

Nearly two weeks later, Grace pushed at the soft, mushy food on her tray. The taste and consistency resembled baby food, since she still couldn't chew properly. Dr. Brady had promised she would be able to in the future. He had also emphasized the importance of eating so that she didn't compromise her health. Listlessly she stirred the carrot-colored section. The unappetizing hospital food certainly wasn't helping.

Dr. Brady was later than usual. He had taken to making his daily visit during the dinner hour, often eating with her. Perhaps he had decided she'd had enough personal hand-holding.

Grace couldn't repress seeds of disappointment. Funny, he was the only person who had thought to offer her physical comfort, to actually take her hand. Even though it was in his professional capacity. Patrick had looked scared to death simply to stand by her side. Ruth was afraid of hurting her. But Dr. Brady seemed to know she needed the tactile contact, the simple human connection.

As the minutes ticked by, she stirred her applesauce

aimlessly. Ruth had gone home for the day. She would be back in the morning faithfully as she always was. But that left a lot of empty hours.

The door whooshed open suddenly. Noah Brady swept inside. "Hello."

"Hey," she replied, her disappointment receding.

He placed his tray on the table, then reached into a white paper sack and pulled out a large disposable cup. "Think I can talk you into a milk shake instead of the usual mush?"

"Chocolate?" she asked, her absent appetite making a revival.

He smiled, a wide grin that revealed even white teeth. "Is there any other flavor?"

"Not for me," she admitted, studying his face. "But something tells me there's more to this than ice cream."

"Ah, the lady is sharp. You're right. It's a celebration."

"For what?"

"I just finished the analysis of your last tests. You're ready for your next surgery."

Fear scorched her insides, much the way the pain of her injuries had. What if these surgeries didn't help? What if all of it was for nothing? She gasped for air as she considered the grim possibilities.

"Take a deep breath," Noah instructed.

She did. Several deep breaths, in fact.

But he didn't seem fazed.

"Sorry," she said, finally calm.

"It's okay. Plastic surgery isn't like an appendectomy. It's rarely routine, we can't always predict the outcome, and in a case like yours there's a lot riding on the success."

"Did you completely skip Bedside Manner 101?"

He smiled again. "That's more like it. Now, taste your milk shake."

She obliged. "It's good."

"Wrong. It's delicious. I'll bring you another one after surgery when you can appreciate it."

Grace awkwardly grasped the cup with her bandaged left hand. "When is the surgery?"

"Tomorrow morning."

Her eyes widened. "So soon?"

"No point in waiting."

She supposed he was right, but what if the surgery failed?

"And right now you're wondering about the outcome, whether it could be bad."

His intuitiveness took a bite out of her fear. "And if it is?"

"Then you'll most likely need even more surgeries than I'd initially believed. But that's possible anyway."

"It sounds like it may never end."

He met her eyes. "It will probably feel that way no matter how tomorrow's surgery goes."

She swallowed. The truth was harsh, but marshmallow-covered lies would be more painful in the long run. "I'm not sure I could do your job, the part about delivering the news to the patient."

"I chose this field because of the patients. It's personal to me."

"But you don't know me."

"I'm beginning to," he refuted. "Already I know you like milk shakes better than baby food."

"That doesn't count. I imagine even babies would prefer milk shakes. Tell me something else."

"You're smart. You're strong. And you have excellent taste in doctors."

She felt a smile forming despite her injuries, then glanced at the cafeteria tray he'd brought in. "Isn't your dinner getting cold?"

"I don't know the difference anymore. I'm so used to leaving meals unfinished that hot food might be a shock to my system." He glanced down at the tray. "Come to think of it, I've had so many carrots and peas it's a wonder I'm not orange and green."

"If you go on that basis, I'll be pure mush soon."

"Nope. The milk shakes will save you."

Grace suspected it would take more than milk shakes, but she didn't want to seem ungrateful for his teasing kindness. Surely he would rather be with his wife or girlfriend than pulling dinner duty in the hospital. "I'll count on it."

He swallowed a forkful of vegetables. "I called Ruth

a little while ago, let her know what time you're scheduled in the morning."

"Isn't that above and beyond the call of duty?"

He tipped his head slightly. "Depends. Every doctor has his own methods."

"But doesn't that take a lot of time away from your family?"

Noah shrugged. "I see my parents when I can and they understand my reasons for a busy schedule."

"No. I meant your wife and children."

"Don't have either."

She was surprised. He seemed like the kind of man who would nurture both. "Your girlfriend, then."

"Not guilty."

Grace studied him as he took another bite of his cooling dinner. "Did you always want to be a doctor?"

"No. I was going to be a lawyer like my dad, only really big time, Ivy League, the whole works. I wanted to be the next household name in law."

That surprised her. "What happened?"

His brow furrowed. "It's a long story."

"I have nothing but time." She paused. "At least until morning."

"Remember, when you're bored to tears, you asked for this story." He paused and she could see the faraway light of memories in his eyes. "It started when I was seventeen. My mother was burned severely in a chemical explosion. Rosewood didn't have much in the way of a hospital—it really wasn't more than a clinic. There wasn't a plastic surgeon in town. And my mother needed extensive care—turned out to be more than a year of surgeries and treatment. That meant she had to be in Houston the whole time, where we found her doctor. My dad couldn't take the idea of my mother being on her own through all that, so we moved to the city."

"That's a pretty big change for a teenager."

"Yeah. I was scared my mother would die. But at the same time I couldn't figure out where I fit in anymore. Here in Rosewood I was the star quarterback with a great future. In Houston I wasn't even bait in a large pond."

So he knew how it felt to be the odd one out, as well.

"Then in my senior year we had a class assignment that was supposed to help us figure out what we wanted to do with our careers. We had to shadow someone in our chosen profession. Well, I didn't really have one anymore because I'd become so unfocused. Law school didn't have the appeal it had back in Rosewood.

"I couldn't go out for high school football because I had to stay home in the afternoons with my younger brothers and sisters. That meant I couldn't hope to be on a college team, which in turn meant I wouldn't be recruited by the pros.

"I went to visit my mother in the hospital, and her surgeon was there. By that time he had worked miracles with her, even though she had a long way to go. And it hit me. If Rosewood had a doctor like him, families wouldn't have to be torn from their homes, away from everything they know, to get good medical treatment."

Grace suddenly wondered if the doctor was too good to be true. "That sounds really noble for a high schooler."

"I didn't mention that the town took up a collection to help us with living expenses and medical care. My family wouldn't have made it without their help. Not to mention that with the accident, moving, assuming most of the care for my siblings, it was a maturing experience."

Although still suspicious, Grace thought of her own losses. "Yes."

"The surgeon let me shadow him. I sat in on late-afternoon rounds and appointments, surgeries. I was able to read what he charted…and it was the greatest experience of my life. I hadn't really expected that."

"Does it still feel that way?"

He hesitated, and she sensed he was retrieving more memories. But he didn't share them, nor did he answer her question. "How about you? We've never talked about your work."

"I'm in… I *was* a public relations rep."

"Did you quit?"

Exasperation bubbled. "I had an accident, remember?"

"I don't see how the two are related. Unless your employer isn't willing to hold your job until you recover."

She flinched. "Public relations means meeting the public."

"I'm sure your job consists of more than appearance. What kind of firm do you work for?"

"Did," she insisted. Grace thought of her job, how fulfilling it had been. But returning to public speaking and networking seemed impossible. "I worked for an independent oilman who wants to give back to the community. So he's a strong charity advocate. The biggest part of my job is…was organizing fundraisers." She swallowed, remembering, hurting for what was gone. "The fund-raisers were for causes that had become very dear to me."

"Why should that change? Clearly they still mean a great deal to you."

Grace remembered how she'd confidently accepted invitations to speak anywhere there was a prospect of raising contributions for the Texas Children's Hospital, cancer research and others. She couldn't imagine how she would ever resume her life—not with an endless stream of pity or disgust from the people she had once inspired to help others.

"Grace?"

Belatedly she raised her head. "Things have changed. Even you can't pretend they haven't."

"Of course they have. But there's a reason for everything."

"You sound like Ruth. No matter how grim things get, she insists it's in the heavenly plan."

"And you don't?" he questioned quietly.

She couldn't face those doubts right now. A promise of long ago echoed in her thoughts. An unfulfilled promise. "I don't know."

To her relief he didn't push. "You've got a lot on your plate right now. But I want you to feel good about tomorrow."

"Do most of your patients feel good about their surgeries?"

His expression darkened. "Depends. The fighters know each one is a step they have to take."

Grace looked at him with the obscured view Patrick's desertion had bred. "And you're so sure I'm a fighter?"

"I believe in you more than you do right now."

She swallowed a sudden lump of emotion. "That's not saying a lot."

"Don't underestimate me."

Grace realized suddenly that the possibility had never even been a consideration. And her doubts flared. Trusting another man, even the supposedly good doctor, could only lead to pain.

Chapter Three

Ruth's anxiety was nearly painful to watch.

"Can't I get you some coffee?" Noah asked.

"It's not me we have to worry about. This child's been through so much loss, so much pain." Ruth glanced down at Grace, who was still sleeping after her transfer from the recovery room. "The way she lost her parents...now this."

"She's strong, Ruth. She'll get through it."

"Physically. But this sort of damage is hard for a woman. It's not something I can explain."

She didn't need to. Noah knew the emotional trauma involved. "I haven't known Grace for long, but I think she's strong emotionally."

Ruth nodded slowly. "Maybe so."

"And like the previous ones, her surgery went without a hitch. I'm very optimistic about her prospects." He glanced at his watch. "Ruth, it's late and you've been here since dawn. Why don't you go home and get some rest?"

Her face was lined with fatigue. "I need to be here if Grace wakes up."

"I'll stay."

"I can't ask you to do that."

Even though Noah was regretting his impulsive offer, he couldn't withdraw it. "Grace will really need you tomorrow. You'll do her more good if you go home and get some rest."

Ruth took one last look at her niece. "She's so dear to me."

"I'll take good care of her," Noah promised. "You can count on me."

She pursed her lips. "You've never let me down before. And I don't expect you're going to start now. I'll take these old bones home, but I'll be back first thing in the morning."

"Good night, Ruth."

Once she left, Noah studied Grace's sleeping form. The bandaged side of her face lay against the pillow. And even though he was well acquainted with her disfiguring injuries, he couldn't help thinking how lovely Grace looked. And how vulnerable.

Noah rarely spent this much time with a singular patient. Not since the experience that had changed him forever.

Still, he found himself drawn to Grace.

He didn't really understand it. She'd struck a chord deep within. That alone should have told him to back off, to put extra distance in place.

Grace sighed and he stepped closer.

Her eyelids quivered with the effort of opening them. She looked at him in confusion, unfocused. She tried to speak, but her lips and mouth were dry.

Noah offered her a few ice chips.

Grace swallowed, then looked up at him again. "Blackberry doctor?" she croaked.

He smiled at the reference. "Yes, I'm the blackberry doctor. And you're doing great."

"Navigator," she managed, her voice still muffled from the anesthesia.

He took the fingers of her left hand, surprised and touched that she remembered these two things. "Yeah. And I'm the captain."

She closed her eyes briefly, then stared up at him. "Where to?"

"Sleep," he replied gently. "And you won't believe how much better you're going to feel before long."

Her eyes drifted closed again.

Good night, sweet Grace.

It took Noah longer than he expected to release her hand. And even longer to finally leave her that night.

Grace could scarcely believe it. Four surgeries later, true to Noah's promise, she was going home. Well, to

Ruth's home. There would be more surgeries to repair her face, but Noah said she was ready to leave the hospital.

"It's so wonderful to see green lawns and flowers." She inhaled deeply. "And nothing smells of antiseptic. I can't wait to take a walk."

"You still have to be careful," Ruth reminded her. "Nothing strenuous for at least six weeks."

Grace knew her aunt was worried. But Grace didn't feel fragile.

"Let's go in," Ruth was saying.

She followed her aunt, who had insisted on carrying Grace's small bag. She was immediately drawn back to her childhood, the visits to this comforting home.

It had been years since Grace had been in Rosewood. Ruth had traveled to Houston for their visits and holidays. First, when Grace's mother had passed away, also spending the summers with her. Then, after Grace's father passed away, Ruth had made the trips because Grace was in college. And the custom continued when Grace became immersed in her career.

She had forgotten how warm and cozy Ruth's home was. Sunshine poured in the oversize bay window. Plump pillows in the window seat invited reading, napping, contemplating.

"It looks wonderful," Grace murmured.

"This old place?" Ruth waved away the compliment. "Pish. I don't think it's changed since you were here last."

"That's what's so wonderful."

"Never having children of my own, the furniture doesn't get worn out. No one to run and play, mess up things."

Impulsively Grace laid a hand over Ruth's. She had never realized not having children bothered her aunt. But the regret in Ruth's eyes was too clear to miss.

"Aunt Ruth, you have me. I couldn't ask for anyone dearer—you've always been there for me. I don't know what I'd have done without you. I'm sorry I've taken that for granted."

Tears misted in Ruth's eyes. "Child, you are a wonder. Let's get you settled on the couch."

Grace wanted to protest. But she *was* exhausted from the trip home. It was ridiculous, but she suddenly felt weak and wobbly. "Okay."

Ruth fussed, draping an afghan over her. "I'll make some tea."

"That sounds good, if you'll join me."

"A cup of tea wouldn't go amiss," Ruth agreed.

The sofa was situated close to the window and Grace took advantage of her position to study the view. Rosewood was a quiet town, a place where neighbors still knew each other and friends dropped by without notice. Grace touched the bandages wrapped over one side of her face, wondering just how much company Ruth usually had. While she was glad to be home, it occurred to her that she

wouldn't be as protected and isolated as she had been
in the hospital.

It seemed nearly unbelievable that she had been in
the hospital long enough for the seasons to change. But
the children playing in their yards were evidence of the
passing days.

The doorbell rang suddenly.

Grace felt her muscles clench at the prospect of
seeing anyone.

Ruth left the kitchen, her shoes an even tapping
sound on the wooden floor as she walked to the front
door, then opened it. There was a murmur of voices,
then the door closed.

Ruth entered the living room, carrying an arrangement of flowers. "Now, isn't this nice."

Grace eyed the flowers warily. "Yes."

"They're flowers, not grenades." Ruth removed the
card, handing it to Grace. "At least find out who they're
from before reacting."

But Grace didn't need to read the card. During her
hospital stay, the large, formal arrangements had come
from her employer, who insisted her old job would
wait for her as long as it took for her to recover. It was
a kind notion, but not practical.

The roses had been from Patrick. His flowers had
arrived regularly, although he hadn't. He phoned Ruth
rather than her, as though scared even to speak to her.
And despite Grace's long hospital stay, he hadn't made

it to Rosewood. As far as she was concerned, Patrick had defected. The roses, she had decided, were to ease his conscience. And were a way to salvage his image.

Glancing at the flowers, she realized the arrangement didn't fall into either category. Fresh, vibrant daisies were nestled into an ivory Victorian vase. Curiosity compelled her to pull the card from the small envelope.

"Welcome home. Noah"

Grace wasn't sure how other plastic surgeons treated their patients, but she suspected her blackberry doctor was one of a kind. He had continued his custom of visiting her each evening, often sharing her dinnertime.

She remembered his pep talk that morning. To his credit, it hadn't sounded like the canned speech she guessed most doctors gave. But then, he wasn't like any doctor she knew.

Grace stared at her stiff right hand. Noah maintained therapy would begin this week. Despite the Houston doctors' diagnoses, Noah insisted she would regain its use. She couldn't see how.

But then she couldn't believe his other assurances, either, that she would recover, that her scars would most likely be minimal. Grace suspected it was Noah's way of being kind. But all the kindness in the world wouldn't make her whole again.

Still, she glanced down at his flowers, reaching out

to touch the creamy texture of the charming vase. Grace wished she could take heart from his gesture, but sorrow had stolen her hope.

A week later, Noah felt he had given Grace enough time to ease back into life outside the hospital. Although it wasn't his custom to make house calls, Ruth had asked him to check on Grace. She had repeated the therapist's report that Grace was resisting therapy. Ruth hoped he could prod Grace into the treatment she needed.

Noah rang the doorbell and waited. It didn't surprise him when Ruth opened the door, rather than Grace.

Her worried expression lightened a bit. "Evening, Noah. It's good to see you."

"You too, Ruth. How's our patient?"

Ruth raised her eyebrows, then nodded her head toward the living room, indicating Grace's presence. "Seems to be doing fine."

Noah entered the living room, his gaze going to Grace. Although she had her legs stretched out on the couch, covered by an afghan, she wasn't a picture of frailty.

Ruth followed him into the room. "Would you like some lemonade or iced tea, Noah?"

"No thanks, Ruth. Grace and I won't need refreshments."

Understanding laced with gratitude flooded the older woman's eyes. "I'll be in the kitchen."

Noah walked closer to Grace. "Hello."

"Hi." Discouragement colored her voice.

"How are you today?"

She inclined her head. "Okay, I suppose."

"And you've probably had all the fussing you can withstand."

Grace smiled faintly. "Pretty much."

"Then you should be pleased to know that I'm not here to fuss."

"Good."

"It's time for some work."

Grace looked surprised. "You might have to arm wrestle Aunt Ruth if you try to get me to do more than lie here."

"She's tough, but I'll take my chances. I want to start therapy on your hand."

Frowning, Grace held up her rigid hand. "It won't do any good."

Noah knew it was time to stop coddling her. "Let me rephrase that. It's time for *you* to work."

Even more surprise covered her face. "You say that as though I've been vacationing in the south of France."

"No. But up until now you've let others do for you. It's time you took an active part in your recovery."

Grace was beginning to rethink her opinion of the kindly doctor. There was a force in his voice and words that was nowhere near benevolent. "Doing what?"

"Today we're going to exercise your hand."

She glanced down at her motionless limb. "The therapist tried. He couldn't induce any movement."

"I can."

"How?"

He took her hand in his, gently but firmly grasping her fingers, stretching them.

The pain was excruciating and she immediately recoiled.

"Grace, this isn't going to be easy."

"You didn't say it would be killing pain!"

"I told you this would be tough. You have two choices. Give up or find the strength."

Grace fought the threat of tears. "From where?"

He met her gaze. "Everyone has a different source of strength."

She knew he meant the Lord, but she hadn't reconciled that yet.

"All right, let's stretch again," Noah instructed when she didn't reply.

"Again?"

His expression became pointed. "For a total of two so far."

"It's not easy," she protested, knowing she sounded wimpy, but not caring.

"If it were easy, it wouldn't be called work," he told her without apparent sympathy.

What had happened to the kind man who had helped her in the hospital? This tyrant had no pity.

She stared at him, frost coating her expression. "I can do it without your help."

He released her fingers.

Still angered, she stretched her hand, determined not to give in despite the pain. However, her hand didn't...couldn't move on its own. And again the pain shot through her. This time she couldn't repress the tears.

He didn't berate her as she expected. Instead, Noah gently wiped away her tears. "I know it hurts, Grace. That's why I called and asked Ruth to give you a pain pill an hour before I arrived. Is it helping at all?"

"I don't know. Maybe. But I hate acting like a wimp."

"You're not. I think it's time to strike another deal."

She glanced at him suspiciously. "I don't think even a milk shake's going to do it."

"Better than a milk shake," he promised. "We're finished for tonight on one condition."

"Anything," she agreed, knowing it was a bad bargaining strategy, not caring.

"That I come back day after tomorrow and we do at least two more stretches than today. And in the meantime, you try to stretch your hand once each morning and afternoon."

She winced. "Isn't there another option?"

"Nope."

"Then I guess I have to agree."

"I'll ask Ruth to elevate your hand on a pillow. That will help."

Grace tried not to think of the pain zinging through her hand. "Thanks."

"You'll get through this."

"If it kills me?"

Noah smiled, picking up his bag. "Well, not purposely. Goes against the oath we doctors have to take."

And despite the pain, she felt her lips twitch.

"Good night, Grace." He raised his voice. "Night, Ruth. I'll see myself out."

She watched as Noah left, wondering what he would have done if he'd been in Patrick's shoes. Throat tightening with an ache she doubted would ever heal, Grace guessed what the answer would be. After all, Noah was a man. Eyes closing, Grace acknowledged that Patrick had broken more than her heart. He'd destroyed her ability to trust.

In the following days Ruth's home remained surprisingly quiet. Grace suspected that her aunt had put a permanent hold on visitors until she could adjust to strangers.

But the transition wasn't going to be easy. The only people Grace saw were ones involved in her medical care.

Like Noah.

He had arrived a little later than she'd expected. But

she could tell why. His pager hadn't stopped beeping since he had entered the house.

Noah clicked off his cell phone. "Sorry about that. It's been a crazy day."

Belatedly Grace realized she was adding to his already overloaded schedule. "Do you normally go to a patient's house?"

"Every case is different. Some need more specialized attention."

She considered that. "Oh."

"I see the wheels turning. No, that doesn't mean you aren't going to recover, just that your hand is a difficult injury. Only concentrated attention will restore your mobility."

Although knowing she probably shouldn't say it, Grace couldn't hold the words in. "All of the doctors in Houston said it would never return. How…"

"How can I be so sure I'm right?" He met her gaze. "You can believe them, or you can do the therapy. It's your choice."

She stared at her damaged hand, her voice reluctant. "The therapy."

"Have you been doing your stretches each day?"

Grace nodded. "It's hard, but yes."

He reached for her hand, carefully stretching her fingers, extending them farther than she did on her own.

Grace pulled back reflexively in pain.

Noah looked at her patiently. "We have to extend your fingers more. Holding back won't cut it."

It felt as though her hand might fall off from the pain if she did as he instructed. Grace started to protest, then saw his determined expression. So she complied.

After a few more horrendous stretches, Grace wanted to kill the once kindly doctor.

But he saved himself the gruesome fate by deciding she had done enough for the day.

Noah rummaged in his coat pocket. "Has the pain medication been adequate since you came home?"

"Until today," she admitted.

Noah handed her a few packets. "Take one of these. It's stronger and it will let you sleep tonight."

"You *knew* it was going to hurt worse today!" she said, suddenly realizing.

"This isn't my first time at the dance," he reminded her. "And don't think I'm going to be the amiable country doctor who will allow you to atrophy."

Ruth pushed open the swinging door from the kitchen. "Noah, dinner's ready and I insist you stay."

"Still afraid I'm not getting enough vegetables?" he teased.

"I know how you bachelors live." Ruth all but tut-tutted.

The smell of her fried chicken wafted toward them. Grace wondered if her aunt's exceptional cooking was going to be a deal maker.

Noah groaned. "Ruth, how can I say no to your fried chicken?"

"You can't," she replied, clearly having decided the doctor had little say in whether he stayed for dinner. Then she glanced at Grace. "You look pale, dear. Would you like a tray?"

Grace could see that Noah was awaiting her reply. Determination fused her spine. "No, you've been waiting on me enough as it is."

Ruth looked at her in concern. "Do you want a pain pill?"

"Luckily the doctor brought some with him," Grace replied, beset by a new round of stabbing pain in her hand. "They're more potent in proportion to the therapy."

Her aunt looked puzzled, then glanced at Noah.

"Therapy's rarely comfortable," he explained. "The new medication should help Grace sleep after a session."

"Ah." Ruth nodded in understanding. "I remember therapy after my back surgery." She glanced again at Grace, but spoke to Noah. "But she's doing well otherwise?"

"Yes. I'm going to have the nurse change her bandages tomorrow. They have to be done more often now—every two days."

Grace began to feel like an inanimate object. "*She's* right here."

"I'm sorry, dear," Ruth replied, obviously contrite.

Grace immediately felt ungracious. "No, I am. I didn't mean to sound like a spoiled brat."

"As though you could," Ruth told her, a note of worry still remaining in her voice.

"Yes, I can," Grace insisted, wishing she could recall the words. Instead she smiled at her aunt. "Your fried chicken smells delicious."

Ruth relaxed a fraction. "I know you like it. And I've cut up some white meat for you so it's easy to manage."

Grace withheld a grimace, hating that she had to be treated like a toddler to get by. But she couldn't say that to Ruth. "Thank you."

Ruth led the way to the dining room.

Noah hung back for a moment, his voice low, reaching only Grace's ears. "This won't last forever."

Grace wasn't so sure, but she *was* surprised that Noah had instantly read her feelings.

"And you're being a real trouper," Noah continued. "I know it's not easy to accept so much help. But you didn't let Ruth know it bothers you."

Embarrassed, she turned her eyes away. "I'm used to being an independent career woman. I've had to learn to hide a lot of my true feelings."

As Grace walked into the dining room, she missed the look of surprise on Noah's face and the reflection that replaced it.

Chapter Four

Noah glanced at the next chart, even though he knew the contents by heart. Grace Stanton was in the exam room, ready for her first post-op consultation since she'd been released from the hospital.

Thinking of the personal therapy sessions he was continuing with her, Noah walked to the exam room.

Grace looked up when he opened the door. He could see the uncertainty and fear in her eyes. Again he was struck by the emotion contained in them.

"Afternoon, Grace."

She nodded, her gaze going to the chart he held. "Afternoon."

"Still doing all right?"

"Yes." But the singular word contained a mass of apprehension as she waited for him to examine her face for the first time since her surgery.

His fingers were sure but gentle as he removed the

bandages and examined her face. The progress was as he expected. "You're healing well."

"And?"

"There's no other shoe to drop."

"So it's all good?" she questioned.

"This surgery couldn't have gone better."

She studied him closely. "And beyond *this* surgery?"

"Each surgery will be unique, but I feel confident we can expect similar progress."

"And the end result?"

He couldn't ignore her directness, nor could he tell her less than the truth. "It's possible you can completely regain your previous appearance and it's also possible that you may have residual scarring."

"Will I be a freak?" she asked bluntly.

Noah sensed the pain behind the query. "I doubt that was ever possible."

Grace shifted impatiently. "I don't want the sugar-coated version."

"That wasn't my intent." He remembered nearly identical words and emotion from years past. "Grace, we're still in the tough stages."

She swallowed, then averted her face. "Yes, I know."

He knew she considered therapy torture. Coupled with today's news, she seemed overwhelmed. He wished Grace could regain the grip on her faith. It would ease this difficult journey. But he didn't want to press and drive her further away.

"Have you gotten out of the house other than to come here?"

Startled, she looked puzzled. "No. But—"

"That's what the doctor orders. Fresh air, change of scenery."

Grace appeared horrified. "Not necessary."

"Hiding, be it in the hospital or in your aunt's home, will inhibit your recovery."

"I'm not ready to see anyone."

He took another unprofessional step. "You've already faced me. Suppose I pick you up after dinner tonight? We can take a drive." He held up his hand. "And I promise you won't have to meet any new people."

Grace studied him suspiciously. "This doesn't sound like typical doctor behavior."

He sidestepped the question, knowing he shouldn't have made the offer. "I never said I was typical. Eight o'clock?"

"I'm not sure what Aunt Ruth—"

"She's crazy about me," he interrupted, knowing she was grasping for excuses, realizing he was a fool to not let her succeed. "She won't mind."

Grace sighed. "I suppose that would be all right. But you're sure I won't have to meet anyone?"

He held up his fingers in the Boy Scout sign. But he didn't feel the responding lightness. "Cross my heart."

"Hmpf," she muttered.

Noah knew that she could easily hide away forever if she wasn't shaken out of her mode.

He also knew he wasn't the person to lead her beyond that.

Nervously Grace watched out the bay window. She had already tried to back out of the commitment, but Ruth had turned as obstinate as a hungry horse headed for the hay barn.

Convinced that the good doctor had taken her on as his "project," Grace was nearly as sure he planned to introduce her to some of the locals. And that she couldn't take.

Meeting strangers was almost as distressing as being considered a project by Noah. She'd hoped he could keep treating her like a normal person. Her hand strayed toward her bandages. But then, she wasn't normal. Not anymore.

Grace chafed at the fact that she couldn't escape this outing. Although it was comforting to be in Ruth's cosseting care, at times it also made her feel trapped. Like tonight.

A sleek Porsche pulled into the driveway and she stared in surprise. She hadn't expected him to drive something so sporty. Grace forgot about the car as she watched Noah stride to the front door.

Long and lean, he seemed very comfortable in his skin. He was handsome—she'd noticed that the first time she had seen him. It was hard to miss. Thick black hair, a bit on the long side, contrasted with his blue, blue eyes. She imagined that he attracted plenty of female attention. Yet he had said there was no special woman in his life.

The doorbell rang. Not hearing Ruth's footsteps, Grace rose. Once in the front hall, she reluctantly opened the door.

Noah's face was noncommittal.

And Grace suddenly wondered if he regretted the impulsive invitation.

She pulled the door open a bit wider. "Hi."

"Sorry I'm late," he began. "Things got pretty wild at the hospital."

"It's all right. I don't have a lot of pressing engagements."

Ruth reappeared from the direction of the kitchen. "Evening, Noah. You kids better get going if you want to have any light left."

Grace exchanged an amused glance with Noah. Funny how easy it was for older adults to reduce them to "kids" in a moment.

"Yes, ma'am," they chorused dutifully.

Once outside, Noah chuckled. "I felt about ninety years old when I arrived. Nice to have some of that fall away."

"Why so old?"

"Bad day at the hospital. I was asked to consult on

a case with a disheartening diagnosis. Sorry. Didn't mean to bring my problems with me."

"How can you not? Doctors are human, too."

"Yeah." The tone of the single word was weighty, so much so that Grace searched his face, but his expression didn't tell her anything.

Noah opened the car door for her, careful to settle her in without disturbing her injuries. "I thought you might enjoy this car more than my SUV. It's practical and roomy, but not very high on the excitement level."

"Not something I worry about anymore." Still, she appreciated the fine driving machine. Grace realized she had been wrong. The Porsche suited him.

Noah drove toward the center of town. Rosewood was a charming, nineteenth-century small town that hadn't lost its appeal with the progressing centuries. False-fronted store buildings were a comforting reminder of that past.

Noah turned on to Main Street. "I don't want to sound like a tour guide. Have you been to Rosewood often?"

"Not really. We used to visit here when I was young, then after my mother died, Aunt Ruth came to Houston. She spent the summers with me and came for all the holidays."

"How old were you when your mother died?"

"Eight," Grace told him, the memory still painful. "My dad did his best, but no one can take the place of your mother."

"Agreed. But I imagine Ruth tried."

"She did. But not in an intrusive way. Somehow Ruth knew I wouldn't welcome that. But she was great about being there for all the mother-daughter things."

"Still rough losing your mother so young."

"Doesn't really matter how old you are," Grace replied, thinking as she always did of the pain and loss associated with her mother. "You're never ready to lose them."

"What about your father?" Noah asked quietly.

"He died when I was eighteen." And she had been devastated. Another promise had died with her father, one she'd never truly gotten over.

"You had hard lessons early."

"And they keep on coming." Grace didn't want to wallow in self-pity, but she couldn't grasp why she seemed destined for tragedy.

"It seems that way right now—"

"What's next on the tour?" she asked, uncomfortable with examining such deeply emotional issues.

"Once we've exhausted the treasures on Main Street, I thought you might like to drive by the lake."

Grace had a fuzzy memory of a happy day on the lake, when her parents had still been alive. There weren't many of those memories. Her vivacious, beautiful mother had died before they could make enough of those mental-scrapbook days.

"Is that okay?" Noah asked when she didn't reply.

She pulled herself out of the past. "Sure."

Like most everything in Rosewood, it took only a few minutes to reach the lake. Noah drove slowly once they reached the gravel road that followed the shoreline; then he parked and turned off the motor.

"Why did you stop?"

He opened his door. "You'll enjoy the lake more if we're on foot."

Grace scanned the surrounding area, but it was deserted at this late hour. "Oh." Still, she was apprehensive as she left the car. She wasn't at all ready to be subjected to the stares of strangers.

The soft grassy slope beyond the road led to the shore. The only activity on the lake was the swimming of a flock of wild ducks. Rays of the surrendering sun made the water appear golden. Noah was right. It was better close up.

Grace felt a portion of her tension escape as they strolled the quiet banks of the peaceful lake. Their presence startled some birds perched nearby and they fluttered upward, taking to the sky.

Unlike so many remembered things, the lake didn't appear smaller or dimmer. The breeze was fresh, filled with the scent of the clean water.

"There's decent fishing to be had here," Noah commented.

Such a male thing, Grace thought with a smile. "Do you fish often?"

He shook his head. "Never seems to be enough time."

"Perhaps you spend too much time on your patients," she remarked pointedly.

Noah didn't meet her gaze. "It's my job."

"Doesn't leave you much time for a social life."

One of his eyebrows rose. "I manage. But there's not the mad rush of a big city to contend with here."

"That's true enough," Grace acknowledged. "It's not all bad, though. Living in the city, I mean."

"I know. I spent a lot of years in one."

"Of course. Is your family still in Houston?"

He shook his head. "We've all moved back here."

"I know you took charge of your younger siblings. Are there many in your family?"

"Five sisters and brothers."

"Whew."

Noah chuckled. "Well said. How about you?"

"I'm an only child."

Noah's expression was reflective. "You don't act like one."

"I suppose that's meant to be a compliment."

"It is."

Grace remembered words from long ago. "My father said there were two types of only children. Terribly spoiled ones who became that way because they didn't have to share either their possessions or their parents' affection with siblings and therefore considered everything solely their own. And equally generous ones, for virtually the same reason. Because they didn't have to share, or fight with siblings for what was theirs, they never felt threatened, so they were extremely generous."

Noah glanced at her. "And which type are you?"

"I guess that's for others to say."

He kept his tone benign. "You don't seem spoiled or selfish."

"Wouldn't be diplomatic of you to say so even if I were."

They passed beneath a canopy of great, green trees. "I suppose not."

Unexpectedly she laughed, realizing that was his intent.

He pointed across the lake. "See that huge oak? The one that dwarfs the others?"

She saw it easily. "Yes."

"When I was seven, two of my friends dared me to climb it. Of course I couldn't refuse. When I got really high in the branches, it was like being on top of the world. Never occurred to me that it wouldn't be so easy to climb down. I was stuck in that tree till nearly nighttime."

"Didn't someone come to help you down?"

"Eventually. My friends didn't fess up until the last minute, figuring they were going to get in trouble."

"Did they?"

"Yep. One of the rescuers was the fire chief—my friend's father."

"Ouch."

"And then some. Of course, my parents weren't real thrilled with me, either."

"But I bet it kept you out of the tree."

"For two more years."

She smiled. "Another bet?"

"Nope. Did it on my own the next time. And I almost made it down without injury."

"Almost?"

His expression was wry. "Only broke a rib. Nothing life threatening."

"Sounds like you led a charmed life."

"Sounds that way."

She remembered his mother's accident. "You liked growing up here."

"Shows, does it?"

"Only a bit."

He tossed a pebble over the bank, making it skip along the water. "It's a good place to raise a family."

Grace swallowed, thinking of her own dreams, ones that were now smashed. "Hmm."

"And it's a town where neighbors still know each other by name and look out for each other."

"Do you ever want more?" she questioned. "Rosewood's nice, but it's so small."

His lips tightened fractionally. "I came back because everything I want is here."

Grace wondered if there was a special girl he hadn't

mentioned. One he hadn't yet made his girlfriend. "Then you're lucky. Most people aren't that certain."

"I wasn't always."

That seemed unbelievable. Dr. Noah Brady always appeared in control, a man who knew what he wanted and went after it. But then she'd once felt the same way.

He took her elbow. "No more deep thoughts. We've done enough excavating for one evening."

It was only after he'd taken her home that Grace realized he'd kept his word. Settling in for the night, she wondered if that was something she could count on. Then she remembered. In her new world, no man could be counted upon.

Chapter Five

Grace watched her aunt, wondering what she was up to. Ruth had been scurrying around all day.

The pit in Grace's stomach grew as she hoped her aunt's behavior didn't signal guests. Ruth had been urging Grace to allow visitors. Still raw from looks of pity while in the hospital, she wasn't ready to face new people.

The more Ruth bustled about, the more Grace worried. She was concentrating so intently that when Ruth called her name, Grace jumped. "Yes?"

"Let's go outside."

"Why?"

Ruth sighed. "It's not a surprise party, if that's what you're worried about."

Grace hid the automatic flinch. "Not exactly."

"I don't want to hurt you, child. You'll know when you're ready to let other people into your life." Ruth's wise eyes held only kindness. "And I intend to let you set the pace."

"I know you're only thinking of my best interests," Grace admitted.

"Then let's head outside." Once out of the house, Ruth went to the side of the garage and mounted the stairs that led above the structure.

Grace couldn't remember what was up there and immediately was curious.

At the top of the stairs Ruth opened a door, and they entered a well-lit room.

Grace looked around in surprise at the compact apartment that smelled of lemon oil and fresh flowers. "I didn't realize you had a garage apartment."

"When your grandmother became ill, we hired a woman to help us care for her. The apartment was hers. Since then I've used it as an overflow guest room, but that hasn't been often."

Strolling to the French doors that opened on to a small terrace, Grace glanced down at her aunt's yard and beyond. "Nice view from here."

"Do you like the apartment?"

Grace turned back around, her gaze encompassing the warm, tidy area. "It's very cozy."

"It's yours," Ruth replied, looking expectant, tremulous and nervous all at once.

"Mine?"

"If you're ready for it," Ruth explained. "I love

having you in the house, but I expect since you're used to having a place of your own, you could use some quiet time without your auntie hovering."

"You don't hover!"

Ruth smiled. "Kind of you to say so, but believe it or not, I was young once."

"You still are where it counts."

Ruth's eyes misted. "And you're still the sweetest child I've ever known." She made a production of straightening a few pillows, then turned to one corner of the apartment. "The kitchen's small, as you can see. Well, everything is—even the piano's a spinet." She glanced briefly at Grace's hands. "And I'll still be cooking, so you won't have to worry about that. I freshened up everything. The colors were a bit dated, so I bought a new throw, curtains, rug and—"

"It's lovely, Ruth. The apartment and the thought. Thank you."

"You're welcome." She sniffed a bit, then turned to Grace with her usual hardy expression. "I've had the telephone man put in a separate line for you."

Grace doubted it would get much use, but she didn't want to spoil Ruth's generous gesture.

"And I've put a few treats in the fridge," Ruth continued. "The sheets and towels are fresh. And I'll take care of the washing and tidying up. And anything else you need, of course." She looked around critically. "I guess that's it."

"I'm overwhelmed," Grace told her honestly.

"I want you to be sure you're ready, though." Ruth fussed. "There's no hurry."

Grace smiled. "I think it's time to kick me out of the nest."

Ruth raised one eyebrow. "Sure you're ready to fly?"

"Yes. And I know where to go if I crash-land."

Ruth looped one arm around Grace's shoulder. "All right, then. We'll have some dinner and get you moved in."

Grace looked at her wounded hands, unable to hide her distress. "Oh."

"Don't mind that. I've called in the reinforcements, just in case you were ready."

"Reinforcements?" Her distress multiplied.

"Noah said he'd be happy to help."

Grace didn't know whether to be relieved that she wouldn't have to face strangers or to be exasperated because her aunt insisted on asking Noah to constantly go beyond his duties as her physician.

Glancing down at her useless hands, she tried to repress the pang that shot through her. The accident had taken more than her face—it had stolen her freedom.

It wasn't as though she'd ever been vain about her looks. She supposed she had been a nice-looking woman before, but that was simply a gift of genetics.

But she didn't know how to deal with dependence.

Losing her parents so early, she'd been forced to become self-sufficient. And now it was more than a habit; it was a way of life.

Despite Noah's assurances, her right hand was still stiff, unresponsive. Again she thought of the Houston doctors, their insistence that the severed tendon wouldn't heal.

Even though she couldn't understand why Noah was so certain they were wrong, secretly she had harbored hope. But weeks of therapy hadn't made any difference.

Now she wondered if his optimistic diagnosis of her face was manufactured, as well.

"Are you ready?" Ruth's voice interrupted the thought.

Glancing up, Grace saw that her aunt stood expectantly at the door.

Ruth took a step back inside. "Is this too sudden for you? I still plan to help you with everything you can't do yet with your hands and—"

"I know I can count on you for help. I'm still having trouble with that concept, though."

Ruth nodded in understanding. "We Stantons are a strong, proud lot."

This time Grace accompanied her down the stairs. Once in the kitchen, she did what little she could to help. She could use the fingers on her left hand, even though she didn't have much strength in it yet. Hearing the doorbell, she glanced at Ruth.

"That should be Noah," Ruth said, bending over the

oven, checking on the rolls. "Ask him to stay for dinner, will you?"

Grace kept the groan to herself. Still, her steps lagged as she walked to the entry hall.

Opening the front door, she gathered what composure she had. "Hello."

"Evening," he replied, his voice and manner easy, comfortable.

"Won't you come in? Ruth asked me to invite you to dinner."

His lips curved in amusement. "That was direct."

Embarrassed, Grace opened the door wider. "Sorry. But I'm afraid Ruth is asking you for too many favors."

"You mean moving your things to the apartment?" He shrugged as he entered. "She doesn't want to make you uncomfortable. I told her you were bound to grow tired of me soon and want to meet other people."

Now Grace felt thoroughly rotten. "I'm not tired of you!"

"In that case, I will stay for dinner. Do I smell homemade rolls?"

"That you do. We didn't churn the butter, however."

Noah chuckled. "What's wrong? Too much *Little House* for you?"

"Not at all. I'm getting awfully spoiled, though. Living on my own, I got used to TV dinners and takeout. Now a quick meal means a sandwich made on freshly baked bread."

"When I was about ten, I did some yard work for Ruth," Noah mused. "She paid me, then set out some lemonade and chocolate chip cookies and told me to have my fill. I ate the whole plate of cookies."

"Ooh. Stomachache?"

"A rotten one. But they were still the best cookies I'd ever eaten. But don't ever breathe a word of that to my mother."

Grace laughed unexpectedly. "I forgot you aren't a lonely bachelor to be pitied and pampered with home-cooked meals. I doubt your mother lets you starve."

"Busted," he admitted. "But I take any rescue I can get from hospital chow."

She glanced out the window at his expensive car. "Surely you can eat out in nice places."

"Yes. But Rosewood or Houston, down-home or gourmet, restaurant fare is restaurant fare."

"I suppose so."

"Do you like the apartment?"

"Very much."

"It's not too…small-town for you?"

She wrinkled her eyebrows in surprise. "Of course not. Ruth put a great deal of thought and effort into making it a cozy, welcoming place." Grace wondered suddenly if he thought she felt herself above what Rosewood offered. "*That's* it," she said aloud. "You think I'm a snob."

"No. But it's not what you're accustomed to, is it?"

Grace thought of the large apartment she'd left behind in Houston. "I've had to become accustomed to a lot of things since the accident. But I'm not attached to belongings."

"I never thought you were."

She remembered his words the evening they had strolled around the lake. He had said then that he hadn't believed her to be spoiled. "Then why do you think I look down on Rosewood?"

"Not look down. Compare."

"The two places are apples and oranges." Grace thought of her fast-paced career. There had been few quiet moments in her life in those days.

"And which do you prefer?" Noah's gaze met hers. "The apple or the orange?"

An unsettling feeling came over her. Throat dry, Grace realized that she was seeing Noah as more than just her doctor. A ridiculous pitfall, she realized. And one she couldn't indulge. Wonderful doctor or not, she was through with men.

"It's all right." He answered for her when she didn't speak. "It wasn't a fair question."

Ruth bustled in, bringing with her the aroma of the newly baked rolls. "Noah! Perfect timing. Dinner's ready. I hope you're hungry."

"Always," he replied, his voice light, sparing Grace one last glance before walking to the dining room with Ruth.

Trailing them, Grace shelved her questions. But she found it wasn't quite as easy to dispel her thoughts.

Noah carried the few boxes up to the apartment easily. Ruth unpacked each, consulting with Grace before putting things away.

Grace remained strong throughout the process and Noah suspected the effort was for her aunt. As he had since meeting her, Noah admired Grace's uncomplaining nature. Sorrow had settled deeply in her eyes, but he wouldn't have expected less.

Even more admirable, she was always concerned about others. Many of his patients ceased to think of anyone but themselves. Noah wondered if Grace realized how singularly astonishing that was.

"Ruth, you must be tired." Grace was looking at her aunt in concern. "You've fussed all day to make everything perfect."

"I'm fine," Ruth insisted. But fatigue had begun to set in the lines of her face.

"Okay, then. *I'm* tired." Grace smiled ruefully at her aunt. "Could we finish tomorrow?"

Ruth couldn't completely hide an expression of relief. "Of course, dear."

"I'll take the empty boxes down," Noah offered.

"That's kind of you," Ruth replied. "I think I'll go downstairs and make a pot of tea."

Noah glanced at the older woman, seeing her

fatigue, guessing she would make another trip up the stairs with tea for Grace. "Ruth, is there a kettle in the kitchen here? And tea?"

"Yes, but—"

"I could bring you the tea…" Grace began.

Noah could see the frustration when Grace belatedly remembered she couldn't.

So he offered instead. "I can bring over a cup for you, Ruth. Give you and Grace both a chance to rest." He glanced between the two self-sufficient Stanton women, imagining each's mental tug-of-war.

"That would be nice," Ruth said finally. "I'm ready for my fuzzy slippers and an early night."

After her aunt left, Grace turned to him. "That was kind of you. Ruth doesn't often feel her age, but she's been overdoing it ever since my accident. I want to help…." She held up her hands. "But I'm useless."

He met her gaze. "Don't sell yourself short." Silently he marveled at the depth of her compassion in spite of her own injuries. "What you give Ruth can't be measured in physical terms."

Suddenly she looked vulnerable. As vulnerable as she had the day he'd first met her. "Do you really think so?"

"Absolutely."

"The lack of independence is one of the hardest things about my accident," she confessed. "I was accustomed to doing for myself and for others. It chafes me to stand by idly and ask for help."

"It's not a weakness, you know."

Her eyes widened, their color tonight taking on the hue of the surrounding blue walls. And again he glimpsed pleading. "But it is for me. It goes against my nature."

"Can't you accept it as a growing experience?" he asked quietly.

"That doesn't make any sense," Grace protested, her lips trembling slightly. "How can it be an asset to become dependent?"

"There's a difference." Noah couldn't ignore the nudging of his faith. "Sometimes we have to ask for help in things greater than we are."

She grimaced, new pain marking the portion of her face that was exposed. "Perhaps *you* do."

"We all do."

Grace bent her head, then turned toward the open French doors. "It's not that black and white."

"You're right. That might be too easy. And faith is more complicated."

Her voice was both small and sad. "Yes, it is."

Noah wanted to probe further, but he could see the agitation in her tense muscles, the pain that was deeper than a physical one. So he crossed the room to the tiny kitchen. "Do you know where the tea bags are?"

"The cabinet over the sink."

The kettle was on the counter. After filling it with water, he put it on the stove. Between movements, he watched Grace as she continued to stand by the French doors. Her tawny blond hair was lit by a stream of moonlight. Her pose was quiet and still. And from his angle, no bandages were visible. She was lovely—a sculptor's vision. But cold marble couldn't do justice to her extraordinary warmth.

Nor could stone convey the depth of her incredibly changing eyes. Noah wondered what color they were right now. He was tempted to cross the room to see if her eyes would be silvery-gray, taking on the cast of the early moon.

The kettle whistled, startling them both.

Grace turned toward him. But Noah didn't see bandages. He still saw the same lovely vision. She was aptly named, he realized. She was full of grace.

Her gaze drifted from the screeching teakettle back toward him.

Seeing the questions forming in her expression, he turned to the counter and poured the hot water. "It should be ready soon."

"I'm glad Ruth's willing to have an early night. She'll appreciate the tea."

Noah put tea bags into the cups. "I'll take hers over now."

It didn't take long to deliver the tea and then return. "Ruth had already put on her fuzzy slippers," Noah reported, going to the kitchen.

He poured the mostly cooled tea from one mug into

a small glass that Grace could get her fingers around. Picking up his own mug as well, he joined her on the small terrace. The fragrance of roses, touched by the day's sunshine, mingled with that of wild honeysuckle, drifting up and over the railing.

"It's so nice out here," she mused, her voice soft. "I miss the fresh air."

"I've told you to get all the fresh air you can tolerate."

"I know. But in the dark, no one can see me, judge me."

"You're so certain they would judge you in the light?"

She paused for a moment. "It's human nature. I've already seen the looks of pity. And curiosity. I've thought back on the times when I saw someone disfigured in some way. I remember the pity mostly. And I've always considered myself a fair-minded person. Still, it was there. Why should I expect any less from other people?"

"It seems you are expecting very little from people."

"I wonder if you'd say the same thing if we traded places."

"I've been very close to where you are," Noah reminded her quietly. "The scars my mother bears were shared by all of us."

Grace met his gaze. "I'm sorry. I didn't mean to minimize your mother's injuries. I suppose I thought they'd occurred so long ago that the memories might have dimmed. It was wrong of me to think so."

"It's natural. My mother's injuries did happen a long time ago. And it changed all of us in different ways. I have the luxury of the viewpoint of a surgeon, but no two people react exactly the same. My mother was consumed by guilt for the stress on the family, all the adjustments we had to make, but she remained strong. Some people become so despondent they never recover emotionally."

She swallowed visibly. "Do you think I'll be one of those people, Noah?"

High above, the stars combined with the moon to illuminate the abbreviated terrace. And he knew he had to offer both gentleness and truth. "No. I think you are the exception, Grace. A true exception."

She glanced up at him, her eyes revealing a touch of hope, and Noah wondered what he was doing. Grace was a patient and he had sworn it wouldn't happen again.

She turned away to quietly sip her tea, and Noah remembered.

It had been four years ago. Noah's life and ambitions were right on track. He had a prestigious position at one of the foremost hospitals in the country. He was making more money than he'd ever dreamed of and his social life was equally satisfying. His relationship with girlfriend Jordan Hall had grown serious. Although Jordan was high-strung, she had a magnetism he hadn't been able to ignore. It seemed everything he touched was charmed.

Then Jordan began a relentless campaign to have him perform cosmetic surgery on her face. Initially he hoped to dissuade her by telling the truth—that she was lovely as she was. Jordan wasn't convinced. Her super-ficiality aside, he told Jordan that he never worked on people he knew, and even if that wasn't so, he didn't perform frivolous operations. He worked only on major reconstructive jobs and birth defects. She continued to cajole him, but he remained firm. Then she told him she was going to another surgeon, one whom Noah knew to be inept.

Noah again tried to convince Jordan to change her mind. She also refused to consider any plastic surgeons Noah recommended. He was the best, she insisted, and she wanted him.

When she wouldn't be swayed, Noah reluctantly agreed to perform the operation. But to his horror, Jordan encountered unexpected complications. She had a heretofore undetected heart valve problem that would have come to light only with an echocardio-gram, which wasn't one of the standard pre-op tests, especially for a young, apparently healthy young woman.

And despite his best efforts, Jordan died.

Noah remembered that agonizing time. Not only

had she died, he had been responsible. Unable to shed the guilt, he had reevaluated his life, left behind his job and status. One thing he had carried with him—the resolve never to mix personal with professional.

Noah glanced at Grace, seeing the melancholy that had returned to her expression. She needed his help.

And he needed to stay far away from the temptation she presented.

Chapter Six

But distance wasn't easy to maintain. Several weeks later, Grace had sunk deeper than ever into her self-imposed isolation. Noah was concerned that her failing optimism would be echoed in her recuperation. As was Ruth.

She had asked for his help again. The voice of the older woman—worried about Grace—had held repressed tears as she'd asked him to intervene.

Against his better judgment Noah had agreed. But luring Grace out wasn't easy. Speaking with Ruth, he learned some of Grace's hobbies. Her favorite was music—playing the piano.

Noah thought of the members of his band. It was a small group he had formed a few years earlier. The four members were all friends, people he could trust.

The band member Noah specifically had in mind was Cindy Thompson Mallory. He felt she was the person most likely to draw out Grace, to ease her back into relating with other people. Hearing Grace's story, Cindy immediately agreed to help.

For the first attempt, Noah decided it was best to have only himself and Cindy. The entire band, even though small, might still be too much for Grace.

He had cajoled Grace into coming with him on the pretext that he needed a pianist. Although she protested she couldn't help with only one hand, he had insisted.

He had spoken of Cindy often while they had therapy. And when he told Grace that she would only have to meet Cindy, she finally capitulated.

Now, in the car, Noah glanced over at Grace, seeing her nervousness. "It's going to be okay."

She fiddled with her shirt, tugging again at the hem. "Sure."

But she didn't look sure at all. Now smoothing the fabric of her skirt, she watched out the window as the houses rolled by. "Like I've told you, Cindy's a good friend."

Grace's head bobbed uncertainly.

"I met her when I needed a friend," Noah confided, not sure where the admission came from. "After I left Houston I was trying to find out just where I fit in again."

Grace finally pulled her gaze away from the disappearing landscape. "That's hard to believe."

He angled his head in her direction. "Oh?"

"You seem very certain of yourself."

Noah considered that. "It's a good cover. But I wouldn't recommend adopting it."

Her head dipped downward. "I doubt any cover will work for me."

He hated the discouragement in her voice. "The bandages won't last forever."

"In some ways I wish they would."

Noah knew that many patients hated the thought of their residual scarring being exposed. He glanced again at Grace. Although only half her face was visible, it was consumed by emotion. He suspected tears were only a breath away and knew she needed a distraction. "How old were you when you began to play the piano?"

She was quiet for a moment. "Five. My mother taught me." Grace laughed softly. "She was as insistent as you are that I stretch my hands."

Noah watched as the memory played over her face. "Smart woman."

"Hmpf." But her lips twitched.

Slowing down, Noah turned into the church parking lot.

Grace squealed. "What are we doing here?"

"This is where the band practices—in the rec hall."

"That's the only reason?" she asked suspiciously, studying the graceful architectural design of the church.

"No hidden motives." He placed one hand on his chest. "Cross my heart."

Grace suspected that Noah hoped some of the sacred ambience the church radiated would rub off on her. But she knew it wasn't that easy.

However, once inside, she felt a rush of memories. Deep in her past she had felt welcome in church. Not anymore.

They walked down the hall toward a small room, and to her relief they didn't meet anyone on the way.

Still she was nervous. "Are there any other people here today?"

"Shouldn't be. The pastor's office is in her home. She has a growing family, so it's easier for her to work there."

"Her?" Grace questioned in surprise.

"Yes. Katherine Carlson. She is our first female minister—one of the best decisions we ever made."

She had scarcely absorbed that when a woman approached them. Grace had a startling impression of red hair and vivacity.

"Hello," the woman greeted her. "I'm Cindy Mallory. It's a pleasure to meet you."

"I've heard a lot about you," Grace managed, the words coming more easily than she expected.

"Yipes," Cindy replied with a wry but warm smile. "That's scary. And yet you came anyway."

Grace found herself relaxing a fraction. "It was all good."

"Noah's too kind," Cindy replied, her warmth compelling.

"I've heard about your triplets." Grace had loved Noah's tales of the precocious girls.

Cindy's face softened. "I shouldn't brag, but they're wonderful children. I'm constantly amazed by their imagination and whimsy. And even though they look nearly alike, they're very different. Especially as they're getting older. Such individual personalities that at times it's hard to believe they're triplets. And don't even get me started on my oldest son. He's the smartest boy in his class, and the baby…" Her voice filled with chagrin. "I'm sorry, I'm going on and on about them."

"I enjoyed it." No longer certain children were in her future, Grace liked hearing the tales of the triplets.

"You're sweet to say so. I know I babble endlessly about the children. My husband just rolls his eyes. It's okay if you do, too."

Grace was surprised but not overwhelmed by Cindy's exuberant personality. "What if I withhold judgment?"

Cindy grinned. "Spoken like a woman after my own heart. I'm glad you're able to sit in on the practice today. Usually I'm stuck with the guys."

"Thanks," Noah responded, sounding properly insulted.

But Cindy didn't seem particularly concerned. "Pooh. You know that you men talk about sports and cars and other equally fascinating subjects."

Grace stiffened. "Will they be here today?"

"Just Cindy and me today," Noah replied.

"I need the extra practice," Cindy explained. "My family takes up so much time that I haven't learned my lyrics." She cocked her head. "Do you sing?"

Grace fumbled with a reply. "Not in your league."

"I asked because sometimes I can't make a performance and Noah could use another singer." Cindy didn't wait for a reply, turning to Noah. "Which reminds me. I can't perform next week. My Rainbow class has a special activity." She turned back to Grace. "The Rainbow class is a pet project of mine. I started it a few years ago for children who need a little extra attention, and it's grown considerably."

"And you love it," Grace guessed.

Cindy's smile softened again. "Absolutely."

Grace could see why Noah had chosen this particular woman as the first person for her to meet in Rosewood. Cindy was warm, open and accepting. A bit more of her tension subsided.

Cindy picked up some pages of music. "Noah told me you play the piano."

Grace swallowed, feeling the weight of her injuries. "I used to."

Cindy didn't look surprised, nor did she give Grace that pitying glance she'd become accustomed to. "Do you think you could pick out the melody line with your left hand?"

"I don't really know." Grace tentatively stretched her fingers. "This hand *is* getting better." She speculated for a moment, then came to a decision. "Why don't I try?"

Cindy and Noah both grinned.

"Don't expect too much," she warned them, walking to the piano. She settled on the bench, then tentatively ran the fingers of her left hand over first the smooth, dark wood, then the keys.

As she picked out the notes of a familiar song, Grace felt a small spurt of her old confidence. Neither Noah or Cindy commented and Grace was glad they didn't feel compelled to cheer her on. She couldn't take any overly inflated rah-rahs.

When Grace finished, Cindy placed a sheet of music on the piano. "Could we try this one? You could play through it before I sing."

Grace nodded. Luckily it was an easy piece. The second time, Cindy added her voice. And Noah came in with his guitar. By the following verse, Grace found herself humming.

Humming, she realized with a start.

It was hard to imagine.

"I think that was pretty darn good for the first time we've practiced together," Cindy declared. She shuffled through the music, lifting out another sheet. "Why don't we run through this one, as well?"

Noah's beeper went off just as Grace accepted the

music. He glanced at the digital readout. "I'm sorry, ladies. I have to run to the E.R." He glanced at Grace, then Cindy. "If Grace doesn't mind, could you give her a ride home?"

"Sure," Cindy replied, looking at Grace.

Relieved that she already felt comfortable with Cindy, Grace nodded. "Fine with me if it doesn't take Cindy out of her way."

"Thanks. Sorry to cut this short." Noah replaced his beeper, then sprinted toward the exit.

"Ah, the life of a doctor," Cindy said with a sigh. "The band has learned to be very, very flexible."

"He doesn't seem to mind the interruptions. But then, I haven't known him nearly as long as you have."

"Noah's a rare and special man."

Grace glanced up at her curiously.

Cindy read the silent question. "No. I was never involved with him. When I met Noah, my heart was already taken."

"Your husband?"

Cindy nodded. "Although he wasn't my husband at the time. Now, there's a story." She paused. "Maybe we could have some lunch, get to know each other."

Grace felt regret laced with panic. "I don't go out."

Cindy wasn't fazed. "We could pick up a pizza and take it home, if you're game."

Unused to fielding social situations in her new condition, Grace hesitated.

"I really am a bull in a china shop," Cindy continued. "If you're tired, I don't mean to press."

It had been a big day for her, agreeing to meet Cindy, entering the church—both had been taxing. But Grace didn't want to turn into a fragile butterfly afraid to even eat lunch with a new acquaintance. "Actually, lunch sounds nice."

Cindy smiled widely. "Great. Now, for the big decision..."

Grace smiled, as well. "Pepperoni or cheese?"

By the time they were on their second slice of pizza, Grace felt she had known Cindy for years. Also a woman without pretense, Cindy was easy to talk to, honest and refreshingly frank. She neither dwelled on Grace's injuries nor pretended they didn't exist.

While Grace had invited her aunt to join them, Cindy had casually gone about setting the table. Ruth had declined, suggesting the "girls" should have some time on their own.

Cindy didn't pepper her with questions. Instead she told Grace about her husband, Flynn Mallory, how she loved his three daughters as her own, and how they'd come to adopt their son.

"Your husband sounds like a very special man," Grace observed.

Cindy's expression grew reflective. "He is. We had impossible circumstances to overcome, but with the

Lord's help…" She paused, then smiled ruefully. "You don't want to hear all this!"

"Actually I do," Grace protested. "Unless it's too personal."

"No, not anymore."

"It used to be?"

"When I loved him from afar, so to speak, I only told my best friend, Katherine. It was too painful to share with anyone else."

Grace studied the other woman. "I realize I've just met you, but you don't strike me as the shy type."

Cindy laughed. "I see you've read me perfectly. No, I'm not shy, but Flynn was married to my sister. We both met him at the same time. I fell hard. He did, too, but in Julia's direction. So I moved here to Rosewood."

"It must have been a difficult situation for you."

Cindy nodded. "I loved Julia with all my heart and I wanted her to be happy. She and Flynn had each other and the triplets. Their life seemed picture-perfect."

"And?" Grace questioned quietly.

"Julia died." Cindy swallowed, sadness flashing in her eyes.

"I'm sorry."

Cindy acknowledged the sympathy with a shake of her head. "Even though I could never love another man the way I loved Flynn, I would never have chosen to lose my sister in order to have him."

"Of course not!" Grace's intuition told her that Cindy had a good heart.

The leap of faith was rewarded with a huge smile. "It helps me to know that I can raise Julia's girls the way she would have wanted."

"I think it takes a special person to do that and to adopt another child."

"Funny," Cindy mused. "I never think of myself as special, just lucky."

"Which is probably why you're special."

Cindy smiled again. "I definitely see potential in this friendship!"

Grace smiled as well, thinking how refreshingly normal their lunch had been. No talk of injuries or the accident.

And Grace read the genuine regret in Cindy's expression when she glanced at her watch.

"I can't believe it's so late! Flynn will be worried if I'm not home soon. He's great about watching the kids, but I don't like to take advantage of him."

"I understand completely."

"Let's do this again soon, okay?" Cindy picked up her purse. "You're so easy to talk to I feel like I've known you forever."

Grace was surprised at how much she'd enjoyed the day. "I feel that way, too."

"We can probably reschedule another band practice for later this week. Would that work for you?"

Thinking of her empty days, broken up only by medical appointments and therapy, Grace nodded. "I think so."

"I'll talk to Noah and call you," Cindy said with a wave.

Noah. Grace had him to thank for persisting until she agreed to meet Cindy. She remembered the other woman's words about him. A rare and exceptional man. Perhaps, but he was still a man. The growing accolades simply made her more suspicious. Noah was beginning to sound too good to be true.

By evening Grace was tired. But in a good way, she thought.

"So, it was a fun day?" Ruth asked, handing Grace a dessert plate.

Grace eyed the cheesecake with an interest she hadn't felt in months. "Yes. And it surprised me."

"Ah. Couldn't foresee that?" Ruth asked sagely.

"I'm not *trying* to be difficult," Grace reminded her.

"No one said you were." Ruth examined her piece of cheesecake critically. "Think this stacks up to the big-city variety?"

Grace took a bite. "It's delicious! I doubt there's better cheesecake in all of New York."

Ruth smiled. "After the final surgery, we'll have to go there and find out."

Grace felt the lump in her throat thicken. "I doubt there's much traveling in my future."

"Pish. I've been waiting all my life to visit New York City. If I can handle the journey, so can you."

"You know it's not the traveling," Grace replied, voice tight.

"Gracie, every day is going to bring more healing. Yesterday you wouldn't have believed meeting Cindy would be fun."

"I suppose. But that's a far cry from traveling."

Ruth carved a second small slice of cake. "One step at a time, dear."

Grace couldn't imagine such a day.

But before she could comment, the phone rang.

"Would you get that, Gracie?" Ruth held up cheese-cake-covered fingers.

Expecting one of Ruth's many friends, Grace was startled to hear Patrick's voice.

"Grace? Is that you?"

She couldn't speak.

"Grace? I thought Ruth would answer."

She cleared her throat, fighting the rush of emotions. She had hoped to hear from him, despaired of ever hearing from him, had imagined her own scathing response should he dare. But now only silence echoed over the wires.

"Grace? I…I'm not sure what to say…."

"Why are you calling, Patrick?"

He seemed stunned by the blunt question. After seconds of silence, his voice was hesitant. "I want to see how you're doing."

"You don't really want to *see* me, do you, Patrick?"

"Grace, it's a bad choice of words. I want to know how you're doing, if you're feeling okay."

"Okay?" The ludicrous choice of words rocked her. "Okay is for a day that's not great, or food that's good, even if it's not your favorite. *Okay* does not apply to a person who's been disfigured beyond repair."

Patrick stuttered for a few moments. But Grace didn't feel any pity for his discomfort.

"Obviously I've called at a bad time." In control of his voice again, Patrick seemed determined to control the call as well. "So I'll say good-night."

"Goodbye."

The click of his phone disconnecting sounded unnaturally loud.

Grace replaced the receiver and turned around. The knowing look on Ruth's face reinforced the discomfort of the call.

"You didn't give him much of a chance," Ruth observed.

"More of a chance than he gave me." New hurt sliced over the old. "He didn't even intend to talk to me. It was a duty call so he can report back to our friends and not look as though he's run away."

"But your friends—"

"Bad choice of words, Ruth. Our social circle is made up of associates, people we networked with. Patrick has an image to maintain."

Ruth hesitated. "Have you spoken to any of them since you've been out of the hospital?"

"No. They sent obligatory flower arrangements, but that's as personal as it will get." Grace reflected on the people she had surrounded herself with in the city. Close friendships from her younger days had withered from lack of care. People moved on and away.

"I'm blessed to have friends in my church, ones I can count on for anything," Ruth commented.

"I'm happy for you," Grace replied tactfully. She didn't need any more hints right now about seeking out the church. Patrick's call only reinforced her feelings. The Lord had turned His back on her again.

Nearly a week later, Grace had a call of another sort. Noah and Cindy needed her for another practice. She and Cindy had spoken several times since they'd met. The fledgling friendship reminded Grace of a time, years earlier, when she'd spent more time with friends than in concentrating on her career. She hadn't thought it was something she missed, but now she wondered.

The pace in Rosewood seemed to allow for more introspection. Grace realized that she had excess time because she wasn't working, but it was more than that.

Every hour of every day in Houston had been packed, brimming with activity.

Now, as she watched out the window, Grace wondered if this was simply part of healing, these different feelings about things once familiar. She would ask Noah.

Expecting him any minute now for what he called a new approach to therapy, she also wondered if it was normal for her to look forward so much to seeing her doctor.

And that she couldn't ask Noah.

The Porsche turned in to the driveway, its sleek lines gleaming in the late-afternoon sun. The sun also lit Noah's dark, thick hair. There was both energy and strength in his movements. It struck her again that it was hard to believe he was still unattached.

Walking to the door, she opened it just moments after he knocked.

"Well, hello," he greeted her, clearly surprised by the speed of her response.

"I saw you coming up the walk," she explained. This man had seen her worst scars, yet she didn't want him to know how much she enjoyed watching him.

"Am I late?"

"No. I'm early."

He didn't question her response. "Then I take it you're ready?"

Grace swallowed, hoping she wasn't making a mistake. "I think so."

Noah had been asking her to come to the church to practice on the organ, believing it would be good for her more damaged hand. Having kept at the exercises he imposed, she was beginning to have some slight movement in her right hand.

And he had convinced her that this was another step in her therapy. In a weak moment, she told herself.

Because she hadn't intended to go back to the Rosewood Community Church, despite encouragement from Noah, Ruth and now Cindy. But it had been difficult to argue against Noah's reasoning.

As they drove through town, Grace marveled at all the people who recognized Noah and waved to him. "I think you could run for mayor and win."

He laughed. "A doctor in a town this size is well-known. Occupational hazard."

"And the Porsche is hard to miss."

"Don't I know it. But it was impossible to turn down."

She turned to stare at him. "You mean it was a gift?"

"From a grateful patient. I refused at first—told him to donate the money to the Rosewood Medical Foundation. He said he'd donate twice the value of the Porsche, provided I accepted the car as well. The foundation was in its beginning stages and I couldn't say no."

She studied him. "That's a big tribute to your work."

"I was only doing my job, which I tried to explain

to him. But when it comes to people's children, emotions overrule logic."

"You operated on his child?"

"Yes. His daughter was burned in a camping accident and he was distraught."

"But you were able to help her?"

Noah glanced over at her. "Yes. And the child has a bright future."

Grace cleared her throat. "Is that a pep talk?"

"*You* asked about the Porsche."

"So I did." She paused. "And maybe I do need a pep talk today."

"Which is bothering you more—therapy on that hand, or going to the church?"

"Everything has been so jumbled since the accident—it's difficult to sort out a lot of things."

"I can understand that."

"You have a unique perspective, having been on both sides of this—patient's family and physician."

"My mother's accident impacted me a lot. Not only did it guide my career, it taught me what was valuable."

Grace remained quiet for the next few minutes as they completed the short drive to the church. Once out of the car, Noah didn't turn toward the rec hall. Instead he walked to the doors of the sanctuary. Taking out a key, he put it in the lock.

Grace watched in surprise.

He caught the question in her eyes. "I have a key

because I'm the music director. And I work with the youth, through the music program, so the key comes in handy."

She realized he was more than a simple churchgoer. He was clearly committed to the church despite his already crowded schedule. "You enjoy it, don't you?"

"Yes. You know how I feel about music. And the kids are a bonus."

"Does that come from having a large family? Liking kids, I mean."

"I suppose so. I just hate the thought of a kid failing or not reaching his potential because no one took an interest in him."

Never having known a man like him, Grace was overwhelmed by his sense of honor.

When she didn't speak, he took her elbow, leading her inside. The sanctuary was quiet, dimly lit. But as she glanced farther inside, she saw sunlight flowing in from the stained glass windows, the bright beams piercing the interior, glancing over the pews.

They walked up the wide center aisle and Grace felt a bittersweet rush of feeling. She could see her mother's smiling face, then the pain on her father's. It was a sense of homecoming, yet a sense of betrayal. Confused, she followed Noah up the steps to the organ.

He gestured to the bench. Hesitantly she sat down. When Noah joined her, she felt immediate relief. It occurred to her that the physical pain of this new therapy might fall far short of the emotional distress.

He leafed through the music, put one piece on top and quietly began to play. The artistry he demonstrated in the operating room spun from his fingers, his song filling the empty room.

Grace closed her eyes against the emotion the notes evoked. Beneath his hands, the music spoke of beauty. It reached out to her, touched her. Swallowing against the sudden lump in her throat, Grace acknowledged how much she missed the tactile feel of the piano keys, the beauty of the notes.

Finishing the piece, Noah took her hand. She would have resisted the gesture, but knew he was acting only as her doctor. The formerly massive bandages had been reduced so that the fingers of her right hand were now fully exposed. They were stiff and unresponsive, but that didn't deter him.

He put her through the warm-up exercises they had been doing. Then Noah stretched out her fingers, gently placing them on the keys. When they didn't respond, he covered them with his own larger fingers, pressing on them gently.

Grace bit her lips. She was used to the pain of stretching her hand, but this wasn't the same.

Aware of his touch in a different way, she held her breath as he carefully moved her hand in unison with his. It was as though they held hands. And, to her surprise, her skin tingled beneath his. Of course it did, she told herself. After all, it had been months since she'd held a man's hand.

Intensely aware of her terribly flawed appearance, Grace swallowed, hoping her feelings would subside. Afraid to look at him, she stared instead at the organ keys, quiet pressing around her.

A sudden noise in the back of the church made them both look up at the same time.

A teenaged boy hurried up the aisle. "Noah?" The boy didn't stop, charging toward them.

Grace shrank back as Noah rose.

"Robert?" Noah questioned as he walked down the steps. "What is it?"

"Your office said you might be here." The boy was breathless, perspiring.

"Take a breath. What's wrong?"

Making certain she couldn't be seen, Grace peeked around the organ, seeing the teenager's distress.

Robert's breathing slowed as he held out a wrinkled piece of paper. "The scores on my college admission tests."

Noah accepted the letter. "You're a junior. You'll have another chance to take them."

"My English scores aren't going to get better if I take the test a dozen times, Noah." The boy's voice dulled with discouragement. "And if I blow the test I won't get my scholarship."

"There are no problems without answers, Robert. You know that."

Robert shook his head. "If I don't get the scholarship, I won't be able to go to college."

"Then we'll have to find you an English tutor."

"You know my dad got laid off. There's no money for a tutor. I give the pay from my summer job to my mom to help out. It's what I want to do, but still that doesn't leave any extra."

Noah placed an arm over the boy's shoulders. "Robert, I promise we'll work this out. I wish I were better at English. Science was my strong suit. We'll think of something, though."

"I never thought about what I'd do if I didn't get to go to college," Robert said in a defeated voice.

Grace felt her heart go out to the young man. Although she had been on her own when only a few years older, the sale of her parents' home had left her enough money to attend college without worry.

She watched Robert as he confided in Noah. The boy should be rewarded for working to help his family, not penalized for their situation.

She admired Noah's deft handling of the boy. Clearly he had a good relationship with the youth for Robert to show such trust in him.

It was a shame that Robert was having trouble with English. That had been her best subject in school.

An idea crashed into her thoughts. *She could help the young man.* And money wouldn't be an issue.

But could she handle it?

Grace was quiet as they finished the day's therapy, distracted by thoughts of the defeated-looking teenager.

As they drove the short distance to her home, Grace kept imagining how it would have felt to be in the boy's shoes, to doubt you even had a future.

"You're awfully quiet," Noah commented.

"Just thinking about Robert. That's a big burden for someone so young."

"He's resourceful."

"He shouldn't have to be. He should be enjoying this time. It's supposed to be carefree, not fraught with worry over whether he has a future." Her mind made up, she turned in her seat. "Noah, I could tutor Robert."

Stopped at a traffic light, he looked over at her in surprise. "You?"

"I'm no teacher, but English was my minor."

He studied her. "I'm just surprised."

"I guess I am, too." Grace knew she might have given up on herself, but not on others. Especially the young man.

"Robert's a good kid. His family's had a rough time, but he's still concentrating on his grades. With the right schooling, I think he'll make a lot of his future."

"Then we'll have to make sure that happens," Grace said with a confidence she didn't feel.

Meeting Noah's gaze, she glimpsed the approval in his eyes.

And was terrified to realize how much that mattered.

Chapter Seven

Grace was nervous. Noah had driven Robert to her apartment, introduced him and stayed for a short while. But now as she closed the door behind Noah, Grace felt unsure of herself.

"Miss Stanton?"

She turned toward the boy.

"Yes, Robert?"

"Well, before we started, I just wanted to say something…."

Grace braced herself.

"It's really great of you to help me. Noah told me about your high-profile career, how accomplished you are. And I want you to know I won't disappoint you."

"Of course you won't," she replied in a rush of relief.

"And I'm going to pay you."

"I don't want your money, Robert. It's my pleasure to help you."

"If you won't take money, then I'll work it off," he insisted.

Seeing the pride in his eyes, she wavered. "I don't have a lot of work that needs to be done. But my aunt Ruth could probably use a hand with her yard."

His eyes lit up. "Sure."

She couldn't prevent a smile at his enthusiasm. "Then I guess we'd better get started. Let's sit at the table."

He followed her instructions and she was relieved that he wasn't staring at her. When they had first been introduced, she'd seen the look in his eyes that struck most people when they saw her extensive bandages. But she guessed that Noah had briefed him, because Robert didn't ask any questions.

As Noah had told her, Robert was extremely bright. And he was a diligent student. But she could see that he would need quite a bit of instruction. His strengths were in science and math. She couldn't help wondering if a lack of interest had caused the deficiency in his literary knowledge.

So she talked to him about his other interests, hoping that she could think of a way to tie them in to the classics he needed to conquer. And Grace found herself relaxing and enjoying the chat.

There was a quiet knock on the door. Grace glanced at the clock, surprised to see how much time had passed.

The door opened and Ruth peered around the edge. "Am I interrupting?"

"Not at all. We're finished for today."

Ruth walked inside. "Great. I brought cookies."

"Umm. Chocolate chip." Grace turned to Robert. "She makes the best cookies in the world. I have milk and soda. Which do you want with your cookies?"

He decided quickly. "Milk."

"The only drink for cookies," Ruth agreed, taking the milk from the refrigerator and filling three glasses.

"Living next door to my aunt is like having a twenty-four-hour restaurant and bakery on the premises," Grace confided as she reached for a cookie.

Grinning, Robert took another cookie when Ruth held out the plate. "Thanks."

Companionably they munched on the cookies.

Robert drained his glass, then reached for his notebook. "I'd better be going."

Grace thought of his struggling family and made her voice casual. "Robert, could you do us a favor and take the rest of the cookies? We're watching our calories and if the cookies are around we'll blow our diets."

Robert seemed to accept her story at face value. "Sure. They're awesome cookies."

After he left, Ruth met Grace's gaze. "He's a nice boy."

"Yes, he is."

"And it looks as though your tutoring went well."

Grace smiled. "I think so. And thanks for picking up on the cookie story."

Ruth shrugged. "You told me about his family. We have enough, and I like to share what the Lord's blessed me with."

Grace sipped her milk, avoiding a reply.

That didn't deter Ruth. "I had a phone call from Patrick."

"Hmm."

"He didn't have the phone number to your apartment. I had a convenient attack of old age and couldn't place your number. Want to tell me what's going on?"

Grace fiddled with the paper napkin. "I didn't think you'd need one after the demonstration the other night."

"I have been wondering why he hasn't been to visit since you've come to Rosewood."

"I wondered about that for about two weeks, then the answer was pretty clear. Remember, he had dozens of excuses while I was in the hospital in Houston."

Ruth frowned. "I assumed you discouraged him from visiting."

"Somewhat. But wouldn't you think he'd come anyway?"

Ruth's face revealed her opinion, even though she didn't voice it.

So Grace pressed. "I see you've got an opinion. Out with it."

"It doesn't matter what I think. This is your life, Grace. I can fuss and hover and love you to pieces, but I can't determine what's in your heart. I will say that I think you deserve a man who's strong…as strong as you are."

Grace looked at her aunt in surprise. "You think I'm strong?"

"Of course you are. You always have been."

Grace thought of the fear and uncertainty that had become her life. "I'm not so sure."

"It's taken a great deal of courage to come this far. Early in your life you faced great loss and stayed strong. You've survived injuries that would have killed most people. And it took strength to offer to tutor young Robert."

Grace started to protest.

Ruth waved away the words. "You risked rejection and that always requires courage, my dear." She paused. "I think the Lord is closer than you're ready to acknowledge. Because He gives us courage."

Looking down at the well-polished table, Grace saw her distorted reflection. Closing her eyes, she thought of all the loss. Her mother, her father…now her life and career as she had known them. And Patrick.

Funny, if their situations had been reversed, she would have glued herself to his side. She'd thought she had tested him in all the ways that had mattered before she had agreed to marry him.

Perhaps there was no man capable of sticking by through such a horrendous accident. A picture of Noah flashed through her thoughts. But that wasn't a fair comparison. He was her doctor. If he'd been in her life simply as a man, he probably would have run as quickly as Patrick had.

Ruth's voice was gentle. "What should I tell Patrick if he calls back?"

Grace looked at her ruined hands. "I doubt it matters." And though she was able to utter the words in a matter-of-fact voice, the hurt still sliced through her.

How could he have claimed to love her, then deserted her?

It was evident to Grace that Cindy and Katherine were good and close friends. Their rapport was easy, natural. Yet Grace was still nervous, meeting yet another stranger.

"Isn't this house fabulous?" Katherine was asking. "Cindy decorated it before she and Flynn decided to get married."

The comment intrigued Grace. She guessed it was meant to. "It's amazing that she knew his tastes so well."

Cindy placed an interesting-looking salad on the table. "It was his way of letting me know he appreciated me for myself, not as a substitute for my sister."

Even though Cindy sounded matter-of-fact, Grace hesitated.

Cindy noticed and smiled. "It's all right. I know the road to our marriage was unusual, to say the least."

"We both chose the hard way," Katherine added.

Grace wondered at Katherine's story, almost as much as she wondered about the fact that she was a female minister. "But you're happy now?"

"Ecstatic," Katherine replied. "And I know how lucky I am."

"Good men are hard to find," Grace agreed, unable to keep all the bitterness from her voice. Immediately she regretted it, not wanting to put a damper on the luncheon Cindy had planned. "Sorry. I'm off men at the moment."

"I've been there," Cindy said, offering a basket of rolls. "And I didn't have any easy answers, either."

Grace looked at the faces of the two concerned women. Faces that were whole, lovely. She appreciated their overtures of friendship, but neither could understand how she felt. She pushed the salad around on her plate, noticing the sunflower seeds and dried cranberries. But she had no appetite.

Katherine and Cindy exchanged an anxious glance.

"I know we can't truly understand what you're going through," Katherine said. "We haven't walked in your shoes, so to speak. But we want to understand, to offer our support."

"That's incredibly kind of you," Grace replied, unable to tamp down the mountain of sadness welling inside.

"It's an occupational hazard," Katherine replied, her eyes filled with concern.

"I don't need a minister," Grace replied. "I appreciate the offer, but—"

"How about a friend?" Katherine interjected.

"Me, too," Cindy added.

Grace felt her throat thicken. "You're both being so wonderful."

"Nothing of the sort!" Cindy objected. "Friends are the treasures of life."

"Absolutely," Katherine chimed in.

"I'm overwhelmed."

"Good. In that case, we can draft you to help with the Rainbow class." Cindy raised her eyebrows to punctuate the remark.

Panic replaced gratitude. "I don't think—"

"Children are very accepting," Katherine told her gently. "But don't let Cindy bully you into helping before you're ready."

"Me? Bully?" Cindy eyed them with mock outrage. "Would I do that?"

Katherine laughed. "When our church was nearly destroyed by fire, Cindy was climbing all over the scaffolding and dragging along anyone she could find to help. Don't fall for that innocent look of hers."

Some of Grace's tension subsided. "I'll remember that."

Cindy groaned. "Katherine, how can I muster volunteers with you around?"

"Oh, I'm quite sure you'll manage," Katherine replied tartly.

Cindy rolled her eyes. "See what I have to put up with?"

"I imagine you hold your own," Grace replied.

Katherine and Cindy both chuckled. And Grace relaxed a fraction more.

Cindy refilled the glasses with a special limeade. "You'll have to meet our husbands."

"Another time," Katherine added. "And the kids, if you want to brave them. We've got quite a tribe between us."

"I'm not sure I'm ready to meet that many new people."

Katherine clucked sympathetically. "Sorry. Our enthusiasm sometimes outruns our good sense. Let's just enjoy today. Tomorrow will sort itself out." She picked up a roll. "Do you know Cindy makes these from sprouted wheat? They're good in spite of that."

Grace swallowed. She was grateful that they were smoothing over things. But it drove home the starkness of the truth.

Her life would never, ever be the same.

It had been a long day. After lunch, the women had talked, exclaimed over the newest photos of the children and whiled the hours away.

Exhausted, Grace wanted to do nothing but crawl under a comforter and relax in front of an old movie. But she knew Ruth would be expecting a report on the visit.

Taking the back way, Grace entered through the kitchen. Seeing it was empty, she pushed open the swinging door to the living room.

And stopped straightaway.

Patrick sat on the couch beside Ruth.

Seeing Grace, he rose.

Ruth's words trailed off as she, too, caught sight of her niece.

"Grace, we were just talking about you," Patrick greeted her.

"I bet."

He looked shocked by her abrupt response.

Ruth's face filled with concern. "Grace, I'm sure you're tired after your long day."

Patrick didn't take the hint. "We have a lot to talk about, don't we, Grace?"

"Do we?"

The smile on his handsome face stretched thin. "Are you going to answer every question with a question?"

"Does that bother you?" she asked perversely.

"I haven't heard about the progress you've made yet." He angled his head, studying her. "You have fewer bandages than I thought you would."

Immediately self-conscious, she lost her edge. "Oh."

"Her surgeries have gone well so far," Ruth interjected.

Patrick's gaze wandered over Grace. "You've already had some plastic surgery?"

Grace winced beneath the layers of gauze. All of the pain she'd gone through since the accident focused into one sharp jabbing wave.

"Grace doesn't like to talk about the procedures," Ruth said hastily.

"Oh…sorry." Patrick looked first at Ruth, then at Grace. "I figured you'd be used to it by now."

Grace found her voice. "I'm not sure that ever happens."

"We can talk about it over dinner," Patrick replied. "Surely there's a restaurant open, even in Rosewood."

Staring at him, Grace wondered how he could be so completely clueless. As though she could possibly feel comfortable in such a situation. "It probably wouldn't be up to your standards."

"Probably not," he replied with a smile. "But I can rough it for one evening."

"I already have dinner started," Ruth intervened. "Why don't you stay and join us?"

Grace wasn't sure whether to thank or strangle her aunt.

Patrick glanced at his watch. "I can't stay too long. I have an early meeting in the morning."

It hadn't occurred to Grace that Patrick would have

driven all the way from Houston for such a short visit. "Ruth, perhaps Patrick and I can talk now. Then he can get back on the road sooner."

Ruth, always a gracious hostess, rose. "I'll be in the kitchen if you need me."

The quiet swish of the door swinging closed behind Ruth was the only sound for a few moments.

"So, what brings you here, Patrick?"

"You, of course."

"Of course?" She angled her head so that the bandaged side was farther away from him. "I don't think that's a given. Certainly not after all this time."

"I was afraid that might be a sticking point," he replied ruefully, his boyish grin urging her to forgive what he considered a mild trespass.

"A sticking point? You weren't even certain I would survive when you walked away. And since then…" Raw pain choked off her voice.

"Look, I'm sorry, Grace. It was a foolish, cowardly thing to do. But I'd never had any experience with sick people."

"I wasn't *sick*. I was injured, nearly killed. It's not quite the same thing as having a tiff that can be patched up with flowers or chocolates."

He frowned. "You sound as though you don't *want* to patch up things."

Her caustic laugh was laced with pain. "That's convenient for you, isn't it? Lay the blame on me. You walk away unscathed, able to tell everyone how you tried and how unreasonable I was."

"Clearly you're not thinking straight. Perhaps I should come back when you're feeling better."

"That may not happen."

Patrick stood up. "I'll call you."

She couldn't reply without lashing out, so she remained quiet.

He walked to the front hall, then turned back for a moment. "Goodbye, Grace."

"Goodbye." It was all she could manage, and even that single word was an incredible effort.

As she watched him through the window, she saw that he checked his watch as he walked to his car. She guessed his mind had already skipped ahead to his next obligation.

That's all she was to him anymore. An obligation. An uncooperative one, at that.

Chapter Eight

Nearly two weeks later, Noah stood at the barbecue pit in his backyard, gazing at the hot coals. Friends were starting to filter through the gate, and the low rumble of conversation scattered around him.

He hadn't invited too many people. The members of his band, friends from church and his family. Then, on an impulse, he'd invited Grace and her aunt.

Although he had intended to broaden the distance between them, he was worried about Grace. Her depression was a visible thing and Ruth had again asked for his help. He hadn't been able to refuse.

He thought Grace would be comfortable at the barbecue. She had met everyone he had invited except for his family. The open acceptance she'd received from Cindy, Katherine, Robert and the members of his band had given her the courage to risk meeting a few people.

When his friends had heard about Grace's unfortunate accident, each had been eager to help her ease into new situations and become a part of the community. Cindy and Katherine had convinced her to meet their families, and she had done well on those outings.

Still, he knew Grace was anxious. This would be her first group situation. He didn't count the numerous times she went to his office or the hospital. There she was in the company of other injured or ill people.

Noah had told Grace that he had also invited his family. When she balked, he reminded her of his mother's accident. His family had heard about Grace and wanted to meet her.

His mother, in particular, had felt an instant empathy with Grace when she'd heard her story. But all of his family was sensitive to the injuries Grace had received.

Even though her anxiety was visible, Grace reluctantly agreed that she would meet them, as well.

Leaving the grill, Noah checked the long table he had set up on the rear deck to hold the food. Everyone would bring a dish—salads, baked beans and desserts. His specialty was barbecuing brisket, a long, slow process that made the meat tender and succulent.

He reached for a few more folding outdoor chairs to add to the ones he had already set up in the yard. The large lawn was one of the many things he liked about his nineteenth-century home. The generous grassy area was only a portion of the acreage that had come with the house. There was still plenty of land in slowly growing Rosewood, so there wasn't a rush to reduce yards to the postage-stamp size often found in larger cities.

For the most part, Noah had kept the integrity of the original house. He liked the faded brick, the tall, distinctive gables and the charm only age could provide.

He had added the wide, long wraparound deck to the rear of the house, but he hadn't sacrificed any of the tall, aged trees that provided enough shade to cool the hottest Texas days. They, along with decades-old rosebushes and gardenias, defined the large space, making it cozy, inviting.

Glancing around the yard, Noah realized he had made more preparations for this barbecue than any social event he could remember.

This fact should have made him reconsider the gathering. He knew better than to invest his emotions in a patient.

Hearing a noise at the side gate, Noah walked across the yard and saw the object of his thoughts. "Grace, welcome."

She smiled, glancing around anxiously. "Hi."

Ruth was only a few steps behind. "Noah, I can smell that brisket a block away!"

Having always liked this spunky, caring woman, he found it easy to joke with her. "Meets with your approval, then?"

"You cooked the beef slow, didn't you?"

He grinned. "Yes, ma'am."

"I may never leave, then," she declared, walking toward the brick pit at the other side of the yard.

Grace glanced around nervously. "Is your family here?"

He took her elbow. "They should be here any time now. My family's really looking forward to meeting you."

He could see her swallow. "Me, too."

"It's all right to be nervous. But you'll see how easy they are to be with."

"It's still so difficult…." She paused. "I want that to change, though."

"Then it will."

"Just like that?"

"You're doing something about it. You could have refused to come today, or to meet the people you have so far."

She nodded reluctantly. "I suppose so. But my behavior is so different from what it once was. I was accustomed to dealing with large numbers of people on a daily basis."

Noah thought of her executive career. "And you thrived on it."

"Yes. But I can't resume my old life with my new face."

He studied her expression. "And if we succeed with the surgery?"

She looked pensive. "I'm afraid to speculate on that."

Spotting Cindy approaching, he didn't comment. If he succeeded with Grace's surgery, she would go back to Houston. He wasn't sure why that was unsettling.

After greeting Noah, Cindy linked her elbow with Grace's and together they strolled toward the deck.

Michael Carlson and Flynn Mallory approached Noah. Both were good friends. At one time Flynn had misconstrued Noah's friendship with Cindy.

But after Flynn and Cindy were engaged, Flynn thawed. And since their marriage, a genuine friendship had grown between Flynn and Noah.

Flynn glanced toward Grace, who was still chatting with Cindy. "She's holding up pretty well."

"It's early, though." Noah casually glanced in her direction, as well. "I hope this isn't too much for her."

Michael's gaze narrowed. "Is there more to you and Grace than doctor and patient?"

Despite his confused feelings, Noah shook his head. "No."

Michael's gaze reflected a shared understanding. "There's no crime in having your relationship evolve into one of another sort. I'm living proof of that."

Noah glanced at her again. "Even if she weren't my patient, Grace is a big-city woman. There's nothing for her in Rosewood."

"I wouldn't say that," Flynn interjected.

"Michael, Katherine's signaling for you."

"Ah. She probably needs help with the lawn chairs in the car."

As Michael left, Noah spotted his parents arriving. Of all the people he knew, his mother could best relate to Grace. But he also wondered if her residual scarring would be off-putting to Grace.

He kissed his mother's taut cheek. Her scars had never bothered him, other than for any distress it might cause her. However, Abigail Brady had assured him she was satisfied with her face. She had been an exceptionally attractive woman before the accident, but she hadn't mourned the loss.

Yet he had offered to find her another surgeon if she wished to pursue more restorative surgery. But she insisted she had made peace with the results.

His father, Joseph, glanced around the yard. "Hello, son."

"She's over there," Noah told him, reading the question on his father's face. "With Cindy."

"Your brothers and sisters should be arriving soon," his mother added. "Danielle has to work late, but everyone else should be more or less on time."

His pack of siblings were as different as the colors in a crayon box. But that made them more interesting, in his opinion.

"Dad, do you want to take a look at the barbecue pit?"

Joseph's glance was pointed. "Subtle, Noah. No problem. I'll make myself scarce while you introduce your mother to your young lady."

Noah raised his eyebrows.

"Fine," his father amended. "Your patient."

Joseph headed toward the old brick pit, and Noah's mother took his arm. "Don't mind your father. You know what a hopeless romantic he is."

"That's because he lassoed the greatest girl on the planet."

She smiled softly. "Don't tell him, but I got the best part of the bargain. So, how's Grace handling the barbecue so far?"

"She looked nervous when she arrived, but Cindy's put her at ease."

"It helps to have a friend."

"I'm hoping you will be one, as well," Noah confided.

"Let's see which way the wind blows, shall we?"

"Mother, I don't think Grace is so shallow that she'll pull back because you have a few scars."

"I'm not suggesting she is. But I remember how it felt at that stage—the fear, the disbelief. It's terrifying to believe you'll never be pretty again."

"You're lovely, Mother."

"And you're a sweet boy. But it's more than a *few* scars. Luckily, treatment has come a long way. And she's fortunate that you're her doctor." Abigail smiled again. "Now, hadn't you better introduce me to Grace before the rest of the pack gets here?"

"That's a wonderful way to speak of your other children," he said with a grin.

She raised one eyebrow. "*Other?* You're one of that pack."

Chuckling, Noah led her across the lawn. He was glad to see that Cindy was off gathering soft drinks. This was an introduction he preferred to have without an audience.

Grace turned toward him, glancing at his mother, as well.

Noah introduced them. To his relief, Grace smiled warmly at his mother. "I'm so glad to meet you, Mrs. Brady."

"Please call me Abigail."

Grace looked at the woman who had raised such a kind, strong son. And she saw the same qualities shining in her eyes. "I'd like that, Abigail."

Noah quietly moved away.

And Abigail studied Grace. "Noah was right."

Grace suddenly felt nervous. "About what?"

"You're warm and friendly."

Grace's lips trembled. "I'm afraid I haven't been since I've come to Rosewood."

Abigail nodded in understanding. "It's hard to be yourself when you're not sure exactly who that is anymore."

It was a tremendous relief to speak with someone who could relate so completely. "I haven't really been able to talk to anyone about it."

"Because they're eager to give you assurances they can't be sure of themselves. And they can't truly understand how it feels."

Grace sighed. "I know it sounds ridiculous, but it's as though I'm the first person who ever faced this. Of course I know I'm not—"

"But it still seems that way. And few of us have someone to soften the way, to clue us in on how we'll feel."

"I've had so many questions, so many doubts...."

Abigail met her eyes. "And those will continue until you're certain of the final results. But that's not a bad thing. I'm convinced it's human nature. I can tell you it gets better, though."

"Were you able to go back to your former life?" Grace asked, hoping she wasn't offending the other woman.

"Yes. And it made me realize how precious each day is. And the feeling didn't fade. I still wake up mornings grateful for my husband and family, for all my blessings."

Grace nodded.

"I imagine it's far too early for you to feel that way. You have more surgeries ahead of you. But luckily you have a premier surgeon to perform them."

Smiling, Grace acknowledged the words. "I think he's far more talented than the doctors in Houston. Look." With great effort she stretched the fingers of her right hand slightly. "They told me this would never happen, but Noah refused to believe it."

"That's my boy."

"And he's an exceptional one."

Abigail smiled, her voice soft. "Yes, he is. Most surgeons of his caliber would still be living in a big city, raking in a fortune. I don't know if he told you, but when I had my accident, it bankrupted the family. All of our money was gone nearly at once with the overwhelming medical bills. And then there was the cost of moving to Houston to get the care I needed. The people of Rosewood donated enough money to make sure we had everything we needed. Without them, well…we might not be having this discussion. Their generosity made a huge impact on Noah. He was driven to give back to them. And he also wanted to make sure no other family had to go through what we did—being uprooted, leaving our home simply to get proper medical care. So he established a foundation."

Grace was intrigued. "I heard him mention the foundation once, but he didn't say what it was for."

"It's to provide money for medical care to any Rosewood citizen who needs but can't afford it. Noah holds fund-raisers to bring in money for new equipment."

"Is the foundation working?"

Abigail smiled. "To date, they haven't turned away a single person in need. And our hospital keeps up with the evolving technology."

"That's amazing." Grace met Abigail's gaze. "You're proud of him."

"He makes that easy." Abigail's voice softened. "And Noah's proud of you."

Shocked, Grace looked at her in surprise. "Me? Whatever for?"

"Your courage. He knows from firsthand experience how difficult that can be to muster."

"I don't have courage," Grace confessed. "I'm scared most of the time."

"It takes courage to simply be standing here today."

"That was Noah's doing!"

"You are a sweet girl." Abigail glanced over toward her son. "Noah was right about that, as well."

Grace guessed that the unbandaged portion of her face was pinkening with both pleasure and embarrassment.

"I was afraid you might have been put off once you saw me," Abigail continued.

Grace looked at her in astonishment. "Why?"

Abigail reached up to touch her cheek that still bore the scars of the explosion. "For obvious reasons."

"This may sound crazy—" Grace hesitated, "—but I could see the kindness in your eyes, and my first impression was how lovely you are."

Abigail's wise, knowing eyes misted. "You are a rare treasure."

Grace bit her lips, willing away the tears of sudden emotion. "I'm going all wobbly."

"Even strong women like ourselves need to lean now and then."

"Thank you for talking to me. I don't know if it stirs painful memories—"

"Not really. The pain is all in the past for me."

Grace wondered if she would ever truly feel that way.

Abigail glanced across the yard. "I'm glad you're up to meeting new people, because my clan's a crowd in itself. My husband and children are headed this way."

Grace could hear the fondness in Abigail's voice and she saw the love shining in her eyes. In that moment Abigail's scarring seemed to disappear.

Noah's siblings were as welcoming as he had promised. Their mother's accident had heightened their sensitivity. And to her relief, they acted refreshingly normal. They joked, laughed and teased her and each other.

It had been difficult to be treated as a fragile flower. Today she was an ordinary petunia, rather than a rare, exotic orchid.

Glancing around the yard, Grace marveled at the number of people she had allowed in her life because of Noah. It hadn't been that long since she had been frightened to meet Cindy. And the circle continued to widen.

These were good, kind people. They were far different from the people she had met while fast-tracking her career in Houston. Those people had sent flowers at the time of the accident, but not one had taken a personal interest.

Yet the people of Rosewood rallied like old friends. Glancing across the lawn, Grace realized the force behind their commitment.

It was Noah who tied them all together.

An unexpected lump lodged in her throat. She was his project. Everything today was evidence of that—the carefully chosen guests, the talk with his mother.

For all that she was grateful to Noah for what he had done, she hated to think she had become a cliché. A patient becoming too attached to her doctor.

And a woman who could no longer trust her own judgment.

Chapter Nine

"I'm honored," Cindy announced the following week, studying her menu. "I've never been part of a therapy celebration."

"I hope I'm not being too optimistic," Grace replied. "But I have a good feeling about the progress with my hand."

Cindy nodded. "I can understand that. You have a great doctor."

Grace thought of all the stories she had heard about Noah from his mother and his friends. "He's beginning to sound like Saint Noah."

Shrugging, Cindy reached for a packet of sugar. "It's hard to find many men like him. He gives up his own social life to hold fund-raisers for his foundation. He's managed to involve the entire community in bake sales, car washes and festivals. Katherine says he does more on his own than her entire fund-raising committee for the church." Cindy stirred the sugar into her iced tea. "And that's only one part of him. He volunteered to be the music director, and not only has it revitalized the choir, he's drawn in the youth. The church isn't large enough to afford a separate youth minister, but Noah's filled the gap. He has a natural way with young people. They trust him and he never lets them down."

Grace thought of Patrick and how he had let her down. "Noah sounds too good to be true."

Cindy's expression grew contemplative. "I suppose so. But he's for real."

Grace drew a line through the drops of condensation on her glass. "Do you see everyone this clearly?"

"Everyone, or men?"

Grace considered hedging, but Cindy was becoming a good and trusted friend. "Men."

"Ah. There I have less than twenty-twenty vision. You've heard my story. But I do have my moments. Why?"

Grace told her about Patrick, the plans they had made and her disappointment in him after the accident.

"Whew. That's tough. Do you think he just got taken for a loop? That he really can come through for you?"

Grace hesitated. "I keep wondering how I didn't see him clearly. And if that means I don't have the ability to judge a man for what he really is."

Cindy searched Grace's eyes. "Do you believe Patrick is without any merit?"

"I think he came upon the most difficult thing he'd ever faced and it was too much for him."

"Could he have changed? Perhaps learned from it and grown?"

"Even if he has, I'm not sure I could ever get over my disappointment in him. And it's not because I don't believe in second chances. It's that I'm afraid I didn't know him as I thought I did." She rumpled her napkin. "I agreed to marry Patrick—that should have been the most important decision in my life. And I made a mess of it."

"I waited to marry because it was just as important to me. I thought I'd made an equal mess of things, too." She paused, then met Grace's eyes. "But I never doubted Flynn."

Swallowing, Grace nodded. She should have had the same faith in Patrick. "How did you know for sure?"

Cindy's voice was gentle. "I prayed about it. He's the only one who knows what our future holds, what is truly best for us."

Grace didn't freeze. But her doubts couldn't allow her to agree, either. Surely a kind and loving God wouldn't want to steal away her parents one at a time, leave her alone, then subject her to horrific injuries that ended the career she loved.

"Why don't you try coming to church with me?" Cindy suggested. "You're not likely to work out your doubts about Him alone."

"It's not that simple."

"It rarely is." Cindy met her eyes. "Flynn no longer believed when he became part of my life. And it wasn't easy. He didn't wake up one morning and decide he was ready to accept the Lord again. He had to work through what had pulled him away. And they weren't little problems. It took a lot of forgiveness and soul-searching on his part."

"And now?"

"He's happier than he has been in decades."

Grace wished she could devise a happily-ever-after for herself. "I don't think that's going to work for me."

Cindy didn't press. "You'll know in your own time what will work. That's the beauty of it. All of the Lord's creatures are individuals with free will."

"Right now I have more questions than answers."

"I think that's true for most of us. And it's an ongoing process. Because every day brings new problems, new questions."

Grace thought of the crushing weight she had felt when her father died, when she knew she could no longer count on the faith of her childhood. "I appreciate your advice, but it's not that easy for me."

"I respect your decision, but if you want to talk to anyone who's been through the same experience, Flynn has a good ear. So does Michael Carlson."

Grace frowned. "They both had lapses of faith?"

"Big time."

"But Michael's married to a minister."

"Which is testament to the fact that even the most difficult situations have a solution."

Grace wished that could be true for her, but she didn't believe it would. Still, she didn't want her new friend to feel rebuffed. "I appreciate you lending an ear. And I'm glad it worked out so well for you and Flynn."

Cindy reached for another packet of sugar. "Perhaps it will work out for you as well…when you've decided who the right man is for you."

Grace swallowed a sip of her soda, staring down at her bare left hand. She hadn't worn her engagement ring since the accident.

So who was the right man for her? One who had panicked?

Or one who had guided her over the most torturous route she had ever taken? The same one who was her doctor, she reminded herself. Who would no doubt be amused to learn that she had fallen into such an obvious trap.

But he couldn't find out—she owed him too much for his friendship.

And she was determined to keep it that way.

A few weeks later, Noah stood at the door of Grace's apartment, lifting his hand to knock. Before he could, the door whipped open.

Tim, one of the boys he knew from church, stood in front of him. "Hey, Noah!"

"Hi, Tim. I didn't expect to see you."

"Grace is tutoring me."

Noah blinked. "She is?"

"Yeah. Robert asked her if she would. I've got to get my scores up on my PSAT."

Still surprised, Noah nodded. "Sure."

Grace walked up behind Tim, her gaze going to Noah. "Hi."

"I didn't mean to come at a bad time. I had some extra time and thought we could get in a physical therapy session." Uncomfortably Noah realized he had come to feel proprietary about Grace's time.

"It's a perfect time. Tim and I just finished his lesson."

"See ya," Tim told them both, trotting down the stairs.

Noah still felt a bit confounded. "I didn't realize your tutoring program had grown."

She smiled. "I didn't expect it, either. But some of Robert's friends needed help, as well. And I've enjoyed it more than I thought I would. Come in."

He did, glancing around the tidy apartment, seeing the books and papers on the small table. "And you're all right about meeting new kids?"

"It's funny, but they don't seem to see the bandages. Even the larger ones after my last surgery. I thought it might be worse with teenagers, but their agenda is improving grades. Maybe it's because they're young that they are so accepting. And I work with each on a one-to-one basis. That makes it easier for me."

"That's great." He reached out, touching a leaf on one of the many plants. "You'll have a jungle in here soon."

"Everyone was so generous sending plants after the last surgery. It was especially sweet of your parents—since I'd barely met them."

"Mom said she feels like she knows you."

Grace's eyes softened. "We share a unique bond. And she was so easy to talk with."

"My friends always liked that about her," Noah agreed. "So, should we start on your therapy?"

"I already began."

Noah tried to disregard the prickle of disappointment. "Oh?"

"I made some lemonade. Juicing the lemons gave my left hand quite a workout. But my right one didn't cooperate. So would you like a glass?"

"Sure. I'm glad you're attempting more tasks."

Grace laughed. "I was, too, until I got to about the fifth lemon. Trying to hang on to the lemons with this stubborn right hand, twisting with the left, which is backward to me anyway… Well, I was about ready to start chucking lemons out the windows."

He found himself grinning. "I'd have loved to see that, especially if Ruth caught you midtoss. Trust me, she's merciless."

Grace continued laughing. "Yet you finagled her into growing blackberries."

"Not everyone has my touch."

"So you say," Grace retorted, handing him a glass of iced lemonade.

He held it up to the light. "Should I sift it for seeds?"

She wiggled the wooden stirring spoon at him. "At the peril of your own neck."

He tasted the lemonade. "Hey, this is good."

"Don't sound so surprised," she reproved him.

"And don't get too cocky or I'll draft you to head up a lemonade booth at the next festival."

Her expression turned thoughtful. "That would be fun, but I wouldn't be able to make enough lemonade with these hands."

Instantly he regretted taking her from her light, playful mood. "No problem. We always have volunteers who want to help out—not to mention an electric juicer. We usually have several people in each booth. You could supervise the setup and preparation."

She looked dubious. "And I could stay in the background?"

"If that's what you want."

"Hmm."

"We need to raise enough money to fund some pretty expensive testing equipment for the hospital. Refreshments have a high profit margin."

"If you really think I can help…"

"Don't try to back out," he countered, seeing the light of hope in her changeling eyes, wanting to keep it there.

Grace smiled in a shy fashion she hadn't employed before. "Okay."

"Give me a list of ingredients and I'll make sure they're at the booth."

To his surprise, she shook her head. "No. I want to do that, my contribution."

Although others often did the same thing, they were permanent members of the community with a vested interest in the outcome. "That's generous of you."

"No. It's generous of you to include me in the community. It makes me feel involved, useful." She glanced up at him. "I never learned how to be idle. I don't think I have it in me to be happy without working."

Instantly he thought of her career and all the big-city perks it offered. Things she couldn't be happy without.

Grace glanced at the clock. "It's later than I thought. Would you like to stay for dinner after therapy?"

"My parents are expecting me."

Her expression dimmed. "Oh."

"Why don't you come with me?" he found himself asking, hating to see the light go out of her eyes. "It's just a casual dinner."

"Your mother's not expecting me," she protested.

"With six kids, you always cook enough for anyone they might bring home. Mom still makes enough to feed a small army. And I know she'd be glad to see you."

Grace's eyes today were the greenish-blue of the outfit she wore. They glided into the color of clear, warm ocean water. "It sounds like fun."

"It's noisy, somewhat crazy—yeah, it's fun."

Grace's lips rose in a smile. "Fun can be good."

Seeing the unaccustomed happiness dancing in her eyes, he agreed. "Yes, it can."

Grace wasn't sure exactly what to expect when she walked into the Brady home. But Noah was right. The noise hit her first. At least a dozen different conversations were going on simultaneously. And they didn't stop when she and Noah entered.

His mother noticed them, and a smile lit her face when she recognized Grace. Skirting the long table, Abigail approached them. "Grace, I hope Noah's brought you for dinner."

"If it's not any extra trouble."

Abigail laughed. "Never in this house. Even though two of my children have married, and they've all left home, I can't seem to cook in small portions." She took Grace's good hand. "You remember everyone, don't you?"

"I think so." Grace noticed that there was constant movement in the Brady home. Snatches of conversation floated by as the siblings caught up on the week's activities.

When she'd been young, Grace had dreamed of

having a large family, a mass of brothers and sisters to enliven the house. But there had been no siblings. That was another prayer that had gone unanswered.

When they settled around the table, Abigail took the place at her husband's right. Throughout the chatter, laughter and clinking of china and silverware, Grace was aware of the tender looks that passed between the elder Bradys.

Grace couldn't help wondering just how Joseph saw his wife. Was he aware of her remaining scarring? Or did he still see her as his unmarred, beautiful young bride?

Either way, she guessed they shared an enviable bond. The house echoed with laughter, and their love had spilled over on their children. It was exactly the kind of home Grace had always dreamed of.

Noah leaned closer. "Do you feel like you're having dinner in Grand Central Station?"

"Yes." She smiled. "In a good way. It must have been wonderful growing up in a big family."

"I didn't know anything else, but I wouldn't trade any one of the aggravating, noisy lot. But I can remember envying friends with smaller families. At the time it seemed as though that meant they got a lot more than I did."

"And now you know differently," she guessed.

"The struggles, problems and joys you share have no equal."

Which was what Grace had imagined. "You have a lovely family."

Noah met her gaze. "Thanks. They mean a lot to me."

So much so that he had dedicated his life's work because of them. Grace admired his noble purpose, the fact that he hadn't let anything stand in his way. He possessed great strength, she realized yet again. A strength that drew her.

Once dinner was over, the family filtered off in many directions. With four pairs of hands in the kitchen, Grace could see her slow, awkward efforts weren't needed.

"Noah, why don't you show Grace around the property?" Abigail suggested. "Then we can have ice cream on the porch."

Noah glanced at Grace. "Sound all right to you?"

"Yes to both."

They left by the back door. Grace felt her feet sink into the lush lawn. A Victorian lamppost shed a circle of light near the house. In the distance Grace could see an aged gazebo. And as they strolled into the yard, she first heard, then saw a fountain of natural rock, the slowly moving water lapping over several levels of smooth stone.

Noah pointed out a neatly tended vegetable garden. "Ever since Mom's accident we've kept the garden going. We never had the severe money troubles again, but Mom and Dad didn't want to take any chances. And, in a way, it was our own victory garden."

The scent of ripening cantaloupes and tomatoes reminded Grace of a charming farmer's market she used to frequent in Houston. She hadn't imagined the lure of having fresh fruits and vegetables just steps from the back door.

"I guess I've lived in apartments or condos so long I'd forgotten how special a garden could be. My dad and I planted a tree in memory of my mother in our backyard. He said that I could always reach out and touch the leaves, just as my mother was touching heaven."

"That's a wonderful sentiment."

It was difficult to dredge up a smile. "I suppose so. But after he died I had to sell the house so that I could finish college. I wasn't able to touch the tree anymore." Nor her mother, or her father.

"There are times when I wonder why some people have so much loss and why others seem to go through life unscathed. But His plan's greater than we can see." Noah stopped. "Sorry. I didn't mean to sermonize."

She brushed away the clinging pain of the issue. "It's all right. Just don't expect me to appreciate that plan."

They strolled past latticework nearly obscured by far-flung bougainvillea. "Everyone to their own time," he replied quietly. "Faith rarely works on a schedule."

If at all.

Moonlight streamed over the gleaming gazebo, making it look like a fantasy arbor.

Noah turned to her. "This was my parents' hideout from us when I was a kid. I'd stumble across them every now and then. They'd be holding hands, talking. I used to wonder how they still had so much to talk about when they'd known each other forever." He chuckled. "Considering I was about twelve, fourteen years was definitely forever."

"It sounds as though they were very much in love." She thought a moment, then amended the words. "*Are* still in love."

"You see it?" he asked, surprised.

"Your father looks at your mother as though…"

"She never had the accident?"

Grace nodded.

"I don't think he sees the scars. I do know that he loves her just as much despite them. When she was hurt his biggest fear was that she would die. He never talked about the disfiguring. I don't think that was important to him, just that she survived."

Grace wondered how it would be to know such all-consuming love. One that didn't require explanation, but was a living, nurturing thing. Her mind flashed to Patrick's behavior after her accident, the difference a sharp pain. "That's how love should be," she murmured. "Just like your parents."

Noah met her eyes, his own dark with secrets she couldn't divine. "That's what I think."

Instantly Grace wondered if that was why he had waited so long to find just the right person, why he still hadn't found her. His parents' ideal was a difficult one to live up to.

"If your mother hadn't had her accident, do you think you'd have stayed in Rosewood?"

"That's a complicated question. I might have been lured to the big city, but I wouldn't have had the insider's knowledge I gained by moving there when I was in high school. Then again, I might not have had the opportunities, either."

"And if you hadn't had the opportunity?"

"I think you know what I believe."

The Lord's plan. "What if a person simply chooses to be daring and bold, picking his own career?"

"I imagine that's done thousands of times every day." He stopped beneath a towering magnolia tree. "Do you know how slowly these trees grow?"

Grace looked at him cautiously, aware of the sudden diversion. "Very slowly."

"This tree has been here for a great many years, growing stouter, taller. It seems so permanent that its destiny must have been preordained. But, in fact, a person planted the tiniest seedling."

"Have you taken to speaking in allegories?"

"No, I've taken to walking in the moonlight."

Grace swallowed suddenly, studying his face. She had been intensely aware of the stars, the moonlight. Of him.

Realizing the danger of her thoughts, she only smiled. Grace knew she couldn't let Noah know that her emotions were shifting, that her thoughts constantly turned to him.

"Are you all right?" he asked quietly when she didn't speak.

She nodded, conflicted about her attraction to him.

As she glanced away from him, she saw a big dog running toward them, his tongue lolling to one side.

"Whoa," Noah commanded. But the large dog stopped by hurling himself at Noah, who took the dog's unwieldy weight with aplomb. "Where you been, boy?"

The dog looked adoringly at Noah.

"Has he been out here all along?" Grace asked, realizing she hadn't seen the dog earlier in the evening.

"Probably started chasing rabbits, then it got dark. Columbus has a tendency to roam, always looking for new adventures."

"Columbus?" she asked, her lips twitching. "As in Christopher Columbus?"

"Yep. Spot didn't suit him, so…"

"He doesn't have any spots," she couldn't resist pointing out.

"Columbus is part Lab, part Boxer and part something only his mother knows. But apparently not a breed with spots."

Grace knelt down, petting the friendly dog. Columbus in turn rolled over, presenting his chest to be petted. Grace obliged.

"You've made a friend for life," Noah told her, crouching down as well, watching as she and the dog became acquainted.

"Columbus seems to be a fine friend."

Noah met her gaze. "So he is."

Silence strummed between them, broken only by the sound of the dog's happy panting.

Grace felt her mouth go dry. Surely she imagined the flicker of interest in his expression, the darkening intensity of his eyes. She supposed all of his women patients fell for him. He was not only strong and handsome, he was their rescuer, the one who hoped to heal the worst of their wounds. Thinking it could possibly be more would simply open her up to more pain. And if he turned out like Patrick… It was unthinkable.

Rapidly she rose, afraid to elongate the moment.

Noah rose as well, the dog scrambling up beside them. "The ice cream's probably about ready."

Grace nodded, afraid to trust her voice, afraid it would reveal husky overtones of emotion.

Noah guided her toward the front of the house. "Everyone will be on the porch."

And they were, filling the glider, chairs and steps. Laughter and conversation colored the air.

"What kind of ice cream tonight?" Noah asked his mother.

"Peach. Took your brothers forever to get it all cranked."

"Cranked?" Grace asked in surprise.

Abigail smiled. "In some ways we haven't kept up with the passing centuries."

"She just spoils me," Joseph said, his arm around her shoulders. "No ice cream can compare to hers."

Grace thought of the kitchen in her Houston condo, equipped with high-tech appliances and yards of stainless steel. It had suited her in the city, but now its memory was stark in comparison to this home.

Noah scooped generous portions into two dishes. "I guess this all seems pretty small-town and hokey, doesn't it?"

She accepted the dish he offered. "What makes you say that?"

"I doubt you spent time eating ice cream on the front porch when you were in Houston."

"You're right. But—"

"You'll probably be glad to get back to the big-city pace after you've recovered."

Grace was saddened by the thought of leaving the close-knit community that had become home. "It's what I'm used to."

He nodded, then glanced at her bowl. "How's the ice cream?"

She dipped her spoon into the creamy mixture and tasted. "Incredible. It puts gourmet ice cream to shame."

"The peaches grow here on the property."

"This house seems to have everything," she murmured.

Again the moonlight seemed to fall between them.

"I always thought so," he replied quietly.

A few minutes later Abigail offered refills, which most everyone eagerly accepted. Grace could understand why her own appetite had withered, but she was surprised to see Noah refuse a second bowl.

When the gathering began breaking up, he glanced at her. "Ready? You have surgery on Friday. Probably shouldn't be up too late."

She nodded and they both rose.

Abigail turned to Grace, giving her a gentle hug. "Now that you know the way to our home, you must come often."

Pulling back, Grace warmed with heartfelt appreciation. As she turned, she met Noah's gaze and faltered. Somehow she didn't think he would be bringing her back soon.

And the pain of Patrick's rejection told her that was for the best. If only her heart would listen to her head.

Chapter Ten

Friday rolled around too soon for Noah. Flashes of the night he and Grace had walked in the garden had continued to nudge him. Pulling on a large reserve of self-control, he had cleared his mind to perform her surgery. But the fact that he'd had to do so kept his mood grim. Better than anyone else, he knew how crucial it was to keep his emotions and his job separate.

Glancing up, he saw the recovery nurse approaching on a run. "Dr. Brady. Recovery room two—stat."

Noah felt a chill in his blood that he remembered experiencing only once before. After he'd performed surgery on his girlfriend Jordan.

He pitched the chart he held onto the unit desk, mindless of the rattling bang it made as it landed. Grace Stanton was in the second recovery room.

Noah's long strides outpaced the nurse's steps. The crash cart was in place beside the bed. Scanning

Grace's vitals, he saw that they were plummeting. Memories assaulted him. In that instant Noah realized he cared more for Grace than he had Jordan. Terrified that he had made a fatal error, he read Grace's vitals again and found they were even worse.

As he quickly processed the possible causes, Grace flatlined.

Without hesitation he picked up the paddles. "Clear!"

The emergency team stepped back.

Grace's body jerked under the electrical charge.

Noah held his breath.

One heartbeat registered. Then another.

Automatically Noah issued instructions for stabilizing Grace, forcing away any other thoughts. The team continued working on her.

As they did, Noah ordered more tests, determined not to lose her. Equally determined to find out what had gone wrong.

Training kept Noah's face noncommittal, his mind focused on Grace's survival. She looked so vulnerable, so alone on the gurney. She had been so very close to death.

He didn't leave Grace's side until hours later. Pulling off his sweat-soaked surgical cap, Noah exhaled. Now he could let his torturous thoughts run free.

He'd almost lost her. Another woman he cared about. And one frozen image kept coming to mind again and again—Grace's frightened eyes the first time he'd seen her, how the terror had turned to trust.

Trust he didn't deserve.

Knowing Ruth was waiting anxiously, Noah pushed open the heavy surgical doors. Mindless of the arthritis that plagued her joints, Ruth sprang to her feet. "Noah?"

"She's stable," he replied.

"Something went wrong, didn't it? You said she'd be out hours ago."

"She was." He pulled at the core of his strength. "But there were complications."

Panic flooded the older woman's face and her voice quivered. "Grace?"

"She's all right. Now."

"Oh, Noah. What happened?"

"An embolus, a blood clot, went to her heart."

Ruth's hand flew upward to cover her mouth. "No!"

"I won't lie to you. It was touch and go."

"But I thought this was routine, without risk."

He sighed. "No surgery is without risk. But you're right. This shouldn't have happened. I shouldn't have let it happen."

Ruth placed her hand on his arm. "Noah. I know this isn't your fault."

He stared ahead into the corridor. Now in the

evening it was quiet, uncrowded. "Don't be so sure of that."

Ruth shook her head. "Noah, I trust you. That's not in question. I just don't understand how surgery on her face could cause a blood clot to her heart."

Noah felt the tension deep in the back of his neck. "I've ordered extensive tests. We'll know more after I get the results."

Ruth bit her lip, deep in thought. "Is it possible that the clot was caused by some of her internal injuries?"

"It's possible. I'm consulting with her surgeon in Houston." But he wasn't looking for an easy out.

"Noah, I've known you since you were a boy. I also know you did your very best in that operating room. Don't go looking for blame where there isn't any."

"We almost lost her, Ruth."

She squeezed his arm. "But we didn't. Let's concentrate on that."

Noah talked with her for a while, knowing Ruth would stay around the clock until she was certain Grace was all right.

As he made his way to his office, Noah replayed the surgery in his mind, looking for errors, not able to find a satisfactory conclusion.

Only one fact could not be refuted. He had allowed himself to become personally involved with a patient. It had almost cost Grace her life.

Guilt and regret dominated every thought.

Hours passed, but Noah couldn't make himself leave the hospital. Instead, he kept in constant touch with the intensive care unit.

When that wasn't enough, he prowled the corridors, finding his way to Grace's side again and again.

Close to midnight, Noah walked soundlessly into the ICU. Grace's vitals had improved dramatically, yet he couldn't find peace in that yet. She was still in a remarkably fragile state. It would take so little to disturb the positive balance.

Long lashes shadowed her cheekbone on the unbandaged side of her face. She didn't have to open her eyes for him to know what they looked like. Her changeling eyes were like magic, blue one day, stormy gray another. They matched both her moods and her surroundings. He considered her eyes to be much like the opening of presents on Christmas morning. You might guess their color, or be completely surprised. Either way, it was like having Christmas every day.

Now, however, she was surrounded completely by white. Since she was in ICU, the lights were only marginally dimmer than during the day. There was no quiet, comforting hush of darkness to help her rest. Under constant observation, she couldn't be shrouded in anything other than light.

She slept deeply, a drugged sleep that kept her deathly still.

Grace had been through more than anyone deserved. And now this...

The soft scuff of rubber-soled shoes told him someone was approaching. Unwilling to allow his emotions for Grace to show on his face, he composed his expression and turned away from the bed.

"Dr. Brady. You have a phone call."

Thanking the nurse, Noah walked to the phone on the wall and picked up the receiver. "Dr. Brady."

"Hello. This is Patrick Holden. Sorry to phone so late, but I just got out of a meeting. I'm calling to check on Grace Stanton."

Noah wondered who the man was. "Information can only be released to a relative."

"Oh, well, I'm not...yet."

"Yet?"

"I'm her fiancé. I wasn't able to reach her aunt, but perhaps you could ask Ruth to call me. She has the number."

"Sure." Slowly Noah hung up the phone. *Fiancé?* How could he have spent so much time with Grace and not have known that important bit of news?

Walking back to Grace's bed, he studied her face again. What else hadn't she told him?

It wasn't only her career that was calling her back to Houston, but a man she had pledged her heart to. It should be a relief, he told himself. He couldn't be distracted by a woman who was engaged. His professional and personal lives wouldn't face the threat of being commingled again.

Feet suddenly leaden, he forced himself to relay the message. He told the nurse and then watched her step outside to locate Ruth.

However, it wasn't relief he felt. He couldn't turn off the feelings he already had for Grace.

A woman he apparently could never have.

Still, he returned to her side. At least while she was sleeping she couldn't see the truth in his face.

Grace sighed, a small sound that pulled at him.

He continued to watch her as he wondered about Patrick Holden. And why Grace had never mentioned the man.

Two days later Grace awoke in that peculiar state that felt as though she were both leaden and floating. It was the medication, she knew. That had been explained to her before.

The previous day had been a blur. Vaguely she remembered they had moved her from one place to another. The room she was in had the familiar look of all the other hospital rooms in the past months.

Unable to remember what Noah had said, she wondered how this surgery had gone. She lifted her left hand, now completely free of bandages, to hesitantly touch the new bandages on her face. She couldn't tell anything from the tentative examination.

The bandages did seem thicker. But that happened after each surgery.

Glancing to one side, she saw Ruth slumped in a chair, having fallen asleep while she stood guard. Grace felt a wave of appreciation for her aunt, who had assumed this burden without a moment's hesitation or complaint.

Although her head felt heavy, Grace turned it, seeing several vases of flowers. She couldn't imagine who had sent them all. She also wondered why she felt so weak.

A muted tap sounded on the door, so quiet she could barely hear it. Her own voice was almost as quiet. "Come in."

Looking uncertain, Robert poked his head in. "Is it okay?"

Grace cleared her throat, yet her voice wasn't much stronger. "Yes."

"They said at the desk that you could have visitors, but I didn't want to wake you up."

"You didn't," she assured him.

He pulled a bunch of handpicked flowers from behind his back. "These are from my yard."

"They're beautiful," Grace replied, touched by the boy's gesture.

He glanced over at the vases of florist-arranged flowers. "Mine can't compare to those."

"And none of those were handpicked just for me." She sniffed the bouquet, lush with fat roses. "Nor do any of them smell so wonderful."

Robert grinned. "How do you feel?"

"Kind of woozy right now. But it's taking me less time to recover each time."

"Have there been many surgeries?" he questioned, his eyes filled with curiosity.

"I'm afraid so. It's not something Noah...Dr. Brady can repair quickly."

"He's the best," Robert replied. "A lot of adults just see past teenagers, you know? Like we're some sort of herd instead of different people."

She nodded.

"He doesn't." Robert hesitated. "And you don't, either."

Grace felt a rush of emotion. "Thank you, Robert. That means a lot to me."

He looked embarrassed, but pleased. "When are they going to spring you?"

She smiled at his choice of words. "I'm not sure. When I know, I'll phone you about resuming lessons."

"Okay." He looked over at Ruth, who was still sleeping. "I mowed the lawn this morning early. I hope it's okay."

"I'm sure it is. You know my aunt Ruth. She'll tell you if it isn't."

He grinned. "Yeah. Well, I'd better get going."

"Thanks for visiting, Robert. And for the beautiful flowers."

"Sure." He disappeared quickly, the limit of his teenage self-consciousness reached.

Ruth spoke from the chair, surprising Grace. "So, I'd let him know, huh?"

Although exhausted, Grace smiled. "I wondered how you slept through that exchange."

Ruth stood. "Figured the boy didn't need an audience. Bringing flowers to a teacher is traumatic enough without a witness."

"He's a sweet boy," Grace replied.

"Well, don't ever tell him that! You'd ruin his teenage standing." Ruth moved closer to the bedside and picked up Robert's flowers. "How are you feeling this morning?"

"A little tired," Grace admitted. "Silly, I know. I barely woke up."

"I'll ring the nurse."

Grace glanced around, wondering why they were surrounded by so many machines. "I don't need anything," she protested. Seeing the lines on her aunt's face, Grace reached for Ruth's hand. "You didn't have to stay so long. You're the one who must be exhausted."

"Nah. I'm a tough old bird. Besides, I'd only worry at home."

Grace felt another rush of gratitude. "I'm glad you're here."

Ruth smiled at her niece. "Good. Because you're not getting rid of me."

The nurse entered, going to the bank of machines surrounding the bed, making adjustments.

"Will I live?" Grace asked, wondering again why she had so many more machines this time.

The nurse didn't smile as Grace expected. "You're on a steady course, Miss Stanton." She looked over at Ruth. "I'll let Dr. Brady know she's awake."

Grace wondered why she was suddenly out of her own medical loop. "Ruth?"

Her aunt turned, walking toward the windowsill where several flower arrangements had been placed. "Do you want to know who these are from?"

Distracted, Grace nodded. "There's quite a collection."

As expected, there was a large arrangement from her employer. There was also a tall, dramatic arrangement of exotic flowers from Cindy and Flynn Mallory, and a flourishing, glossy-leafed plant from Katherine and Michael Carlson. Noah's parents had sent a spring bouquet filled with bright color.

Surprised and touched, Grace listened as Ruth read all the cards. She came to the last one, roses from Patrick.

Ruth hesitated after reading the card.

"What is it?" Grace asked, seeing something else in her aunt's expression.

"Patrick called to check on you."

"Oh."

"I haven't called him back yet. I thought you might want to do that."

"Could you handle it, please?"

Again Ruth hesitated. "Fine. But he'll call again."

"I can't face hearing his excuses just now. I only want the truth from now on." Grace closed her eyes. "Just the truth."

Chapter Eleven

Noah stared at the book in his hands, not seeing the words. His focus was shattered. It had begun to fissure immediately after Grace's brush with death. When he was away from the hospital, it was all he could think about. What if Grace hadn't made it?

He had replayed Jordan's death a hundred times since Grace's surgery. All the what ifs, the unanswered questions.

Noah knew he had to put those thoughts aside so that he could find the best doctor for Grace. It would mean she would return to Houston, but that was a small price for her to pay to receive top-notch care. Glancing at the pages of names, Noah knew he would recommend only a precious few. He had already spoken to his first choice and Trevor Scott had agreed, despite a long waiting list, to add Grace to his caseload.

Now he just had to tell Grace.

Knowing he couldn't put off giving the news, he replaced the book on the tall wooden shelves flanking the door and left his office.

It didn't take long to reach Grace's room. Shaking off any personal thoughts, Noah adopted his most professional mode as he pushed open the door.

Looking somewhat stronger, Grace smiled when she saw him.

Ruth's tired expression lifted, as well.

Noah kept his tone benign. "How's the patient today?"

"Okay," Grace replied. "How's the doctor?"

"Fine." He moved to the bank of machines, noting the readouts.

"Don't feel you have to elaborate on that," Grace told him, her voice puzzled.

"I'm here to discuss your health, not mine." He was glad to see that the purplish tinge beneath her eyes had faded.

Ruth drew her brows together, but remained silent.

"Your vitals look good," Noah reported, wondering if Grace was strong enough yet to learn about her close call.

"Good." Grace glanced over at her aunt. "Now maybe Aunt Ruth will stop fussing. She's been acting as though this were my first surgery, instead of the zillionth."

Noah met Ruth's gaze. "There's a reason for that." He paused. "Grace, everything didn't go well this time."

Her fingers flew up to touch the bandages.

"The restorative work wasn't the problem."

Grace's eyes widened, but didn't show fear. "Then what?"

"A blood clot. It was nearly fatal."

Puzzlement rather than the expected shock entered her eyes. "But I'm all right now?"

"At the moment."

"Noah—" Ruth began.

"Grace deserves the truth, as well as the best care possible."

"That's what I'm getting," Grace protested.

"No. Rosewood Hospital is an adequate facility. But we can't compete with the Houston Medical Center. There you will have the best of the best, both in completing your restorative work as well as making certain you don't have any more residual effects from your internal injuries."

"Noah Brady!" Ruth chided.

"You said nothing went wrong with the surgery on my face." Grace struggled to sit up straighter. "And this hospital's been just fine so far."

Noah's face and voice remained tight. "Hardly. I've been consulting with your surgeon in Houston, apprising Dr. Burger of the developments in your case."

He was shocked to see a wave of hurt flash in her eyes. "I'm not going back to Houston."

"I don't want to be blunt, but you don't have a

choice in the matter. I'm turning your case over to Dr. Burger."

Ruth took a step toward him. But Grace's words hit him first. "You can send every X ray, test and file you have on me to Houston. But I'm not going."

He tamped down his frustration. "There's no point in being stubborn."

"You walk in here and announce that you're shipping me back to Houston, that I have no say in the matter, and you call *me* stubborn?"

Noah knew this was an argument he had to win. For her sake even more than his own. Not only had he crossed the line by having feelings for her, those feelings had grown beyond caring. Beyond anything he'd expected. "Grace, the issue isn't debatable."

Determination replaced the hurt in her eyes. "I'm not a package you can pop in the mail."

Noah turned to Ruth. "Will you talk to her?"

Ruth's expression filled with disappointment. Disappointment in him, Noah realized.

Realizing he could say no more that would convince her, Noah left Grace's room. His heart heavy, he kept seeing the hurt in Grace's eyes. Trust had turned into pain. And he had only himself to blame.

A week later, Grace was relieved to be back home. In Ruth's home, that was. Her aunt hadn't been willing to let her stay alone in her apartment the first few days. Ruth had been hovering ever since Noah had dropped his bomb.

Grace couldn't understand why his defection hurt so. She now knew that men couldn't be trusted. Despite that, she had begun to believe that perhaps Noah was an exception.

And she had no idea what she was going to do about her medical care. Noah maintained that he wasn't going to change his mind. Grace couldn't imagine leaving the safety Rosewood and her aunt offered. The thought of facing strangers in the city horrified her.

The doorbell rang, and Grace couldn't stop the spurt of hope that it might be Noah. She heard a masculine voice mingling with Ruth's. But it wasn't Noah.

"Hello, darling," Patrick greeted her.

"Patrick."

He didn't seem to notice the lack of enthusiasm in her greeting. "Looks like you came through it all right."

She wondered briefly if he knew she'd nearly died. As quickly, she decided it really didn't matter. "Yes. I'm fine."

He angled his head, studying the bandages. "Looks like you have more wrappings on your face than before."

Grace kept her tone even. "That happens after each surgery."

"So, you're just skating through the surgeries?"

Ruth made a strangulated sound.

Patrick turned to stare at the older woman. "What?"

Ruth sent an apologetic look to her niece. "Grace had complications."

"What kind?"

"Just a clot," Grace answered mildly.

He glanced again at Ruth. "That so?"

Grace let Ruth off the hook. "Apparently it could have been serious."

Patrick frowned. "What does your hick-town doctor say about this?"

Grace squashed down the sudden impulse to defend Noah.

But Ruth didn't have the same self-control. "Noah Brady is an excellent surgeon! In fact, he wants to send Grace to the medical center in Houston to make sure it doesn't happen again."

"Finally!" Patrick replied. "I guess you're relieved, aren't you, Grace?"

She clenched her teeth. "Not exactly."

"Patrick—" Ruth started to add.

"No offense, Ruth, but this is hardly the place for Grace to get the medical care she needs. This Dr. Brady—he's the only plastic surgeon in town, right? No one to consult with? I know you like the guy, but that doesn't mean he's qualified. Besides, Grace doesn't belong here. Her life's in the city."

Grace stared at Patrick, unable to believe how entirely clueless he was. Again she wondered how she'd come to be affianced to a man who knew so little about her. "Patrick, I don't intend to return to the city now."

"You're being ridiculous," he replied.

Stung, she stared at him.

"Sorry. Didn't mean to be so blunt. But you've got to face facts, Grace. If this doctor thinks you need more competent care, then you'll have to go to the city."

Her back up, Grace made a sudden decision. She wasn't leaving. Neither Noah or Patrick could force her. If Noah refused to treat her, she would find another way. But she wasn't going to be pushed into a corner. "I'm afraid not, Patrick."

He let out an exasperated hiss. "I don't understand you anymore, Grace."

She kept a bitter laugh contained. "Anymore?"

Shaking his head, he stared at her. "You're not thinking clearly. Maybe after you've had time to really process what this means you'll come to your senses."

Grace felt the same overwhelming disappointment she had since the accident. Knowing that, she remained silent.

Patrick stood suddenly. "I rescheduled a meeting to come here today, but it appears to have been a waste of time."

Even though she knew he wasn't the man she'd thought him to be, his words hurt.

He pushed a hand through his immaculately styled

hair. "Didn't mean it that way, Grace. Look, I'll get going and we'll talk when you're feeling better."

He strode to the door, Ruth trailing behind him. This time Grace didn't even glance toward the window to see him leave.

Ruth returned, her expression somber. "I admire your pluck, Gracie. But what are you going to do if Noah won't reconsider?"

"That can't be an option," Grace replied with far more assurance than she felt.

The church sanctuary was quiet, still. It was a time Noah savored. Although he valued the fellowship of fellow members, he could always reach deeper to what was in his heart when alone.

Choir practice would start in just over an hour. Until then he could relish the solitude. He sat in a pew, rather than at the piano. But the peace he expected didn't descend on him. His troubled emotions were still irretrievably tangled.

Deep in thought, he was surprised when a shadow fell over him. Glancing up, he was even more shocked to see Grace.

"What are you doing here?"

"Hello to you, too," she replied mildly, glancing at the empty space on the pew beside him. "Can I join you?"

He nodded. "I wasn't expecting anyone."

"I know."

Thoroughly baffled, he studied her expression. "You do?"

"Cindy told me. She said that when your schedule permits, you like to come here before choir practice."

"Ah. Not too many secrets in a small town."

"But plenty of good friends."

He eyed her warily. "Yes."

"I thought you were my friend."

Her arrow hit his already wounded heart. "Yes."

"And my doctor."

He could feel the scowl as it crossed his face. "Not anymore."

"So you're willing to concede that the doctors in Houston were right? That I'll never regain full use of my hand?"

"Of course not."

Her eyes shifted color. They were pewter now, and challenging. "Then how am I supposed to regain its use without you?"

He hesitated. "I'll help with your hand, but that's all."

"So you're going to make house calls in Houston?"

Angered frustration edged his voice. "You're treating this as though it's some joke. We almost lost you, Grace. Don't you understand that?"

She gasped, a soft mewing sound. Wary tenderness lingered in her expression. "You say that as though you care."

"Of course I care."

"Then help me. I don't want to go to another doctor, someone who looks at me as just another patient—"

"That's exactly what you need!" He didn't care that he'd raised his voice enough to shatter the hushed quiet of the sanctuary.

"You'll have to explain that."

"Grace, no doctor should allow the line between personal and professional to become blurred. I knew that, but I still did. Four years ago I was crazy about a woman in Houston—Jordan Hall. I thought she was everything I'd ever wanted—talented, compassionate. She was beautiful, too. But she didn't think her beauty was perfect. Essentially she blackmailed me into performing frivolous cosmetic surgery." Remembering emphasized the raw pain his mistake had caused. "And she died."

Grace's hand reached out to cover his. "I'm so sorry, Noah."

"Me, too. I vowed then it would never happen again."

"But you were in love with Jordan," Grace protested.

He stared into her eyes, now soft silver, glowing with compassion. "So I was."

Grace glanced away and he felt the blow to his heart.

"Noah, you told me there's just one final surgery. I don't want another doctor."

He shook his head. "That's impossible."

"Look around you, Noah. Can you sit in this church, the one you've urged me to return to, and refuse? Is that what the Lord would want you to do?"

Shaken, he examined her expression and found only sincerity. "Don't ask me to risk your life again, Grace."

"And if He asks?"

Noah had no answer. Only the realization that whatever he decided, it could mean the life of the woman he loved.

Chapter Twelve

Only a few weeks later, Grace could scarcely believe it. Her tutoring had grown, one student at a time, from two to eleven in a relatively short time. And she was continually receiving inquiries to tutor even more children.

Caught up in the demands of her former career, Grace had almost forgotten her love of literature. Before her father had died, she had planned to become an English teacher. But her focus had changed. Teaching had become intertwined with the pain of her past. So Grace had left that decision behind with the rest of her dreams.

Now she wondered. How different would her life have been if she had allowed herself to pursue the course she had initially planned? Even though she was only their tutor, Grace found immense fulfillment in teaching her pupils. Could that sustain itself on a full-time basis?

Hearing a knock on the door, Grace glanced at the clock. She wondered who it could be. Perhaps Robert, hoping to put in another hour's work. But she didn't mind. He had proven to be not only bright and quick—he also challenged her. And he nudged her memory, reminding her how it had been to be his age.

She whipped open the door. But her smile faded.

"Hello, Grace." Patrick stood at the top of the stairway, favoring her with his boyish grin.

Instinctively she took a step back. "Patrick. I wasn't expecting you."

"I took a chance that you might be home."

Reluctantly she gestured to the living room. "Come inside."

He followed her, looking around at her tiny apartment. Mentally she followed his thought process, seeing him size up her new accommodations that were a far cry from her sleek Houston condo.

"Not what you expected, is it?"

He shrugged. "I doubt there's much to choose from in a burg this size."

"Perhaps you shouldn't judge something you know nothing about."

"I didn't come here to fight, Grace. I know things haven't been right since the accident, but it's taken me a while to process all the changes."

"And you've worked them out now?" she asked, feeling at once angry and vulnerable.

"Not completely. But I'm trying, which is more than I can say for you."

"Excuse me?"

"You don't seem very happy to see me when I come to visit."

"This hasn't been a particularly *happy* time for me, Patrick."

He gestured around the apartment. "You act as though you like this place, this town. It's not you, Grace. None of it. Your career, your friends, everything you could want is back in the city."

Grace pictured what he described, what she'd given up.

"I can tell you're thinking about it. I don't know what hold this town has over you, Grace, but you can shake it, move on."

She reached up to touch the bandaged portion of her face. "Not quite yet."

"I'm going to be visiting on a regular basis until we can straighten this out."

Patrick and Rosewood. The two didn't seem to belong in the same sentence, Grace thought inanely.

"Why don't we take a walk?" he suggested. "Maybe you can show me what it is you like so much about this place."

Reluctantly she agreed and they drove to Main Street. It seemed awkward. Both because she was with Patrick and because of the noticeable bandages on her face.

He was looking at her now as though trying to read her mind. "Penny for your thoughts."

"They're not much of a bargain."

He didn't try again. Instead he parked in one of the many open spots. They strolled beneath the full, tall trees that lined Main Street. Dusk was descending, but it didn't discourage the shoppers and strollers.

Early fall in Rosewood dictated baseball and ice cream. Since the game was finished for the day, most of the spectators gravitated toward the ice cream parlor. Built in the 1800s, the quaint old place boasted a marble fountain, tall bar stools and root beer floats big enough to dive into.

"This place is hard to believe," Patrick commented. "Looks like a movie set from about sixty years ago."

Grace tried not to take offense at his words. "The pace is slower here."

"Slower? I think it's stopped completely."

She felt defensively protective about the town that had opened itself so warmly to her. "That's not really fair."

"It's picturesque, I suppose. But surely you're about to go stir-crazy." Another expression overtook his face. "Unless it suits your recuperation."

Grace hid the grimace she felt. Why was it that Patrick's every reference to her injuries grated?

When she didn't reply, he looked pained. "I don't know what to say to you anymore. Things seem so different."

"Things *are* different. *I'm* different."

"But you'll be back to your old self soon."

Grace felt the truth pushing at her. "No. I won't. Not just on the outside, either."

"What do you mean?"

"I've changed."

His expression grew thoughtful. "That makes sense. It would be difficult to go through that much pain and not be affected. But you're still *you*, Grace."

She couldn't really argue with that logic. "I suppose I am."

"You've been thrust into a different set of circumstances that seem appealing because you've been recuperating."

Grace started to shake her head.

"Think about it," Patrick argued. "Don't you miss your job, the adrenaline rush of pulling together events the entire city talked about for weeks?"

"You're not suggesting that I can just step back into my old job?"

"You told me they're holding your position open."

She met his gaze. "And you expect me to stand in front of huge groups of people with my scars all aglow?"

He couldn't disguise his horrified reaction, though he tried. "Maybe you could have an assistant do that part of your job."

"An assistant that good would be capable of doing the job on her own."

"Well, something related, then."

"Patrick, everything about PR means people contact. You know that."

"Don't just dismiss it out of hand."

"Out of hand?" She looked at him with disbelief. "I've lived with what's happened to me on a daily basis. While you were 'working things out' I was having surgeries and treatments. It didn't go away for one minute of one day. So don't think you can assess the situation in a matter of minutes."

"I wish I could turn back the clock, make things better for you."

Struck by one of his few empathetic responses, she felt her anger deflate. "Thanks. But there's no point in trying to wipe away the past months."

"You act like you don't want to forget. Is there something else you're not telling me?"

Immediately she thought of Noah. "It's not just one thing. I'm not the same person I was when we planned to get married."

As they walked together, Patrick didn't attempt to take her hand. He acted as he had since the accident—as though if he touched her she might break. Bewilderment and irritation had segued into sadness. Was this how all men saw her?

Even as the thought progressed, she had an instant image of Noah as he took her hand and made her feel like a real person.

Grace heard someone call her name.

Cindy and Flynn Mallory, along with their children, had spotted her. Glancing over at Patrick, she saw his surprise.

"Does everyone in town know everyone else?"

She resented the irritation in his voice. "It's a very social place." Still, Grace was relieved that Patrick behaved in a charming manner when she introduced the Mallorys.

"We're headed toward the ice cream parlor," Cindy was saying.

"I'm having sprinkles," one of the triplets announced. "Bunches of 'em."

"That sounds wonderful," Grace replied, captivated by the children.

"Would you like to join us?" Flynn asked.

"Yes," Cindy encouraged. "Please do."

Grace knew Patrick would play along, but she also knew he wouldn't mix well with the Mallorys. "I think we'll enjoy walking for a while."

Cindy picked up on Grace's mood, smiling graciously. "Enjoy. It's a beautiful evening."

Patrick watched the Mallorys as they walked into the ice cream parlor. "Rosewood's a real family-oriented place, isn't it?"

"Now that you mention it, I guess it is."

"You didn't notice it before?" Patrick asked in surprise.

"Not particularly." She paused. "Does that bother you—the family thing?"

"No. Just that in the city we socialized with other career couples who understood our goals."

Goals she hadn't examined closely in a while. Goals, it occurred to her, that she'd never questioned before.

They continued walking, glancing at the storefronts and the other people who strolled down the quiet street.

"I wonder what it would be like growing up here," Patrick speculated.

"Comforting," she replied, realizing the word had slipped out without thought. Then she remembered Noah's words. "And fulfilling."

Patrick's eyebrows drew together. "Fulfilling? I doubt there are a lot of opportunities here."

"I suppose that depends on your definition of opportunity." Grace thought of all the people who came together to help each other as well as members of other communities. Her tutoring had been an incredibly satisfying experience.

Patrick looked at her as though she were a stranger. "I thought we agreed on what we believe opportunity is. A chance to grow in our careers, to establish contacts, to build our lives."

Had that once been so important to her? To build her life solely through her career? "I don't see things like I once did," she admitted.

"I've read that people who are ill… I mean have a long recovery, well, that they're not always themselves for a while."

Her smile was sad. "Who do you think I am, then?"

Patrick looked as though he wished he knew.

Grace took pity on him. "Perhaps you're right."

He brightened a fraction. "It's a big adjustment. I know that."

For which one of them? Grace wondered. And why did the prospect fail to stir her?

As they strolled farther down the street the conversation dwindled to nearly nothing.

And though she walked beside Patrick, he didn't occupy her thoughts. Instead her mind filled with a sudden desire to see Noah. Logically she couldn't reconcile the two, but her heart wasn't listening.

Chapter Thirteen

Noah was pleased by the attendance at the festival fund-raiser. It wasn't a surprise. The townspeople always supported the events that funded their hospital.

As he walked toward the refreshment booths, Noah told himself it was to check on all of them. But he headed straight for the lemonade stand Grace was supervising.

He had called and given her an out in case she didn't want to participate. But Grace had insisted. She hadn't wanted to be involved in taking the drink orders or ringing up sales—that was still too public.

Although Ruth was with her, Noah was concerned about how Grace was handling the festival. It was by far the largest public event she had attended. Person by person she had eased into the community. But this was a giant step.

Noah found her at the back of the booth, mixing a

batch of lemonade. Ruth was at the opposite end of the same table. She'd had the foresight to bring a juicer to speed up the process.

"Hello, ladies."

Grace glanced up, the unbandaged side of her face flushed. "The lemonade's selling well."

"I'm not surprised. It tastes great."

She smiled, her bottom lip trembling a fraction. "How about a complimentary glass?"

Searching her eyes, Noah felt a fist of emotion hit his gut. This was real. She was that singular woman he had searched for all his life. He cleared his throat. "Sure."

Grace poured lemonade into a paper cup. "We're using crushed ice. That's part of my secret."

He lifted the cup to his lips, realizing he could be swallowing kerosene for all the attention he paid to the drink.

"What do you think?"

"Wonderful," he murmured, swamped by his feelings for her. Then he settled his voice into a more normal tone. "Really wonderful."

Her smile spilled sunshine across his soul. "I'm glad."

As Grace held his gaze he saw questions flicker in her expression. She gestured vaguely toward the batch of lemonade. "I should be—"

"Sure. And I have things to check on."

Her eyes didn't leave his. "Of course."

Noah made his way out of the booth, conscious of Grace's gaze still fastened on him. It wasn't until he'd walked to the other side of the festival that he realized they hadn't discussed anything medical…or personal.

And that maybe, just maybe, he had a chance.

Inside the lemonade booth Ruth studied Grace's face. "Have you told Noah about Patrick?"

Grace slowly shook her head. "I never considered it an issue. You know, it's funny. Immediately after the accident all I dreamed of was having Patrick come after me, realizing he couldn't live without me. I wanted him to be my knight on a white horse, charging in to claim me, to proclaim his undying love regardless of what had happened."

"And now?"

"Now I realize that he never was the knight-on-a-white-horse type. I expected qualities he didn't possess."

Concern hovered in Ruth's eyes. "What about Noah?"

"I'm sure he can have his pick of whole women."

Gently Ruth tipped up Grace's chin. "Regardless of how your injuries heal, you *are* a whole woman. A woman any man would be proud to call his own."

Tears trembled in Grace's eyes. "I wish that were so." She bit her lips to stop their quivering. "Oh, how I wish that were so."

Chapter Fourteen

The church was quiet. Midweek, early in the day, few people came to the sanctuary. Noah knew that he could have chosen somewhere else to conduct Grace's therapy. But he continued to hope that her contact with the church would bring her closer to reconciling her faith.

"Have you thought any more about attending church?" he asked.

"Have you reconsidered your decision to remain as my surgeon?" she countered.

For the next few moments the only sounds between them were the random notes of the organ as Grace picked through an unfamiliar song.

She reached for a higher note on the organ than usual. "I can stretch my fingers farther than the last time without any pain. I've been able to for days."

Surprised, he stared at her. "Why didn't you share that with me?"

She kept her head averted. "It's not always easy to tell something, even when you want to."

Noah felt a familiar fist to his stomach. "Such as?"

Finally, reluctantly, she lifted her head. "I haven't told you about Patrick...my fiancé. Well, he *was* my fiancé. I'm not sure exactly what to call him now."

"No, you haven't told me about him."

She swallowed visibly. "When I first had the accident, Patrick came to the hospital. But he was shaken, unsure of himself, of what had happened. He said that he wanted to stand by me, but the look on his face... He was horrified. I could see that he couldn't deal with my accident."

"And then?"

"It was as though he didn't know how to deal with me once I was disfigured—like I wasn't the same person."

Noah silently called the man a fool, but aloud he forced himself to remain neutral. "And now?"

Grace went very still. "He keeps coming to Rosewood."

Noah felt the crush of conflicting emotions. "To pick up your relationship?"

"So he says. I'm sorry I didn't tell you earlier about him."

"It wasn't essential to your recovery."

She cast her face downward, seeming to stare at the keys of the organ. "No. I don't suppose it was."

"I imagine you and he share a lot of common interests, living in the same city."

"I suppose so," she murmured. "Patrick wouldn't fit into a small town."

Noah hid his flinch. No doubt Patrick would find them all backward and hokey. "Not everyone does."

Grace lifted her face, her eyes searching his. "No. I guess not."

He wanted to tell her that she fit, though. That everything about her was right for Rosewood and for him. But in light of her revelation about Patrick, he knew it wasn't the honorable thing to do.

Instead he gently touched her hand, positioning her fingers over the organ keys. On the outside he remained professional. But inside he could feel the quaking of his heart, the splinter of its breaking.

The quiet sanctuary seemed to welcome the mellow notes of the organ as Grace picked them out with more and more certainty.

And Noah tried not to dwell on how forlorn the lonesome sounds would be without her.

Chapter Fifteen

Grace hadn't ventured to Noah's house on her own before. Aside from the barbecue, she had been there only to sit in on a few band practices.

But she felt compelled to come here, to speak with Noah. She needed answers to the questions Patrick continued posing. Grace hesitated as she approached the house. The side gate to his backyard was ajar. On instinct, she stepped through.

She could see Noah beneath the tall chinaberry tree at the edge of the lawn. Smoke curled lazily from the massive brick barbecue pit. But the table wasn't set up for entertaining.

Still Grace was hesitant as she approached, not wanting to intrude on anything he had planned.

Before she could speak, he turned, as though sensing her presence. He looked surprised, but not displeased.

"I took a chance you might be home," she began,

feeling suddenly nervous. "Your office said you were off today. Am I interrupting anything?"

He shook his head. "I was about to put a burger on the grill for lunch. Should I make it two?"

"Okay. Can I help do anything?"

"Eat," he replied.

She relaxed a fraction. "Do you always fire up the barbecue pit for just yourself?"

"Depends. Sometimes I think the great smell beckons company."

"Cross my heart, I headed over here *before* I smelled the mesquite."

His gaze met hers. "Either way, you're welcome."

Her throat dried and she found it difficult to swallow. All the words she had rehearsed fled. "You have a way about you, Noah Brady."

His eyes darkened. "A good way?"

A very good way. But she could only nod.

Their gazes connected. Noah finally broke the moment. "Would you like some iced tea?"

She welcomed anything that would relieve her emotion-parched throat. "Please."

It didn't take Noah long to fetch the tea. Standing beside him, she sipped the sweetened brew. As she did, Grace listened to the bright chirping of the birds, the quiet sounds of the occasional car that drove down the street.

Noah stirred the fire. "It should be ready soon."

Then he turned toward her. "I have the feeling that you've got something on your mind."

She fiddled with her glass for a moment. "Noah, can you tell me why you're so content in Rosewood?"

He didn't answer immediately. And his voice was slow when he did reply. "Well, you know about my mother and family, my debt to the community."

She leaned forward. "That's *why* you're here. I suspect you've repaid that debt a dozen times over. Yet you stay. What is the source of your happiness?"

He met her gaze steadily. "The true source of all my happiness is the Lord. He makes everything else possible. Friends, my work with the youth in our church, the caring attitude of the community."

She was silent, considering his response.

"Grace, I know you don't like to talk about it, but can you tell me why you've drifted away from your faith?"

She wanted to close up as she always did, but this was the man who had shared the worst of her fears. Her voice stumbled as she began. "I was eight years old when my mother died from cancer. I questioned why God let her die. My father told me that it was His will, that we didn't always understand it, but we had to accept what happened. When I didn't want to accept it, my father promised that I would never be alone. He said that I could get through my mother's death and any other bad thing because he would always be there for me, to help me understand God's will." Grace paused, remembering the pain—old, but still sharp. "When I was eighteen my father was killed in a small plane crash."

Noah stepped closer. "I'm sorry, Grace."

Ridiculously, she felt the sting of tears over what had happened so long ago. "I know it sounds childish, but I clung to that promise, and when my father died it shattered my world. I couldn't understand why God had let that happen."

As her tears increased, Noah put his arm around her shoulders, bracing her up.

Grace released words she had kept locked up for years. "And even worse, it was as though God had betrayed my father, as well. I couldn't understand why He made my father break his promise."

"Oh, Grace." Noah pulled her close, letting her cry against his shoulder. He didn't offer platitudes or false comfort.

The hot rush of tears dampened his shirt, yet he held her. And she didn't sense any judgment from him. Finally she pulled back, needing to know. "Do you think less of me?"

"For suffering terrible losses and losing your way?"

She ducked her head, then slowly lifted her face to look at him. "The accident was the final straw. It seemed that neither God nor Patrick wanted to stand by me."

He flinched, and instantly she regretted her mention of Patrick.

Yet Noah ran his hand gently over her disheveled hair. "You're weighted by burdens greater than we can bear alone."

"I just don't know," she murmured, wanting to have the trust he did, but burned by her past.

His pager beeped and Noah sighed. "It's like a fifth appendage." He scanned the digital readout, his face tightening.

"What is it, Noah?"

"A train wreck. It's bad. Lots of injuries. I've got to get there right away. I'm the emergency medical coordinator."

"Let me come with you," she offered impulsively.

He frowned. "Bystanders get in the way."

"If I can't help, I'll leave," she promised. Grace flexed her bad hand, demonstrating its improved state. "And I can do *something.*"

"All right. But you can't allow ash or any other foreign matter to get past your bandages—you'd be risking infection. Understand?"

She nodded, following as he jogged to his car. Once inside, she glanced back at the house. "Oh! What about the fire in the barbecue?"

Noah was already backing up. "The advantage of an old brick pit. It's completely contained. This isn't my first emergency when I had it going. The fire will burn itself out."

Speeding down the quiet residential street, Grace

felt a sudden qualm of fear, envisioning a derailed train scattered over the surrounding homes. "Could anyone in town have been hurt by the wreck?"

"Not likely."

The possible effects of the tragedy kept them silent as Noah raced through the town. A few blocks from the site, a burning stench filled the air. Glancing over at Noah, Grace saw his face tighten even more.

The train was derailed. But the actuality was far worse than what Grace had imagined. It wasn't only the smoldering heaps of twisted metal. Shattered glass covered the ground. And personal belongings were strung out like a macabre yard sale.

Wounded and dazed passengers struggled to stand. Others wandered aimlessly, ineffectually trying to stanch flowing wounds.

Horrified, Grace followed Noah as he grabbed his medical bag and jumped from the car, running toward the fire chief. Immediately Noah drafted two paramedics. "We have to set up a triage," Noah told them. "On this side of the big oak." He glanced up at the fire chief. "Is help on the way?"

"I've contacted all the surrounding towns, but no one can get here for hours." He didn't have to say that distance was the problem.

Noah snapped open his cell phone, punching in numbers. "I'm going to call for help in Houston and send our helicopter."

Relief flashed over the chief's face. "Good thinking. This is bigger than anything we've ever handled."

"Call the school and city hall. Have them make announcements and ask for volunteers," Noah told him. "I'll phone the hospital, ask them to call in all off-duty staff."

As the chief nodded, Noah spoke into his cell phone, getting arrangements for the helicopter going.

Grace was filled with admiration for his competence and leadership. Looking around, she desperately wanted to help and not be in the way.

Noah closed his cell phone.

She spoke quickly. "Noah, would it help if I guided the walking wounded to a safe place?"

He rapidly scanned the area. "Over by the tree next to the big oak. It's close enough to where we're going to set up triage without getting in the way. Have them sit and keep still."

Then he was gone, searching for the most seriously wounded.

Grace walked quickly toward the train. Suddenly a flashback of her own accident hit with such intensity that she felt her knees buckle. Calling on her strength, Grace straightened, determined not to give in to the weakness.

Seeing a woman wandering toward her, Grace quickened her stride and gently took her arm. "Ma'am?"

Dazed, the woman remained unfocused.

"Let's get you to a safe spot." Grace spoke softly, sensing the woman's shock. Glancing up, she saw townspeople running toward the railroad tracks. Many carried first aid kits. Others brought pillows and blankets.

Michael and Katherine Carlson arrived. As Grace helped the woman, she saw the duo check with Noah, then begin organizing the volunteers.

An ambulance screeched to a stop, the attendants jumping out. They headed toward Noah. It seemed everyone knew that he was in charge.

Grace settled the woman and went to fetch another person.

As she did, Cindy rushed up to her. "Katherine sent me over here to help you. They're not sure how many people may be ambulatory."

"Are you here alone?" Grace asked, not seeing Flynn.

"Since we have a plane, Noah called Flynn and asked him to organize the other small planes at the airport to fly to nearby towns and collect help. Houston's sending help, but this is massive."

Grace looked out over the wreckage. "It's the worst thing I've ever seen. There seem to be far more patients than doctors and nurses."

Cindy nodded grimly. "Thank the Lord for Noah." Then she left to help an elderly man wandering nearby.

By the time Grace returned to help another possible patient, there were as many townspeople as passengers in the scattered wreckage.

A nurse had been assigned to oversee the passengers brought to the safe spot beneath the tree, separating out those who needed to be sent to triage.

Between Noah and the volunteers he put in charge, the damaged landscape soon began resembling a *M*A*S*H* unit. Still the cries of the wounded, along with those of frightened babies and children, mingled with the shouts of volunteers and firemen.

The most seriously injured began to be transported to the hospital via ambulance as well as by volunteers with vans and SUVs.

Why had this happened in Rosewood? she wondered. It was too small to handle something so massive, so horrific.

Just then Grace spotted her aunt. She was organizing a pillow-and-blanket brigade.

Suddenly an explosion rocked the ground, pitching Grace off her feet. Stunned, she lifted her head and saw that one of the engines had blown. New shards of glass and metal spewed out, a free fall of blowing shrapnel.

Immediately she looked for Ruth, her heart in her throat. She couldn't bear to lose this one last member of her family. Surely God wouldn't be that cruel. Not seeing Ruth, Grace felt a sob crowd her chest.

Weakness started to overtake her. Then she spotted Ruth being helped up by a young man.

Scrambling to her feet, Grace looked up to see Cindy's concerned face.

"Are you all right?" Cindy asked, holding out a steadying hand.

"Yes. You?"

"It scared me to death." Cindy squeezed her hand in encouragement.

Grace left her and ran across the sandy width of the railroad embankment. Reaching Ruth, she hugged her, silently uttering thanks for her aunt's safety.

Pulling back finally, Ruth tried to scold, but her voice betrayed her concern. "Child, what are you doing in the middle of this mess?"

"Same thing you are."

Ruth's eyes ran over Grace, making sure she was okay. "I guess you come by it naturally. Be safe, though."

Grace hugged her again. "You, too." Then she ran toward someone who was stumbling from the nearest train car.

She helped that man and the next. Person after person until she wondered how there could be so many of them.

Hours must have passed, she realized later. Because ambulances and paramedics from the closest towns had arrived.

And a second plan was already taking shape. Members of the community volunteered to open their homes to the uninjured. Grateful passengers left with their new sponsors.

As the sun began setting, Grace met up again with Ruth.

Looking fatigued, Ruth patted Grace's arm. "Grace, I want to do something, but I'm worried about you."

"Me?"

"Yes, dear." Ruth hesitated. "I'd like to offer our home to some of the passengers."

"Of course," Grace agreed instantly. "But why are you concerned about me?"

"Well…the accident, the reminders."

"Bad things are always going to happen." Grace swallowed. "I know that. But I can't hide from life forever. It's funny, you know. Since we arrived at the train wreck, I haven't thought once about my bandages, about what people would think."

Ruth took her hand. "I wish you knew how very special you are, child."

Grace smiled. "If so, I came by it naturally."

Ruth smiled at the echo of her own words. "Then shall we bring home our guests?"

"I suppose you have someone already picked out for us to take home."

"You'll like them," Ruth assured her.

Grace spared one more glance in Noah's direction,

knowing he must be tired, also knowing he wouldn't stop until the job was done. In that instant Grace realized she'd never known a man like him. A man of noble purpose living a life dictated by honor and faith. A man determined to keep her at arm's length.

Chapter Sixteen

It took a while for Rosewood to settle back to normality. The uninjured train passengers had returned home and only a few remained at the hospital. Which meant Noah had time to seek some solace.

Normally he could find that at his own home or at the family house. But discontent traveled with him. So he had come to the church for the peace he needed.

Once inside, he passed by the pews, going instead to the organ. As he played the last song he'd practiced with Grace, he pictured her hands stretching for the notes. She had persevered beyond the pain, determined to make the hand work normally again. He could envision her earnest expression, the determination in her eyes.

Caught up in his thoughts, Noah was startled to feel a gentle touch on his shoulder. Abrupt silence replaced the music as he whirled around.

"I'm sorry to disturb you, Noah." Grace looked at him with those entrancing eyes. "Please continue playing."

Unable to pull his gaze from her face, he gestured to the bench. "No, this is your song."

"Oh." Hesitantly she sat beside him, flexed her fingers and began to play.

Her hair smelled of vanilla, he decided. A scent so delicate he might have imagined it.

Grace finished the song, and the final notes trailed off in the surrounding silence.

"How did you know I was here this time?"

She smiled, a tremulous lifting of her lips. "You weren't at home, so I drove on. Your car's parked out front."

The distinctive Porsche. "Hard to miss."

"Yes." She fiddled with a slender bracelet on her wrist.

He hadn't seen that piece of jewelry before. Stiffening, he wondered if it was a gift from Patrick. "Is that new?"

Grace glanced down as though surprised to discover the unconscious gesture, and stilled her fingers. "No. Very old. My father gave it to me."

Instantly he remembered the pain she associated with his passing. "It must be very special."

She nodded, then lifted her head, seeking his gaze. "Noah, I need to talk to you."

His gut tightened. Was she about to tell him that she'd decided to marry Patrick? "What is it?"

"I've come to ask you to reconsider your decision to not perform the final surgery."

He wondered how relief could blend so completely with angst. "Grace—"

"Don't answer just yet. I know this is a difficult decision. But I need you."

"I can't understand why you won't go to the doctor I've recommended. He's the best—"

"He's not you," she replied with quiet conviction. "And I'm guessing you've followed my progress since the last surgery."

Since Grace refused to see the other doctor, Noah had had an associate monitor her case as she'd come in for regular bandage changes. "I've already made my decision."

"I've made one of my own, Noah. If you won't perform my final surgery, I won't have it done."

"That's ludicrous! You're so close. Why would you risk the final outcome?"

Grace met his gaze. "I've had a lot of trouble with trust since the accident. And I trust you. Not a strange doctor in Houston. *You*."

He wondered at the undercurrent of her words. "I've explained before why this is impossible."

"Only if you make it so."

"You're not listening, Grace."

Her eyes pleaded with him. "You're wrong. I've listened to your reasons for not performing the surgery. I've also listened to what you've said about the Lord. And now I'm wondering…have you listened to Him, as well?"

Noah thought of the chaos his thoughts and feelings had been in. Maybe Grace was right. "I don't know."

"Noah, it has to be you."

He met her gaze, feeling lost in her eyes, finally speaking reluctantly. "I'll think about it."

"Oh, Noah—"

"I said *think* about it. And pray."

She placed a hand over his. "That's all I can ask."

No, she could ask for his heart and it would be hers.

Grace stood. "I'll leave you alone, then."

Noah watched as she left. It was a decision he couldn't put off. And one that Grace was right about. It was time to take it to a higher power.

Noah stared at Grace's still body. Still but healthy. There had been no surgical complications this time, no clots that threatened her life.

Choosing to perform her surgery had been one of the most difficult decisions of his life. But after prayer and reflection he knew it was the right one.

She stirred.

Noah stroked her arm. "It's all right, Grace. You're going to be fine this time. I'm watching out for you.

No matter what you decide, no matter who you choose, I'll be there for you. Always."

It wouldn't be long until she awoke. And based on her current progress she would be transferred to a room shortly afterward.

Noah added another blanket, knowing she would be chilled. He also knew he should move on, attend to other things, but it was difficult to leave her.

The recovery room was cold. Grace shivered beneath layers of blankets. The room echoed with the sound of beeping machines and the faraway buzz of voices.

She'd had an accident, Grace realized. A terrible accident. In a train. Or a car.

But that was an opportunity.

Opportunity? The word floated in and out of her consciousness.

A deep male voice spoke her name and soothed her. It was a voice she knew. Her knight, she recognized. Noah, not Patrick. He would spirit her away and make everything all right.

Because it was his opportunity.

No, hers.

The machines beeped more loudly. Her aunt Ruth must be worried, she thought, the fog of anesthesia still clouding her mind.

But she shouldn't worry.

Because it was an opportunity. Noah had said so.

* * *

That evening Grace's hospital room was quiet, the door closed against the intrusive noise of the corridor. And in the solitary confines of her room Grace had been thinking. She remembered the word that had been on her lips from the moment she awoke.

Opportunity.

And she didn't think it was the vague wanderings of her medicated state. In the time since Noah had told her that his service was an opportunity, the concept had been nagging her.

And now she knew. The car accident wasn't God's punishment. It was His blessing. Tears slipped down her face, wetting her bandage, salting her lips.

If not for the accident, she would never have come to know the joy of living in a caring community of friends. Or the simple joy of a day, unrushed by a pace spiraling out of control. Nor would she have rediscovered her dream of teaching.

And she would never have met Noah.

Grace stared out into the darkness beyond the window. He had changed her life in ways she was just now beginning to understand.

Hearing the door open, she withheld a sigh. She knew they had to come in often. But sometimes she felt like a Sunday roast, being prodded, her temperature checked, everything short of being basted. Silly thought, she realized. Much like the first one she'd had about Noah.

"Grace?" Noah spoke softly.

"The blackberry doctor," she blurted out before she could stop herself.

In the low light she could see the gleam of his teeth as he grinned. "I'd been advised your anesthesia had worn off. I'll have to recheck your chart."

"I didn't think I'd see you tonight."

He glanced about the empty room. "I can't let my favorite patient fend for herself."

Her voice was soft. "Is that what I am? Your favorite patient?"

Noah studied her face. "You're a strong, courageous woman who I admire tremendously."

Without warning, her lips trembled.

He stepped closer, his face drawing into a frown. "What is this? Tears?"

"No…" She began to protest.

But he had already perched on the side of the bed, reaching out to gently wipe away her tears. His touch was a balm to more than her physical wounds.

And he didn't speak for a long while, allowing her to recover her calm.

When she had, he met her eyes. "Would you like me to sit with you for a while?"

Suddenly that seemed like the best thing she could imagine. "It's late," she protested weakly. "I imagine you're tired."

"No," he corrected her. "Not just late, *very* late."

The stars seemed to pop out, one at a time, while she listened to Noah as he told her warm, comforting tales. She wasn't sure if it was the medication or her newest revelations, but never had she felt so secure.

And for just this time she could believe it was forever. That, somehow, Noah might come to love her as she loved him.

Grace's postsurgery hospital stay was without incident. However, even once she was home, the time seemed to pass in an excruciatingly slow manner. She still avoided mirrors, yet she was conscious of her appearance nearly every moment.

Because this was it.

In a matter of days she would know her fate.

She couldn't help picturing Noah's expression when her bandages came off for the final time. Would his eyes fill with understanding and sad kindness? Then her stomach would lurch as she envisioned pity.

And her mind filled with her rediscovered faith. All along she had believed she was battling outside forces—the accident, fate—but she knew now that wasn't true.

She had been battling inner demons.

Ones that had been with her since she lost her faith. In some ways she wanted to share her discovery with Noah. However, it was still too new, too fragile.

Grace also knew she could pick from a dozen other

people—Ruth, Cindy, Katherine and more—to discuss her faith. But she needed more time to reflect, to hold the revelation close before she shared her feelings.

Patrick called from Houston, and Grace realized she was already treating him like a friend. Without knowing it, she had distanced herself emotionally from him long ago. Since the last surgery she had searched deep in her heart. It truly wasn't a grudge and it was no longer a matter of his betrayal.

Grace wanted a deep and abiding love. One that would remain strong as they grew old together, one that could withstand anything, no matter how bad it was.

She wanted Noah.

The phone rang. When she heard his voice, her hands began to shake even though she knew he couldn't truly read her thoughts.

Noah was calling on his cell phone. He was in his car, only a few blocks away. Grace agreed to his stopping by shortly for her therapy. Replacing the receiver, she stared at her hand, the scars still red. Angry, her mother used to call scars. Red and angry.

It wasn't often she could remember her mother's words. She had died so very long ago. And it occurred to Grace that she never associated memories of her mother with anything other than pain. That really wasn't fair to the wonderful woman her mother had been.

Her smile had been wide and quick. She had

laughed a lot, Grace realized. Warm, caring, her arms always ready for a hug. The pain had come only once she was gone. But that shouldn't have been her legacy.

Hearing a car in the driveway, Grace knew it was Noah's Porsche. The distinctive engine couldn't be mistaken.

Her heart quickened as it never had for any other man. And she rushed to the door, opening it just as he reached the top of her stairs.

"That's getting to be a habit," he greeted her.

Embarrassed, she stepped back. "My mind's so full, I think it's spilling over."

He didn't seem to find that particularly strange. "Filled with what?"

"I was just thinking about my mother, actually." She took one of the chairs and he followed.

"And?" he prompted.

"Just that in the past, whenever I've thought of her, all I felt was hurt and loss." She paused. "And today, just now, I was thinking about her smile. It was wonderful."

Noah's eyes met hers. "I can almost see it."

"And her laugh," Grace continued, caught in his gaze. "It was magical."

"Yes," he agreed.

She pulled her glance away, trying not to reveal her feelings. "And until today I never thought it odd that I only remembered the bad."

"And now you do?"

Grace remembered. "My mother was so special. Why do you suppose I didn't think about that instead?"

His gaze was thoughtful. "It's my feeling that faith helps us deal with the loss of loved ones. It's difficult to think about them if you don't believe you'll eventually be reunited…if you're not certain they're in a better place."

"I just always thought of her as gone," Grace said, realizing this suddenly. "Forever."

"You asked me once how I could believe," he said quietly. "I don't understand how someone can't. It must be a very difficult life."

She swallowed. "I'm beginning to think you might be right."

Hope flashed in his expression. "Grace?"

"I'm not sure I'm ready to talk about it."

He searched her face, his own filled with understanding. "That's okay. It's enough that it's in your thoughts."

Ridiculously, she felt tears threaten. How did he always know the right way to respond to her? And how would she ever replace him in her life?

But he didn't let her wallow in her emotions. "Have you kept up your stretching exercises this week?"

She managed a wobbly smile. "Yes. I didn't want to get in trouble with my doctor."

"Pretty tough, is he?"

"Murder," she replied, grateful for his light tone.

"Then we'd better start working." He took her hand, holding it a bit longer than necessary before starting the exercises.

She felt her pulse increase, and her throat was dry. Unable to speak, she followed the slow movements of his hand over hers. She wasn't sure whether she was relieved or disappointed when they moved to the piano.

Surprisingly, Noah began playing. It was a song she had never heard, but she liked the gentle, evocative tune.

When the last notes faded away she glanced up at him. "I like it, but I haven't heard it before."

"I'd be surprised if you had. It's one of mine."

"I didn't know you composed music!"

"Time restraints don't allow for it much anymore."

"Did you write this one a long time ago?"

His expression grew more thoughtful. "No. I was inspired to write it recently."

With a sickening thud she wondered if he had written it for a special woman in his life.

Noah didn't speak for several moments, either. And when he did, he surprised her. "Would you like to play something?"

Usually he made her go through scales and other stretching techniques, waiting until the end of the session for the free play. But she didn't protest. Instead she chose a piece that had been her father's favorite. It always comforted her.

When she finished, Noah was quiet again.

"Is something on your mind?" she asked softly.

"Just restless tonight." He turned toward her. "Would you like to play hooky?"

Grace took heart. "Doing what?"

"Taking a drive…maybe a walk by the lake."

He had combined two of her desires. To be away from anything to do with her injuries…and to be with him. "I'd like that."

They drove through the uncrowded streets. Children played on well-tended lawns and older people sat on their porches, watching the day end.

"Everything seems back to normal," she marveled, calmed as always by the peaceful town. "It's as though the train wreck never happened."

"Quiet, nothing happening."

"I meant that in a good way," she protested.

He glanced over at her. "You won't get an argument from me."

They approached the vintage downtown center, and Grace remembered Patrick's unwelcome comment. "Someone told me he thought Main Street looked as though it had been plucked from an old movie set."

"I guess it does." Noah turned in the direction of the lake. "Never thought about it before. It's just the way Rosewood is."

The road curved, the incline increasing, then dipping as they passed through the gently rolling hills.

Huge fields of long grass carpeted the knolls and tall trees congregated over the last of the summer wildflowers.

Feeling as though she'd had her eyes opened for the first time in many years, Grace saw there was beauty all around her. As she watched, a deer darted from the scrub oak, then loped up the hill.

"Look!"

His gaze followed hers. "White-tailed deer. They're all over these hills."

"I had no idea."

Noah turned on to the road leading to the lake. "All kinds of wildlife out here."

"The closest I used to get to wildlife was the poodle in the condo next to mine," she admitted.

"I didn't know a poodle was considered a wild animal."

"You don't know Bootsie," she replied. "That dog went nuts over everything and nothing."

He smiled suddenly.

Seeing the grin, she smiled herself.

Then they were on the last turnoff that led to the lake. It took only a few minutes to reach the shore. Climbing out of the car, they started walking by mutual, silent accord.

They left the gravel road and climbed toward the sandy banks. Tall stalks of reedy grass fluttered in the mild breeze. A pair of mallards chattered at each other.

"They sound like they're arguing," Grace said as she watched them.

"It's the last of the season for them. They'll be flying farther south soon."

That took her aback. "The months have passed more quickly than I thought."

He remained quiet for a bit as they strolled farther along. Then he looked at her. "The next few days will pass just as quickly."

Swallowing, Grace tried to read the subtext of his words. And again she wondered how he would react to her final appearance. "Actually, the days are crawling."

"Not like in Houston with a busy pace and a reward-ing career to fill the days."

Days that would never be repeated. But Noah wouldn't want to hear that. It sounded too pitiful. And pity was the one thing she didn't want from him.

The sun had begun its slow descent. The golden rays gave way to pink-and-purple-tinged fingers in the sky.

Noah glanced over at her. "You're quiet."

She pushed away her thoughts. "Just rediscovering how beautiful everything is."

He looked surprised. "It's the same as it was the last time we were here."

But then she hadn't considered the gifts of life. "I didn't really see it before."

Noah searched her face, but didn't question her. Instead they continued walking, accompanied only by the sounds of the last birds of the day singing their final songs.

And the silent echo of Grace's longing for the man who had gone from rescuer to mentor…to thief of her heart.

Chapter Seventeen

Patrick glanced around the room. "I didn't think the restaurant would be this crowded."

"I've been out in public since the accident," Grace reminded him. "It doesn't bother me as much now."

"Hmm." Patrick didn't meet her gaze, instead studying his menu.

It hit her a beat later. Patrick was embarrassed.

She closed her own menu. "We don't have to stay."

"Of course we do. You said we needed to talk. And I'm ready to listen." He met her gaze and had the grace to look ashamed. "Sorry, Grace. I'm just not accustomed to this yet. It will take some time."

She didn't reply.

"Think there's anything on the menu that won't clog our arteries?"

"I'm sure they'll have something," Grace murmured, wishing Patrick didn't have to pick the place to pieces.

"Don't you miss decent restaurants?"

"Not particularly. Rosewood has a lot to offer in so many other ways."

He groaned. "I'll have to take your word for that. I can run an extra two miles tomorrow to work off this dinner."

She wished her troubles could be solved so easily.

"Is something wrong?" Patrick asked when she remained silent.

"Not wrong exactly." She met his gaze. "My last surgery was probably the final one."

It was difficult to read the stream of emotions that crossed his face. But his voice was cautious. "Isn't that a good thing?"

"Yes. But this is pretty much it. I'll know the results, good or bad."

"I know I blew it before, Grace. But I won't this time."

She looked deeply into Patrick's eyes. He was doing his best to be sincere, she realized. It wasn't his fault that she no longer fit into his well-ordered life.

Although she'd once thought she loved Patrick enough to accept his proposal, her original feelings for him paled against those she had for Noah.

She loved the person Noah was. A man who gave up riches to devote his incredible talent to his small town. One who volunteered for the church, helped children and teenagers, and whose heart was true.

A man who possessed the courage, strength and nobility that she now knew was paramount to her happiness.

"Grace?"

"This may be hard to believe, but I don't have any hard feelings about what happened before."

He pushed aside the dinner plate and leaned forward. "Good. This time—"

"Patrick. Please don't."

His face went still. "What do you mean?"

"I want you to believe that I truly don't hold a grudge. But I can't plan a future with you. I've changed."

"I told you I could deal with it," he protested.

She bit her bottom lip. "That's not the change I mean." Gathering her courage, she lifted her gaze. "I don't love you, Patrick."

He looked stunned. "This is just a reaction to your final surgery."

Grace shook her head. "No. Regardless of how the surgery comes out, I'm sure."

"This is because of the way I acted immediately after the accident, isn't it?"

She searched for the truth. "Partially, but I really have changed."

He still looked stunned. "I can't believe that I'm not going to be part of your life."

Grace glanced down, fiddling with her fork. "Please don't make this more difficult."

He stilled the nervous gesturing of her fingers. "Okay, how about a truce for the evening? I promise to be on my best behavior."

"Okay." She hadn't really wanted to accept his invitation, but he had been insistent. "I haven't asked. How have you managed to take so much time off from work? You've been popping up here to Rosewood on a regular basis."

"I shifted some of my accounts to Stevenson for the interim. He thinks they're his for the long run, but—"

"He thinks wrong," she finished for him, with a smile for remembered times. "He doesn't have your talent or your tenacity. They're still your accounts."

"Tenacity. My best quality, you once said."

Grace looked at him, sad for what they had once had. "You have many great qualities, Patrick. That's not why my feelings changed. It's about me, about how different I am now."

"Quite a truce, isn't it?" he said wryly.

"I do think it's one time your tenacity isn't going to work."

"You're so sure?"

"Absolutely. Patrick, I think it's time for you to go home."

"But your bandages come off in a few days."

She sighed. "I know. But either way, I'm not resuming the life I once had. And, generous as your offer has been, I don't need your shoulder. I've come to peace with my accident…and the near certainty that I'll be disfigured."

"But—"

Grace took his hand. "I've found something else here in Rosewood, Patrick. My faith. And that's going to enable me to deal with whatever happens."

"You shouldn't be on your own."

"Don't you see? Even if I didn't have Ruth and all the wonderful, caring friends I've made here, I've got the Lord to lean on."

"Grace—"

"Please. Do it for me, Patrick. I would feel better knowing you're home, doing what you love, doing what you're so great at."

"You're a very special woman, Grace." Belated regret simmered in his eyes.

She leaned over, kissing his cheek. "Goodbye, Patrick."

As Patrick clasped her hand for the last time, another man watching from the entrance turned abruptly and left the restaurant as quickly as he had entered.

Once outside, Noah sucked in deep breaths of the fresh night air. And called himself a fool.

The following days crawled for Grace.

On the day before her bandages were to come off, she had scheduled only two tutoring sessions in case she had any last-minute errands or qualms. Now Grace wished she had filled the day with lessons.

Ruth had questioned if she would be all right with a little company for dinner. Grace welcomed any distraction.

She had hoped that Noah would call. But the phone was remarkably still. Of course she would be seeing him the next day. Still, she had thought he might offer some words of encouragement.

Glancing at the clock, she realized enough time had passed that she could go over to Ruth's to help with dinner.

A wheelbarrow and garbage can blocked the path to the back door. Guessing that her aunt must have some project going, she headed for the front door instead.

She heard a flurry of voices and realized the guests had already arrived. An apology for her tardiness on her lips, Grace rounded the corner into the living room.

A circle of women stopped talking and broke into applause.

Stunned, Grace stared at them.

Ruth and Cindy walked out of the group, each taking one of her arms.

"What is this about?" Grace asked, still baffled.

"We're here to applaud your courage," Cindy explained.

"And tell you how much we love you," Ruth added, her eyes glistening with a sheen of tears.

Katherine approached. "You've been a wonderful example for all of us, demonstrating grace, courage and strength. And we want you to know that our hearts will be with you tomorrow."

Grace felt the tears slip from her eyes as she looked at these women who had become so dear to her. "I *never* cry," she finally managed.

Everyone laughed, surrounding her, offering hugs and hankies. These were the women Grace had joined to make memory books for a town that had been flooded, losing all their sentimental treasures. She had been part of their efforts to help the victims of the train wreck, gathering clothing, providing a warm, welcoming home. These and other projects had woven Grace into their community. And tonight she knew that wasn't a temporary thing, that she was truly part of the town.

"This is so amazing," she told Ruth after a few minutes. "Thank you."

"You've always touched my life, child. Now you've touched theirs, as well. I'm so proud of you."

Grace swallowed the threat of more tears. "I'm going to be completely waterlogged soon."

Ruth hugged her. "I'll settle for that."

A delicious-looking buffet had been laid out on the dining-room table. And each woman had written her a few special words on slips of paper. All the papers had been placed in a heart-shaped container of cloudy pink glass.

"When you need a pep talk, or a smile, or to know we're close, just pull out one of the slips of paper," Cindy explained. "And know you're in our hearts."

Incredibly touched, Grace accepted the gift, knowing she would treasure it as she did these friends.

Memories, dear to each person, spilled out as they talked and talked. And by the end of the evening Grace was overwhelmed by the outpouring of support.

"We'll be praying for you," Cindy and Katherine promised as they left.

And Grace knew she would be doing her own praying, as well. It would be a special prayer. One for herself, it was true. But not for an unscarred face. Rather for an unscarred love.

The morning dawned, bright and clear. Grace's appointment was early, just after Noah completed morning rounds. Ruth accompanied her to his office.

When Grace's name was called, Ruth clasped her hand. "Do you want me to go in with you?"

Grace shook her head. "No. I need to do this by myself."

Both understanding and concern hovered in Ruth's eyes. But she squeezed Grace's hand one more time before releasing it.

Noah didn't make Grace wait long in the examining room before he joined her.

"Hi," she greeted him, unable to keep the nerves from her voice.

"It's going to be all right, you know."

She smiled bravely.

"Are you ready?"

Girding her strength, she nodded. "Yes."

His movements were careful and deliberate as he began removing the bandages. She was accustomed to the process. The only difference today would be that she would finally look in the mirror.

Grace held her breath as the final bit of gauze was removed. She saw a spark of joy in Noah's eyes and felt a leap of excitement. Then his eyes filled with incredible sadness.

At least she finally knew. Releasing her breath, Grace battled her disappointment as she accepted the mirror he extended.

Closing her eyes, she reached deep inside for courage. Finally ready, she pulled the mirror closer and opened her eyes.

She stared at her image. Her full, unabridged image.

Puzzled, Grace wondered if she was imagining what she saw.

Hesitantly her hand strayed to her face.

Noah's voice was gentle. "The two small marks will mostly fade in time."

She moved the mirror even closer. The marks were so small she could barely see them, just their red stain. Unable to understand Noah's saddened reaction, she glanced up at him. "Why aren't you happy about the results?"

"But I am," he reassured her.

"Then why do you look so incredibly sad?"

He searched her face, his expression tight. As though pulling himself from some faraway place, he cleared his throat. "Because now you're ready to return to your life in Houston."

"No, I'm not!"

"But you and your fiancé have waited for this day."

"Patrick isn't an issue." She met Noah's eyes, her own pleading for him to understand. "What we had is over—and has been for a very long time. He returned to Houston two nights ago. Patrick is part of a past life I've left behind."

"After he sees you, he won't let you go."

"Is that how you judge a woman?" Suddenly it was terribly important to know this about him. "Simply by her looks?"

"The eyes are important," he replied solemnly. "For they reveal the heart." He stepped an inch closer. "And the lips, because they speak either in kindness or to wound."

"And the nose?" she asked, entranced by his words.

His lips edged upward. "Very important. I can't abide snobbish women."

"And how do you see me?"

He swallowed and she glimpsed tenderness in his eyes. "Ah, Grace. Woman of infinite beauty, that's an unfair question."

Her heart pounded so loudly she wondered that he didn't hear it. "Why is that?"

"Because you're leaving soon."

Finding a confidence she thought was lost forever, Grace put her heart on the line. "Can you think of a reason for me to stay in Rosewood?"

His eyes locked with hers. "Do you need a reason?"

Solemnly she nodded, praying he could read her thoughts.

He touched her newly healed cheek. "How about the fact that I love you?"

Heart thrumming, she felt a surge of newfound hope.

Regret infused his face. "But that's not enough."

"Why?" she cried.

"You can't be happy in my little one-horse town." He met her gaze, his eyes shining with naked love. "And I can't ask you to give up everything for me."

"I've grown to love Rosewood and the people here nearly as much as I love you." Her lips trembled and her eyes filled. "And because of that, I've also found my way back to God. I know now that you were right about opportunities. The Lord blessed me with an opportunity greater than I could ever have wished for." She reached up, tenderly touching his jaw. "And He led me to you."

Noah's hands folded into her hair as he pulled her close. "Grace, I love you so much. I see your smile each day when I wake, I dream of your changeling eyes each night as I sleep. But I never thought you could be mine. Are you sure?"

"More sure than I've ever been of anything. You *are* my life now, Noah. And my love."

Noah tenderly fitted his lips to hers, his soul filling with thanksgiving, unable to believe this lovely, wounded bird was to be his.

Grace took hold of the dream that she had once despaired of, grasping it close to her heart. She would keep it there, tenderly securing it along with her love for this noble man. Her knight, she realized with new wonder. Who would stand by her forever.

The sunlight that streamed through the examining-room window seemed to glow as though cast from heaven itself. And together their hearts took flight—not away, but upward on the wings of a love destined to last for all time.

Epilogue

The church that had become hers radiated with hope and love. Massive bouquets of flowers decorated the altar. Their fresh scent mingled with that of newly lit tapers.

Grace looked out at the crowded pews of wedding guests. She was still unable to believe how many friends she had made in the town that was now her home.

Noah's family had welcomed her warmly as one of their own. Along with Ruth, they provided her the family she had always dreamed of.

It was a perfect day for her wedding, filled with sunshine that etched an elaborate tapestry as it pushed past the stained glass windows.

Joyous organ music resonated in the aged, beautiful sanctuary. The mood of the music fitted the jubilation of the day, the joy Grace knew would fill their union.

So much had happened while the wedding arrangements were being made. Grace's former employer had decided to become a permanent endower of the Rosewood Medical Foundation. Although he maintained he could never replace Grace, he had embraced the foundation with his usual generosity.

Robert had excelled on his scholarship exam—surpassing all their expectations. His father had found employment and the entire family was doing much better. Grace still tutored Robert, though. He would always be special to her—her first student. He had been enormously pleased when they'd asked him to be an usher for the wedding. Grace noticed that he had taken special care escorting Noah's parents to their pew.

With Noah's encouragement, Grace was securing her teaching certificate. It had been scary at first, returning to school. But she enjoyed the challenge nearly as much as substitute teaching. She could hardly wait until she became a full-fledged teacher.

The music swelled again and Grace felt her throat tighten with joy. It would only be moments now.

Cindy, her matron of honor, walked up the aisle, taking her place opposite Michael, Noah's best man.

Ruth patted Grace's arm. "I think they're about to play our song."

Grace smiled, pleased that Ruth was walking her down the aisle. It might be unorthodox, but Ruth had been both mother and father to her. They had shared so much. It was only right that they also shared the beginning of this newest path.

"I don't know if I would have agreed to give you away if you weren't marrying Noah," Ruth added, her eyes glistening.

"You're gaining a son, not losing a daughter," Grace told her gently, wanting Ruth to know she had been so much more to her than an aunt.

Tears spilled onto Ruth's spare cheeks and she reached for her already rumpled handkerchief. "Thank you, child."

The music swelled once more. Grace used her now fully recovered hand to squeeze Ruth's arm. "I think that's our cue."

The guests rose as Grace and Ruth moved up the aisle. But Grace didn't watch their faces. Her gaze was fastened on the man soon to be her husband. He stood tall and handsome.

And her heart called out to him.

Noah's deep blue eyes signaled his reply.

Her smile widened.

They reached the front of the church.

"Who gives this woman?" Katherine asked as the notes of the organ faded away.

Ruth squeezed Grace's hand one final time, said, "I do," then stepped away.

With no one left between them, Noah took her hand in his. And Grace savored the rightness of his touch.

Then they both gazed at Katherine, who smiled at them before beginning the age-old words.

Sunbeams pierced the stained glass windows, punctuating each sacred promise.

"Will you take…from this day forth…"

Grace and Noah steadily repeated their vows.

When the words *in sickness and in health* were to be echoed, Grace felt the emotion lodge in her throat, her voice tremulous as she spoke.

But Noah's eyes filled with promise.

Lips trembling, she didn't take her gaze from his.

"I do," Noah uttered, his strength flowing through to her.

Two such very small words. Carrying with them the promise of forever, Grace realized, blinking back the tears before she, too, repeated them.

"I now pronounce you husband and wife."

Noah lifted his hand to tenderly cup Grace's cheek.

Somewhere in the distance she heard the sighs of guests.

"You may kiss the bride," Katherine told them, her voice filled with joy.

Noah's lips gently covered Grace's, sealing them with a promise of devotion and commitment she thanked God for. Eyes misting with overwhelming happiness, she looked up at the man who was now her husband.

Triumphant strains of music flowed from the organ, seeming to reach the very beams of the old sanctuary.

"I now present Mr. and Mrs. Noah Brady," Katherine concluded.

Grace placed her hand in Noah's larger one, knowing he would always make her feel as safe and loved as she did at that moment.

"Shall we?" he asked, his gaze lingering on hers as though searing this memory for all time.

Hand in hand, they took the first step of their new lives. Walking down the aisle, they smiled at friends and family.

As soon as they passed through the double doors that led from the sanctuary into the foyer, Noah pulled Grace along with him to the empty bride's room.

Turning, he drew her into his arms. "My bride...my wife."

Without warning, her eyes misted. "I love you so."

Again he cupped her cheek, gazing deeply at her. "I had to fix one thing in my memory."

"What?"

"The color of your eyes on the most important day of my life."

She felt her heart stutter with a wealth of emotion for this rare and wonderful man. "And?"

His look was tender. "The color of heaven."

"One thing about me will never change, Noah. My love for you."

He lifted her scarred hand, one she had chosen to leave as it was, a reminder of what had brought her a new life, a renewed faith, a love like no other.

Gently he kissed that hand. "Forever, Grace. We have forever."

It was a gift from above, one they could share, as matchless as the golden sunlight that fell around them.

Her hand clasped in his, they walked from the tiny room to greet their friends and family. Connected by touch, by hearts, by spirit, their smiles reached out to all those watching.

And like the sunshine, their love was radiant. Also matchless, a joy that reached to the sky and beyond.

Forever.

* * * * *

Dear Reader,

This story called out to me because it's one of change. Like many of you, I feel surrounded by change—in our world, our country. I'm not usually the first one in line to embrace change, so it made me wonder about a woman who would have to deal with change in every aspect of her life.

Even as the familiar comforts us, I wondered, could change possibly comfort us even more?

I invite you to join my journey of promises, friendships and, most especially, love. And I hope that all your changes are joyous.

Warm wishes,

Bonnie K. Winn

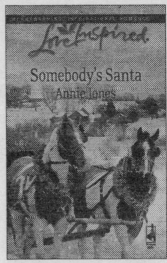

Playing Santa was not workaholic Dora Hoag's idea of a good Christmas. But how could she refuse Burke Burdett's request for help in fulfilling his mother's dying wish? Especially when all Dora wants for Christmas is a second chance with Burke.

Look for
Somebody's Santa
by
Annie Jones

Available October wherever books are sold.

www.SteepleHill.com

Steeple Hill®

LI87499

Love Inspired
HISTORICAL

INSPIRATIONAL HISTORICAL ROMANCE

Years after being wrenched from Alice Shepard's life due to his lowborn status, Nicholas Tennant returns to London. Now wealthy and influential, he seeks revenge on Alice and her family. Alice is now a beautiful, grown woman and a loving single mother, and Nicholas cannot deny his feelings for her. Can he abandon his thirst for revenge and become the man most worthy of her love?

Look for

A Man Most Worthy

by

RUTH AXTELL MORREN

*Available October
wherever books are sold.*

www.SteepleHill.com

Steeple
Hill®

LIH82797

Love Inspired
SUSPENSE
RIVETING INSPIRATIONAL ROMANCE

Seeking ancient ruins in Desolation Canyon, Kit Sinclair finds her plans going awry when tribal police officer Hawke Lonechief threatens to arrest her if she enters the dangerous gorge. When she risks his wrath by going alone, he finally agrees to lead her. Yet someone else is watching them, and they grow closer to danger with every step....

Look for

Forsaken Canyon

by MARGARET DALEY

Available October wherever books are sold.

Steeple Hill®

www.SteepleHill.com

LIS44309

REQUEST YOUR FREE BOOKS!

2 FREE INSPIRATIONAL NOVELS
PLUS 2
FREE
MYSTERY GIFTS

YES! Please send me 2 FREE Love Inspired® novels and my 2 FREE mystery gifts (gifts are worth about $10). After receiving them, if I don't wish to receive any more books, I can return the shipping statement marked "cancel". If I don't cancel, I will receive 4 brand-new novels every month and be billed just $4.24 per book in the U.S. or $4.74 per book in Canada, plus 25¢ shipping and handling per book and applicable taxes, if any*. That's a savings of over 20% off the cover price! I understand that accepting the 2 free books and gifts places me under no obligation to buy anything. I can always return a shipment and cancel at any time. Even if I never buy another book, the two free books and gifts are mine to keep forever.

113 IDN ERXA 313 IDN ERWX

Name _____ (PLEASE PRINT)

Address _____ Apt. #

City _____ State/Prov. _____ Zip/Postal Code

Signature (if under 18, a parent or guardian must sign)

Order online at www.LoveInspiredBooks.com

Or mail to Steeple Hill Reader Service:
IN U.S.A.: P.O. Box 1867, Buffalo, NY 14240-1867
IN CANADA: P.O. Box 609, Fort Erie, Ontario L2A 5X3

Not valid to current subscribers of Love Inspired books.

Want to try two free books from another series?
Call 1-800-873-8635 or visit www.morefreebooks.com

* Terms and prices subject to change without notice. N.Y. residents add applicable sales tax. Canadian residents will be charged applicable provincial taxes and GST. Offer not valid in Quebec. This offer is limited to one order per household. All orders subject to approval. Credit or debit balances in a customer's account(s) may be offset by any other outstanding balance owed by or to the customer. Please allow 4 to 6 weeks for delivery. Offer available while quantities last.

Your Privacy: Steeple Hill Books is committed to protecting your privacy. Our Privacy Policy is available online at www.SteepleHill.com or upon request from the Reader Service. From time to time we make our lists of customers available to reputable third parties who may have a product or service of interest to you. If you would prefer we not share your name and address, please check here. ☐

LIREG08

AN UPLIFTING ROMANCE SET DURING THE 1860s
LAND RUSH ABOUT THE POWER OF FORGIVENESS...

ROSANNE BITTNER

To provide a better life for her young daughter,
Clarissa Graham joins a wagon train headed west. But as the
trail turns increasingly dangerous, Clarissa fears her decision
could cost them their lives. Help comes in the unlikely form
of a jaded ex-soldier, Dawson Clements, who knows nothing
of grace, forgiveness or even love. Now Clarissa is about to
face an even greater challenge. Can she convince Dawson to
remain by her side for a journey that will last a lifetime?

WALK BY *Faith*

"Bittner is one of those writers whose talent has
grown over the years; that talent truly blossoms."
—*Publishers Weekly*

Available wherever paperbacks are sold!

Steeple
Hill®

www.SteepleHill.com

SHRB634

Love Inspired

HISTORICAL

INSPIRATIONAL HISTORICAL ROMANCE

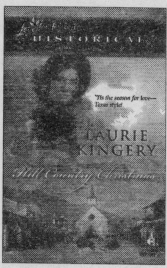

Overnight, Delia Keller went from penniless preacher's granddaughter to rich young heiress. Determined to use the money to give herself the security she'd never had, building a house by Christmas is her first priority. That is until former Civil War chaplain Jude Tucker starts challenging her plans—and her heart

Look for

Hill Country Christmas

by

LAURIE KINGERY

Available October
wherever books are sold.

www.SteepleHill.com

Steeple Hill®

LIH8279